THE GREAT WILD

THE GREAT WILD

— Phantasm Book IV —

CHRISTOPHER HALL
AKA MAXLEX

Podium

Cover design by Amanda Shaffer

ISBN: 978-1-0394-5877-2

Published in 2024 by Podium Publishing
www.podiumentertainment.com

THE GREAT WILD

A FRESH START

People are weird. We think of ourselves as perfectly rational beings, but underneath a thin veneer of civilization, we're a messed-up mishmash of emotions, poor decisions, and instincts. If you built a robot that wanted to tap its feet when it heard a beat, you'd call that a backdoor hack, or at the very least an Easter egg. Perfectly normal for humans, though.

Or take the herd instincts, developed on the savanna, but still just as relevant today. The instinct to obey someone with power or status was at its most powerful when it was unacknowledged. Subtle signaling that we did, consciously or unconsciously, that informed all of us herd members who was in charge, and who had to obey.

The people of Ryvue, human and otherwise, *shouldn't* have had the same instincts. From all accounts, they hadn't evolved. They were created out of whole cloth by the gods in much the same form as they were today. Normally, I'd smirk at such a creation tale, but I had reason to believe the gods were real, so I had to give the story at least some consideration.

Part of that story was that they'd been created by the Goddess of Creation right before she committed suicide, which might explain some of the design failings. Unexplained, though, was the similarity to the humans from Earth.

Not just a similarity. As far as I could tell, the two races were identical, right down to the collection of instincts that by rights the Ryvuans shouldn't have had. Did Ix create humanity from a template stolen from Earth? Nobody knew, not even the gods.

There were some differences, but they could be easily explained by the different environments. Here, instead of subtle cues coming from the confidence that status brought—or masterful acting by those who had no status—people responded to social skills. Or, more accurately, the product of your Level Skill and Charisma. There was some pushback at first, manifesting as Social Contests, but once people got used to the idea of who had the highest total, they let the herd instincts take over and knuckled down under whoever was on top.

At this time, and in this place, here in the town of Talnier, that was me. Which was why I was carefully keeping my mouth shut for most of this meeting. If I said anything, that would be the end of the discussion, as everyone would immediately agree with me. By keeping quiet, I allowed the others to make the points that they had come here to make. They felt included in the decision, and on the off chance that they actually had a point that I hadn't considered, I'd get to hear it.

The matter under discussion was the expansion of Talnier. Talnier was growing, and not slowly. This time, though, I wanted to do it properly. Sewers, paved roads, and *then* buildings. Oh, and walls. To my 21st-century mind, they seemed superfluous, but I had to admit that there were monsters out there that needed to be defended against.

The land outside the walls wasn't owned by anyone. The Tribes to the north had a claim on it, but they didn't want to go near civilization, so their claim was only nominal. They were happy to waive it in return for some minor concessions on dungeon use. Concessions that the town was happy to give since the dungeons were growing. Growing because of all of the mana that had started flowing our way, once the Tribes had stopped focusing that mana on creating monsters in the forest.

With the Tribes' assent, the Town Council could claim as much land as we needed, dig out the sewers, plan out the streets, divide it up into packages, and then sell it to people to fund the whole development. If the new immigrants didn't have *enough* money, well, the newly formed Bank of Talnier was ready to lend it to them.

All of this could have been accomplished any time in the last twenty years, if the relevant parties had just been willing to *talk* to one another. None of the people here had been responsible for that particular bit of pig-headed nationalism, though, so I held my tongue, smiled, nodded, and waited for the meeting to come to a conclusion.

To pass the time, I called up my status. My abilities hadn't changed at all recently.

Abilities
[Strength]: 4
[Agility]: 4
[Finesse]: 5
[Soul]: 3
[Intelligence]: 6
[Charisma]: 10
[Unspent Ability Points]: 10

Past level five, you didn't get Ability points with each level. I still had a few points from past levels coming my way, but it would be another six months before I saw anything on that front. My abilities were pretty high, considering, thanks to the Worldwalker trait that gave me plus one to each ability. That hadn't been worth that much at the lower levels, but abilities cost more to improve each time one of them went up. Having one added to each ability *after* I spent the points was a huge bonus.

Traits

[Worldwalker]: Level prerequisites for Professions are overridden. +1 bonus to all stats.
[Gift of Tongues]: All languages are understood.
[Female]: +1 bonus to Charisma.
[Silent Casting]: Allows you to cast spells without a chant.
[Subtle Casting]: Allows you to cast spells without gestures.
[Disease Resistance]: You are more resistant to diseases of all types (upgradeable).
[Extra Spells] : 15 more spell levels per Casting Skill Level.
[Socialite] : +1 bonus to all social skills.

[Unspent Development Points]: 22

I did have some points to spend on traits, but I hadn't settled on what to get. There were too many options, just as I had too many skills.

[Body Development]: 3	[Run]: 4
[Stamina Development]: 5	[Stealth]: 3
[Perception]: 4	[Memorize]: 4
[Identify]: 6	[Bargain]: 5 (6)
[Scribe]: 4	[Advanced Mathematics]: 3
[Calculate]: 5	[Intrigue]: 4 (5)
[Mana Sense]: 5	[Persuasion]: 5 (6)
[Mana Development]: 7 (8)	[Sing]: 2
[Illusion Magic]: 6 (9)	[Teach]: 3
[Creativity]: 3	[Intimidate]: 3 (4)
[Disguise]: 2	[Enchant]: 3
[Weapon Mastery: Dagger]: 4 (5)	[Research]: 2
[Deceive]: 3 (6)	[Cook]: 3
[Charm]: 4 (6)	[Weapon Mastery: Triggered]: 2
[Conversation]: 4 (6)	[Water Magic]: 4
[Dodge]: 4	[Theurgy]: 4
[Jump]: 4	[Bureaucracy]: 4
[Climb]: 4	[Craft (Smith)]: 1

The number of skills I had was basically unbelievable to anyone from this world. I'd learned a lot of things during my twenty-four years on Earth, and some of them translated into skills. If you convinced the System that you could do a thing, it just gave you the skill, no points required. This was something that people from this world could do, but few bothered. I know if I'd been able to learn statistics in an instant by spending a skill point, I wouldn't have spent years at uni learning it.

Once you bought a skill, it improved with use—faster if you used it in dangerous situations. I saw a lot of dangerous situations, which helped me to catch up with other people. Everyone born in this world had years more than me to develop their skills. I shouldn't complain; it wasn't like I didn't have my own advantages.

Dismissing the blue boxes from my vision, I looked around at the Town Council. Delmar Balend and Cheney Labelle had finished arguing over the exact number of land packages and the mayor, André Michaud, was looking at me expectantly.

"So that's decided then?" I asked brightly. Everyone nodded and muttered agreement. "Very well, I'll note that the new development is to be divided as determined here."

Thanks to Memorize, I didn't actually *need* to make a note, but I would be writing up the minutes for the meeting. I was the Secretary, after all; that was my job.

"Is Anas ready to see me?" I asked my assistant, Huette, cuing up my next meeting as soon as I was back in my office.

"Yes, ma'am," she said, managing to convey her disapproval of the man without saying or doing a thing out of place. In the few months since I'd gotten back from Dorsay, Huette had become *much* more concerned with propriety. I think it was my Bureaucracy settling in. As the staff learned more about the procedures of the organization, they became functionally immune to social skills, as long as they were following policy.

That had to come as a relief, but I thought it might be resulting in a group of people that were more hidebound and conservative than they otherwise would be. Policy couldn't be set in stone, after all. So it was good that she was dealing with people like Anas. We were on friendly terms with him, but he definitely didn't fit into our bureaucracy.

"Lady Secretary," Anas said, stepping carefully into my office. It wasn't quite the closet that it once was. The new building had been completed, so I had room for a desk, another room for Huette, and a room for people to wait for me in, so they didn't have to block the corridors. It was still a far cry from a corner office in a skyscraper, but give me time.

"Anas," I said warmly. Anas was the *speaker* for Tinidan, the Tribal Elder who was our main contact with the Tribal Nation. In practice, that seemed to translate to apprentice, but since Tinidan spent most of his time with his Tribe, we got to speak with Anas, who held no official title.

"Have you spoken with the Elders?" I asked. I wasn't sure if he *actually* spoke, either by some communication magic or fast travel spell. Tinidan wasn't anywhere nearby, but Anas had *some* way of getting in touch.

"I have," he said solemnly. "They have agreed to your terms."

"Oh . . . excellent," I said with a smile. "How soon can the shaman get here?"

"A few days, perhaps a week," he told me. I nodded understandingly. I would have to keep some time clear in my schedule until then. So far, Dorsay Palace had been the only organization I found that ran on any kind of punctuality. The Guild weren't too bad but most Latorran deadlines needed a few days' wiggle room. The Tribes had even less concern for dates. The shaman would show up when he arrived, and there wasn't much I could do about that.

"Are you sure you'll be able to meet their demands?" he asked.

"It should be fine, as long as I can get sufficient mana," I said.

We were talking about the placement of what would be my new dungeon. Negotiations with the King about how much mana I could get had not gone well. "Count not on the gratitude of kings," was now an expression that I had personal knowledge of. He had cited a number of factors when refusing my petition. The dire mana situation in the capital, the conflict with Shadthe, and the fact that building an unfortified dungeon in a town was generally frowned upon.

Feh. If there was one thing I wanted my dungeon to be, it was *convenient*. Building it out in the wilds was all very well for Mandel, but I wanted—needed—to interact with people. I couldn't hide out in the dungeon all day; I had things to do.

But when one door closes, another opens. The Tribal Council had been more receptive to the idea of sending more mana my way. Cleaning up the deliberate mess that they'd made around Talnier was proving more and more beneficial. And they were quite keen to make sure that the benefits didn't all flow towards Latora. That didn't mean they were willing to do it for free, of course.

"Actually, something might have come up. The Council might be willing to reduce their demands if you can help out with something."

"Oh?" I said, raising my eyebrows.

"This is all very preliminary," Anas cautioned. "But would you be willing to travel into Tribal lands, if asked?"

"In principle, sure," I said. "But I suppose you're not able to give more details on where in the forest, how long it would take, or when it would be?"

"Not at this stage," he admitted. "There is still heated discussion of the wisdom of asking you for help. But if Lady Kaito remains unavailable . . ."

Last I'd heard, Kaito and her girls had headed east. First to check that the treaty was holding, and then for more adventure farther east. Kaito had expressed some interest in fighting sea monsters, which . . . well, each to their own.

"I understand," I said. "So your Council needs a Champion, then?"

"I'm not sure of the details," he confessed. "I was just asked to sound you out. Don't take this the wrong way, but not all of the Elders have . . . positive feelings about you."

"Oh? I wasn't aware I'd done anything to piss them off, specifically."

"Some Tribes are not in favor of the trade deal," he told me. "Some Elders still remember the war and don't want closer ties with Latora. They are in the minority, but the Council operates on consensus, so . . ."

"Well, that sounds like somebody else's problem," I said brightly. There were so few of those. "But if your Council can get its act together enough to ask something from me, I'll see what I can do."

WE LIVE IN A SOCIETY

"We want a Party Leader," Koenig said, as blunt as ever.

"Why, Guild Master," I deadpanned, "you want me to lead this group into a dungeon? I thought your adventuring days were over?"

I was in another meeting, this time in the Adventurers Guild offices with Martin Koenig and his assistant Nadine Lagacé. There was an apprentice there as well, taking notes. Altogether, we would have made for an *interestingly* balanced party.

"Don't be obtuse, I'm talking about a profession," Koenig replied, rolling his eyes. "We want it to be available at a low level, and for it to include Leadership."

"Oh . . . that was a bit of a sore spot with the old King, wasn't it?" I speculated. Leadership was something of a cheat skill, a way to get levels quickly and without necessarily putting in much effort. It was mostly confined to professions that required either a noble title or a high rank in the King's service. There were some unaffiliated professions that had it, but they had very high level requirements.

As the leader of Talnier—a fuzzily specified designation that was determined by the System—I had the ability to create professions that were available to citizens of the town. Nobles had the ability to do this for their own domains, and the King could make professions available for the entire Kingdom. But they didn't *know* about it, and the Guild was very keen on keeping them from learning. They felt, not without reason, that the nobles would use the ability to further entrench themselves in power.

How this had remained a secret was beyond me. Just two words in the right ear would be all it took to break it. Perhaps that was why the Guild had gotten so antsy when they learned that I *knew* those two words. I'd agreed to consult with them before I made any further modifications to professions, and I guessed this was the discussion we were having now. I'd thought it was to discuss new dungeon developments, but maybe we'd have that later.

"You might say that," he agreed. "We're not sure if it was a deliberate attempt to keep the common folk down, but King Nestor felt strongly about keeping leadership limited to the upper social order."

King Nestor had once held some strong feelings about many things, notably the unsuitability of his heirs. He had left the secret of territory status with the Guild, and they had not passed it on.

"You don't think it would give the game away to the nobles?" I asked sipping my tea. The Guild might get most of its income from selling alcohol to adventurers, but they also served excellent tea. Just as well, as I wouldn't want to be having this discussion drunk.

"You already did that, with your Talnier official," Nadine said. I looked pointedly over at the apprentice. Given that she could read and write, I'd bet gold that she had the Scribe profession. Nadine had the decency to blush. "Not that making the Scribe skill more widely available was wrong, but the secret is out now."

"Is it?" I asked. "I haven't heard anything about it outside of you two. It could be that Scribe is beneath their notice. I doubt Leadership is."

"Maybe not," Koenig admitted. "But I'm confident now that you're not going to give up the secret if they come looking. I think we can trust you."

"How gratifying," I said sourly. "And me, not even geased."

Koenig shrugged, uncomfortably. That had been a bit of a sore point. The Guild put an enchantment on their higher levelled members, to keep this, and other secrets, safe. Which reminded me of another topic that I should bring up. But first . . .

"I'm not sure that giving it to adventuring parties is the best plan, though," I said. "You're not really getting the full benefit with only four followers."

The average size of a party was five people. Leadership wasn't a one-way street; the followers did get a bonus to one skill that the leader had. An adventuring party, though, was comprised of people with diverse skills.

"If your Party Leader is a swordsman, he's going to want to give a boost to Weapon Mastery: Blade. That's not going to do much for the Wizard, the Healer, or the Rogue. Or even another fighter, if he's wielding an axe. Now, if the Party Leader was a mage . . . an entire team of mages would be interesting."

"They could get a type of magic, or they could get Mana Development," Nadine pointed out, spoiling my fun. "Either way, they wouldn't be able to cast spells."

"Good point," I allowed. "Anyway, it's a bit of an ask to donate your experience to someone if you don't get anything useful back."

"I suppose," Koenig muttered. "Do you have a suggestion?"

"What about a Militia Captain?" I asked. "We could give it a requisite of Weapon Mastery: Spear, bonuses to the same . . . maybe Bureaucracy."

"Do you want to give that to *all* the professions in Talnier?" Nadine asked curiously.

"Not *all* of them," I replied, equivocating a bit. There wasn't a need to, when I could start Teaching it. "I do think, though, that it's one of the missing elements that holds this society back."

"How so?" Koenig asked.

"Well, between social combat and actual violence, it's hard, here, to have organizations that stand up to any sort of pressure. Bureaucracy lets you make institutions up of lower-levelled people without having to worry that some level six is going to sweep them away."

"That's why the Guild uses it," Koenig agreed. "But is there really a need for more permanent organizations?"

I looked at him blankly. "Let's just say, yes," I said. "Give me a second to price up a Militia Captain."

It didn't take long. While I hadn't actually made any new professions, I'd been playing with the interface in my spare time.

Profession Name: [Militia Leader]
Profession Description: Band together to save the town!
Prerequisites: [Level 2] [Charisma 4] [Weapon Mastery: Spear] [None]
Skill Unlocks: [Leadership] [Bureaucracy] [Tactics] [Scribe] [+] [-]
Skill Bonus: [Weapon Mastery: Spear +2] [Leadership] [Tactics] [+] [-]
Special: [+]
Territory Point Cost: 0
Development Point Cost: 5

"Why Scribe?" Nadine asked, once I'd read out the result.

"Captains have to write reports; at least they do if they're in any sort of decent organization," I replied.

"Just how much paperwork are you going to burden these folks with?" Koenig asked. "And there's not much use for spears in a dungeon. Too cramped."

"It's not for adventurers," I said, gazing thoughtfully at the blue box that only I could see. "It's for people who are willing to defend the town. You want spears on a wall, I'm told."

"Any kind of mass combat," Nadine agreed. "And that is the arena where Leadership shines."

I nodded. I wasn't sure exactly how Leadership worked, but it seemed obvious that the more troops you commanded, the better the experience gain. There also seemed to be some benefit from layering Leadership skills, having leaders following other leaders in a hierarchy. I wasn't sure what the benefit was, though—people with Leadership tended to be nobles, and were closemouthed about it.

"Hmmph," Koenig snorted. "It's easy enough to qualify for, but do we need the spear prerequisite?"

"It keeps the costs down," I told him. "One for being a prerequisite, and it also reduces the cost of the bonus. Without those cost savings, I'd have to pay Territory Points to create it, and I want to save those."

New professions were all very well, but the real value of Territory Points was buying customizations. Unfortunately, the good ones were really expensive. I'd gained a few Territory Points, but nowhere near enough.

[Territory Name]: Talnier **[Territory Type]: Free City** **Population: 2,306** **[Territory Points]: 4** **[Roles]** **[Customization]**	**Liege: Kingdom of Latora** **Vassals: None** **Threats: Hector Rodakis, Duchy** **of Arryen, Duchy of Bargougne** **[Infrastructure]** **[Defenses]** **[Treasury]**

Not that I'd started obsessively checking to see if my points had gone up. Part of the problem was that the really good customizations, the ones that applied bonuses to your entire population, increased in cost as your population went up. Since population increase was one of my main sources of Territory Points, ever affording one of those bonuses might be forever out of my reach.

"I suppose it's an easy enough skill to get," Koenig allowed. "Very well, I'll accept it."

I raised an eyebrow, but didn't say anything. I'd agreed to *consult*, not defer to them. Still, if this satisfied them, then I could move on to other topics.

"So about Reynard," I said. "Has there been any word from Dorsay?"

Reynard was supposed to be sequestered away somewhere, getting punished or reeducated, whatever it was that the Guild did with misbehaving officials. They weren't supposed to be *able* to misbehave, what with the geas and their contracts and so on, but Reynard had managed it.

Now he'd managed to escape their custody. What had happened to him had been an idle curiosity when I'd seen him in Dorsay, but he'd jumped up several places on my priority list when I'd seen him wandering the streets of Talnier.

"Ah. Him," Koenig said, looking embarrassed. "He's not responding to his geas."

"What does that mean?" I asked.

He scowled. "I shouldn't even be telling you that he *has* a geas—and I *wouldn't* be if you hadn't already figured it out."

"Ifs, buts, candied nuts," I said, not bothering to work out if the rhyme translated. "I *do* know, so spill. Is he a criminal now? Can I have the guard arrest him?"

"No, is the short answer," Koenig replied. "As for . . . escaping custody shouldn't have been something he could do under the geas. He must have been free of it when he was interacting with you."

Yes, my little secret of what I'd been up to in Oakway was out. The King had passed it on to his Guild Master, who'd passed it down to at least this minion.

"Is that a surprise?" I asked. "Isn't the geas supposed to stop him from secretly profiting from a dungeon's expansion?"

"Well . . . there are loopholes," Koenig admitted. "We're still not sure exactly what he was up to, but he may have been able to work around the geas. Escaping, though . . . and there are other functions that aren't working. The link has been broken."

"But you said no arrest . . . don't you hunt down rogue Guild members?"

"It's not normally necessary," he said. "In this case . . . well, you reported that he was working for Countess Rankin."

"Yeah . . ."

"She has extended her protection over him, as her vassal. That wouldn't have meant much a few months ago, but since the . . . incident in the capital, Lady Rankin is high in the King's regard."

"So you can't touch him. Don't you want to know how he broke your geas?"

"We do. There are some ways to do it. A Theurge, dungeon items. The Countess presumably has access to one of them."

"So you're just going to leave it at that?" I asked.

"We can't do anything overtly, and Reynard is a careful man. He'll be on the lookout for any kind of . . . less overt activity. It will take time to arrange. I'd advise against just arresting him as well. You don't want the Countess taking action against Talnier."

"I'm not going to arrest him if he hasn't committed a crime!" I protested, ignoring the fact that I had just proposed that. Abandoning the Guild might actually have been a crime, but I couldn't consider it as one.

"Even then, I'd advise against it. Not that you'd be able to; Sir Hector is probably all too aware of the man's special status."

"Hector Rodakis commands the soldiers on the wall," I said frostily. "He doesn't get to decide who gets arrested or not."

Koenig raised an eyebrow. "Is that really true?" he asked. "In that case, I have to wonder what he's been doing on the streets."

THE LAW OF THE MARKET

Hector was going to be a problem. *Part* of the problem, the smallest part, but the part that was often uncomfortably at the forefront of my mind was that I was calling him Hector. Not Captain Rodakis. He had become familiar to me, both in our working relationship as Talnier officials and as a consequence of his pursuit of my hand in marriage.

He hadn't been subtle about it, but neither had he been too pushy. With Tom having done a disappearing act, Hector no longer had competition. That might explain why he was content to play a slow game, just making sure that I knew he was there, and that he was interested. I honestly thought he might give up if I ever gave him a clear indication that the answer was no.

The reason I couldn't *do* that was the bigger part of the problem. Hector was listed as one of the "threats" to Talnier, or to my leadership of it. The interface wasn't exactly clear, but it wasn't telling me anything I didn't already know. The nobility wanted Talnier back, and Hector was the point man for at least one noble faction.

Having to question the loyalty of the head of your military was either a leader's worst nightmare or something they did as a matter of course. I was still new to this leadership gig, so I wasn't sure. I was sure it was something that I needed to worry about. My hope was that as long as he thought he had a chance, he wouldn't do anything rash, like open the gates for another noble's forces.

That said, I couldn't let him get *too* confident. I didn't want him to get the idea that I was just playing hard to get and that a coup was what I "really wanted." I was walking a fine line, and the days that it was *visible* were the good ones.

In the meantime, though, I had to contend with Hector spreading his influence any wider. According to our Charter, the King was responsible for garrisoning the city and maintaining a guard on the wall. In theory, that put the King in direct control of the local forces, without having to go through the treacherous hierarchy of dukes, counts, and barons. In practice . . . well, at least I wasn't the only one who had to worry about Hector's loyalty.

The town guard, which had previously worked for the Baron, was now only responsible for keeping order in the town itself. The reduced responsibilities had allowed us to shrink the force, but only a bit. I had aspirations of turning them into an actual police force, and they were a tight-knit group that would have responded badly to any drastic cuts.

Still, it had allowed us to cull a few of the more corrupt and incompetent members from the ranks. They were a pretty good guard, if I did say so myself. It wasn't a surprise that Hector wanted to take control of it. He'd made a proposal twice now, to the Council, and had been rejected both times.

The arguments about both forces working in unison during emergencies and such weren't actually bad, but they weren't persuasive to me, and the rest of the Council was even more firmly against it. We were all quite friendly with the current head of the town guard, Captain Alain Guertin, and he wasn't happy with the idea of getting demoted to lieutenant.

However, it seemed that, instead of taking no for an answer, Hector had been out on the streets, administering . . . something.

"Is there something you want to tell me about this expense list?" I asked Marlon, my information broker. He scowled and screwed up his mouth as though he was going to spit.

"Cost of doing business sometimes," he said. "It's a reasonable expense."

"I don't doubt it, but if you're in some kind of trouble, I can do more than just pay for the healing potions."

He thought about it for a bit, long enough to make me wonder if I was going to have to use a skill. I tried to avoid that, especially among those whom I thought of as my people. Pushing someone with Intimidation or Persuasion might not be as painful as slapping someone around, but no one liked a bully.

"Might as well say," he admitted. "Captain Rodakis has been sniffing around for dirt . . . he's more fond of fists than gold for getting answers."

"Do you want to make a complaint to the magistrate?" I asked, my voice carefully neutral.

This time he did spit, aiming it behind the table we were sitting at. I winced. This was one of the nicer taverns; I didn't envy the server who had to clean it up. "I know how it works, with his type. A complaint won't get me anywhere."

"Maybe," I said. "It might go the other way. You're a local, he's an interloper. I can put in a good word for you. But he is the King's man, so the odds aren't good."

"Like I said, it's the cost of doing business. Long as you pay for fixing it, we're good," he assured me. "Besides, now that he's shown me the error of my ways, there shouldn't be too much of that from now on."

"You talked," I stated.

"'Course I talked. Not like I know anything damaging to you. Not that he asked much about that. Mostly he wanted to know . . . about the same stuff you did, at the start."

"Who's doing what, how this town works," I said. "He wants to get his feet under him."

"I suppose," Marlon agreed. "I told him where the remaining gangs hang out, but I haven't heard of his men doing any raids."

"They don't have the authority to do so," I explained. "Any more than they had the authority to beat you up."

"A noble's sword is its own authority," he muttered.

"True. It might be that he's just waiting for the right . . . exigent circumstances to use that information."

Knowing where the criminals lived was one thing. Without evidence of a crime—something the Guard was only just starting to grasp the need for—all you could do by raiding the place was bust some heads. For now, the guard was focused on catching the criminals in the act.

Marlon shrugged again. "Is there anything you want me to keep from him . . . or anything you want me to tell him?"

I shook my head. "Use your own discretion for now. If something comes up, I'll let you know. If you find something damaging to me, I presume you'll contact me to charge me more."

He looked away. "Maybe not," he said after a pause. I raised an eyebrow.

"You were right, before," he said, "about the business."

I didn't say anything, curious as to where he was going with this.

"The town's booming, and townsfolk want to know about everyone else," he said. "Businesses want to know about their competitors. Not criminal stuff, but how well they're doing, what their contracts are, that sort of thing."

"Information is the lifeblood of commerce," I said, quoting a line from my first orientation session at the company. "That's what *I* pay you for."

"Yeah, and it turns out there's a whole lot of people that will pay for it as well. So it looks like you were a good bet after all."

"Good to hear," I said.

"So all that I'm saying is that it doesn't make sense to bite the hand that's feeding you, you know? You're gonna keep growing the town, keeping my bottom line in the black. If something comes up that's gonna put an end to that, I'll make sure you know. No charge."

"Thanks," I said, touched by his sincerity. "Now, about the rest of those reports . . ."

"Yeah, sure, boss. Your other guy was right on the money. Brennan and Betard are definitely getting extra money from somewhere." He scowled. "Wish I knew who he was."

I just smiled. Marlon had already asked, and I'd refused to answer, saying that two informants kept each other honest. The truth was a little difficult to admit to.

My other source of information was the Town Status interface. Additional sections had become available over time. The Treasury section had been added when the Council had gotten some funds, the Defenses section had arrived when Hector and his troops showed up, and the Infrastructure section had appeared after we built our first building.

It might have been nice, if a little difficult to explain, if the Infrastructure section had allowed me to spend Town Points on buying new buildings. I wouldn't have put such a thing past the System. What it *did* do was provide information about all the *existing* infrastructure.

Maybe infrastructure was the wrong word. It wouldn't be the first time that I thought the interface was badly designed. What the section showed was a long list of every constructed feature of the town, and every *business* operating in the town.

Now, all the businesses were listed, but not all of them were *named*. To be named, you had to be registered in some way by the city. Merchants, for example, signed in whenever they brought goods in or out of the town. That was mainly for tax purposes, but it also made their name appear on my list.

Local businesses, on the other hand, might not be named. I was finding ways to encourage businesses to register, but Marlon's enterprise was probably going to be forever known as "Unnamed Information Broker 13." I could tell it was him because his income went up every time I paid him money.

That was the really useful part of the list. Each business had four numbers next to it: Foreign Income, Foreign Expenses, Domestic Income, and Domestic Expenses. Domestic didn't refer to Latora; it was limited to my territory.

The other part of the list was the various features and infrastructure of the town. These listings showed what the town paid to maintain them, and what they generated for the town.

For example, the docks and the town gates generated tax income from goods passing through. The numbers matched what was reported manually. I wasn't yet sure if that meant that no one was skimming or if skimming wasn't reported.

For something like the town walls, what was generated was *lives*. How the System calculated that, I did not know, but there had been a few wandering monsters that had been stopped at the walls. Each time, lives saved had ticked up by a few people.

Those numbers weren't everything I would have liked for an economic analysis of the town, but they were updated in real time, and Marlon could fill in some of the blanks. I'd been working on a model in my spare time. Calculate and Scribe weren't an *entirely* adequate substitute for a spreadsheet, but I was getting there.

I went over Marlon's reports, comparing his data with what I already had. The few meetings we'd had so far were almost a refuge from this crazy world. As I crunched the numbers, I could almost believe I was back in my finance industry job. Almost.

There were still a few areas where Marlon had declined to help me. Reminders that he was still beholden to criminal interests. Because the criminals were listed, too. "Unnamed Criminal Gang," "Unnamed Fence," "Unnamed Alchemical Provider." Crime in Talnier had taken a beating once the Baron was no longer there to protect it. I liked to think that my promotion of actual policing was also taking a bite out of it. But my interface was a reminder that it was still there, and would be a part of my town until I rooted it out.

Before then, Marlon would have to take a side. Today gave me some hope that it would be the right one.

BUSTLE AND HUM

I didn't spend enough time here. I had my office in the town hall, and it was comfortable enough. People knew to find me there—most of my time was as scheduled as we could be without digital clocks, but there were always a few free moments to be found. It was . . . fine, I supposed. Politics wasn't my thing, but my skills did make it easier. Being accessible was part of being a politician. I didn't have an *open* door, exactly, but I could be reached, if I wasn't busy, during office hours. I couldn't spend all my time there; I had a business to run. Most of the Council members did; the Mayor was the only one who lived off of his salary.

Now, the rules at the bank were quite different from the ones at the town hall. For one thing, I didn't meet with *anybody* who wasn't going to make me a lot of money. Investors, depositors, clients looking for a loan, and that was it. Oh, there were a few personal exceptions that the staff knew to let through, but if you weren't here for business, I didn't want to see you.

Another thing was that my office here was quite a bit more luxurious than the town hall one. There, I was a servant of the people, selflessly foregoing luxuries so that the money might be spent better elsewhere. It was nonsense, but it worked. People trusted me the more for it.

At the bank, on the other hand, it was the other way around. I wouldn't say people trusted private wealth, but they felt reassured by it when it came time to entrust their wealth to me. I'm not sure why, even though I'd felt it myself, back at the company. The aura of wealth that the higher-ups had possessed was a powerful thing. It made you want to trust your money to them, when really what it should have told you was that these people were adept at separating wealth from their clients.

So my office was as luxurious as I could make it. Richly polished wood paneling, cut glass around light stone lamps. They hadn't invented deep shag wall-to-wall, but the rug on the floor was such a work of art, it felt wrong to put furniture on it. There were even some paintings on the wall. Phantasmal ones, a Monet and a Vermeer. They made for quite the talking points. Latora wasn't quite ready for impressionism, though most people would agree that the picture of the bridge was quite beautiful.

The Vermeer confused them even more. I had to explain several times that it was an illusion of a *painting*, and not of a milkmaid.

Today, I didn't have anyone to meet at the bank. I could relax in my leather-bound chair and go over final approvals for loans. Territory Status sometimes gave me useful insight into the finances of applicants, so it was worth going over them, even if my staff had done their jobs correctly.

Going over paperwork is more entertaining than you might expect, when you stand to gain considerably from each application. Still, I wasn't upset when I was interrupted.

"Guys! Back from another dungeon trip?" I said as my companions trooped in. I gave them a mock glare. "You'd better not be tracking dungeon guts on my good rug."

It was a fake glare, not because they'd never gotten my rug dirty (they had), nor because the rug wasn't expensive (it really was), but because Water Magic was pretty good at cleaning. There wasn't a specific spell for it, but my control was pretty good now, and I could soak, scrub, and dry an object without damaging it. Or a person, if they happened to be a misbehaving and particularly filthy orphan.

"You know it!" Felicia said, holding her hand up for a high five. Hanging out with me, she was picking up some Earth mannerisms here and there. I ignored the hand and gave her a hug, having already noted that they'd cleaned up before coming here.

"There weren't any problems?" I asked, but she shook her head. They were actually a pretty good team now. Cloridan, Cutter, Janie, Maslin, Kyle, and Felicia. Three fighters, two mages for distance and swarms, and a healer. Cutter had made level five, and Maslin was closing in on it quickly. His reduced share was more than made up for by the high-threat monsters the team was going up against.

"We're going to catch up to you at this rate," Felicia said. "How long before you come down with us again?"

"A little while yet," I mumbled. "Things are starting to come together, but it's still . . . fragile."

It wasn't that I'd given up adventuring, I still went down with my crew occasionally. I wasn't really adding that much value, though. Cloridan was a terror when he was invisible, of course, but Cutter became less effective, as he had to avoid actions that might put Cloridan in harm's way. When you added in that I took a greater share of experience, thanks to my higher level, I felt that I was holding them back when I joined them.

Felicia pouted. We'd gone over this before, and there wasn't much point in rehashing it.

"Just get Fire Magic if you're that hung up on contributing," she said. "You've got the skill points now, right?"

"Hells, yeah!" Janie said. "Imagine the flames, with three of us burning everything in sight!"

"I don't know that I'd be *contributing* anything at that point," I said wryly. "Just adding to the mayhem isn't constructive."

More than that, though, I didn't *want* to burn people to death. It was bad enough cutting up monsters for parts, but I'd made my peace with it. I could appreciate the efficiency of Janie's methods without wanting to emulate her.

"No, if I pick up another magic, I'll look for something like Shadow or Air," I said. "Flying or teleportation, I can't say no to that."

Janie scoffed, but she knew she wasn't going to get anywhere with this argument.

"Anyway," she said. "Are you ready?"

"Yeah," I replied. "Did you think it would take all of you to drag me to the dance hall?"

"Nah, miss," Cutter said. "We just wanted to see the fancy digs is all."

I rolled my eyes. "Well, let's get going, wouldn't want to be late to Isabel's first performance."

There was quite a crowd outside the entrance to the dance hall. Part of me felt bemused at that, but I knew better. This world just didn't have the entertainment options that mine did. No movies, few books, and barely any music. You could call dungeons adventure playgrounds, but only if you had a *very* lax attitude to safety standards.

There were plays in the cities, but very few travelling entertainers. Bard was not a well-regarded profession, as it provided little experience. A Bard got most of their XP from the monsters they slew on the road, which wasn't a great advertisement for the profession.

Bringing Isabel here had been as much accident as planning. I'd needed someone to take care of the orphans I'd saddled myself with, and she needed to get out of Dorsay before she had to choose between starvation and prostitution. Setting her up in Talnier had been a risk, but it was one that the Bank of Talnier could afford to take.

I noted with approval that the children were managing the door. Child labor laws were a long way away; you worked to live. Not all of them had Calculate, but enough did to handle counting the money and giving change.

I flicked up my interface to check and was pleased to note that the income of Isabel's dance company was finally ticking up. Not a bad start, but we'd have to see if our projections held up.

Felicia nudged me as we got to the head of the line. "Don't get lost in the finances," she warned. "We're here to see the dance."

I shrugged and ignored the way that the kids straightened up as I became visible, with whispers of "the Headmistress" getting passed around. I wasn't sure why I rated all that reverence. I may have been responsible for keeping them fed and warm, but the only classes that had been run since they got here were Isabel's.

That would change just as soon as I could get the second Tower of Learning up and running again. I gave a slight smile at the thought, which no doubt started a few rumors about the kids. I let it go, and let myself get escorted to our table. The show was about to begin.

The applause was loud and sustained, which boded well. A packed house on the first night could be explained by simple novelty, but the applause suggested the crowds would be coming back. Isabel had done well.

She carried the show. Her apprentices had Dance, but skill level counted. They did pretty well as a support, though, and they would improve with time.

I held off on analyzing the night's take, as our table was being approached by one of the performers. Not one of the kids, but the Bard that Isabel had hired to accompany them. She'd worked herself up into a tizzy to ask for the budget for him, but our conversation had amounted to "Well, of course, you need music to dance to," and her preparations had been wasted.

This was my first time meeting him. He'd been busy with rehearsals, and I'd been . . . busy. I only knew who he was because I'd seen him on stage. He was about forty, handsome enough in a kind of disreputable way. He bowed as he approached.

"Madame Councillor, If I might present myself. I am Stephen Durr, a humble Bard. I hope that our modest melodies have entertained you."

I refrained from snorting or rolling my eyes, but I'd seen what we were paying for those so-called "humble" melodies.

"It was quite the show," I told him truthfully. "You were very accomplished." I refrained from mentioning that I planned on having them perform with recordings once I could get an enchanted music box built. It seemed to me that it would be easier to dance to a recording that never changed. Plus, it would be a recording of Taylor Swift, so better all around.

"I'm so pleased you approve," he smarmed, bowing again. I winced, but only to myself. This was probably the start of an extended period of sucking up to the rich patron, which I wasn't looking forward to. At least, at his age, he wasn't going to try and sleep with me . . . I hoped.

"I was asked to pass on my regards," he continued, which deviated from the script a bit. "A colleague of mine, and an acquaintance of yours," he said.

I raised an eyebrow. "A colleague?" I asked. The only one I could think of was . . .

"Aesrideu," he confirmed. "He spoke fondly of you, and asked me to pass on a missive."

He held out a letter, which I did not immediately take, frowning suspiciously at it.

"Last I heard, Aesrideu was making good money Can't he afford to pay for a Courier?"

Durr shrugged. "He heard I was being hired by you, and took the opportunity to write a note."

"You've been in town a while," I noted. "Couldn't you have gotten it to me sooner than this?"

"It's a favor for a friend," he explained. "When I took it, he asked that I give it to you directly. Both your Council office and your place of business were quite willing to pass on a letter, but they declined to let me meet you."

He gave me a dazzling smile. "I wanted to fulfill the promise to my friend, but I also wanted to see if you were as beautiful as he said."

This time I did roll my eyes. "Well, I hope that I don't disappoint," I said, plucking the envelope out of his hand.

"Your beauty exceeds even his fulsome description," he assured me.

He *was* going to try and sleep with me. "Well, thank you for the letter," I said. "As you can see, I'm with some friends at the moment . . . and I've already got a Rogue in this party."

"Thank you for this small moment of your attention. I will remain in your service," he said. He bowed again and then backed away.

"He was a bit old, but he seemed nice?" Felicia said, grinning.

I scowled at her. "Better than the envoy of a psychotic ice mage or the man who wants to betray this small town's democratic process," I agreed.

Felicia giggled, and Janie laughed out loud.

"When you put it like that, they sound pretty bad," Felicia admitted. "They are handsome, though."

"No need for those blackguards," Cloridan put in, "when you have the perfect companion right under your nose."

I gave him a sceptical look. "Aren't you still seeing Alicia? Or was it Belitere, the cat girl?"

He coughed. "Belitere was simply a passing fancy," he said with an embarrassed look. "And Alicia . . . found out about Belitere."

There were some jeers and boos around the table, but Kyle called a halt to it. "Not that Cloridan doesn't deserve it," he said. "But who is . . . Esridoo, and why does he have a weird name?"

"Aesrideu," I told him. "He's an elven Bard that I met in Anchorbury."

"An elf?" Felicia said.

"You picked his brains, as I recall, instead of his pants, like half the noble ladies of Anchorbury," Janie said with a smile.

"Was he . . . pretty?" Felicia asked. Janie laughed.

"Hard to tell with all the ladies in the way," she said.

"But why is he sending you a letter?" Kyle asked, cutting through the nonsense.

"I dunno," I said. "I guess there's one way to find out."

FİΠALLY

Honored Mistress Hammond,

    I hope this missive finds you well, and I also hope that it reaches you in a good and timely manner. You might find it strange that I should use such an unreliable and roundabout method of writing to you, but I have my reasons. It pains me to admit it, but I am a fugitive. Not from the law of your country, but of my own. Courier networks are one way that the hunters, spread thin and wide-ranging, catch the scent of people like myself.

    I wish that we could meet again, but by the time you read this, I will have left Latora for greener pastures. Sadly, the life I have chosen does not allow me to stay in one place—one country—for long.

    The reason I am writing to you, aside from passing on my best wishes, is that I have heard that you might be visiting my homeland soon. I'm hoping that I can prevail on you to contact my sister, Jesridae, to let her know that I am alive and thinking fondly of her. We have been out of touch for many years, and she must be worried.

    Like me, my sister chafes under the restrictions of the Grove. Unlike me, she was unable to find her way out. She is a person you can trust. If you mention that you are a friend of mine, I'm sure that she would help you to the full extent of her abilities.

    Your servant, Aesrideu

What is going on here? I thought as I let the letter drop to the table. The others were looking at me expectantly, so I passed it over.

"I can't believe you're friends with an elf," Felicia said. "Why didn't you mention this before?"

"It wasn't a big thing," I told her. "I just had some questions about demons that he helped me with . . . we were friendly enough, but it was nothing special."

"So when are you going to Elfland?" Janie asked.

"It's called the Glade," Felicia corrected. "But yes, when?"

"That's the *really* weird thing," I said. "*Most* of it is weird, but it all kind of makes sense if you accept that part. I don't have any plans to visit . . . the Glade. I don't even know where it is."

"North of here," Felicia said. "On the other side of the Tribal lands."

Janie laughed. "Someone's got a thing for elves," she snorted. Felicia flushed.

"I . . . may have read some stories when I was younger. If I'd known there was an elf in Anchorbury, I might have visited sooner."

"I suspect that if you had known, he wouldn't have been there for much longer," I told her. "From the sound of it, as soon as word spreads outside the town that he's there, he's gone."

"Besides," Janie added, "even if you had been there, you would have had to fight your way past all the hungry upper-class ladies."

"He wasn't that hard to talk to," I said, scowling at her. She rolled her eyes in response.

"She plays this town like it was a musical instrument, and she thinks she wasn't special just because she was level four at the time? Trust me, those vultures knew better than to mess with you."

"Well, maybe," I admitted. "The fact remains that I *don't* plan on visiting the elves, so who told him that I did?"

"There's one obvious answer," Cloridan said. "Well, seven."

I scowled and looked at the letter as if it were a snake.

"It could be a devious plan by one of your enemies," Janie tried. "That got . . . leaked to your elf-bard. Didn't you say that one of the people you were worried about was a countess? She might have slept with him and let something slip."

"He wouldn't have—" I said but stopped myself. *I* wouldn't have, but I had to admit that she was pretty and rich. Normally it only took one of those. "Okay, he might have," I admitted. "But if he was really trying to warn me, wouldn't he be more . . . specific?"

"It's a stretch," Janie agreed. "But if you're looking for something *other* than 'the gods have got plans, and this is their way of booking out your calendar,' that's all I've got."

"Maybe he was worried that if he mentioned the Countess, the hunters would have a lead on tracking him down?" Felicia speculated.

"That's so convoluted that it gets us right back to having been organized by a god," I groaned. "Well, it's not like we can do anything about it. I'll just try to avoid travelling to the Glade."

"What if that's what they want you to do . . ." Cloridan said slowly. "Either the god or your enemy. Keep you in the city, or away from the elves, whichever one is their goal."

"When you put it like that, I guess that there really *isn't* anything to be done," I groused. "Can't go with the flow, can't go against it, can't even write back to ask what's going on."

"Just keep your eyes open?" Felicia suggested. "Make the best decision that you can with the information that you have available."

"Yeah," I agreed. "That's all I've ever been able to do."

I stood at the center of the hidden . . . temple? Tomb? Fortress? I didn't know. It might have been any of those, or none. Most recently, it had been a bandit base, and now I was claiming it for my own.

I bent down and placed Rhis on the stone floor.

Sufficient mana detected. Instantiate mana construct? [Y/N]

[Y], I thought. There was a momentary pause, and then I was in the white room.

"This isn't really sufficient, Mistress," Rhis said, scowling.

"It's enough to work with, right?" I asked. "We're well out the Order's collection range."

"It's about what I had at Oakway," he admitted. "But that amount was so *limiting* back then. I'd hoped for more . . ." He tried his puppy dog eyes.

"Don't worry so much," I said, laughing. "I'm going to get you more mana. I just wanted you already in place before the shaman arrives. I'm hoping that when he gets close, you'll be able to draw the mana stream closer to you and use it, without having to rely on his enchantments the entire way."

"I suppose that is possible, depending on what you mean by *close*," Rhis said thoughtfully.

"The farther the better," I replied. "The farther out you can grab the stream, the less certain of your location he's going to be."

"I see," Rhis said, nodding thoughtfully.

"So for now, just focus on expanding to cover this structure."

"That will take quite some time with my current levels," Rhis informed me.

"Oh? Have you got an estimate?"

The white room flickered, and then we were standing back in the underground base. This version of it was lit with a sourceless bright light, instead of my own light spell. Everything could be seen clearly.

"I should be able to absorb most of what you see here *and* register a second floor with my existing mana," Rhis said. "After that, though, I will only be regenerating 24 mana a day. I can only guess at how much more there is to absorb, but it will take six days to accumulate enough mana for a third floor."

"That slowly? This doesn't look much bigger than that dance hall."

"The mana levels are much lower. This instantiation, there wasn't enough free mana to start me with full mana. Please consult your Dungeon Status"

I did, and saw that he was right.

Dungeon Name	Tower of Learning		
Level: 7 Current Mana: 80 Dungeon Traits	XP: 38,736,321 Mana Cap: 120	Next Level: 100,000,000 Mana Regeneration: 12	Floors: 1 Upkeep: 0.0
Name	Rank	Effect	
Spatial Control		Teleportation, Portals, Expansion (8)	
Monster Classes	10	Lizards, Goblins, Insects, Mammals, Fish	
Treasure Classes	5	Coins, Gems, Ores, Mystic Crystals, Crafted Items	
Trap Classes	5	Simple, Advanced, Natural, Magical, Lava	
Environmental Classes	5	Desert, Jungle, Swamp, Forest, Mountain	
Mana Efficiency	5	10% bonus mana regeneration per rank	

"That is low," I admitted, wincing. "Increasing your floors will increase your mana regeneration, though, right?"

"Yes, but there is a diminishing return. It costs more for each floor. At current mana levels, I estimate I can create no more than five levels. The fourth floor will take seven days to save up for, and the fifth, nine more days. After that . . ." He paused. "The cost for the sixth level will be more than the mana cap."

"How much would you need for the portal?"

"At current levels of mana, I would need . . . seven levels to create such a device."

I sighed. "Well, we'll just have to get you more mana, won't we?"

He nodded eagerly. "That would be ideal. Shall I proceed with the expansion and the second floor?"

"Yeah, I'll be back in a bit." I turned to head outside.

"Mistress? You're leaving me?" Rhis asked anxiously.

"Just for a bit." Belatedly, I remembered that I was in the white room, and walking away wouldn't do anything. With an effort of will, I shifted my perceptions back to the real world. Connected *to* my will, Rhis seamlessly shifted realms as well, crafting an illusion of himself without missing a beat.

"I've got to place that enchantment up top, to conceal your mana funnel," I told him.

"But, but, there might be beasts or monsters down here that could steal my core!"

"I doubt there's anything more than a couple of rats," I assured him. "There's no food."

"One rat is all it would take, though," he said. "They just have to touch the core, and then . . . I'm gone."

"That . . . is a good point," I said. "Do you want me to get the others in here to guard you?"

"That would help with my mana regeneration," he said automatically, "But are you talking about Felicia, Janie, or Kyle? They've all been casting covetous glances at me when you aren't looking. You can't leave me alone with them."

This again. Refraining from rolling my eyes, I pulled up a monster from my memory. "Fine. I'll let you have *one* Phantasmal monster, to scare away any beasts."

I used the dungeon to cast the spell, which would allow Rhis to take control of it. The Phantasmal alien appeared between us, flexing its claws and dripping Phantasmal slime on the floor. It didn't actually *hit* the floor, just smoked away into nothing.

"Ooh," Rhis said. "Can I get a real one of those?"

"I hope not," I said. "This should be scary enough for you."

Rhis nodded eagerly, and I left him to his work.

My apparently untrustworthy companions were camping outside of the crack in the cliffside. Felicia waved at me when I emerged.

"Everything go well?" she called.

"Yeah, it's fine, just got to plant that enchantment now," I said, looking up. Free-climbing was never my thing back home, but I had a few advantages now. I eyed a likely handhold, about three meters up, and jumped.

Climbing like this . . . maybe I should take it up as a hobby. It was easier to see what people saw in it, now that I had the physical capacity and the skills to make it easier. I swarmed up the cliffside like an Olympic athlete on speed.

When I got to the top, I was in for a surprise. There were structures here. Ruined ones, long overgrown with brush and trees.

Interesting. These have got to be connected to the structure below, right?

I took a quick look but couldn't find anything that looked like a way down. As overgrown as they were, though, that didn't really mean anything. Any shaft or passageway was likely to have collapsed or been covered with rubble from the building containing it. Maybe Rhis would find something going up.

That wasn't what I was here for, so I didn't spend too much time on it. Rhis's mana funnel was clearly visible. It wasn't as big as the one in Dorsay, but to the right eyes, it would be visible from a long way away. However, it was easy to conceal with the enchanted item that I'd made back then. I propped it up in one of the corners of a building that had most of its walls and then positioned a few loose stones to conceal it.

I climbed back down and invited the others inside. Rhis would just have to get used to his paranoia. I broke out some wine, and we clinked Phantasmal crystal goblets together.

"Stage one is complete!" I declared. "Stealth Dungeon has been achieved! Now we just need some more mana."

LOST IN A FOREST

There was a problem with meeting the shaman, and it lay in the fact that I didn't know where my dungeon was. Little inconveniences like this don't trouble you in a world with GPS and Google Maps, but I don't think I could have even explained how they worked, let alone duplicate them here.

I knew how to *get* to my dungeon . . . probably. Between memorizing the landmarks and walking there a few times, I thought I could get there on my own. I hadn't actually put that to the test, though. On every trip so far, I'd relied on Cloridan and Cutter, our most outdoorsy types, to take us on the roundabout route that led to the secret entrance.

That was one thing. Ask me to point to the spot on a map, however, and I'd be stuck pointing to some vague area covered in hills and trees, and saying, "Somewhere in there." And that was supposing I managed to find a good map. Most of the maps of the northern forest were bad copies of Empire-era maps, with the increased extent of the forest added in green.

If I'd wanted to take the shaman to the dungeon, that wouldn't have been a problem. I could have led him there, or, more likely Cloridan could have led us both there. Regardless, we would have found our way there. But I didn't want to lead him to the dungeon. I wanted to meet him some distance, say a mile, from the dungeon and see if Rhis could suck in the mana river that he was leading closer.

A little-known fact is that in a world without GPS, you can't just start at one place in a forest and "go north." There are trees, hills, and cliffs in the way. You get lost. You lose track of the sun because the trees are too thick. You have no idea of how far you've travelled, and since it isn't in anything like a straight line, even knowing it won't do you any good.

Fortunately, all of this was explained to me before I tried to do just that. I thought that maybe someone with a decent Hunt or Gather skill could do it, but apparently the expertise those skills granted told the user not to try something so stupid.

So we cheated, making use of two advantages that I did have. One was the use of a Griffin Rider. The riders didn't exactly answer to me as a Councillor, but I *was* on good terms with their captain. A quiet word, a little extra money, and I had access to a rider who could be discrete. I didn't want to call it bribery; I felt that closer cooperation between the civil and military administrations was something to be encouraged. Hector could have learned from us, if we had been inclined to tell him.

The other advantage I had was that I could see through my own illusions. This made it easy to identify my dungeon's location from the air. Then all we had to do was fly a mile or two north and find an appropriate clearing to land it.

At this point, what would hopefully be the final flaw in my plan showed itself. There was no clearing. Fortunately, griffins didn't need clearings to land in.

I screamed my lungs out as the griffin folded its wings, plunging a short distance through the upper canopy. I hadn't gotten to my second breath before it caught itself on a branch or the main trunk. I wasn't sure which, but at this point, I was hanging at a strange angle, clutching at my harness for dear life.

Whatever perch we were clinging to was not so firm that it didn't sway as it absorbed our momentum. The sensation was sickening, but I quickly found myself missing it, as my ride reoriented itself and then jumped to a lower branch. The rest of our descent was . . . nerve-wracking to say the least. At least it was over quickly enough that I managed to not vomit.

"Are you sure I should just leave you, ma'am?" the rider asked, as I reacquainted myself with my best friend, the ground.

I ignored him for a moment. The forest floor wasn't the *most* comfortable ground around. There were too many roots and not enough grass. Still, I took a moment, and then a moment more, to appreciate its basic solidity before pulling myself together to answer the man.

"I should be fine," I assured him. "They told me that the shaman would be able to find me, as long as I was in this general location. You can find this place again?"

"Aye," he said. His voice was doubtful, but it wasn't his own abilities that he was doubting. "Messie can smell out the tree she landed in, no problem. Even if it rains, if it's just a day it'll be fine."

"Then I should be fine as well," I told him. "The shaman probably heard me coming down and is on his way."

"Might not be the only thing that heard you come down," the man pointed out.

"I can hide from anything too big for me to kill," I told him. I threw up a Light spell to make my point. It was the least of the spells I'd be casting here, but it was necessary. The canopy was thick around here, and while some light made it down, it wasn't enough to read by.

"We're not near any mana streams," I said, glancing around with Mana Sense to make sure. I'd checked from above, but the forest was quite hard to see through. This area was quite low on mana, with a smooth flow that suggested where the nearest stream was. "There's not likely to be any monsters around."

He looked at me doubtfully but then shrugged.

"All right then. I'll be back around this time tomorrow," he said. He climbed back onto his saddle and started strapping himself back in.

"Are you going to . . ." I started, not willing to finish the question.

"Yep!" he said brightly. "This is what the straps are for, really. Not much call for flying upside down on a normal flight."

I took a step backward, as the griffin waggled its hips and then jumped twenty feet straight up onto the trunk. It clawed its way up the tree, with its rider seemingly entirely unfazed by the ascent.

I'll have to go through that tomorrow, I told myself and shuddered. To distract myself, I started setting up camp.

I travelled light—when travelling by griffin, there was no other way—but that didn't mean I needed to camp without equipment. Not when I had Phantasmal Object at my disposal.

My first priority was a chair, based on any number of camping chairs that I'd seen. I could have just placed an Aeron chair down, but that seemed excessive. Next was a table to put my food and drinks on—I wasn't a savage, to leave these things on the ground.

If I'd been planning to stay here longer, I would have made a tent and a bed and a sleeping bag, but those could wait for now. Instead, I thought about a fire. It *was* pretty cold. The forest canopy seemed to be keeping any snow away, or it was just a bit too warm for it. I didn't know how it worked; I wasn't a weather forecaster.

The ground . . . seemed a bit too dangerous for fire to me. It was pretty damp, but it was mostly wood, either roots or fallen branches. Maybe an English boy would have said *Nah, that'll be fine*, but my instincts were made in drier forests.

So, a brazier then. A Heat enchantment would have been safer and more efficient, but I'm not made of money, and my enchantment budget was taken up with other things. Alchemy was cheaper.

First, the brazier itself, made with Phantasmal Object. Next, a cloth, treated with an alchemical substance that made it practically immune to heat. Draping that over the brazier would protect it from the fire that would otherwise keep chipping off its hit points until it vanished. Then I needed to gather some dry . . . ish branches, and then all I needed to do was light the fire.

I did manage to get badges in Girl Scouts, but we mostly used matches when we went camping. Flint and steel were all very well for primitives, but Alchemy came to my rescue again. A small vial of liquid, poured over the wood, quickly started to smoke and then burst into flame. And with that, I had a nice little campfire.

I couldn't eat Phantasmal food, of course, but my ring could easily hold three days' worth of cold rations and cordial. Wine had seemed ill-advised. This place wasn't *entirely* safe.

I'd been entertaining myself for a couple of hours, practicing my Water Magic, when I heard the faint sounds of song. Looking around for the source of it, I noticed a bird that hadn't been there before. That I hadn't noticed arriving.

> **[Identification]: Fell Raven – Threat: 12 – Properties: Flight, Shadow Aspect (Bonded)**

Ah. I've been found. Tame wasn't part of the official Shaman skill set, but Shaman tended to be a profession picked up late in life. They generally had other life skills.

As the singer grew closer, I realized that "song" might have been an overstatement. There was a tune, but the words were meaningless. Not just *la-la-la*, more of a *lo-lie-de-dum*. I might have assumed it to be in another language, but the fact that it didn't get translated ruled that out.

I stayed seated since the incoming shaman seemed to know where he was going, and shortly thereafter, the man himself appeared. Not on the ground, as I expected, but perched on a tree branch. A grey-furred cat-kin, if I was any judge.

"Woot! They said she was a looker, but this is ridiculous," he said as he looked down at me. "Makes me wish I was sixty again!"

I frowned. The language he was speaking wasn't Latorran, and it didn't sound like the common Tribal language. It must have been his Tribe's tongue, which he couldn't have expected me to speak. Unless he knew—or suspected—that I was a Champion? More likely he was just being rude.

"I'm sorry, I assumed the shaman they sent would be able to speak the common tongue, at least," I said.

He shrugged. "I speak Latorran," he said in Tribal Common. "But you speak the common tongue pretty well, for a human. Let's use that, Council Member Hammond."

I smirked. I knew very well that I spoke his language *perfectly*. If I wasn't focused on it, I spoke in exactly the accent he was used to.

"The common tongue is fine," I said. "Now—"

"You must be pretty brave coming out into the forest alone," he said, grinning down at me. "Or pretty stupid."

He showed no sign of coming down to talk. Were we going to have some kind of face-off? I relaxed my suppression of my level six aura. I'd been practicing it, not because I'd gotten it working, but because that was what you needed to do to get it to work.

He didn't look impressed, which was no surprise. I'd probably gone from a 5.8 to a six . . . which was where he was as far as I could tell. Hopefully, *he* wasn't suppressing *his* aura. I'd need to do something else to impress him.

"I can take care of myself," I said, but I didn't say it from where I was. Instead, I said it from above, my Phantasmal Emissary appearing silently and without any warning on the branch above. Thanks to Conceal Mana, there was no sign of a spell to be seen with his Mana Sense.

He jumped and looked up. I waved to him before cancelling the spell.

"So I see," he said slowly. He looked back at me, trying to figure out what had happened. Illusion Magic wasn't a common path in the Tribes. There were too many people with high enough Perception to see through the illusions of a beginner Illusionist. Someone as young as me, with illusions that he couldn't see through, wasn't something he could come to terms with easily.

"Did you bring the mana?" I asked. I actually knew that he had. I could see it. The mana levels here hadn't changed much, but I could sense how the flow of it had changed. It was all being sucked up into a wide pipe, the sides of which were out farther than I could see.

"I did," he said. Shaking off his thoughts, he jumped down to me. He was pretty spry for someone as old as him. Sure, he groaned as he straightened up, but that jump had been twenty feet down. "I am known as Filnas. Did you bring my payment?"

"Right here," I said and handed him a leather sack. My negotiations had been with the Tribal Council and hadn't been for anything as petty as gold, but the expectation that the man doing the work would need to be paid had been passed on.

"Dungeon gold," he mused, pulling out one of the coins and looking at it. "These have become a lot more common since the trade started."

"I was told gold would be preferred," I said. "If you need beast cores instead . . ."

"No, this is fine," he said. "More common is good. More Tribes are becoming familiar with it, more Tribes are desiring it to trade with. Where shall I send this river?"

"Can you send it underground?" I asked. "I'd like for it to not be visible."

He raised his eyebrows. "I can . . ." he said thoughtfully. "Mana goes easily through the ground. The beasts, though, they cannot travel that way. With nowhere to go, they will break out of the confinement."

"The beasts?" I said uneasily. I hadn't been worried about them up until now, but I suddenly realized that I was in a mana river, the sort that monsters travelled through.

"None will arrive for some time yet," he assured me. "But thinking ahead is required for shamans."

"Right, right," I said. "Can you make . . . an offshoot? That links back in? That way the monsters will just go around and around?"

He nodded. "Normally, that would cause a dangerous buildup . . . but you are planning to absorb most of the mana . . . I think that can work."

"Then send the river into that ridge, and we'll see if we can take hold of it from this distance."

"As you say," he said and started up his song again.

Moving mana like this, it felt like a breeze that didn't touch anything physical. What it *was* touching, what I was feeling, I didn't know. But I felt it.

"I feel it," Filnas said, making me jump. "Something is taking it . . . it is gone."

"Is that it?" I asked. "Are we done?"

Filnas laughed. "Oh no. I still have to do the loop, and I will need to mark the trees here to fix the stream. But you have your mana."

BUILDING BACK BETTER

Dungeon Name	[Tower of Learning]		
Level: 7 Current Mana: 17 Dungeon Traits	XP: 38,045,236 Mana Cap: 675	Next Level: 100,000,000 Mana Regeneration: 67.5	Floors: 3 Upkeep: 0.005
Name	Rank	Effect	
Spatial Control Monster Classes Treasure Classes Trap Classes Environmental Classes Mana Efficiency	 10 5 5 5 5	Teleportation, Portals, Expansion (8) Lizards, Goblins, Insects, Mammals, Fish Coins, Gems, Ores, Mystic Crystals, Crafted Items Simple, Advanced, Natural, Magical, Lava Desert, Jungle, Swamp, Forest, Mountain 10% bonus mana regeneration per rank	

"That's better," I said.

"Yes, Mistress," Rhis answered. "I should have enough for a fourth floor in about five hours."

I nodded. "And then?"

"I'd like to get another floor, but there is still expansion to be done if you want me to take over this whole complex. Those extra floors are only nominal right now."

"Is there any problem with keeping them nominal for now?" I asked.

Rhis looked at me reproachfully. "Not as such," he said. "But without floors, I don't have room for defenses. Right now, once you've gone back to town, I'm going to be entirely defenseless."

"We'll get something in place before I go," I said. "And the gang will be staying to protect you."

"Whom did you think I needed protection *from*?" Rhis muttered, entirely performatively. Some quirk of the interface meant that Rhis's voice always came through perfectly clearly, regardless of how he spoke. Not that he didn't want me to hear him in this case. I just continued on, ignoring his trust issues, which didn't show any sign of going away.

"How long before I can return to town?" I asked.

"One portal is under the mana cap now," he replied. "Five hours of regeneration and I can start on it, if you want to delay the next floor."

I sighed. "We should get the others inside you, to help with the regen."

"That would help, a little," Rhis agreed. "It would help more if they could occupy the lowest floor, but . . ."

"But the third floor is just nominal," I finished for him. "All right, it looks like we'll be staying the night. Get another level, then do some expansion. See if you can have a portal ready by the morning."

"How long is that? I don't have access to the surface yet."

"About eighteen hours," I answered and turned to leave.

"Mistress!" Rhis exclaimed, looking at me with pleading eyes. "You're not going to camp outside and leave me alone, are you?"

"I'm *just* going outside to let them know the plan," I said. "We'll camp in here for tonight. Devote some mana to making some of the rooms habitable, and . . . is there something you can do to make a fire safe?"

"I can handle it," Rhis said. He didn't look *entirely* pleased at the thought of the others coming in, but he seemed to like that idea better than me leaving.

"Then some sort of common area where we can cook and eat." Not for the first time, I was simultaneously pleased and creeped out by the fact that I didn't need to give Rhis *specific* orders. I knew that he would arrange the rooms appropriately and not turn them into subtle traps or nightmarishly decorated torture chambers. The sad look he gave me told me he *wanted* to, but he would follow my wishes.

The next morning, we had some decisions to make. The portal was ready for us to take back. Knowing that we were going to be carrying it, Rhis had made it as light as he could, but there was only so small you could make something designed for people to walk through.

"Couldn't you have made something that folds up?" I asked. Rhis shook his head.

"The two portals need to be *exactly* the same size and shape," he said. "So it has to be rigid—and tough. If you *do* manage to dent it on the way, you'll need to bring it back."

"I've heard of portals that did that, though."

"Those aren't the same thing," Rhis sniffed. "That would be a free teleport to a beacon, not a linked passage. They cost more."

I wanted to ask how much more, but there wasn't much point. This was what we had, and not using it would be a waste of the mana.

"How heavy is it?" I asked, reaching out to find out for myself. "Oh, it's light!" Light was a . . . relative term. I doubt my previous self would have been able to lift the corner of it. The new me, however, had four times my old strength. That put me, disappointingly, still within the normal human range, albeit at the top of it. I could lift this on my own, but carrying it for half a day's travel was probably a bit much. Not to mention it was an awkward carry for one person.

"Cutter and I can take it back," Cloridan said. "You can stay here with the dungeon."

Rhis nodded in eager agreement. I hated to disappoint him.

"I've been away for three days already," I said. "Talnier has probably burned down by now. Besides, we need to set this up in my offices, and you two aren't allowed in there on your own."

"You don't trust us?" Cloridan said, his grin taking the sting out of his words.

"As far as I can throw you," I said, with the same amount of humor. "Actually, I'll probably have to grant you guys some access once we set it up, but right now it's the vault. No one gets in there without a good reason for it."

"Well, we have a good reason," Cloridan said.

"Yeah, but they're specifically forbidden from letting someone in just because they say I said so," I told him. "Happens more often than you'd think."

"Well, three is better than two for carrying, and your delightful presence is always welcome. Won't Rhis miss you, though?"

"Sooner we leave, the sooner I can get back," I said firmly, ignoring Rhis's pouting. "Let's go."

I'll gloss over the trek back. Suffice it to say that carrying a door through the wilderness isn't as you might think. If you think that it might be pretty hard, well, it's harder than that. There weren't any challenges that couldn't be overcome, it was just that they came every minute of that long, long trip.

But we made it. Carried that damned thing all the way through the forest, through the gate, under the curious eyes of the guard, and up to my bank. Procedures were properly followed to allow my access (I knew better than anyone not to trust what I saw), and we mounted the portal against the stone wall that had been ready for it.

I looked at it uncertainly. It didn't *look* dented. Some engineering had gone into it, I knew. It was both lighter than a rectangle of metal should be and stronger than a hollow version would have been. Despite a few . . . accidents, it looked as good as new. There was only one way to tell, though. I touched the panel on one side and started feeding it mana.

To my relief, it wasn't long before the space within the doorway shimmered and flickered blue. The shimmering intensified, and then Felicia's face was looking back at me.

"Hi, Kandis!" she said. "Everything went well?"

"Yes," I replied, and swallowed. This had been my idea, and my . . . minion who was responsible for creating it. This wasn't an experimental device, it was part of a long tradition of magical creations. There wasn't any question about it being safe. But I still hesitated to trust it. Only for a second, though. If there was any doubt, I wanted to be the type of leader who didn't put her friends through a risk I wasn't willing to take.

I stepped through and found myself back in the dungeon.

"It works!" I said, with a little more excitement than I should have felt.

"Of course it works," Rhis said, a little snippily. "If something was wrong, the passage wouldn't have even formed."

I grinned at him. "I'm just not used to magic being this convenient," I told him. As I spoke, Cutter and Cloridan came through the portal as well.

I looked around at the group. "We've got a lot of work to do. Well, Rhis and I do; you guys are mostly going to stand around and guard the entrances."

"No problem!" Felicia said, doing a terrible impression of a town guard salute.

"Two entrances," Rhis complained. "Are you sure about this, Mistress?"

"As I'll ever be," I said. "Let's get to work."

Is there a better place to put your vault than in a dungeon? That's an interesting question, one that for most would be purely philosophical. It's true that a dungeon is a never-ending source of traps and monstrous protectors. But it's also true that adventurers delve dungeons *all the time*. Some of them reach the end.

It was possible that I could design a dungeon that would stop adventurers in their tracks. I hadn't gotten off to a great start, already making decisions that reduced my security. But I had some hope that I'd get away with this. A vault in the city wasn't only defended by stone walls and magical traps. It was protected by the law.

Most adventurers were law-abiding. Happy to operate in areas that were *beyond* the law, sure, but most of them respected the idea of property that was held by other people. *More* of them respected the idea that the guards or the King's men would come after them if they broke the law. That left the thieves, but thieves were surprisingly rare in the ranks of adventurers. There was something about spending your time risking your life grasping for treasure in the deeps that didn't mesh well with the idea of stealing other people's hard-earned gains.

That wasn't to say they were all honest. But enough were that it kept the others mostly in line. Right now, my dungeon was protected by obscurity, and not much else. But given enough time, I'd add magic, traps, and monsters to the equation.

But the best protection I could give myself would be to become an institution. Valued by all, especially by the ones who could bring me down.

"How's the expansion going?" I asked Rhis.

"I've taken all of this chamber," Rhis said, gesturing around the octagonal room, "and all the rooms coming off it. Both on this floor and the upper one. I haven't extended yet down that passageway, I'm told that there are more rooms in that direction."

I looked up at the balconies above us. "This big central shaft is going to compromise our layout if we make it two floors, right?"

Rhis nodded. "There are ways around it," he said doubtfully.

"Nah, let's make this entire thing the first floor," I said. "Including those rooms down the passageway. They looked like monk cells; they should be fine for bunking children in once we clean them up."

Rhis nodded again. "I have found signs of a collapsed staircase in one of the upper rooms. Your theory about this structure being linked to the ruins upstairs may be correct. Should I expand upwards?"

"No . . ." I said slowly. "We don't need three entrances, at least for now. Seal it up and reinforce it, and clean everything up while you're at it. Let me know if you absorb anything interesting."

"As you wish," Rhis said, bowing. "There were a few copper coins scattered about. And . . . something you might find interesting."

He pointed to one of the rooms on this level. Shrugging, I walked over to it. It would have been easier in the interface, but I kept it real for now.

"This was almost entirely covered in dirt and smoke," Rhis said. "Easy enough to clean."

Indeed, the wall had become clean, smooth, granite, as clean now as the day they were carved. One wall, though, wasn't granite. Various flat colored stones had been fused with the wall somehow. It might have been a mosaic technique like we had on Earth, but just looking at it, I suspected Earth Magic had been used. As I walked closer, I could see that it wasn't just colored stone. Words and symbols had been carved into it, covering the whole wall in a picture of remarkable complexity. Actually, not a picture.

"It's a map," I said.

TRICK OR TRAP

A map?" Rhis asked. "I don't see it."

I gave him a look. "Are you comparing this to all the dungeons you know? Or rather, all the dungeons you've *been*?"

"Of course I am," he said. "And this doesn't look like any of them."

I sighed. For all of Rhis's intelligence, he had some gaping blind spots. "No," I explained. "This is a map of the territory of where all your dungeons *are*. Or were, as the case may be."

"So it's a security risk?" he asked. I shook my head.

"If someone is looking at this, then they already know where you are," I told him.

"With respect, that's not exactly true, Mistress. With the portal, intruders can find their way in without knowing . . . my location." He gave the map a dubious glance as he said this.

"That's a good point," I admitted. "But then, I don't know if this location is even marked on this map . . ."

Looking more closely, I could see that there were fine grooves carved into the colored rocks. "You've got soot in your inventory, right?" I asked.

"Yes, Mistress."

"Can you . . . fill in all of these grooves with it?"

"Easily. One moment." Rhis stared fixedly at the wall for about five seconds before the change started to occur. Black lines and letters sprouted across the map, filling in the details of roads, borders, and settlements. The map was suddenly more clear, and also labelled. Labelled in a script and language I wasn't familiar with, but that made no difference to Gift of Tongues. Just looking at the strange characters made their meaning appear in my mind.

"This is pre-Empire," I said. "See, the duchies are separate kingdoms. Or maybe it's just from before they were conquered?"

There was a larger nation to the north and west of the three duchies. It was labelled as Imperial territory and extended quite a bit further south and east of the river that formed the current Kingdom's border. The duchies weren't alone in being reduced, though. The forest that dominated the northeast half of the peninsula in the current day was then easily half the size it was now.

"This place wasn't even in the woods back then," I said. "If the river is there, then this place would be . . ."

My finger drifted into the foothills on the map and stopped at a marked location that I thought was in the right place.

"Here," I said. "Torian Monastery."

"The God of Knowledge?" Rhis mused. "Interesting coincidence, given the name you gave us."

I frowned, but I didn't say anything. I knew there weren't any coincidences when the gods were involved, but at the same time, I couldn't see how Toriao would have arranged this. Nor could I see how this place being an ancient temple of hers made any difference to anything.

Instead, I started scouring the map for other points of interest.

"Look, the map goes far enough north to show the elven lands," I said. Talnier was short of such maps. Nobody went there, so the fact that it was past the Tribal lands was all that anyone cared to know. And if the beast-kin made maps, they didn't share them.

"Hmph," Rhis replied, profoundly uninterested. "Where are my other locations?"

Amused, I pointed them out. "Oakway didn't exist when this map did, but it would be about here," I said, pointing to a spot quite near the old border.

"Dorsay did exist . . . I heard that it went back a ways," I said, pointing it out on the map. It even had the same name, although the knowledge in my head told me that this collection of letters was supposed to be pronounced "Dorshay." I wondered if the word had changed, or if the Imperials had gotten the foreign name wrong.

Talnier was also not on the map. Either the tower had been built after this, or it wasn't important enough to rate a mention. Those were the only locations Rhis cared about, so after I'd identified them, I was free to return to examining the elven lands.

I'd heard that the elves changed slowly or not at all, so of all the map, this was probably the part that was most likely to be still accurate. It was depicted as being mostly forest, with some cleared areas. Just five settlements, with no indication of size. Gaeleath, Nieven, Talthhaln, Inialos, and Aneirn. And one more place.

I stared at it for a bit and then blinked. The symbols didn't go away, and the meaning of them that was lodged in my head stayed the same. It was strange how that worked. The System seemed to know what was meant, not just what was written. The names of the elven cities were *names*, so they came through as the sounds that they made. At the same time, I knew that the sounds had meaning. So Gaeleath *meant* "safe haven," and I knew that as well.

The one remaining elven place was different. It didn't have a name, or if it did it wasn't marked on the map. Just a description.

Portal to the other world.

"Well, it's obviously a trap." Janie leaned back in her chair as she delivered the words. We had gathered in what I'd dubbed and furnished as the meeting room, one of the smaller rooms leading off the main hall. The table was phantasmal, but the chairs were real. Sitting on a Phantasm would cause it to gradually accumulate damage, and I didn't want to have to keep track of how long my chair was going to last.

"More like bait," Felicia disagreed. "There might be a trap, but it might just be because a god wants you to do something there. We were already warned that one does."

"It's not exactly subtle, though, is it?" I asked.

"It actually is . . . from some points of view," Kyle put in. "It's a message that only you could possibly get. Especially if the map has always been there."

"It could have been changed right before we arrived," I said, sighing. "Rhis didn't see any sign of it, but he admits that he wouldn't detect a god meddling."

"There's supposed to be limits to how much they can meddle, though, right?" Janie said.

"The other part that's subtle is knowing whether this is going to make you go or not," Kyle continued. "Given that it is a message from one of the gods, does that make you want to go, or not?"

"I do want to avoid this Great Game of theirs," I said. "But I don't think I can avoid checking this out."

"Do you want to get home so badly?" Felicia asked, a little hurt.

"It's not just that," I told her. "Fyskel told me I *couldn't* go back, that my real body was left behind. Ashmor told me that opening a gate outside this universe would break it, and kill everyone. The fact that a portal existed—if it did exist—is huge. Even if it's no longer around, even if it doesn't lead to Earth, confirming that it's not just words on an old map would tell me a lot."

"Maybe this is some god's way of discouraging you from going," Cloridan said, speaking up for the first time. "Maybe you were going to find out about this when you visited the Tribes, and learning about it this way primes you to avoid it."

I glared at him. "Well, that clears things up," I said sarcastically. "Whichever way I go, I'm falling in with some god's plan."

"Trying to outsmart the gods isn't recommended in the stories, as a rule," Felicia told me. "But . . . they can't be all-knowing, can they? Or there wouldn't be a point to their game. They'd already know how it ends."

"There must be a limit," I agreed. "Or . . . differences in their ability to predict my—anybody's—actions. That's where the actual game must lie."

"But *we* don't know who's best at it or who's pushing you which way," Cloridan said thoughtfully.

"And even if we did, I don't think I want any one in particular to win," I said. "Whoever my patron is, they can take a hike."

By now, I had a pretty good idea of who my patron was. There was only Silence, Death, and Knowledge left to choose from. In this pantheon, Death wasn't considered particularly evil. He wasn't interested in hastening people's end—that was Ashmor—but concerned himself with the processes that started after death. Decay and rot if you were unsympathetic, but also the renewal that comes from returning nutrients to the ecosystem.

In many ways he was a foil for Ashmor, seeing (and seeding) new life from destruction. There were worse patrons to have, but I hadn't seen any signs that my life was being directed by the God of Destruction.

The God of Silence was more of a possibility. Tondeni was supposed to be responsible for Illusion Magic. The lack of communication was also a characteristic sign. Not much was known about her goals, though, so it was hard to tell if I was being directed by her. She would have been my first pick if it wasn't for Toriao.

It hadn't escaped my notice that the biggest problem I had with this world—other than the inescapable violence—was probably shared by the God of Knowledge. The lack of institutions—financial, legal, and academic—was crippling this country, and who knew how much of this world.

My actions and goals were very much in line with what I thought Toriao wanted. The torrent of advice her priest had given me when I'd gone to see him was another sign. Since then, I'd avoided her clergy . . . religiously.

The main strike against her was the silence. She was supposed to be all in favor of information sharing. Fyskel had hinted, though, that keeping quiet was uncharacteristic of my patron, so if he could be believed (he couldn't) that was another sign that she was the one.

"I shouldn't try and second-guess them at all then," I finally said. "I should just get on with what I want to do and let the chips fall where they may."

"That sounds better than running around in circles," Felicia agreed. "So where does that leave you? Are you going or not?"

"I will go," I decided. "Not immediately, though. If it exists, this portal has waited, what, three hundred years? It can wait a little longer."

"So nothing's changed, then, except you'll want to make a detour if and when you get to visit the Tribes," Cloridan said.

"Yep. Get Rhis established and absorb the rest of this complex. Get the cells habitable, and move the kids in. Get the kiddy dungeon up and running and have them start delving into it. Get the lower floors stocked with higher-level monsters for security and start storing the gold down there. Work out some procedures for getting the gold in and out."

I took a deep breath. "It should go pretty quickly. Rhis should be ready to start excavating the lower levels in a couple of days, and he'll start feeling more secure once he's got some decent monsters. We've planned out where the spacial distortions are going to go, so it's mostly a matter of mana generation now."

"You're really going to operate your bank out of a dungeon," Felicia said.

"The customer-facing stuff will stay in the building," I said. "I'll move my office and the vault inside, and there will probably be some staff in here. We'll reduce the security at the portal entrance but not remove it entirely. The kids will be going in and out occasionally, so the main security will have to be in the dungeon."

I sighed. "I'm going to have to keep switching between my office here and the town council one, for at least the foreseeable future."

"We'll be able to delve the lower floors, right?" Kyle asked. I nodded.

"I don't think I want to open them to the general public any time soon, but you guys are fine. I might try and find some other trusted individuals to delve as well."

The more delvers I had, the more experience I got from the dungeon. The kids would be providing a modest income, but the real gain would be from delvers like my party members.

"Well, get cracking on that one, then," Janie said. "We're going to be mostly standing around until you do."

I shrugged. "Standing guard is important work, and it's not like I can trust this to mercenaries. I'm hoping you have a nice quiet few weeks, and then I can move on to the next item on my agenda."

THE NEXT ITEM ON THE AGENDA

Something was off. The question was, though, did it matter? I was standing outside of the walls of Anchorbury, staring at the southern gate to the city.

The *southern* gate, because it was the least likely gate to be on the lookout for me. It wasn't that I thought they were looking for me, or that they could find me. Given what I was up to, it was best that I took all the precautions I could. The southern gate wasn't *that* far out of my way. Not when I could jog faster than Usain Bolt could sprint. By the same token, it wasn't that unexpected that I'd use it, so I'd been watching it carefully before I approached, looking with both regular vision and Mana Sense.

I hadn't seen anything to suggest I couldn't just walk straight through while invisible. But I had noticed something odd.

Right now, two people were walking up to the gate. They were both carrying massive backpacks, making them look like distorted snails. That wasn't that odd. Enhanced strength was common enough that unless you were carting metal around, the limiting factor to how much you could carry was the bulk of your cargo. Merchants, or people out to make new lives, got a cart and pulled it themselves. Anyone else, with loads less than their own body weight, just threw it over their shoulders and started running.

What made them odd was that in the fifteen minutes I'd been watching the gate, three more pairs had come through wearing identical backpacks.

They weren't in uniform, but I thought they looked like soldiers. They'd all been carrying identical longspears, paired with shortswords for close-in work. Despite Koenig's disdain for the weapon, adventurers *did* use polearms. They loved the reach and high damage, and just avoided dungeons with tight spaces. What you didn't get was the *same* weapon. Delving teams liked to be prepared for everything, and doubling up on one weapon reduced the team's overall flexibility.

Mercenaries were another possibility, but again . . . they tended not to get their equipment from a central store. A well-organized mercenary company, perhaps, but in that case the difference between that and regular soldiers was pretty academic.

Deciding that solving the mystery was worth a little extra time, I followed the pair through the gates. The guards never saw me, and like the other pairs that had passed by, the guards only gave these two a cursory glance-over once they saw the men's papers.

The guards directed the men down the main street. Eventually, they encountered another guardsman, standing in the street, who directed them down a turnoff. And so it proved, all the way to the final destination.

At least this indicates that Aubert is aware of whatever is going on here, I thought, slightly relieved. I could do without this piece of déjà vu, though.

The building the men had been directed to, and subsequently entered, was the same building that had housed the mercenaries that had tried to depose Aubert's father. There were a few differences, though.

For one, the main door was guarded by soldiers. Not wearing the uniforms of Aubert's men. It took me a moment to go through the jumble of descriptions I'd heard at various times and conclude that these were probably the men of the Duke of Bargougne.

Aubert's boss.

That made all this official *and* suggested the reason behind what they were doing. Bringing in troops, not secretly but *quietly*, and lodging them in town instead of camping out in the field. Aubert had warned me. I'd believed him, too, but there wasn't much I could do about that I wasn't doing already. This was the first concrete sign I'd seen that the Duke was coming for my head.

I wondered if they would wait for spring. I wasn't sure how military logistics worked in this world. A company could carry all the supplies it needed for a good while on its back. How much, I didn't really know, but it was a given that an army here could march for longer, and travel faster, than back home. Without carts to get stuck in the mud, they probably didn't worry about winter as much.

That said, they did have siege weapons that would need to be carted about . . . probably? I did have a capable military advisor at home. Too bad

I couldn't trust him. For now, I should see if the castle held any answers. I was unlikely to find the Duke bunking down with his men.

They say the way to a man's heart is his stomach, and after a bit of thought, I fancied the same might be true of castles. The kitchens were easy to find, and from there, I figured, I could just follow the path of refreshments to wherever either the Duke or Aubert were. The kitchen provided meals for everybody, of course, but I figured I could just go to whoever ordered the fanciest snacks.

Or the maid that I followed in could just announce to the room, "I need a bottle of red wine and a basket of bread and cheese for the Duke." Easy.

As I slipped in behind the maid, I thought to put a bit of Phantasmal filler in the doorjamb, to prevent the door from latching properly. I think she noticed when she left, but she wasn't in a position to fiddle with it. Slamming the door wouldn't have been unobtrusive service, so she pulled it closed as best she could and left it at that.

I had already started observing the two men in the room, sitting on opposite sides of a table covered with papers. Looking at him now, I saw that Aubert seemed to have fully healed, and had grown, a bit. His dark hair was still artfully tousled, and his skin was still too pale, but he had stopped wearing those ridiculous outfits. He was also no longer so gangly, filling out a bit of his height with either muscle or fat. Probably the former, if he was still delving. He had a sulky look on his face, but under the circumstances, I felt that was a positive.

The other man was, as I'd suspected, Duke Victor de Bargougne. He was dressed more expensively than Aubert—though not as badly as Aubert at his worst—and was still dyeing the tips of his hair.

"I expected better intelligence than this," he said sourly. "Haven't we gotten someone close to her yet?"

"No," Aubert replied. "And we're not likely to, not unless we seek aid from specialists." His face twisted with disgust. "Like Finley did."

I wondered if the dead didn't rate titles, or if he just hated the guy too much to use them. The Duke didn't comment.

"What about Sir Rodakis? He keeps saying he's on the verge of winning her over."

"That's . . . probably not the case, sire. All our other reports state that the Councillor is keeping him carefully at arm's length.

Aside from a very brief interaction with the King, this was the first time I'd seen Aubert sucking up to his superiors. He'd managed to be respectful to me, at times, but even then I'd gotten the feeling that doing so was beneath him.

The Duke snorted. "Thinking with his prick, hey? But these other reports, they're all thirdhand or from a distance."

"You wanted her to remain unaware she was being watched, and she is good at picking up even subtle watchers. We tried to get people into her organizations, but she's set them up with her Bureaucracy skill. Any attempt to suborn someone will notify her of a rules violation."

"How in the hells did she even learn that skill?" Victor complained.

"Like most of her skills, it's a mystery," Aubert told him. "We're pretty sure she had it before the new professions showed up in Talnier."

"*Just* in Talnier," Victor said.

"As you say, sire. It's like the specialist professions that show up in the Tribes, we don't know how it happens."

"Nor do the Tribals, at least not the ones we've captured," the Duke said sourly.

"With respect, sire, there's a lot we don't understand here. Wouldn't it be best to hold off? The King—"

"The King's writ runs thin right now," Victor spoke over him. "Executing Lord Finley like that . . . he had the right, no one would gainsay it, but it rubbed us all the wrong way. He's fighting brush fires all across the realm at the moment, placating his own people and the duchies. Now is the perfect time to snatch the prize and seek the King's blessing after the fact."

"I suppose so, sire," Aubert said listlessly. The Duke stared hard at him.

"We'll talk on this later," Victor said, standing. He'd hardly touched his wine and cheese.

I followed him out. I wasn't ready to show myself to Aubert, and he wasn't going to give anything away to an empty room. Besides, I wasn't going to abandon the *actual* reason I was in the castle.

To my consternation, though, the Duke seemed to have the same destination that I did. It made things a little easier for me, as closing doors behind him was beneath His Grace, but I didn't particularly want company for my little mission.

Company was what I had, though, because the Duke was meeting one of his men in the library. I could tell he was the Duke's man because of the uniform but little else, because for some reason he was wearing partial plate mail, including a full helm.

"Are we alone?" was the first thing he said, as he sat in one of the leather-bound chairs. The guardsman carefully closed the door.

"Yes, sire," he said, his voice muffled by his helm. "I've checked every nook and cranny."

"Then take off that ridiculous helm," the Duke said. "No one suspects?"

"No sir," the man said, taking off his helmet. I widened my eyes in surprise.

"Who needs Illusionists, when a simple disguise will do the trick," the Duke said smugly.

"People see what they expect, my lord. No one is expecting to see me here, least of all as one of your guards," Guillaume Duvost agreed.

How are you here? I protested silently. *You're supposed to be in jail!*

Duke Victor snorted with amusement, but quickly turned serious. "It is as you said, your cousin is reluctant to go against the woman. I suspect that Sir Rodakis is not the only one thinking with his prick."

"She is quite charming, my lord." Guillaume didn't seem to have suffered from his spell in prison. He was still a taller version of Aubert, better looking for being stretched out a tiny bit.

"Don't tell me I have to worry about you as well."

"I remember her role in my downfall quite well, my lord. You need have no worries on my account."

"Good. Everything has been proceeding?"

"I've been showing your men the key locations, choke points, and hideaways. Should it prove . . . necessary, they'll have all they need for a quick takeover. Is that going to be the case?"

"I haven't decided yet," Duke Victor said. "For the moment, your cousin is cooperating. If he does make a stand, I have you ready to take his place. Should he come to realize where his best interests lie, I can find you another position. I always have a use for loyal subordinates."

"As you say, my lord," Guillaume said. There was a certain *brittleness* to his smile when he said that. The Duke didn't seem to notice; he just got up and clapped Guillaume on the back. They left together, Guillaume putting his helmet back on.

Well, that's a fine kettle of fish and no mistake, I thought. *At least they finally left me alone.*

I looked around at the silent shelves. I would have to do something about . . . all of that. Save my town, maybe even save Aubert.

But first, I thought, *I need to rob this place blind.*

CONSISTENT CHARACTER FLAW

Of course, I wasn't actually going to *steal* anything. Probably. What I was going to do was known as piracy back home, but I didn't think there was a word for it here. I hadn't tried it, but the System translator was probably smart enough not to refer to it with whatever word they had here for robbery on the high seas. It would probably get translated as "copying" or something similar, which would lead to confusion as I tried to explain how that could be a crime.

Maybe. Or maybe not. My brief interaction with the priest of Toriao had hinted at knowledge being deliberately restricted, against her wishes. Maybe, with a law against disseminating *some* knowledge, they had a word for it.

Whatever. They could hardly object if they didn't find out about it. The first step was to take inventory. Memorize had a strictly limited storage space for . . . magical knowledge. I needed to figure out which texts I wanted to Research here and which I wanted to Memorize. If there were more texts than I could absorb, I'd have to think about whether I wanted to take them. That was a last resort, though. As long as I wasn't detected, I could keep coming back here for more texts, once I'd cleared out the old memory banks. I wasn't sure how long it would take for a missing book to be missed, but it wasn't never.

At least I didn't have to deal with misleading or absent titles on the book spines. I could just Identify them. Given that they were all unique objects, it was probably good practice for the skill.

> [Identification]: History Text, *Origin of the Family* – Quality: Good –
> Properties: None
> [Identification]: Romance, *Danger in Dorsay* – Quality: Damaged –
> Properties: None
> [Identification]: Mathematical Treatise, *Principles of Calculation* –
> Quality: Mediocre – Properties: Teach (Calculate)

To my surprise and irritation, the books were in no sort of order at all. Just scattered randomly on whatever bookshelf that would fit them. The bookshelves themselves weren't arranged for easy perusal. Mismatched and badly sized, the books were jammed into whatever corner or cranny they would fit into, leaving dead ends and nooks that I'd have to explore before I could finish.

It took a while, but I was eventually left with a shortlist. There was a book on Illusion Magic, which I didn't need. Two books that taught Water Magic, which added further insult to Aubert gifting me that text on that . . . less useful magic skill.

Of the others . . . well:

> [Identification]: Magical Text, *Ignis* – Quality: Average – Properties:
> Teach (Fire Magic)
> [Identification]: Magical Text, *Master of the Tempest* – Quality:
> Damaged – Properties: Teach (Ice Magic)
> [Identification]: Magical Text, *Philosophy of the Deeps* – Quality:
> Average – Properties: Teach (Earth Magic)
> [Identification]: Magical Text, *Born Out of Light* – Quality: Average –
> Properties: Teach (Shadow Magic)
> [Identification]: Military Text, *Considerations of Battle* – Quality:
> Mediocre – Properties: Teach (Tactics)
> [Identification]: Spell Book, *Miscellanea* – Quality: Average –
> Properties: Mixed-Type Spells
> [Identification]: Spell Book, *Stone Tools* – Quality: Average –
> Properties: Earth Spells

By now, I thought I was getting a headache from using Identify too much. Or it was just from reading all the screens? I ignored it and thought about what I wanted to do.

The texts needed someone with the Teach skill to use. I had that, so I could teach myself. I only had two skill points, though, courtesy of my last level, so there was a limit to how many of them I could learn.

Fire Magic and Tactics I could dismiss. I had military advisors at home, and Janie had both skills.

The spell books actually held spells I could learn using Research. I was pretty sure this method didn't cost me any spell points, which was a huge help. As long as the miscellaneous one had useful spells, or I wanted to take Earth Magic.

I didn't *not* want to take Earth Magic. It was on the same level as Ice Magic for me. They both had good offensive and defensive options. Shadow Magic, on the other hand, had a few good synergies with my illusions. I brought up the spell list to make sure.

---

5 Lesser Cloak: Gather shadows to cover an object. Light will dissipate shadows after duration. (5 mana) (5 minutes)

10 Stain Shadow: Make a shadow resistant to light. Effect Level is Light Level. (10 mana / 10 mana per minute)

15 Cloak: Gather shadows to cover a person. Light will dissipate shadows after duration. (15 mana) (5 minutes)

15 See Shadows: Allows the caster to see into one shadow and look out of another, nearby shadow. (15 mana)

20 Shadow Step: Step into, and out of, the same shadow. Immaterial and invisible while in the shadow. If the shadow is dissipated, you will take damage as you are expelled. (20 mana)

20 Enshroud: Allow a Cloaked object or person to be included as the caster for any Shadow Magic spell (20 mana) (lasts while Cloaked)

20 Inspire Fear: Causes fear. The target or the caster must be shadowed. (20 mana) (5 minutes)

25 Shadow Walk: Step into one shadow, step out of another. Must be within one minute's walk. (30 mana)

25 Umbral Bolt: Releases a bolt of Shadow Energy that can cause 25 damage. Unresisted. (50 mana / 10 mana per minute)

25 Umbral Claws: Covers fists in Shadow Energy that can cause an additional 25 damage that is unresisted. (50 mana / 10 mana per minute)

25 Umbral Weapon: Covers a weapon in Shadow Energy that can cause an additional 25 damage that is unresisted. (50 mana / 10 mana per minute)

25 Scry Shadow: Look into one shadow and see out of a much farther away shadow. (25 mana)

30 Greater Cloak: Gather shadows to cover a building. Light will dissipate shadows after duration. (30 mana) (5 minutes)

30 Enter the Shadow World: Enter the world of shadow. (30 mana)

Most of the spells seemed to have a set duration, and those that didn't were expensive to cast. There looked like a complicated relationship with the spells, where you wanted to cloak things in shadows in order to affect them with the spells. All I really wanted, though, was Shadow Walk. Seeing through shadows would be useful as well, I supposed.

I wasn't sure what to think of Enter the Shadow World. No duration, just . . . enter.

What wasn't there was Air Magic. Which I also wanted for just one thing—flying. Not for the tactics of it, just because it was . . . flying. If I took Shadow and Earth, I wouldn't be able to get Air until my next level, which was . . . some time away.

I resolved to brood over it tonight, and just take Shadow Magic for now. It was going to take a few hours to learn it, and I wanted to get out of here before they shut the doors for the night. I found myself a nook where I'd hopefully stay undisturbed and started reading.

[Shadow Magic] Skill unlocked.
[Shadow Magic] Level 1 purchased.
For gaining a skill level, you have been awarded 1 XP.

My profession only gave me spell points for levels in Illusion Magic, but my Extra Spells trait gave me fifteen spell points for each level of *any* magic. That wasn't enough for Shadow Walk, but when I took Earth Magic tomorrow, I should have enough. It felt like a bit of a cheat to gain points through one magic and spend them on another, but I'd already done it with Water and Illusion. The spell book should give me some useful Earth spells.

I slipped out of the castle and found a quiet place to cancel Invisibility and cast Disguise. Then I wandered into one of the nicer inns as a merchant and paid for a room and a good meal.

There was a lot of talk about the influx of soldiers. Having them enter the city quietly might have stopped anyone watching from outside from seeing them, but the townsfolk weren't so easily fooled. Soldiers had been spotted in the city, in the Duke's livery, working with the existing guards. No one seemed to have realized the full number of soldiers, but if I'd been a spy, it couldn't have been hard to find out.

I went back up to my room and started brooding. I knew I'd be taking Earth, but I wanted Air, damn it!

> [Earth Magic] Skill unlocked.
> [Earth Magic] Level 1 purchased.
> **For gaining a skill level, you have been awarded 1 XP.**

In many ways, Aubert's guests made things easier. There were more people to dodge as I moved about, but most of the enchanted alarms had been disabled, at least during the day. I'd expected that I'd have to work my way around the ones in the library, but Duke Victor apparently preferred to hold his secret meetings there. It made my studies a little awkward, but they weren't checking out the books, so I could remain tucked away in my little hidey-hole, listening with half an ear to the Duke complaining about Aubert's lack of enthusiasm to both his lieutenant and Guillaume.

It wasn't even a lack of cooperation he was complaining about. The only thing Aubert was guilty of was a lack of eagerness to lead his troops against my town. It got me curious enough to attend another planning session.

"I'm worried that even if we make it through the gate unopposed, we'll face fighting from the Adventurers Guild."

"The Guild never interferes in the business of nobles." Duke Victor scowled at Aubert across the table. This was the third objection that Aubert had made to an immediate attack. "Why would they do so this time?"

"This isn't a fight between nobles," Aubert countered. "The Talnier Council holds a Charter from the King, just like the Guild. It would be only natural for the Guild to consider them natural allies."

"And," he added, as Duke Victor opened his mouth to dismiss him, "Councillor Hammond *is* an adventurer, when it suits her. She might well have thought to make arrangements with them.

I sniffed, but only in my head. Then I remembered that my invisibility covered sound, so I sniffed for real and added in a silent "Hmph" for good measure. From my discussions with Koenig, I knew the Guild was more than willing to "interfere with noble business," just not overtly.

"Adventurers are never going to stand up to our formations in the field," the Duke said.

"Right, but we won't be able to keep those formations once we move into the town," Aubert pointed out. "If it devolves into street fighting, they'll have the advantage. More magic, and more levels."

"What would you suggest then?" the Duke said sourly.

"We should wait until she's out of town," Aubert said earnestly. "Our reports suggest that she's preparing her organizations for a long-term absence. She's been meeting with the Tribal envoy. I think she might be planning a trip into the Great Wild."

"We should wait longer? She's a trickster, she doesn't have any military training or ability!"

"If she's absent, the coordination between the town and the Guild will be greatly reduced," Aubert said. "And, we won't have to worry about reporting her death to the King."

Duke Victor waved his hand dismissively. "She's hardly going to be on the walls," he said.

"Accidents happen when a town gets sacked," Aubert countered. "Do you really want to take that risk?"

"It *is* a risk," Victor conceded. "But we can hardly hand over our time-table to the enemy!"

"There is a limit to how long we can wait," Aubert allowed. "But leaving it to, say, the second week of spring shouldn't be too disruptive."

"Perhaps," Duke Victor said slowly. "I will think on it."

Yeah, that doesn't sound ominous, I thought to myself. I slipped out of the room and headed back to the library. I wanted to get those spells researched before the shit hit the proverbial fan.

That was why I was holed up in the library, muttering silently to myself about annoying distractions, when Duke Victor met up with his henchmen.

"I've had enough," he said. "Set everything in motion tonight."

BUY IN

If this had been a movie, I would have leapt into action at the Duke's words. I could have appeared out of nowhere, struck down the evil noble, and put an end to his plans once and for all. As if. More practically, I could have rushed off to warn Aubert of his impending doom. There were a few reasons I did not do so.

Most immediately, I still had spells to learn! I wasn't sure how long it was going to take to go through two spell books, but I was guessing hours at least, possibly days. If I didn't want to take the risk of people noticing the books were missing, I needed to buckle down and start studying.

That may have seemed as if I was putting a few spells over a man's life, but that wasn't the case. I'd been listening to their plans and contingencies over the last two days, and Aubert's life wasn't to be taken. Guillaume had argued strongly for it, but Victor had insisted that Aubert was to live. Given that he was the Duke, he hadn't needed to give a reason.

Some people probably would die during the coup, but it wasn't as though they were planning a bloodbath. Every man would be needed for the assault on Talnier, after all. That was another reason to let the plot go forward. Every man who died here was a man who wouldn't go on to attack my city.

Fear was a part of it too, of course. I'd been ghosting my way around these halls with impunity, but that was only because no one was looking for me. There weren't many direct counters to invisibility, but there were a lot of ways that they could make things harder for me. Just keeping doors shut, for one.

Janie and I had talked about her Detect Invisibility spell, but it wasn't that funny when I thought I might be on the other end of it. You just filled the room with fire and looked for the person-shaped void. Ironically, the screaming wouldn't give me away, but only because the spell would be muting it.

There were other easier ways to find an invisible person, but I was pretty sure the Duke had fire mages in his army. I didn't really want to take action and then run the risk of being discovered.

So I ignored it all and kept my nose in my book. Opening up *Miscellanea* caused my Research skill to wake up. I probably didn't have to actually *read* the book, just let my skill do the work. I let it have its head, and a notification for the first spell popped up.

Research Spell: Boulder Strike (30) (4.17 hours) [Y/N]

A genuine combat spell! I could have looked it up, but I didn't need to. I'd skimmed the basics. Crushing my enemies with a giant boulder—from a distance—was probably one of the less icky ways to kill someone. It was a pretty high-level spell, though. I'd pass on it for now and come back for it later.

Research Spell: Water Whip (20) (2.78 hours) [Y/N]

Another combat spell, but this one wasn't that good. It didn't do any more damage than a whip, though it did have a longer range and used your Water Magic skill instead of a weapon skill. What else was there?

Research Spell: Flight (25) (3.47 hours) [Y/N]

I grimaced with something like pain. I wanted this, but without Air Magic, I couldn't use it. Next!

Research Spell: Shape of Stone (20) (2.78 hours) [Y/N]

I hesitated. This was the basic stone shaping spell, usable on up to a cubic meter of material. It was generally useful and I could cast it. I might find a lower-level spell if I kept looking, but it probably wouldn't be as useful. I indicated yes.

My hands turned the pages, going unerringly to the right section, and I began to peruse the words and diagrams written there. This wasn't learning as I knew it; I got the impression that the text was only an excuse. It did have meaning, but my slowly crystalizing understanding of it was coming from somewhere else.

I let it go on. Time passed. Just as I knew that I had finished, another box popped up.

> **[Research] Level 3 acquired through use.**
> **For gaining a skill level, you have been awarded 1 XP.**

Well, the first couple of levels are the easiest, I told myself. I wondered if I was getting an experience boost from using the skill in a somewhat dangerous environment. I didn't feel particularly threatened, but most libraries didn't have even the smallest risk of discovery and capture.

I shrugged and went to steal some lunch. The coup hadn't started yet; it wouldn't until nightfall. I got the impression I wouldn't be getting much sleep tonight.

The next spell out of the book was a disappointment.

> **Research Spell: Unseen Sound (5) (27.78 minutes) [Y/N]**

I had to run into some duplicates eventually. Next.

> **Research Spell: Detect Earths (15) (1.39 hours) [Y/N]**

An odd name, but it wasn't a typo. This spell let you look for a material, specified at casting, that fell under the categorization of earth. That included metals, gems, and different types of stone or dirt. It only gave you a direction and a distance, and the range was quite limited, but it was quite useful. I decided to take it.

One point thirty-nine hours later, I was ready for my next spell.

> **Research Spell: Wall of Stone (25) (2.31 hours) [Y/N]**

An advanced version of Shape of Stone. Ten cubic meters. Sure, why not?

> **Research Spell: Slingshot (5) (27.78 minutes) [Y/N]**

It was getting late, but I could spare half an hour. Slingshot was a pretty nice beginner's spell. It only did as much damage as a normal dagger, but what did you want for level five?

After I finished with that spell, I had a decision to make. They would be closing the front door soon, making it a lot harder for me to get out. Should I head back to the inn now? It had been easy enough for me to steal bread and cheese from the kitchen during the day, but a proper dinner would be much harder to steal.

After some consideration, I decided that risking a good dinner was worth it, and kept going. The kitchens would probably be in chaos once the coup started. I returned to my book.

Research Spell: Iron Dart (20) (1.85 hours) [Y/N]

Another decent combat spell. Yes.

Research Spell: Illusory Room (25) (2.31 hours) [Y/N]

Oh, an Illusion spell, and one I don't already have. Nice. While I was learning this one, I started to hear shouts from about the castle. Thankfully, Duke Victor wasn't using the library as his command post.

The fighting was still going on when I snuck out to get some dinner. The kitchen was closed. All the staff were cowering somewhere instead of cooking. Fair enough, and this would make it easier to steal something once I got inside. However . . .

I eyed the locked door with some distaste, and then gave a silent chuckle. No longer would doors be my nemesis. Fifteen spell points from each of my new magic skills meant:

You have learned the spell [Shadow Walk] (25 spell points spent).

I'd been meaning to get this for later, but it wouldn't hurt to get some practice in. I focused on my new spell. I could see shadows. Scratch that; *everyone* could see shadows. I could . . . *sense* the shadows on the other side of the door. Throughout the castle, in fact, within a limited range.

Not for the first time, I wondered if some sort of dimensional shenanigans were responsible for how magic worked. The shadows weren't *just* shadows, they were also paths.

It was quite dark in the kitchen, I knew, but there was a torch burning right in front of the entrance. I stepped away from it, looking for darkness.

Shadow was a misnomer, I sensed. What mattered was the light level. The brighter the area, the harder it was to slip through to the other side. With only one in the skill, I was limited to dark areas, but my Intelligence and level brought me up to a respectable total of thirty-six. High enough that, standing in the darkest part of the corridor, my own shadow was dark enough to step through.

I stepped out into the darkness of the kitchen and swore. I quickly cast a Light spell to confirm what I'd felt.

My Invisibility spell had been broken, as well as my habitual Conceal Mana spell. There wasn't anybody in the room, and I didn't sense any hostile magic, so this must have been a side effect of the dimensional jumping. I'd have to watch out for that.

I glanced around again, but the kitchen was empty. I quickly got on with the task of raiding the pantry.

On the way back, I practiced a little with my new shadow sense. Since it was a sense for "places I could teleport to," I could sort of discern walls and people. A well-lit room was the same as a block of solid stone to me, but many places were not so brightly lit. People were large, moving blocks of inaccessibility, as I couldn't teleport right next to them. I wasn't a point object, after all.

It was . . . kind of useful for scouting, I supposed. There was information there, just not complete or particularly detailed. Things seemed to have settled down by the time I got back, so I settled in to finish my book.

Research Spell: Ice Golem (30) (2.78 hours) [Y/N]

Ugh. Another spell I couldn't learn. I could have gone back to the spells I'd skipped, but I was curious to see if the *Stone Tools* spell book had any spells I hadn't seen.

There were two, both of them Earth spells, of course.

Research Spell: Stone Sight (10) (55.56 minutes) [Y/N]

Research Spell: Fortress of Stone (30) (2.78 hours) [Y/N]

It was quite late by the time I'd finished both of those. They'd extinguished the lanterns in the library, so I'd had to continue using my own light source. It was time to go check on Aubert.

I was fairly sure I'd find him in the dungeons. Honored prisoner or not, Guillaume had been fairly vocal about reclaiming his "rightful" place, so I didn't think they were going to lock Aubert up in his own bedroom. I wasn't familiar with the dungeons, but they were dark, so they were pretty easy to find.

After a bit of searching, I found an underground passageway with rooms coming off of it. It was blocked off from the main castle by an inaccessible section, which I took for a lit guardroom. Since I didn't need to speak with them, I just stepped through to the darkest part of the dungeon.

I didn't have my invisibility, but it was dark, and shadow jumping didn't make any sound as far as I could tell. I looked around furtively, but there wasn't any sign that people had noticed me. I could see the faint light of the guardpost, but all the cells here were dark.

First things first. I didn't want to be disturbed by the guards. I crept forward and saw there was only a single one. Easy. I cast Phantom World on him, showing him . . . just what he was already seeing. Like the old trick of looping the video cameras, he'd just keep seeing and hearing that. I'd have to keep maintaining the spell to account for his own actions, but that was pretty easy.

Finding Aubert was a little less easy. Each door had a little barred window so you could check on the prisoner inside, but there were a lot of prisoners in here with fancy clothes. They must have been his loyal supporters.

Eventually, I resorted to sending in a Light spell, dimmed so as not to wake them up, so I could get a look at their faces. Aubert was the fifth one I checked. I looked him over. He didn't seem injured, just asleep.

I thought about the final reason I hadn't stopped the coup. My old manager had been fond of giving advice to the green graduates he'd been in charge of. Simple, obvious rules to keep in mind because breaking them was what caused spectacular losses.

Never buy into a falling market, he'd told us. Easy to say, hard to do. Looking at Aubert right now, though, I was fairly sure this market had hit rock bottom.

The cell doors didn't have locks, just bolts well out of reach of the window. I pulled it free, as quietly as I could, which wasn't very. Aubert, and who knew how many of the other prisoners, started to stir.

"Wakey-wakey, eggs and bakey."

ROCK BOTTOM

Aubert glared at me through sleep-sodden eyes. The poor dear had probably only just managed to drop off.

"You?" he managed to mumble. "What are you doing here?"

"Oh, I was just in this area, checking out the local coups, and I thought I'd tour your dungeons," I said smugly. "They're very nice."

He shook his head to clear it, probably ignoring everything I said.

"You're here," he repeated. "No one thought you'd dirty your hands with your own espionage. But we were wrong."

"Don't flatter yourself," I told him. "I came here for the library."

"The library . . . *my* library?" His outrage cut through the fog of his thoughts. "You're stealing my books?"

"Not stealing," I said. "I just needed to pick up a few skills."

"*More* skills?" How do you have so many skill points?"

"I got two with my new level, remember?"

"I remember *that*," he said indignantly. "But most people use those skill points to fill in their gaps. You needed more magic skills?"

"I couldn't possibly comment." Getting skills for free by demonstrating competence was a bit of a blind spot for these people. Even though some of them did it for Scribe and Calculate, they discounted the possibility of doing it for other skills. I suppose it was because they started spending skill points at such an early age. It was so much easier to just spend points on Run, Jump, and such than it was to actually do the work. Aubert, though, was still going.

"You fight, you have the full list of social skills—"

"I don't have Seduction," I interrupted.

"What? But you . . ." He broke off, blushing.

"I don't," I insisted. I had a *bonus*, which took the skill up to one. Paired with my stats and level, that took my total up to sixty, which wasn't much compared to my other social skills, but was a hell of a lot better than the fat zero a normal person without the skill would have. I wasn't going to explain that, though, so I just stared at him until he dropped the subject.

"Fine. But you still have too many skills," he mumbled. "It's almost as if . . . wait . . ."

"What?" I asked suspiciously.

"Champions are said to have more skills than normal . . ." he said slowly.

"Are they? Are you sure that's not just the legends talking them up?"

"Maybe," he admitted. "But you were so friendly with the ones in the capital . . ."

"They're friendly people," I countered. "Kaito has five companions that are very much *more* than friendly."

"It would explain so much," he said, looking at me intently. "The way you overtook me in levels . . ."

"Even if I was, don't you have bigger problems right now?"

"I . . . suppose so," he said, remembering where he was. He looked around his cell warily. "Shouldn't there be a guard?"

"Glamoured," I said, waving a hand airily. This world didn't have fairies, but I trusted the term would get translated. "He's not going to notice anything for a while."

"Then . . . what are your intentions here?"

"Hmm," I said thoughtfully. "Why don't you fill in a few details first? Why did Victor want to keep you alive?"

"*Duke* Victor," he said, frowning at me. I just raised an eyebrow and met his gaze. Eventually, he sighed.

"I don't know, exactly," he admitted. "Killing me would be more unusual; these matters are normally settled bloodlessly."

Remembering the sounds of fighting from earlier, I figured we had different definitions of bloodless. Aubert did seem mostly uninjured, which was probably what counted for him.

"Keeping me here serves as insurance against setbacks," Aubert went on. "If the King objects, or the people revolt against whatever puppet he sets up in my place, he can set me back in place, no harm done."

I was learning so many new definitions for words today.

"You didn't know?" I asked. "He has Guillaume with him."

"That snake!" Aubert spat. "He changes masters as easily as he breathes."

"Well, Duke Finley *is* dead," I pointed out. "I imagine swearing loyalty to whoever could get him out of prison seemed like a pretty good idea."

"He should have died with him," Aubert growled. "I'll make sure of it this time."

"Will you," I said, looking him over. He did look in pretty good shape. "That eager for a rematch? Think it will go better a second time?"

"Maybe," he muttered, looking at the ground. "We were taken off guard earlier. If we'd known, maybe we'd have had a chance."

"Say that's true," I said. "If you do beat him, which is a pretty hard sell given he's level seven and you're level *five*. If you do manage that, and don't kill him because you want to keep it bloodless . . . then doesn't he just order you to stand down? Isn't he still your liege?"

"He stopped being my liege when he dragged me from my bed!" Aubert protested hotly. "But also . . ." He trailed off, confused.

"Just what is your legal status right now?" I pressed. "Does Victor get to decide who the Count of Seren is?"

"If I'd done something wrong, perhaps," Aubert said slowly. "Tradition decides . . . the Duke has his say, but the King confirmed me. Unless I break my oaths, Duke Victor has no right to depose me."

"So he just sends a message to the King saying that you broke your oath, so he replaced you with Guillaume."

"I wouldn't have thought him capable of such a thing . . . until now. But yes, that would be accepted."

"So if you're out of prison," I mused, "and, say, back at Dorsay, saying to the King that Victor deposed you for no reason, what happens?"

"Well . . ." Aubert said, thinking.

"Don't worry, I know this one. Duke Victor outranks you, so his word gets taken and you're right back in here. Right?"

"That . . . might be true," Aubert admitted despairingly. "The King would not look kindly on someone who showed up as a beggar. It might be different if a Champion were to speak on my behalf, though?" He looked at me imploringly, but I dealt with real puppy dog eyes every day.

"Not for your entire county," I told him flatly. "I'm not getting entangled in politics in the city. Again. Let's talk about what happens if you manage to win here. What and where are the forces involved?"

"My main garrison in the town has probably not been informed yet," he said thoughtfully. "They probably plan on sending Guillaume there tomorrow to inform them of the change of leadership."

"That'll just work?" I asked.

"He is a Duvost, and the Duke's men will be standing by his side. My men will have no reason to doubt what he's saying. If I was there at the time, it would be different."

"Right. So what does the Duke have in town?"

"About half my numbers," Aubert said. "He had more troops outside, but we've been bringing them in quietly to avoid notice."

"And in the castle?"

"I had only a tenth of my garrison stationed here," he said. "Those that yet live are probably confined to their barracks, for now. They may go over to my cousin, but the circumstances of tonight's events will make them wary of swearing a new loyalty. Duke Victor has probably brought in about the same number of his own troops."

"What about your high-level people?" I asked.

"Imprisoned down here as well." The voice came from outside the cell, from one of the locked rooms. I stepped out and saw a number of faces looking through the barred windows. The man who'd spoken before continued, allowing me to identify which one had spoken.

"We're willing to fight again for his lordship, but we'll be needing healing potions," he said. "We went down fighting to protect him."

I looked over at a relatively unscratched Aubert.

"I surrendered only when it looked hopeless," he said, wilting under my gaze. "Which was after my guards were beaten."

"Whatever," I said dismissively. "So it sounds like you've got three options. You can fight him in the town, with two-to-one odds. Beat him there, and you can bottle him up in your castle until he surrenders. I've no idea how easy it will be to take the castle from the town, but I assume it's designed to make that hard."

"It is," Aubert sighed. "And we'll have to fend off attacks from his men outside as well. At least we'll have the walls for that."

"Sure. Or, you can try and take the forces in the castle with what you've got here. That's . . . less than even odds? Assuming you can get weapons and healing potions."

"But if we win here, we win," Aubert stated. "The Duke can be forced to order his men to surrender, Guillaume can be executed, and rightful authority restored."

I didn't know where to start with that statement, so I just let it pass. "If you capture the Duke, does he just say, 'You won, good game,' and everything goes back to how it was before?"

"I'm not that naive," Aubert said sourly. "If we captured him, I would have to take him back to Dorsay to bring a case before the King. He would have to make a ruling."

"And you'd just have to hope that he ruled in your favor," I said. "Not to mention, you'd have to escort the Duke all the way to Dorsay, through territory filled with his men."

Aubert opened his mouth and then closed it again. "That would be challenging," he eventually admitted.

"What if you killed him during the fighting?"

"That's not very likely," he told me, with just a hint of condescension. "He is level seven, after all. We might be able to overwhelm him, but if that looks like happening, he will probably surrender."

"Humor me," I said flatly. "What would happen if he did?"

"Then . . . command would revert back to the highest ranking officer. He has a son with the troops in the town—not his eldest, but of high enough rank to be listened to. A new duke would need to be confirmed, taking precedence over the current operation. They might be willing to leave in return for receiving his body."

Aubert took a deep breath. "And then, either I would be summoned to Dorsay to answer for the murder of my liege, or I would have started a blood feud with the Bargougnes. Since they are the ducal house, it would be less than a year before I found the entire duchy raised against me. They would raze my city to the ground and kill every man, woman, and child named Duvost."

"So . . . bloodless victory is preferred," I said.

"Indeed," he replied.

"Does the King have to worry about that for Duke Finley?" I asked.

Aubert shrugged. "He is more powerful than a ducal house," he said. "He had the right, no matter how transparent his motivations were. The King chose to pay the costs he is facing now because of his actions."

"I suppose. So anyway, how did you want to proceed?"

"You said there were three options."

"Oh, right. Well, the third option was if you wanted to kill Victor. Sneak a small group in and kill him. You could try for a capture, but he does have that level gap. A small group will be at a disadvantage."

"None of the options appeal. What is your advice?"

"Did you mistake me for one of your advisors?" I said, amused. "My advice is option four. Sneak out of the castle and leave the noble life behind. Start a new career as an adventurer."

He grimaced in disgust. "Why even suggest such a shameful thing? And if you're not here to help, why are you here?"

"I already told you why I'm here. If you're asking why I'm talking to you, it's because I'm trying to find a path where Talnier doesn't get attacked. I'm helping you only if it helps me."

I gestured around me.

"You're in charge of these poor fools, of the poorer fools in the barracks right now, and the unsuspecting fools in town. They'll obey you, not me. What are you going to do with that power, and is it going to help me?

"Or is it just going to get all these fools killed?"

COUNTER COUP

B-but . . . but . . .” the guard stammered.

"Are you refusing my order?" I asked mildly.

The guard blanched, as well he might. After all, as far as he could tell, he was talking to Duke Victor. I didn't know the man well, but I suspected that he might have a certain reputation with his underlings.

"But your orders, sire!"

"I know what my orders were," I growled. I didn't, of course. Perhaps some sort of rule to make sure that they weren't infiltrated by an Illusionist?

"Now, my orders are for you to open that door and stand at attention!" The *or else* was implied and didn't need to be any more than that. Just the presence of an angry duke was more than enough of a credible threat for Intimidate to get its claws in.

"Yessir!" the guard said over the clatter of bolts being thrown, and I swear that his voice was an octave higher. It only took a moment for the armory door to open.

I swept inside. My eyes flicked to the alarm rope, a simple system that would ring bells elsewhere in the castle. But my attention focused on the rack of healing potions, right where Aubert said it would be. It wasn't as full as he'd described, but that was to be expected. There had just been a fight here, after all. Not all of the Duke's men would have rated an expensive healing potion, but some of them would.

"This is where the effects of the prisoners are being held?" I asked. The two guards nodded and pointed at a table piled high with gear. Two guards *was* a little light, but it was the middle of the night and they must have been short-staffed with all of the recent fighting.

"Excellent," I told them. "Now, you"—I pointed at the guard nearest to the rope—"stay there and choke yourself unconscious. You just stand there for the moment," I said to the other guard.

Both guards stared at me. My Intimidate skill was pressing at them, but that wasn't what made one of the guards start to choke. Now the second guard was staring at the first in consternation, aghast at the sight of the man apparently following my orders.

An invisible man applying a chokehold doesn't look *exactly* like a man choking himself through sheer willpower, but it's close enough that the second guard took way too long to figure out what was going on. By the time he figured it out, his partner was already slumping to the ground.

He made the right move when he snapped out of it, lunging for the rope. But his partner, or more relevantly *my* partner, was in the way. And I'd had plenty of time to prepare a response.

"Improved Blind," I cast aloud, so as to not give too much away to my invisible friend. He was the least injured of Aubert's retainers, Seraphin Durand, the Vigilant Guardsman.

As for the guard, he wasn't doing too well. His shouts were muffled by my spell, he couldn't see, and I'd just tripped him.

[Unarmed] Skill unlocked.

Had I really gone this long without unlocking that skill? Also, that was a decent trip! I should have gotten a free skill from competency. There was no arguing with the System, though, so I just watched as Seraphin finished the job. He gave me a look, which I took to be a complaint about the second guard landing on him. Or he was taking issue with having to do all the grunt work. Whatever it was, he quickly broke off and headed for the potion rack.

He grabbed the first potion in the rack and slammed it down. Then he started grabbing bottles to take down to the prisons.

I checked on the guards. They were still alive, so I pulled out some manacles I'd liberated from the cells and applied them. They were of Excellent quality, so they should hold.

The whole "take them alive" aspect of conflict between nobles only applied to the nobles themselves. Perhaps valuable retainers that you wanted to use later could also be included. Not so much random guards. I'd insisted, as part of the price of my participation, that deaths were to be avoided, if at all possible.

Thanks to a bit of trickery, it was easily possible in this case, but I had no illusions about how much longer that would go on. Maybe that was why Seraphin was glaring at me; it would have been much easier if he could have just snapped these guys' necks. Maybe I should lift my spell, so he could make his complaints known.

Looking over at him, I giggled. Maybe there was another reason to lift the spell.

"You look like a floating bag of potions," I told him, repressing a giggle. If he'd been able to hide the bottles in his shirt, the invisibility would have covered them, but he was currently lacking most of his clothes.

I cancelled the spell, and he returned to visibility. He was quite a sight. Tall, with broad shoulders and rippling muscles that were not at all concealed by the remains of his shirt, he looked battered but still unbeaten. His face was somewhat weathered, and marred by a jagged scar across his left cheek, but the short grey hair and the salt-and-pepper beard made him look distinguished.

"We need all of this," he told me, gesturing at the table full of gear. "I can't carry it all."

I glanced at the pile of gear. He probably *could* carry it, if we had a container to put it all in. Glancing at his biceps, I didn't think the weight was going to be a problem. I looked around for a crate or something and then realized I was being an idiot.

"Summon crate!" I chanted while casting Phantasmal Object silently. To Seraphin's obvious surprise, the spell worked and a crate appeared, sized to my hastily estimated dimensions.

"You have a spell for that?" he asked, but didn't question me further, starting to pile weapons and armor into the crate. It turned out to be an awkward carry, but well within his capacity. Unfortunately, it was also too big to be covered by the Improved Invisibility spell.

"I'll go first," I said. I was still disguised as the Duke. "We didn't run into anyone on the way here, but if we do, I'll try persuading them to look the other way."

He nodded resignedly, I think expecting that he'd have to silence a witness along the way. He was back to full hit points, though, so I thought we'd be okay if we did get into a fight.

We dragged the guards to the back of the armory and then made our way back to the cells. Our return was uneventful. The one person left on guard at the cells had been overpowered and secured in Aubert's cell. Aubert and Elena, another one of his retainers, were waiting nervously for us to get back. He had two more captured retainers, but they were too injured to be moved safely.

While Seraphin treated the others, Aubert and Elena equipped themselves. Elena pulled on a tight leather jerkin and started strapping hard leather armor pieces to her arms and legs. Aubert's rapier was missing—I'd lay odds that Guillaume had it—but he didn't complain, just grabbed the ordinary rapier that we'd found and added to the pile.

Then the rest of the party came out, healed by the miracle of alchemy, and we discussed the plan as they got dressed.

"I won't be of much use in the fight," Edric Bertrand said. He was a cleric of Duit, if the robes and the staff were any guide.

> **[Identification]: Brikenwood Staff – Quality: Perfect – Properties: Blessing of Duit**

He looked the oldest of Aubert's retainers, with silver hair and a slight frame. He still moved easily, though, and his green eyes were still alert.

"I'm out of mana and Faith. I won't have much magic until I've had a chance to rest," he added. "I would be best for alerting the garrison in town."

"You can't sneak over the walls, though," Elena told him. "Main door will be shut and guarded, you can't walk out."

"If you can climb the walls, though, I can make you invisible," I offered.

He gave a sigh. "Alas, I had a sheltered childhood and never picked up the Climb skill," he admitted.

"I'll go," Elena said. "I don't need a spell, and the garrison knows me well."

Aubert nodded. "Then we will wait for Lady Hammond's distraction, and then attempt to free the garrison here."

A bit of scouting by yours truly had identified where the troops were bunked down. Aubert's troops were locked in the barracks, while the Duke's troops were camping in the courtyard. That meant the prisoners had better sleeping quarters, but the barracks were secure, something that couldn't be said for an open-air courtyard with connections to most of the castle.

"Are you sure you don't want to wait until morning, my lord?" the final retainer asked. He was Emeric Stormrider. I wasn't sure if he'd taken the name or if he came from a family of Storm Arcanists. That profession had a requirement of Water and Air Magic, granted Ice Magic, and gave a bonus to all three.

The man himself was tall and lean, with wild black hair. But his most striking feature was his eyes, a pale and electric blue, that seemed to glow in the dim light.

"I'm out of mana as well," he admitted. "I can fight, at least, but our chances will be better in the morning."

Aubert shook his head. "The same is true for our opponents," he pointed out. "Lady Hammond's distraction will be more effective right now, so we can't waste any time."

"Very well," Emeric said, and the rest of them murmured agreement.

"Right then, I'll be off," I said. "Just remember what we agreed."

"My lord!" the guard exclaimed as I came up the stairs onto the outer wall. I was still disguised as the Duke. Anchorbury's fortifications were, I thought, a little odd. Not that I knew much about medieval fortifications, but instead of building a city around the strong point of the fortress, Anchorbury was built between *two* strong points. One of them was the fortress around the dungeon, and the other was the Count's castle. Both of them had walls stronger and higher than the city walls, so it sort of made sense that both of them formed part of the outer defenses.

That meant that I could stand on the castle wall and stare out into the night at Aubert's lands. Not that I could see much. The night was cloudy and it was dark, and aside from a few walled homesteads, there wasn't much to give off light.

I ignored the guard standing next to me, awaiting my orders. I could get used to this sort of deference. Though, in fairness, I was getting a fair amount of deference back home. I didn't spend any time basking in it, though; I was here to make a distraction with my new spell.

First, though, I looked back at the castle. I hadn't gone rummaging through Aubert's private quarters, but I knew where they were. Guillaume had probably claimed those, and the Duke was probably in the honored guest quarters. They were close enough together for my purposes. No lights were showing. I guess they were sleeping off a hard day of usurpation. Good. I cast my spell and was pleased to note that there were no changes that I could see.

I turned back to the dark landscape outside. I'd picked up this spell before coming here, with the points I'd received from raising my Water

Magic to four. I'd figured that it would come in useful when Talnier was attacked, and this was close enough.

I frowned. "Do you see that?" I asked the guard beside me. He looked out obligingly, and I cast my new spell.

[Illusory Terrain].

Lights bloomed in the darkness below.

Small Distraction

Illusory Terrain had one of the vaguer spell descriptions.

> **[Illusory Terrain]: Create large-scale illusions.**

Once I had it, though, how it worked became intuitively obvious, even though none of my other spells worked that way. I could *split* my spell total between what I'd call believability and the volume that the spell affected.

Believability was the normal default for Illusion spells. Beat a person's level times Intelligence times Perception, and they couldn't see through the illusion. There were exceptions, like Phantom World, where any serious doubt about what they were seeing broke the spell.

Thanks to my high Charisma, and the bonus to Illusion Magic from Phantasmal Artificer, I hadn't faced many opponents who could see past my spells. Now I could use my monstrous spell total for something else at last.

Two hundred seemed like a safe amount to spend on believability. It was night, the illusion was far away, and the men on the walls were either level three or four. That *left three hundred and forty* points of spell total, which translated to a *radius* of that many meters.

Or thereabouts. The spell description wouldn't confirm it, but some of the other spells made mention of meters instead of a more fantasy-appropriate measurement like yards or furlongs. The point was, it was a huge volume, even if I wasn't using most of it. Centered on the ground, it was a huge *area*, and that area was now filling up with the torches of my illusionary troops.

"Sound the alarm, and get all our men up on the walls," I calmly remarked to the man beside me. He didn't question an order from his Duke and ran off, shouting.

Alarm bells were already ringing along the wall. The Duke ran an alert army. They were probably still keyed up from the recent coup as well. People started running up to me for orders, so I started directing things as best I could.

It wasn't the normal practice to put *all* your men on the wall at once. You needed to take shifts to give the men a chance to rest. I thought it was believable to get them all out here at the start, though. The enemy's numbers were huge, and sleeping in shifts wasn't going to help if the wall was breached.

That caused a certain amount of chaos, of course. The sleeping shift wasn't happy about being woken after only a few hours of sleep. Runners were being sent to the rest of the city, sounding the alert and asking for reports. Those probably wouldn't be coming back, assuming the garrison loyal to Aubert was doing its job. They could keep the Duke's troops in the city isolated and without orders for a little while. Not forever—there were elites in that group, and they'd take action on their own eventually. Long enough, though, for something else to fail first.

Like my own little deception. I was well aware that impersonating the Duke in his own (if stolen) castle was a trick with a limited shelf life. I'd done what I could to extend that by casting my first illusion on his quarters.

This was an illusion of silence. You could use the general-purpose spells to accomplish the same things as the specialist ones. It would have been a waste of a level forty spell, though, if I hadn't needed the huge volume to cover for my lack of knowledge about where the targets were.

Normally, a simple silence spell would have caused some disruption and not much else, but circumstances mattered. Duke Victor and Guillaume were, hopefully, asleep. Casting silence on their rooms meant that they didn't *wake up*.

It would have all been for naught if a servant had knocked on their doors and realized that they weren't making any sound, but with the Duke out here making noise and giving orders, it would delay that realization for priceless minutes.

Minutes that Aubert and his men could use. Use to free his own men and start his counter-coup. While the Duke's forces were focused on the threat outside, the real danger could strike.

I was just starting to get panicked reports of fighting inside the castle when the house of cards started crashing down.

"Arrest that impostor!" Duke Victor shouted as he came up the stairs. He seemed angry. This was still within my projections so I was prepared, making sure that I was near a darkened corner. Noting what he was wearing, I quickly used my one and only Shadow Magic spell to step into the shadows.

And out again, into an unoccupied storeroom at the bottom of the tower. Taking a moment to adjust my Disguise, I strode out bellowing orders.

"The Duke on the wall is an impostor!" I yelled, probably matching what the actual Duke had been saying on his way up. "Get more men up there to deal with him!"

"But sir, the barracks—" someone protested.

"Those are our allies against the Tribals outside, you fool! You've been tricked into attacking them!"

I wasn't sure if that made sense, but making sense wasn't the point. The point was to sow confusion and keep moving. I kept going like that for maybe ten minutes more until I turned a corner and ran into a bunch of Aubert's men.

They attacked me, of course. I was the Duke! I didn't like my chances of convincing them of anything, so I Shadow Stepped into another unoccupied dark place. Despite the whole castle being up in arms, not every nook and cranny was lit up.

[Shadow Magic] Level 2 acquired through use.
For gaining a skill level, you have been awarded 1 XP.

Nice. I decided that my agreed contribution to this endeavor was done. I could sit back now and let Aubert do the work. At least, that was the theory. In practice, I now had a lot riding on Aubert winning. If he didn't, I'd taken on all that risk for no reward.

With a sigh, I started Shadow Stepping back up to the central tower. That should give me a line on where the final battle was going to be held. The tower was practically deserted. Some of the rooms were occupied, I assumed by Aubert's family. The doors were locked and the rooms dark, but I was getting adept at noting the volumes where a shadow-blocking person was standing.

Getting to level two in Shadow Magic had doubled my spell total, and increased the light level in which my spell would work. I wouldn't be stepping in broad daylight anytime soon, but it made it easier to get around the badly lit battleground that was my current environment.

One thing that became clear as I reached the top level was that my silence spell had gone, probably broken the first time that I Shadow Stepped. As expected, but annoying. It meant that my illusionary army had disappeared as well. It had done its job, at least.

Looking around, it seemed that the battle was going well. There was one knot of fighting that seemed to be intractable, though. It was hard to tell, but I thought I recognized Seraphin in the middle of it.

I looked for an appropriate place to step through. Not too close, since I wouldn't be coming out invisible. There.

I stepped through, the sound of fighting becoming much louder. Turning invisible seemed prudent, so I did. Then I stepped around the corner.

Jackpot. I was actually behind Duke Victor as he defended the doorway I'd seen Seraphin fighting on the other side of. He was . . . winning? It didn't look like he was losing, anyway. Even as I watched, the man he was fighting cried out and fell back, to be replaced by another. There were three other soldiers in the room with him, but with Victor occupying the choke point, there wasn't much for them to do except look alert.

Guillaume was here as well, looking decidedly less than alert. He'd taken an injury at some point and was leaning against a wall, trying to stay on his feet.

Not knowing how many men Aubert had to lose, I quickly cast Blind on Victor. Annoyingly, perhaps even dismayingly, it didn't make an immediate difference. He was shocked by it, sure, but his opponent was just as shocked by the appearance of a black void around the Duke's head. Too shocked to take advantage of the brief moment of distraction. By the time he attacked, the Duke had recovered his poise, if not his sight.

It turned out that even without his sight, the Duke was more than a match for an average soldier. Which seems incredible, but when you use a skill, the System is the one that moves you. Victor was getting a penalty— a significant one—but his skill was just too high.

Then Seraphin stepped up. I wasn't sure if it had taken him this long to press through the crowd, or if he'd been waiting for Victor to become disadvantaged in some way. Whatever the reason, he was here now, and the Duke was *not* good enough to fight him off while blinded. He started taking blows, and he was forced to fall back.

Now the Duke's soldiers had something to do. They fell on Seraphin from both sides as he forced his way into the room. He blocked two strikes and took one, but he kept on pressing forward, allowing his companions to enter.

Now the room was filled with fighting. Incredibly, Duke Victor was still holding his own. He was taking wounds, sure, but they were small ones and didn't seem to be wearing him down. Aubert entered the room now, a better fighter than the average guard, but not a patch on Seraphin. He was the only one who could touch the Duke.

It was Aubert who made the difference, cutting down one of Victor's guards, allowing the other three to be overwhelmed by superior numbers. The fighting started to die down. Of his side, only Duke Victor still stood, still blinded, still managing to lash out at any incoming strike. Aubert's men stayed well back from him. Seraphin was the only one brave enough—or good enough—to approach, keeping Victor pinned against the wall with occasional probing thrusts.

Aubert strode over to where Guillaume was leaning against the wall, glaring at him. Angry looks were about all he could manage as Aubert came up to him, placing his sword against his throat.

"Cousin," Aubert said flatly.

"Usurper," Guillaume spat.

"Weren't we family a year ago?" Aubert said wonderingly. "Was that all lies?"

Guillaume didn't say anything in reply. Aubert sighed.

"Councillor, will you lift the blindness?" he asked.

I complied, and Duke Victor shook his head as his sight returned. He looked around the room warily.

"It is over, my lord Duke," Aubert said wearily. "The traitorous cat's-paw you thought to replace me with is under my blade. Your forces in the castle have been comprehensively defeated. Your mages are out of mana, and your force in the city has been isolated, with no knowledge of what is going on."

Aubert's mages were out of mana as well, but he didn't mention that. Unless he was counting *me* as one of his mages. I frowned at the thought but didn't interrupt.

Victor looked at Seraphin, slowly up and down, carefully evaluating him. Only once that was complete did he turn his gaze to Aubert.

"Turning a blade against your liege is treason," he said. "All of you are guilty."

It was strange. I could see the effect his words had on the room, but I didn't feel them. Aubert staggered as though he'd been shot, and the others flinched. Even Seraphin grimaced from the pressure of the Intimidation that he must be feeling. But standing there invisible, I wasn't in the room in a social sense, so I felt nothing.

An absence easily rectified.

"Don't even try it," I said, appearing out of thin air and letting my own Intimidation skill come to life. I'd faced Duke Finley when I was level five, and Victor's skill total was comparable to that. At level six, it wasn't a problem.

Around me, I felt spines stiffen and blades were raised once more.

"Your oath as my liege was broken when you put me in my own cell for not showing you enough deference," Aubert said. "It's not treason to take back what's mine."

"You think you can break with Bargougne?" Victor asked, amused. "Go running to Arryen perhaps? You killed each other's fathers, so you have something in common."

"Where I seek to place my allegiances is no concern of yours anymore. Put down your sword. If I become responsible for toppling two of the nation's pillars, people will start to talk."

They glared at each other for a moment more. Finally, Victor grimaced and threw down his sword. I swear I wasn't the only one to breathe a sigh of relief. Seraphin sheathed his sword and pulled a pair of manacles out of his belt. Always be prepared, I guess, and we did just come from the prison.

"That would appear to be that," I said. "My lord Count, I'm sure you've got a lot to do. I'm going to retire for the night. I'll see you sometime tomorrow about my payment. Probably"—I yawned—"sometime in the late afternoon."

THE IMPORTANT BIT

It was late morning before I stirred from my room at the inn. The staff were a little surprised to see me, as they hadn't seen me come in last night. It had been so late, I saved everyone some sleep by just Shadow Stepping straight to my quarters. Nobody inquired how they had missed me; I just saw some puzzled looks as they served me the leftovers of the breakfast meal.

Fed and rested, my next order of business was a visit to the Ironworkers Guild.

"Gustave!" I said warmly as I entered his office. As a senior guild member, his minders had waved me right in.

"My word! Mistress Hammond, as I live and breathe!" he replied, his hand jerking a little on the document he was writing. He carefully put the quill in its holder. "With all the excitement we had last night, I should have known you were in town."

"I'm sure I don't know what you mean," I said, taking a seat opposite him. "Did something happen?"

He winked at me. "Reports are scarce, but apparently the Duke's troops in the city were arrested on the Count's orders. Their weapons and armor were confiscated, and they're to be expelled from the county tomorrow."

"Weren't they here secretly?" I asked. He gave me a little grin in return.

"You can't have troops without arms and armor, and you can't move *those* without the Ironworkers finding out about it. You'd have read a letter from me about it by now if the Count hadn't cut off all traffic to Talnier."

"That was thoughtful of you," I said.

"Unnecessary, as it turns out." He made an exaggerated expression of displeasure. "The extra money to travel a more circuitous route was entirely wasted. I doubt either the Count or the Duke are in a position to conduct any unwise military ventures this year."

"I've some business that might make up for that tiny loss," I said, amused. Was he going to try and get me to refund the postage? "I have need of your—of the Guild's—legal advocate. I can pay for his time, of course."

"Oh? You need another contract written? Not with us, I hope?" His eyes widened in mock horror.

"No, no. This would be a contract between the Town Council of Talnier and your own Count. Given its official nature, I want to make sure that all the legal niceties are followed."

"I see. Well, in that case, I shall let him know to bring his sharpest legal implements."

Since Gustave needed a little time to arrange for the advocate, I was able to visit Elodie and her apprentice, Lundy. We had a nice chat and a quiet lunch before I collected my advocate and headed up to the castle.

"We're expected," I said to the guards. "Where can I find Count Aubert?"

Surprisingly, they didn't just let me wander the castle, so we ended up cooling our heels in a waiting room before they showed us into a larger room where Aubert was looking harried.

"Remember, you wanted the job," I said idly as I came in. "You could have been wandering the countryside by now, free as a bird and beholden to none."

"I remember," he muttered. "Who is this?" he said, looking at my companion.

"This is the man who'll be writing down the formal contract outlining our new relationship," I said brightly.

"Was my word not enough?" Aubert asked, irritated.

"Of course, but I've got to take this to the Council. Your memory is fallible, my memory is fallible. They can misunderstand the details of what I tell them . . . better to have the whole arrangement written out so we can agree."

Admittedly, my memory was a lot less fallible than it used to be, but the "Contracts are Good" speech hadn't changed since I was a first-year. Not that I was lying. Our agreement had covered the big picture, but there were a lot of nuances that needed to be hashed out. The devil was in the details, and the devil worked for Goldman Sachs.

I wasn't going to get a *better* deal here than I had gotten in Aubert's jail cell. I could tell already that he regretted making it. But his word was his bond, so there wasn't much he could do about it.

Back then, I hadn't pushed as hard as I could have. Bargain told me that I could have ended up with Seren county as a vassal of Talnier. As crazy as that sounds, a county becoming the vassal of an ex-barony, it was a testament to how Talnier's importance had grown. We were still smaller than Anchorbury in terms of wealth and population, but we were growing, quickly.

It was also an indication of the power that Aubert felt that I held, personally. Now that he had broken with the Duke, he needed another protector. He had ended up seeking the protection of the King, but he did see me as someone with that kind of power. Part of my side of the deal was a letter, written to support his application for direct vassalage.

Flattering as that was, I didn't want his vassalage. Instead, we were crafting a mutual alliance. How much that would be worth was anyone's guess. We weren't in a position to offer Aubert much in the way of military aid, and there was a good chance that his county would be gobbled right up again by one of the duchies that had it in for me. It was a start, at least.

The tax considerations were much more valuable.

"Honestly, this is going to benefit you more than you can imagine," I said as I watched Aubert wincing as the modified rates went down. "Less tax means more profits, which means more trade."

"So you've said," he said grumpily. "I'll believe it when I see it. And do you need to take the entire library?"

"That library is wasted on your family," I told him. "It's just gathering dust when it could be granting skills and educating people."

"It is—was—a symbol of my family's history and status. To have collected so many books—"

"That library is going to make real differences to people's lives," I told him. "I can't believe you think it's worth more as some sort of a trophy."

"Those people aren't going to help *me* at all."

"Then I guess they can count themselves lucky that you needed my help."

"You know, I was only in that cell because I was protecting you," Aubert said. "I think that our deal should reflect that—"

"I don't think that's true at all," I said. "Duke Victor brought Guillaume with him, after all. I think he was just looking for an excuse to replace you."

Aubert scowled. "Perhaps," he admitted.

"Incidentally, you really should be more careful who you let in your house. Concealing his identity with a full-face helm? That's amateur hour."

"I can see that I have a lot to learn about intrigue."

I narrowed my eyes. "I'm not going to be your tutor again, Aubert."

I stayed long enough to watch as the Duke and his men were expelled. I was a little worried about letting them go, but the locals had a procedure for it. As it happened, the Duke had one of his sons here, so he served as a hostage. He would be guarded until it was clear that the Duke and his army had left the county. Then he'd be given a small escort out as well.

The confiscation of the arms and armor was an interesting twist. The Duke and his men were of sufficient numbers to deal with any wandering monsters or bandits they encountered. Without weapons, though, they'd be hard-pressed to be a danger to a military force. And good quality equipment was one of the more expensive parts of raising an army. I'd have to mention Aubert's surplus to my commanders and see if they were interested in acquiring some of it.

Before they'd been allowed to leave, a runner had gone out, the fastest one that Aubert could find. We had correspondence—a lot of correspondence—that needed to go to the King. There was Aubert's plea for protection, my recommendation that the King grant it. There was a complaint about the release of Guillaume without Aubert being notified of a trial. And there was another bundle attached to a complaint of my own. A bundle of evidence.

"How soon do you think he will respond?" I asked.

"Not as soon as I'd like," Aubert admitted. "If nothing else, he will probably wait until he hears Duke Victor's side."

"And if Victor just rearms and comes back for you?"

"That will take time, too. A purchase of equipment that large isn't easily made. I've also sent letters to the other counts, letting them know what happened here. I don't think . . ."

Aubert trailed off uncertainly. "I don't think that he'll be able to easily raise the duchy against me. I have some small reputation, and the other counts will want assurances that what happened to me won't happen to *them*.

"That lot," I said, gesturing at the departing army. "They were Victor's personal troops, weren't they?"

"Yes. From his ducal estate. He has more men than me, but not much more than twice as many. And he needs to keep some at home. If he wants to crush me, he'll need the other counts."

"Which takes more time."

"Yes. And if he starts gathering support, I will probably hear of it, which would give me grounds to appeal to the King for more haste."

"So . . . this is going to work?"

"It might." He gave a nervous laugh. "He might act in time. He *might* refuse my plea, or . . . I can't think through all the possibilities. But it might work."

"You're gonna make me feel bad for leaving you to wait it out," I pointed out.

He laughed again, just as nervously.

"Just be ready to pull me out of a cell again, and all is forgiven," he said.

I pretended to consider it. "Yeah, all right," I finally said. "Can't say I won't charge you for it."

"It was a fair price for my life, all things considered," Aubert admitted. "I'll try to avoid having to pay it again. Good luck with your own battles, Councillor."

"Thanks," I said. "Remember to keep in touch. We're allies now, partner."

Every time I came back to Talnier, I expected to be greeted by the sight of the town in flames. I'd timed my run to arrive just after sunset, which meant that getting past the gate was even easier than it had been on the way out. The walls themselves were fairly well lit, but there were plenty of shadows on either side.

"You're back!" Felicia was the first person to greet me as I showed up at our house. "How much of the library did you steal?"

"All of it," I said smugly.

"Kandis! We agreed that you weren't going to steal *any* of it!" she exclaimed. "And you can't fit all of it in your ring, anyway."

The others were gathering—Kyle, Cloridan, Cutter, and Maslin. Janie must have been doing guard duty at the tower.

"Some things happened," I admitted. "Long story short, the library will be arriving in the next shipment from Anchorbury."

"I guess you'll have to tell us all about it over dinner," she said.

"Sounds good," I replied.

*   *   *

All things considered, the King's response—to one of my requests, at least—was processed quickly and efficiently. I had to wait just three days after I got back to Talnier for a response, so it couldn't have taken him much longer than that to come to a decision.

I'd set up a messenger to let me know whenever a griffin flew in with some mail, but in this case, it wasn't necessary. The missive came directly to me. Fortunately, I was in my Council office at the time, so the courier didn't have any problems finding me.

I looked up at him as he waited, slightly out of breath, while I held the document. He wasn't leaving.

"I'm to report that you have read the document, and take back any reply," he said in response to my raised eyebrow. I nodded and broke the seal. There was another seal at the bottom of the document I noted. I read the contents carefully.

"Thank you," I said to the courier. "You can tell His Majesty I'll act on this immediately."

SURPRISE MOVE

I gathered my forces before I went to beard the dragon in his den. Alain Guertin, commander of the city guard, was the man to see. He would have given me the men if I'd just asked, but I showed him the order anyway. I didn't want there to be any misunderstandings.

"Right," he said, taking a deep breath. "I'll get the men."

He started bellowing orders. Tasked with keeping order in town, half of the guards were out on the street at any one time. The other half were asleep or resting. It sounded as though they were getting woken up.

"We're not going to be fighting the whole garrison," I said mildly.

"You hope," he said bluntly. "When it comes down to it, who knows how many of them are loyal to their captain instead of their king?"

"Not *all* of them, I hope," I said uncertainly. If it *was* all of them, then we might be in trouble. I didn't think that the guard could take the garrison in a pitched battle.

"The more force you show, the less force you need to use," Guertin said. "Are you going to be coming along, ma'am?"

"I fancy I'll be of some use," I said. "But I'll let you and your men take the lead."

He nodded gratefully. "He's not likely to hole up if you're there," he said. "If we move quickly, most of them will be without arms and armor. Might be over quick and easy."

He didn't sound quite as reassuring as he might have meant to. Slightly spooked, I borrowed one of his runners to take a message to the Adventurers Guild. Not asking for help, just apprising them of the situation.

Collectively, the Guild was the strongest military power in Talnier, and while the Guild Master didn't *lead* them, he could suggest a course of action. They hadn't gotten back to me by the time the guards were ready.

"Let's go," the commander said. I fell in behind the squad as they marched to the garrison.

The guards at the gate were surprised to see us, but they stiffened to attention when they saw me. Intimidation was running at full blast, and while this squad wasn't a threat to the entire garrison, it was certainly one to these two.

"Open up," I said, "We're here to see Hector."

One of them moved to open the door instinctively, but the other was made of sterner stuff.

"I don't think that you'll all fit in his office, ma'am," he joked nervously.

"Then you had better fetch him down, hadn't you?" I smiled thinly. He agreed nervously and disappeared inside, through the door his companion had just opened. We marched inside right behind him.

We paused right behind the doors in an open area that had served as a reception hall before the Baron was chased out. A wide open door to one side led to what had been the banquet hall, now converted to a barracks. Most of the soldiers that guarded the wall were quartered there, except for the ones with night duty. They got to sleep in the old, smaller barracks during the day.

All up, roughly a quarter of Hector's men were hanging around in the barracks, looking at our intrusion curiously. It was an awkward few moments, finally broken by Hector's arrival.

He came down the stairs looking wary but confident. Calmly coming up to me, he walked through the protective ring that the town guard had formed and bowed.

"This is quite the surprise. What brings you here, my lady, with such an entourage?" he asked.

"Aubert Duvost has shared your correspondence with me," I said. I held out some documents. He snatched at them, but his face didn't change until he looked at what he held and recognized them.

He grimaced and tried to tear the documents in half. The look on his face when he failed to was amusing. Then he exerted more force. Damage over time was one weakness of Phantasmal objects, so it didn't take more than a moment for the documents to disperse into the ether.

"Forgeries," he said grimly.

"Copies," I admitted. "The King has the originals."

I held up the King's warrant so that he could see the seal. I kept it out of his reach though.

"You're not serious," he said.

"Hector Rodakis, you are charged to answer to the King for your actions," I said loudly, so all his men could hear. "You have betrayed the post that you have been charged with."

I was pushing hard with all the social skills I could muster. Not just on him, but on all his men. I must have seemed quite the forbidding authority figure right now. It might have been wiser to focus on Hector, but I really didn't want anyone else starting a fight.

I could beat Hector, in this realm at least, but he was no pushover. He fought me every step of the way.

"Aubert Duvost is the *true* ruler of these lands," he said. "He is the King's vassal! It can't be treason to pass information to him!"

"Duvost's loyalty is why he reported you to the King," I countered. "If you want to make a claim about the legality of your actions, you're going to have to make it at your trial."

His shoulders slumped. For a second, I thought I'd won, but . . .

Where's the notification? Even as I thought that, a bottle blinked into existence in his hand.

He has a spatial ring? I'd never seen him wear one. But he mostly wore gloves when on duty. Or were they gauntlets? For just a moment I was distracted by the useless question while the rest of my brain tried to identify the bottle. Oh, wait.

[Identification]: Fire Trap Potion – Quality: Excellent – Properties: Ignite, Sticky, Fire Damage

---

"No," he said. "I don't think I will."

The bottle came down, thrown not at me, but at my feet.

As the flames swept up at me, my first thought was for the document in my hand. A quick thought sent it safely away into my ring. Admirable perhaps, but not the best move tactically. The warrant wasn't a magic scroll; its power didn't go away if it was destroyed. Enough people had seen it to *know* what the King had decreed. Failing to act on that because the document had been destroyed would be foolish.

You have taken 23 damage!

Almost as foolish as ignoring fire, even for a moment. I was backing away but the fire followed—my dress was on fire. As were a few of my guards, but they could take care of themselves right now. My dress had been designed to convey importance, competence, and stability to those who saw me wear it in the Council offices. It had not been designed to be fireproof.

> **You have taken 58 damage!**

I wasted precious moments by screaming, trying to bat out the flames, and then screaming some more. None of these things helped, and in fact only made things worse. When I tried to suck in a fresh breath of air, I only choked on the smoke, which forced me to bend forward as I tried to scream and cough at the same time.

> **You have taken 76 damage!**

At some point during that embarrassing display, my mind actually caught up to what was going on. I had a solution to this. It was lucky that I didn't need words or gestures to cast, as my body was pretty much acting on its own right now. Nor did the skill need any of my attention to use. Just my *intention* was enough for the skill to take over and cast Water Stream.

The spell gave a fair degree of control over the direction, spread, and flow of the stream of water. Directing it at yourself was an unusual application, but it was definitely called for here. I went for maximum dispersal and flow, which resulted in a cone of heavy spray that I directed at myself. Then around the room at the others who were burning, and then back on myself when I remembered that you were supposed to use running water on burns.

Only then could I spare some attention for what was going on in the rest of the room. All around me, I could see guards, both Hector's and my own. It looked as if they had all been fighting the fires, which were now out. Hector was nowhere to be seen, and I could see that everyone was trying to work out what their next course of action was.

I needed to speak, needed to tell them what to do. But my throat was closed up from smoke, and I needed to do something about the pain that seemed to be coming from all over. Every part of me *stung* as if I was still on fire. I quickly brought a healing potion out of my ring and into my hand.

Pain. So much . . . why?

I stared in confusion and disbelief as the potion fell out of my nerveless grasp and shattered on the floor. As soon as I'd grabbed it, my hand had flared up with agony. I stared at my hand. Was my skin always that red and blistered? I . . .

Then everything fell away and the pain stopped for a little while.

"It's just as well you didn't take the potion," Felicia said. "Burns are tricky to heal. Without a mind to direct the repair, you'd be looking at scars for sure."

"Ugh," I attempted to croak, only to find that my throat was working fine again. Felicia did good work. "Thank you. What happened?"

"Nobody died," she told me. "The Council is paying the Guild for healing, so all the guard's injuries are taken care of."

"What about Hector?" I asked.

"He was gone before I arrived. Really, Kandis, what were you thinking trying to take him on alone?"

"I wasn't alone, I had an entire squad of guards," I said testily.

"I mean without your team," she corrected herself.

"I thought . . . it was Council business, not adventuring. I'm trying to keep them separate."

"Hmph, it's not like I'm asking to do your paperwork for you. But when you're going into dangerous situations, you need to have us around. And you need to work on your instincts. You would never have fallen for that play if you'd been on your guard."

"Maybe not," I admitted. "I was worried about him switching from social to real combat, but I expected him to do that by drawing his sword."

"Which is why he didn't do that," Cloridan said, entering the room.

"Hey, there's healing going on here!" Felicia protested. "She could have been naked!"

"That's what I was hoping for," Cloridan said with a grin, "I'm a little disappointed to see she's covered up."

I was covered up, but only with a blanket. My dress was nowhere to be seen, and given its state the last time I remembered seeing it, I wasn't surprised. I sighed and cast Disguise.

Cloridan made a sad face as I sat up. "Lech," I said. "But you're forgiven if you can tell me what happened to Hector."

"He's gone," Cloridan said, suddenly serious. "He's taken eleven of his most trusted men and slipped out of the city."

I very much doubted that *slipped* was the right word. The tower we'd confronted him in had access to the wall, so he and his men could have walked up the stairs and jumped down from there. Their level was sufficient to easily make that jump.

"And the rest of the garrison?" I asked.

"Confused, but loyal," he told me. "A few of them saw the King's seal before everything went down. The temporary commander is keeping everyone to the barracks and a new commander has been requested, assuming that one isn't already on his way."

"The warrant appointed his deputy to take charge," I said. "I'd guess that he was one of the eleven?"

Cloridan nodded.

"So do we know where he's gone?" I asked.

"We've sent messengers out to the nearby towns to keep a look out for him, but the guards on the walls did see what direction they headed," Cloridan said.

"Where?"

"Into the forest," he replied. "They've gone into the Great Wild."

POST-INCIDENT MEETING

"So I suppose this is where you tell me that you don't have an extradition treaty with Latora."

Anas looked at me curiously and flicked his ears. "I don't know what that is, but since we don't have any kind of treaty with your kingdom, I can assume that's true."

I waved my hand dismissively. "It was a joke. I know your people don't control your borders."

"Does anyone? If your kingdom had been able to control the exit of Captain Rodakis, we wouldn't be having this problem."

"True," I admitted, ignoring the bristling from the Latorrans in the room that his statement caused. "I guess the difference is that we make an *effort* to control them."

"A wasted effort," the wolf-kin told me. "That said, individual Tribes do exert control over their territories. We can send out messengers to let them know about the Captain. However, what they do with that knowledge will depend on how they feel about me and your experiment here."

"So they're just as likely to send him on his way with a meal as they are to arrest him?" I asked.

He shrugged. "I think most likely is that they deny him access. Few Tribes think well of Latorrans, but some will offer hospitality to travellers. Arrest is more likely if we have sent a warning, but even then I would not count on it."

He paused in thought and then continued. "If he's still dressed in the King's colors, hospitality is less likely. They might attack him."

"It's not just him, remember, he's got a dozen men with him," I pointed out.

"Yes, but they can claim to be exiles from Latora, not raiders," Anas said. "In the right places that claim might hold some weight."

"I don't understand why he would run into the Tribal lands in the first place," Delmar, my fellow council member said. "He knows they hate him, and he holds them in contempt."

"There's a lot about his actions I don't understand, and that's one of them," I agreed.

"He might not be heading into Tribal lands," Captain Alain said. "It's a common tactic to detour through a border so that the forces chasing you can't follow. It could be that he plans to double back into the Kingdom once he's lost the trackers."

"That's not going to happen, though, since we're working in cooperation with the Tribes, right?"

"That's right," Guild Master Koenig confirmed. "We sent out Guild-accredited hunters paired with Tribal ones. They shouldn't have any trouble moving on either side of the border."

"I don't know if he'll be travelling along the border," Cloridan said. He'd come in without knocking and had just caught that last sentence. He had come in carrying a bunch of variously sized papers, which he quickly started laying out on the table.

"What have you found?" I asked. Since the town guard didn't actually have an investigation team, I'd tasked Cloridan with going through Hector's office while I put this meeting together. He'd seemed quite pleased at the idea of rummaging through the man's stuff in an official capacity.

"First of all, he was not only gathering information about Talnier, he was also paying for as much information about the Great Wild as he could."

Cloridan laid some more papers down, these ones covered in dense notes. "Including maps."

"Those are a map?" I asked. I could read the notes, but I kept that to myself—they weren't written in Latorran. They read like a mix of bad poetry and a Google Maps direction list. "They're not like any map I've seen."

"They are more like guides," Anas said, examining the papers closely. "Pictures do little good in the forest, directions are hard to discern. The guide describes a path to take that gets you to your destination. These would need to be translated, though, and they are old, besides."

"Yeah," Cloridan said. "I figure that's why they were left in his office and not taken with him. Chances are he's got more up-to-date, translated versions."

It wasn't so much that the forest changed over time, although I suppose it did. Quicker than that, though, were the mana streams. The shamans had turned the Great Wild into a maze with invisible walls. If you knew the routes, you could travel in relative safety. If not . . . well, adventurers appreciated the experience of fighting monsters all the time.

"Why, though?" the mayor asked. "As Councillor Delmar said, he hates the Tribes."

"Because that's where Tom went," Cloridan said, pointing at a separate stack of papers. These were small and tended to have just one thing written on them.

"Is that where he went to?" I asked.

Tom had disappeared shortly after I'd gotten back from Dorsay. Envoys from the Ebon Order were not currently welcome in Latora. Tom had vanished just before the arrest order had gone out. That order had gone through Hector, not me—there might have been some concerns about my impartiality. Tom had his own sources, though, and had skipped out just ahead of the guards.

That Hector was still looking for Tom wasn't a surprise. That he was hiding out with the Tribes was.

"So what are you saying?" I asked Cloridan. "Do you think he's gone to capture Tom so the King will forgive him?"

"Maybe," Cloridan said. "Maybe he was planning an expedition and decided to start it early when you forced his hand."

"Why, though?" I asked. "Why run at all?"

"Accusations of treason are a serious matter," Captain Alain said. "And we know he's guilty, so . . ."

"Is it really that serious?" I looked about the room. "Maybe for everyone here, but Hector is a noble. He may not have a title, but he's born to a house like all of them. Does anyone really think that he's going to be punished severely?"

Everyone looked as though they were thinking it through, so I continued.

"Hector was passing information to another of the Kingdom's nobles and was probably going to open the gates for them. He was betraying his oath, but he wasn't betraying the country. Duke Victor was planning on *attacking* us. And yet, he thought he was going to get away with it. Aubert couldn't even look me in the eye and say he won't still!"

"What's true for dukes isn't necessarily so for untitled captains," the mayor pointed out. He wasn't the sharpest tool in the shed when it came to governing, but he had a keen sense of politics. "He was part of Duke Finley's faction; he may have feared following in his patron's fate."

"That's another thing that bugs me about this," I griped. "As soon as Finley's dead, he starts passing information to Victor. Wouldn't his allegiances normally pass to Finley's son?"

Shrugs all around. "Maybe he was always playing both sides?" Cloridan suggested.

"Maybe," I said. "It just feels like we're missing something."

"We can ask those questions if we manage to catch him," Captain Alain said impatiently. "Until then, it's just speculation."

"True." I looked back at Anas. "Are you sure there isn't anything the Tribes can do to help?"

Anas managed to look apologetic. "For the help you want, it would take a proclamation from the Council, and they wouldn't do such a thing lightly."

"They still want that unspecified favor from me, don't they?"

"*Some* of the Council do," Anas admitted. "I don't know if more than my mentor are in favor."

I narrowed my eyes. There was something Anas wasn't telling me. Bargain was stirring. It smelled a quid pro quo . . . somewhere.

"What would it take to get that proclamation?" I asked.

Anas looked uncomfortable, folding his ears back. "I'm not really authorized to say such things . . ." he started.

"But?" I pressed.

"My master did say that . . . if you were to speak with the Council and volunteer to help with this problem, they would be so grateful that they'd do whatever you asked in return."

"When did he say that?"

"Before all this started. I didn't mention it because it was just something that *he* said, not an official offer."

"An official offer," I said wryly, "might mention what this job is. But! I don't have an invitation to visit the Council."

"You don't *actually* need one," he said slowly. "No one can be barred from the meeting grounds unless they bring violence. And . . . we don't control the borders."

"So I can just walk right in?"

"Yes, but . . . you need to know where to go, and I can't tell you."

"It's a *secret* meeting place?"

"No, but if I help you get there then that would be seen as my mentor exerting undue influence on Council decisions. Many of the members would turn against us."

"And ..."

"The same is true for any Tribal member here in Talnier," he admitted. "I have influence over them, just as my mentor has over me."

"I'm starting to understand why the Kingdom never made a treaty with you," I said sourly. "You make everything so *difficult.*"

"Well, I do apologize," he said stiffly. "Our traditions are important to us, as is maintaining the independence of the Tribes."

"I'm sorry, that was uncalled for," I said. "I was just frustrated. So you're saying that *if* I can make it to your gathering place and *if* I agree to help with ... whatever it is that is bugging your master, then I *might* be able to get the help of the Council to catch Hector."

"You did ask if there was *any* way to get them to help," Anas said reproachfully. "I wasn't planning on bringing it up as a possibility."

"That's true," I agreed. I turned to Captain Alain. "So how badly do we need the Council's help?"

Alain grimaced. "Ask me in three days. By then, they should have either caught him or lost the trail. If they're not back by then, then either they still have the trail but he's travelling too fast for them, or ..." He trailed off.

"Or?"

"Or they've caught up with him and aren't coming back," he said grimly.

"Right ... but it will take, what, three days to get to the gathering place?" I asked Anas.

"I don't want to be too precise ..." Anas trailed off as I glared at him. "Perhaps three to five days?"

"Fine. So if we wait for the hunters to report back, it'll be a week before we can do anything. And how long will it take to spread the word among the Tribes?"

"Oh, word spreads quickly once the Council makes a decision. And I can keep Master up to date with the news from here if you do decide to go there."

"Huh." Of course, I knew such communication methods existed, but they didn't jibe with what I knew of the Tribal style. Then again it was probably tree-speaking or something.

"So if I spend three ... to five days getting there, Elder Tinidan can fill me in on whether Hector's been captured or what. If we don't need the help, I can pass on his mystery job, or just get paid with concessions on the trade deal."

"I'm not sure why you're thinking about this," the mayor said. "Catching criminals is not the responsibility of the Council."

He glanced over at Captain Alain, making clear just who he thought *was* responsible.

"Normally, I'd agree," I said. "But in this particular case, I suspect the King has certain . . . unspoken expectations of me."

"Ah." The mayor's expression was a combination of sympathy for my plight and smug delight that he hadn't been the one to meet the King. "Fraternizing with royalty does bring duties as well as benefits," he said.

I refrained from rolling my eyes. The King's expectations were entirely born of the fact that I was a Champion and hence caused disruptive troubles just by existing. He expected me to clean up any mess in my general vicinity as well as any other troublesome events that happened elsewhere on the grounds that it might be "Champion Business."

Not that I was averse to the notion in this case. It looked as though there was the potential for profit. And I owed Hector for setting me on fire.

Koenig cleared his throat. "One problem," he said when we all looked at him. "All the people I know of that might be able to guide you there got sent out looking for Hector."

"*Really?*" I asked. What sort of multi-stage quest was this?

"I'm afraid so," he said. "We can put out another call and see who shows up, but . . ."

Anas looked at me apologetically. I sighed. "So the first thing I need to do is find a guide."

COMMUNITY OUTREACH

I didn't want to be here, but sacrifices needed to be made. Every hour I spent outside of the Tower of Learning was an hour I wasn't getting that slow trickle of experience. It wasn't going to kill me or anything, but as time went by, I was starting to see why people like Aghen Shadthe never left the comfort of their dungeons.

That wasn't an option for me, though. I still had a business to run. While the essence of banking was to let the money do the work *for* you, I had a lot more work to do before the money was ready to do that. Eventually, maybe, I would be able to run the bank in a more hands-off manner.

But I was also a politician. Something that I was trying to impress on my fellow Councillors was that a politician needed to be available to their constituents. More than that, I wanted to establish it as a norm, a tradition that got passed down. The best way of doing that was to lead by example, which meant that I needed to spend a certain number of hours a week in my less comfortable office, doing paperwork and making myself available.

No more walk-ins, though, I thought to myself when I saw who just walked through the door. I needed to establish some sort of appointment system.

My Bureaucracy skill stirred at the thought, eager to set up some rules and regulations for governing Talnier. I pushed it aside—I had more immediate concerns.

"Morning, Councillor Hammond," Reynard said as if it was just another day. He ambled in and took a seat without any ceremony.

"I preferred our previous arrangement," I said. "Where you skulked about on the outskirts of my town and didn't bother me. This change is unwelcome."

I made sure to talk over the Unseen Sound I was casting to let my assistant know that this man could be trouble. There was a startled clatter from her desk, and Bureaucracy itched at me again, wanting to set up security and safety procedures. I ignored it in favor of paying attention to the man in front of me.

"Ah, don't be like that," he said, smiling. "It ill behoves a Champion to be so unfriendly."

I didn't let my face change at all. If Aubert had started to guess, then others couldn't be far behind. I'd wager, though, that it was his noble patron who had passed that little piece of information along.

"I'm not advertising it," I said coldly, "But I'm not the weak level two that needed to hide any more. There's not many left that I'm worried will use me, and most of those already know."

Numbers one and two on that list were Aghen Shadthe and the King. Since I'd taken sides in the conflict between them, though, I was less worried about Shadthe using me and more worried about him planning a messy assassination attempt.

The main reason I wasn't advertising my status was that I feared I would become *too* popular. People were already bowing in the street. If I added the cachet of being one of the gods' Chosen, they'd throw away democracy and acclaim me as the town baron without a second thought. The King would go along with it, too; he'd already offered me the position.

There was a flicker of a grimace across Reynard's face as if he'd actually been hoping to hold that over me.

"I'll keep that in mind," he said. "But I'm actually here to *help* you."

Bargain informed me that we were starting a negotiation. It wasn't that the skill tapped me on the shoulder; I just knew that Reynard wanted a deal and that he was starting his pitch. From the feel of it, he actually had Bargain, but not to my level, and certainly not paired with my Charisma.

It felt rather like settling into the cockpit of a top-of-the-line sports car at a racing track, looking over and seeing that your opponent was driving a nineties Corolla sedan. *What is he even trying to get out of me?* I wondered, focusing on the skill. That was exactly what Bargain was for, after all. *Oh no. No way.*

"I heard that you were looking for a guide into the Great Wild," he said blandly.

"I wouldn't trust you to find your own way out of this building, let alone lead me into the biggest forest in the world," I said.

He frowned. "Is that a disparagement of my skills, or do you just think I'm going to ransack the place on my way out?"

"The latter," I assured him.

"Oh good, because I assure you that my skills *are* real. I'm a real Ranger, I've travelled the wilds before, and I have no association with the Tribes. That is exactly what you need right now."

Now it was my turn to frown. "How do you know about that last requirement?" I asked. Koenig knew about it, of course, but I was fairly sure that he wasn't advertising it while he was looking for guides for me. Then again, this guy wasn't coming to me from Koenig. He may have acquired the protection of a noble, but I didn't think he was going to tempt fate by coming within fifty feet of the Guild Master. That was just asking for an "axeident."

"A little bird told me," he said lightly. I probably wasn't going to get anywhere with that. Somebody in the meeting may have talked; it wasn't like we were keeping it a secret. Or he might have worked it out from Koenig's rejected applicants.

"I notice you didn't take issue with the 'robbing me' part of my statement," I said sourly.

He shrugged. "I can't do much about your own prejudice," he said. "Though I will point out that I'm doing quite well for coin. I've no need to steal your silverware."

"You broke an oath that can't be broken," I said. "There's no way I'm going into the forest alone with you."

"Not an oath so much as a mind-control spell," he said bitterly. "The Guild that you're so happy to work with, they've already tried to get you to agree to it, haven't they? Are you really going to fault me for getting out from under it?"

"I—" . . . had to admit that I was torn on that one. Still. "You used that freedom to commit crimes, stealing an extra floor's worth of wealth out from under the Guild's nose."

"They owed me ten times what I took, if it comes to that," he said. "But as it happens, I needed help to get out. She had a price, and I was glad to pay it."

"Countess Rankin, right? How did she do it?"

He looked at me for a long moment before answering. "An amulet. Made by her dungeon, or so she said."

"Do you still have it?" I asked.

Another long moment passed before he pulled it out of his shirt. I didn't waste any time.

> **[Identification]: Mind Shield Amulet – Quality: Perfect – Origin: Caverns of the Serpent's Embrace – Properties: Restricted**

Huh. The name checked out, but why were the properties restricted? It seemed sus. I already had Mana Sense active, but now I cast Dispel Illusion.

Sure enough, a concealed mana string appeared, heading back in the general direction of Dorsay. Just like the Guild members.

"You're still working for her," I said, not at all asking a question.

"I'm lucky to be so. She was generous to keep me on after my failure at Oakway."

"This is all on her orders," I realized. "She *sent* you to Talnier . . . to do what?"

"Keep an eye on you," he admitted easily. "A task that should be remarkably easy if I accompany you on this trip."

"Yeah, that's not a hugely persuasive reason to take you."

"It doesn't need to be." He shrugged. "You don't have a choice. Well, you could always not go, of course."

I narrowed my eyes. "*How* do I not have a choice?" *Is this an offer I couldn't refuse?*

"For one thing, as I said, you're not going to find another guide. Not in the time you have. For another, if you find a way to go without me, I'll just follow you."

"What?"

"The same as I did when you went to Anchorbury just recently."

"You're guessing," I challenged. "I was invisible the whole way."

"Still left tracks, though," he pointed out. "I couldn't follow you into the castle, but I did figure out which inn you were staying at."

I stared at him. "I never saw any sign of you."

"There's other ways to hide than being invisible," he told me. "I didn't have to stop you, or talk to you, I just had to keep an eye on you, as much as I could."

He waited for me to respond, but I was a little too shaken to do so. He continued on.

"So your concern about my trustworthiness isn't relevant. I'm going to be out in the forest with you, either by your side or about half a mile back. Which would you rather?"

I found my voice. "You're going to stalk me, and you're just admitting it ahead of time?"

"I don't know what it's like where you're from, but that's not a crime. Not here, and especially not in the Wild. I don't know if they mentioned it, but—"

"The Tribes don't care who travels through the forest," I finished for him. "Yes, it's been mentioned."

He grinned. "Now, going into a Tribe's territory would be another matter, but I think I might do a little better than you there. After all, I've been through before, and you haven't."

"I'll get you arrested, have them hold you until I leave."

"On what charge?" He chuckled. "Didn't I hear some pretty speeches about how we were all equal under the law? Assuming your guards can catch me, they can't hold me long enough for your trail to go cold. And that depends on having someone else to guide you."

"Trusting you to guide me would be insane," I said. "You'd lead us into danger, or just around in circles until Hector's gone."

"I promise I won't," Reynard said, holding up a hand. "Dangerous places, they're mostly behind a mana boundary, which you can detect on your own. Circles is where you'll go if you try it without me. You may be able to see the dangerous areas, but finding your way through them . . . takes a guide."

I glared at him in silence. Eventually, he got to his feet.

"Well," he said, "I've said my piece. Think it over for yourself. You'll see I'm right, eventually. Try not to take too long, though; Hector's only getting farther away."

He turned to leave, only to find his way blocked by the recently arrived guards.

"Whoop! Guess I won't be getting a chance at the silverware after all!"

He looked back at me. "These guys sending me to a cell, or throwing me out?"

I took a deep breath. "Out. Escort him outside, please," I said. I wanted to give a different order, but corrupting the rule of law for my own convenience was not something I was going to do. Not over this. I did put advocating for anti-harassment laws on my to-do list, though.

He left without any trouble, and I thought long and hard about what he had said. Koenig had been doubtful there were any guides left in town, but Reynard had been *sure* that there weren't. Had he already asked around? Or had he made sure that anyone who was left wouldn't volunteer? Either way, it implied that he'd known I was going to be looking for a guide for quite some time, at least *before* I knew.

How much of the strangeness of recent events had he been responsible for? Could he have manipulated Hector? I didn't see how. Perhaps the Countess was responsible. She had seemed quite close to Duke Victor, back in Dorsay.

Something was going on, and all the signs pointed to the Great Wild as the place where it would get resolved. Part of me wanted to opt out entirely, but the part of me that had wanted to be a trader reminded me that risk wasn't always a bad thing. If you didn't put the investment up, you wouldn't reap the rewards.

AFTER-ACTION ANALYSIS

What just happened?

I had just been beaten at my own game, by someone who could barely boast of a skill total.

No, really. What happened?

There had been no notification after the fact. I hadn't lost a Social Contest. I hadn't been Persuaded, Intimidated, or even Seduced (ugh). That had been a . . . Bargain?

That *was* the skill that had fired up at the start, I recalled. But where was the deal? He had offered to go with me . . .

No, I realized. That wasn't what he was *offering*, it was what he *wanted*. What he was offering was . . . to take me where I wanted to go.

That didn't seem *right*, but it was *true*. Bargain, as always, cut through to the heart of the matter. That was what he wanted, that was what he was willing to pay. It just hadn't gotten through to me in the moment because it made no sense.

He *couldn't* take me where I wanted to go *unless* he accompanied me. They were the same thing. Structuring the deal that way made no sense.

For a moment, I considered the possibility that his Bargain was sufficiently high to feed me false information. It didn't seem likely, though. We were even on level, and I was higher on Charisma. He might have a higher base skill than me, but I doubted it. I had a bonus, so even if he had more time to devote to practice, he couldn't be that much higher than me.

So I had to assume that the information I was getting from Bargain was correct. His offer was genuine. Maybe that was why he'd structured it that way. It let me sense that he intended to be an honest guide and that all he wanted was to accompany me. If he'd had an ulterior motive, I was pretty sure that I would have picked it up.

That didn't mean I was in the clear, though. Bargain only covered what was currently known. If the Countess had lied to him, and planned on ordering him to kill me . . . that wouldn't show up. But he had to be fairly confident that she *hadn't*, or that doubt would have shown up in his offer.

This was where Intrigue should be kicking in, I realized. That it wasn't meant either that the Countess wasn't intriguing against me, or that she was significantly better at the skill than I was. That sounded . . . disturbingly plausible.

If I assumed that the Countess was intriguing against me, then things started to make more sense. Reynard didn't have the full story. He was just told what to do, not the reasoning behind it, so I couldn't pull it out of him.

My threats against him had not been plausible, blunting the skill's effectiveness. I supposed I should be grateful that implementing something like a proper rule of law was preventing me from acting like a tyrant, but I had to admit that it chafed.

I wasn't yet rich enough for Bargain to help. I couldn't outbid a noble family that went back forever. Persuasion was always a possibility, but I would need some arguments to use against him. He didn't seem like the type to be swayed by appeals to his higher principles.

That was pretty much it for acting directly against Reynard. Oh, I could attack him, of course, either physically or with illusions. I wasn't going to do that, though, any more than I was going to lock him up on trumped-up charges. I was better than that, and he hadn't actually *done* anything.

So the best way of dealing with this would be . . . to do nothing. Don't take the attractive bait. Finding Hector wasn't that important, and the hunters might yet turn up something. Diplomacy could wait for another day, a day when I could be officially invited. There was no reason for me to let myself be led into a trap.

Three days later, I was looking at a letter. After spending far too much time on greetings and discussions about the weather, Aubert finally got down to business. There were a few bits of important news in the envelope, but one in particular stood out.

As you suggested, I questioned Guillaume about the reasons why he switched his allegiance from Finley to Bargougne. The answer he gave . . . was that he had always been working for Bargougne. Some of the things he told me about the night my father died contradicted my own memory of events.

It is possible that our methods were ineffective, but I would swear that he was telling the truth. This casts serious doubt on the nobility of Duke Victor, but I am unsure of how to proceed.

I didn't have any answers for him, and I had my own concerns. It had been three days, and none of the hunters had returned. It was time for another meeting.

"Where does this leave us?" I asked. "We've given it three days, and we still don't know anything."

"We would have heard from the border towns if he'd doubled back," Captain Alain said.

"I've had time to make . . . a few inquiries," Koenig said uncomfortably. "A lot of the men we sent out had . . . dealings with Rodakis."

"What sort of dealings?" I asked.

"We don't really know," Koenig said. "We know he was preparing for an expedition. He met with a lot of guides, both local and from the Tribe. A few of them are still here and tell us that he was just asking questions about prices and available knowledge, but . . ."

"He may have made arrangements with the ones who went after them."

"None of them mentioned the connection when I hired them," Koenig said. "That might have been because they feared I wouldn't hire them if I knew . . ."

"Or it might be because they had something to hide," I finished for him. "Did we send him reinforcements instead of hunters?"

"We don't know," Koenig admitted. "He might have turned just a few, enough to either lead the others astray or get them killed in an ambush."

"I've been keeping the Elder Tinidan informed," Anas put in. "There has been no word of Rodakis or his force. He's still working on getting you an invitation."

Charm helped me restrain my childish urge to throw a tantrum. Instead, I passed Aubert's letter to Koenig.

"What do you make of this?" I asked.

He read it swiftly and made a face. "Mind Magic," he said with distaste. "I wouldn't have thought it of Duke Victor."

I raised an eyebrow but didn't comment. From what I'd seen, nobles had few scruples about the methods they'd use. Victor had been fine with drugging me, and he hadn't batted an eye at the loss of his men. Finley had sacrificed an entire company of his men, just to make a point.

"This could explain Hector's change of heart," I said.

"It could explain any amount of his odd behavior," Koenig agreed. "But that would require the Mind Mage to be in Talnier. Guillaume must have been turned when he was locked up in Dorsay.

"I still want to know how he got released," I muttered. I'd sent a letter to the Chancellor but had yet to receive a reply.

"Noble's games," Koenig said dismissively. "They never stay down for long. The mentalist in the city is of far greater concern."

"I'm not aware of the history your country has with Mind Magic," I said carefully.

"It was banned by the last king," Koenig said. "Shadow Magic and . . . ahem, Illusion Magic are not well regarded by the Kingdom, but they aren't illegal. Mind Magic is. Your Count Aubert is wondering if he should start a witch hunt in the capital."

"When he says he is uncertain of how to proceed? And he's not *my* Count."

"As you say, my lady," Koenig said, but his smirk told a different story. "If word gets out of a mentalist in Talnier, we'll have an inquisitor or three here in no time. Trouble is, they're hard to ferret out."

"They'll change an inquisitor's memories so he thinks he's questioned them." Captain Alain put in. "Or change them so he thinks someone else is guilty."

"You need to be on the lookout for people with wrong memories," Koenig said. "Look for the commonalities. It takes a while, and it gets nasty. Every person a possible victim, every person a possible suspect."

"In this case," I mused, "Duke Victor was the beneficiary of both Hector and Guillaume's odd behavior. So would he be the main suspect?"

There were frowns and shaking heads all around the table, except for Anas, who didn't have much of an opinion on Latorran politics and was looking on, bemused. He'd no doubt have a lot to report to Tinadan later.

"Nobles don't like getting their hands dirty *or* spending a lot of time learning magic," Koenig said. "He's more likely to have hired one."

"I wouldn't want to negotiate a contract with someone who can change my memory of what I signed," I pointed out.

"Historically, it doesn't turn out well, hence the ban," Koenig agreed. "But that's what they did then, and I don't see them doing things any differently this time."

"There's also the fact that Duke Victor wasn't in Talnier during the period when Rodakis changed allegiances," Captain Alain said.

"What about Reynard?" I asked Koenig. He frowned, while the others looked mostly blank.

"What about him?" he asked carefully.

"He was in Dorsay, at the same time as I was," I said. "Since then, he's been swanning about around Talnier, seeing the gods know who, and doing the gods know what. Mind Magic could explain his . . . unique status, couldn't it?"

"It could," he said coldly, glaring at the rest of the table who weren't privy to Guild secrets. "But I've read his file. The man only took Scribe when he was appointed deputy administrator. To have gotten Mana Sense and Mind Magic *and* to have trained the skill sufficiently in that time . . . it doesn't square with what I've read."

I frowned. I'd have to talk privately with Koenig later about the magic item that Reynard had shown me. If it did more than shield from mental influence . . . speaking of which:

"I do have some enchanted items that protect against mental influence," I said, staying vague about the exact numbers. I only had amulets for each of my team, but I could make more.

"That might help," Koenig said. "Dungeon-made or your own work?"

"The former."

"Then I'll caution you—dungeon work is more sophisticated than what mortals can manage, but the protection tends towards the weaker side. On the brighter side, they tend to warn you if they've been overcome."

"I haven't really had a chance to test them, at least as far as I know," I said.

"Still, did you want to distribute them?"

"Not for free, not at this point," I said, wincing. There were too many people that would need one. "Maybe at cost, if the Council wants to authorize the budget for it."

Murmurs around the table. *That* was going to be a long discussion, especially once I calculated the price. I decided to throw them a bone.

"If we decide to form a task force to hunt down this Mind Mage, I'll see if I can supply protection for them."

That should limit the number of amulets to something manageable at least. Of course, this kicked off *another* topic of discussion—whether to form a task force—at the same time. It took a while to get everyone to stop talking over each other. Once that was done, we could start discussing the new matters.

It was going to be a long afternoon.

BAİT

In the end, it was my diplomatic concerns that proved to be the final factor. We needed to forge a strong bond with our neighbors, which meant getting as many of the Council members on our side. My side, if I was being honest. The Charm offensive that I was planning only worked on a personal level, which . . . wasn't the worst thing in the world. If I was the linchpin on which all hopes of prosperity rested, then I could count on a lot of friends to keep me safe.

Not that the current plan left me feeling terribly safe.

"There are lots of signs that the mentalist only wants to make a move when you're outside of the town," Koenig had said. "And other signs that suggest they're trying to get you out of town."

"Right, so why are we doing exactly that?" I'd asked.

"Because if we're expecting a move, we might be able to catch them in the act and work out who they are," he'd insisted. "If you have Mana Sense, you can see it in use, so if we just keep some wizards looking out for key personnel, we might just catch them."

And if it is Reynard? I thought to myself in the present. I kept my thoughts to myself, because the man himself was in front of me.

For our second meeting, I'd elected to name the time and place and brought some support. Kyle and Cloridan were with me. Whether a pair of level fives could take a level six was an open question, but if the level six was blinded, I thought our odds got a lot better.

Not that there was going to be any fighting. We were in a public place, the Golden Goose tavern. We'd arrived early so that I could place everyone where I wanted them.

"I told you that you'd hire me," Reynard said smugly as he took his seat.

"Yes, you're very astute," I said sourly. "Before we agree to anything, I would like some assurances that you're not going to get orders later that cause you to betray me."

He started speaking, but I wasn't really listening. I willed Charm to have me make appropriate noises, and I willed Bargain to not agree to anything and let me know if anything he said threw up a red flag. I was focused on other things.

I had been keeping Mana Sense active, of course. The tether of his magic item had been restored to invisibility, but that was easily fixed. While I gathered my resolve, I looked him over for other items.

His sword, of course, was enchanted. His armor wasn't. It was leather armor, sourced from something called a bellious beast. Like a lot of light armor wearers, myself included, he was relying on the improved protection that came from using the skin of powerful monsters. I was due for a similar upgrade, something I was hoping to do on this trip. The Tribes were the acknowledged masters of the style, due to both their craftsmanship and the abundance of suitable monster skin.

He had a spatial ring, I noted, which concealed any magical items he might hide inside it. Hopefully, it was filled up by his bow and arrows, which weren't in evidence at this meeting. There was something magical in his belt pouch, something small that he evidently kept close at hand.

And there was the amulet. Sitting under his armor, but that wasn't an impediment to Mana Sense. I could see it, and now I could see the tether that headed off towards Dorsay.

Since I was sitting to the southeast of him, the tether went right by me. I focused on Theurgy.

The first spell was the easier one. I made my hand . . . sticky to mana, was how I thought of it. Mana threads tended to avoid entanglement, but with this spell in effect, I could make a quick gesture, as if I was warding off a fly, and scoop up the tether in my hand.

That was necessary to reduce the range for the second spell. I don't think I could have done it at range, but with my target in the palm of my hand . . .

> **Your effective spell total of 20 was sufficient to dispel the mana construct!**

I felt a presence. The touch of a mind, startled for only a brief instant before the feeling faded. The tether dissolved, at least the part of it I was holding. Both ends started to retreat back to their sources. Reynard showed no reaction at all.

What had I just accomplished? I didn't know what that amulet did, but I did know that Reynard—or the Countess—wouldn't be able to reestablish it without bringing it into the presence of whatever it was linked to. That *had* to spoil her plan.

I allowed myself a moment to feel irritation at the notification. An "effective" spell total of twenty when my Theurgy total was 144 was an annoyance that never ended. The moment passed, and I returned to the conversation.

"All right, Reynard, when can we leave?"

There was one more thing that I had to do before leaving. Okay, there were about a hundred things, and even with the others handling what they could, I was run off my feet. One more important thing. One more meeting.

"To what do I owe the honor of a visit from the great Champion?" Priestess Tonet asked archly.

I rolled my eyes. Word was getting out, evidently. There wasn't much point in asking if she'd worked it out for herself, been fed the detail from her information network, or if her goddess had decided that the information embargo had been lifted. So I just ignored it.

"I'm hoping to obtain your help," I said, taking the seat that she indicated for me. I had gone to see her, so we were sitting in a nook of the lushly overgrown garden that occupied the entire interior of her temple. "I'm about to leave on a diplomatic trip to your Council."

"The Glade of the Conclave?" she asked, pouring us both some tea.

"Is that what the place is called?" I asked. "The envoys have been surprisingly reticent about naming it."

"Every Tribe has a different name for the place," she said. "They've never been able to agree on what to call it, and they don't like revealing that fact to outsiders."

"You're . . . not joking," I said. That did sound like the Council. She nodded sympathetically.

"The Glade is the priesthood's name for the place, although that strictly only applies to the glade where Naldyna spoke directly with the Elders . . . a long time ago," she said. "There has been a lot of development around the Glade since then, of course."

"Do they still meet there?" I asked.

"No . . . it's a little small to hold every Elder," she said. "But, according to tradition, no decision is official until it has been read out by a representative in the Glade itself. Not that Naldyna needs them to be there to hear it, they just want to remember their roots."

"There are worse traditions," I said noncommittally.

"True. Were you looking for a guide to the Glade?"

"No. I was told that, in the absence of an official invitation, any help from a member of the Tribes would be seen as an undue intervention coming from whatever Tribe they happened to come from, prejudicing my case."

Tonet giggled. "That does sound like the Council," she said. "Surely it would be better to wait for an invitation, then? What's the hurry?"

I gave her a cool look. "I'm sure you've heard about Captain Rodakis."

"Mmm," she murmured. "You've not given up on him, then?"

"What do you know about his current whereabouts?" I asked.

"Very little. I heard in which direction he escaped, of course, and the questions he'd been asking about the Great Wild suggest that he plans on staying there for a while."

"You get news from the Wild, don't you?"

"I have a few contacts, yes. None of them have mentioned him."

"Would they, if you asked?"

"Perhaps . . . but I think not. If he were a normal traveller, then yes, but the silence that I've heard thus far makes me think that a village is *hiding* him, for some reason."

"Why would a Tribal village hide a Latorran officer?" I asked, confused. "Everything I know suggests that they should be enemies."

"You'll have to ask that village when you find it, I'm afraid," Tonet said with a sly smile. "We're an independent and diverse people."

It felt a little odd to hear her say that, seeing as she was human, and humans were a tiny minority in the Tribes. However, despite living in a human town, Tonet had always made her allegiance clear, at least to me.

I sipped my tea and calmed myself. This was not the time for a rant about how unreasonable the Tribes were being.

"So, what help *did* you want from me?" Tonet asked, after a pause.

I took another breath and started my spiel.

"You've been . . . fairly cooperative since we last spoke. With a few notable exceptions."

"How could I be otherwise, a humble priestess in a foreign town?"

"I know you trade in illegal alchemicals," I pointed out. "I know the attack on Hector's people when they arrived was your doing. Since then, though, you've been quiet."

"I hope you don't expect me to respond to such outrageous allegations," Tonet said, amused. "You made certain representations when you started, and while you haven't fulfilled them, you have been moving in the right direction."

I took another sip of my tea. "It doesn't seem to be common knowledge yet, but the terms of our Charter are written to give Tribal residents a vote for *our* Council, once that time comes around again."

Tonet blinked. "Why would..." Then her eyes narrowed. "There aren't *enough* residents for that to make a difference. Especially if their vote is split between candidates."

"True," I said. "Which is why this proposal is being discussed right now."

Pulling some papers out of my ring, I passed them over to her. She skimmed over them quickly.

"This is proposing... voting districts?"

"Yes. You divide the town up into a number of districts equal to the number of Council members you want and then each district elects one member. It helps prevent the kind of disenfranchisement you were about to complain about."

"And the Charter permits this?"

"The details of how the Council is elected are decided by the Council, according to the Charter."

I'd suggested the simpler system for the first vote since everyone was new to voting, but I thought we were ready for the next step.

"Why haven't I heard about this?"

"The next election is months away," I said, shrugging. "There's no point in advertising this until closer to the vote. And right now, the Council is arguing over where to draw the districts. They seem fine with the general idea, though."

"Then... why are you *telling* me about this?"

"People always say that politicians have no loyalty," I told her. "It's always *what have you done for me lately*. That's wrong, though."

I gave her a wide smile. "Politics is actually all about what are you *going* to do for me."

Finance as well, really, the only difference being that the correct answer was always "pay me lots of money." No wonder bankers and politicians got on so well.

Tonet smiled back. "And so, finally, we get to what I can do for you."

"We do," I agreed. There was no point in asking her if she wasn't going to say yes. "My problem is that we suspect that one of the nobles is going to make some kind of move while I'm away."

"Please, don't overwhelm me with detail," Tonet said sarcastically. "I suppose that you want me to cooperate with the people here and foil any 'move' that gets made."

"Exactly," I said. "We've some ideas about the form it will take, and who's behind it, but it's all speculation at this point. Let me start with what we know . . ."

THE GREAT WILD

This wasn't the first time I'd been in the Great Wild. I'd entered the forest many times, travelling on short, well-known paths to get to the two dungeons that sat on the edge of beast-kin territory. I'd even penetrated quite deeply on griffin-back, flying over miles of deep green to get to Mandel's workshop.

Even my dungeon was located in the Great Wild, only a little deeper than the two open dungeons. Travelling to that was the closest I'd come to what I was doing now.

Experiencing the forest. Travelling on foot under its branches, wandering its meandering ways. Living *in* it, instead of passing through. Forced to capitulate to its terms, we were becoming one with nature.

Don't get me wrong, it was a wondrous experience and all, but I gave it three days before I would murder someone for a bath.

Reynard led us at a brisk pace, leaping from root to root, in that odd manner of movement I'd seen him use before. I learned later that it was quite common in high-strength adventurers. Faster and less predictable than running, or so they said. I had my doubts about it in normal terrain, but it was certainly easier to jump over the tangled mess of roots and hillocks that we were travelling through than clamber over them.

With less strength, Felicia and I couldn't jump nearly as far, so Reynard's speed was limited to what we could manage. He didn't show any sign of impatience, though, simply pausing between each jump while we made two to catch up.

"Let me know when you're running low on Stamina," he said at one point. "We're on a safe route, but you never want to be at zero."

Good advice, so that was what we did, resting for fifteen minutes every hour. Jumping really took it out of you. I was looking forward to at least one level of Stamina development before the trip was over. Probably one of Jump as well.

Ideally, I would be practicing Shadow Magic—I could Shadow Step farther and faster than I could jump—but not only would that mean leaving Felicia behind, it would let Reynard know that I had the skill. It seemed wise to keep it in reserve for now.

Cloridan and Kyle were with us as well, of course. Janie had stayed behind. She had joined up with a temporary party in Talnier to keep busy delving.

"Too many bugs in the forest," she'd complained. "And too many people that complain when you clean the bugs out with fire. Give me the city and a nice nonflammable dungeon."

I sighed. Cloridan was a city person, but he'd come. As had . . . Cutter. Against my objections.

This world didn't really have age limits. Someone who was level five, like Cutter, was ready for anything the world could throw at him. All you needed to drink in taverns was money, and the same was true for . . . other activities.

Cutter had finally chosen Duellist as a profession, and he'd paid for the twin sabers that hung at his side. He might not have received all of his first-level points, but he was as dangerous as any of us.

Reynard might have been a little bit more dangerous, but he was behaving so far. According to him, we were making pretty good time, and we were on track to get to Mossridge Gather before nightfall.

"Surprised by something?" he asked during one of our breaks.

"You're just so . . . professional," I confessed. "It is surprising."

He snorted. "I was a Ranger for years before I got caught up with the Guild. Escort contracts are bread-and-butter for a level four Ranger."

"Why did you get sent to Oakway?" I asked.

"Nothing in particular," he said, shrugging. "Oakway had a jungle level, which called for someone with wilderness skills to manage it. It was more about . . ."

He scowled, looking at nothing in particular. "Before they let you gain levels, they want to make sure that you're . . . sound. That you'll follow orders, that sort of thing."

"That seems like a reasonable precaution to me," I said. "I'm not sure that it works, though," I admitted, thinking back to all the high-level

Guild members I'd seen running amok. Even the geas hadn't kept Reynard under control.

"I hadn't heard that *you'd* signed up, though," Reynard said. "It's the smarter move if you can get your levels elsewhere. I couldn't."

"Until you could," I said.

"The Countess has been generous," he agreed. "Shall we get moving again?"

Reynard alerted us to the fact that we'd reached Mossridge Gather when he saw the first stone. Flat-topped, they had been inserted into the forest floor, held fast by tree roots and mostly level. Together they formed a winding path that led into a more deeply shadowed grove.

"Stay on the stones," he told us. "There are traps on the more direct routes."

He was the expert, so we followed him, returning to a normal walking pace. The trees grew high here, so the forest canopy was far above us, lit by the fading sun. I imagined I saw movement up there—we were probably being watched.

Reynard led us along the path until we came to a small shelter covered with vines.

"We wait here," he said, taking a seat. "Someone should be along to bring us into the village."

"You've been here before, then?" I asked.

"Many times," he said. "It's the closest village to the border; most of those that travel between here and the Kingdom pass through. I've friends here."

I raised an eyebrow. "I guess I have problems thinking of you as anything but a criminal."

He snorted with amusement. "Get used to it then, girl. I'm liked well enough here, and back home I've got the backing of a noble. It's only the Guild that thinks badly of me."

I was spared from replying by the approach of one of the villagers. He was a . . . deer-kin, I guessed. The antlers were a bit of a giveaway. They weren't as large as the ones I would expect to see on a stag, but they were just as elaborately branched, and I thought they might be just a bit more pointy. They would probably be awkward to use as weapons, but I wouldn't want to be impaled by them.

"Greetings," Reynard said, bowing. To us, he said, "This is Urnmor, chief of this village."

He then introduced us all by name, leaving off any titles. Well, *my* titles. The others didn't have any posts or positions to speak of. I wondered if I should change that.

"Greetings to you all, travellers," Urnmor said with a deep and resonant voice. "What brings you to our village?"

"We're travelling to meet with the Council," I said. Mentioning our actual destination was apparently a bit of a faux pas.

"I see. Then you have a ways to travel yet. For tonight, will you rest in our village?"

"If you can spare the food, Chief. We have our own supplies . . ."

"Nonsense, you shall not eat dried rations tonight. We shall host you, and you shall repay our hospitality with news and stories of the outside world."

"If you wish, Chief," I said bowing. Inwardly, I breathed a sigh of relief. The ritual had gone just as Reynard had said it would. Not that they were going to kill us if we got the wording wrong. But following custom made the process go more smoothly and reassured them that we were the sort of people who respected their customs. Or at least that we were the sort of people who listened to our guide.

Urnmor led us into the village proper along a flower-lined path. The forest floor was quite dark by now, and the flowers had closed up, but I thought I could make out a faint glow from them that helped keep us on the path.

"Behold our humble village," Urnmor said as we came around the final bend. Despite his words, there was a lot of pride in his voice.

Charm kept a smile on my face as I saw where we would be spending the night.

Oh, good. A tree house.

It was . . . about what I'd expected, really. The Tribes' affinity for nature and living close to the land wasn't exactly a state secret.

The trees rose even higher here, comparable in size to the giant mountain ash trees that you get down in Victoria. There were about twenty of them that I could see from this vantage point. Each tree that I could see sprouted platforms about halfway up. Some of the trees just had one platform that went all around the trunk; others had multiple platforms that jutted out like enormous bracket fungi.

Villagers were climbing down, or in some cases gliding down, to meet us. There were three types of beast-kin in this village—deer like the chief, squirrels, and owls.

The owls were new to me. They had wings . . . sort of. Much like bats, they had a feathered structure extending back from their arms. Exactly how their arms bent the way they did was a mystery, but I doubt their joints were anything like either owls or humans. They couldn't fly on their own, but Air Magic was pretty common for them.

I learned this at the feast that was quickly put together in our honor. On ground level, fortunately. We made a quick trip up to our assigned tree house, managed by a squirrel-kin called Cerine, to drop off our packs of supplies. They did have a basket that could haul up the infirm, but our Climb skills were up to the challenge.

Whether that would still be true after the feast remained to be seen.

The toasting started after everyone had been given a chance to take the edge off their hunger. Identify could tell me the names of the meats we were eating, but since I'd never heard of the animals, it didn't tell me much. They were tasty, though.

The chief toasted to our health, and we toasted him right back. We were drinking a slightly fermented berry juice. It tasted like a really fruity wine. Hopefully, it wasn't too strong.

Storytelling duty seemed to fall to me. Reynard was off talking with his hunting buddies, Cloridan was drinking, and Felicia and Kyle seemed to get tongue-tied. That was fine, though; I had stories to tell.

I told the village about what we were trying to do in Talnier. They would have heard of us, of course, but through rumor and secondhand accounts. I felt better knowing that they had the details from me.

Then I moved on to more exciting stories. I told them about Shadthe's attack on Dorsay and Duke Victor's attack on his own vassal. I left out the details of my involvement in those stories, much to Reynard's amusement. I caught him grinning at me from the other side of the feasting table. Hopefully, he wasn't blowing my cover with his drinking buddies.

The really popular story turned out to be the one about Kaito fighting her way into Duke Finley's dungeon. No one questioned how I knew about it enough to describe all the battles. They loved it, especially the final desperate battle against the giants. Just when all hope was lost, the dungeon break ended, saving them all.

In fairness, they probably would have loved a story about how Kaito went to the pub just as much. She was super popular here, and probably in the rest of the Wild.

Telling stories all night meant that I was able to avoid drinking too heavily, so I was easily the least drunk of all my companions when we retired for the night. Cloridan and Cutter managed to climb up on their own, but Felicia and Kyle needed help. Reynard was sleeping elsewhere, which was all for the good as far as I was concerned.

Despite my fears, the beds turned out to be soft and the blankets warm. The primitive tree house managed to be not at all drafty. It was all, in fact, remarkably comfortable. The last thought that passed through my mind before I drifted off to sleep was that these Tribals might know what they were doing after all.

TREETOP MORNING

You got used to waking up in civilization. Latora was a very *poor* excuse for a civilization, but that was what it was. It had beds and glass windows. Streets, and people selling stuff on them. It was *worse* than back home, but pretty much the same thing. I'd grown accustomed to it, but I'd never stopped comparing how things were now to how they were back home.

Occasionally, back then, I'd gotten out of the city. Just for a week, or a weekend, I'd get a room in some resort out in the mountains or further south. Hardly uncivilized, but wilderness adjacent. It didn't take long before I was itching for the hustle of the city, but for a brief period, it was a nice break. A way to decompress.

Waking up in Mossridge Gather was like that. And unlike life in the Kingdom, the experience was not a degraded one. The smell of the air was *different* from that of an eucalyptus forest, but not *worse*. The birds that greeted the morning were undoubtedly different from the ones back home, but I couldn't tell the difference.

Well, except for the lack of a kookaburra.

Sitting on the balcony, sipping the tea that our host Cerine had provided, I could look out over the forest canopy. We were still *under* the canopy, but the trees in this area were taller than those around us. So the morning light could illuminate us, and I got to experience an incredible view. Crisp winter air, the mist rising through the foliage. Nothing but nature as far as the eye could see. It was peaceful.

I could have done with a coffee, though.

Eventually, everyone was up and the magic of the dawn was covered over by the mundanity of getting breakfast and getting ready to leave.

When I saw Reynard talking with one of the hunters, I assumed he was getting the latest details about the next leg of our trip. Their discussion got animated, though, and he soon brought the owl-kin over to speak to me. I thought I recognized him from last night, but Reynard had monopolized him then and I hadn't been properly introduced. I had gotten a chance to be startled by his big yellow eyes. They seemed to shine even in daylight.

"There's a problem," Reynard told me. "One of the hunters from last night's patrol hasn't returned."

The owl-kin started speaking as well. He spoke in the Tribal common tongue, which I spoke, but I let Reynard translate for the others.

"This is Turem Thornclaw," Reynard said. "He's asking if you can hold off on leaving until they find out what happened to the missing hunter."

"Aw, come on!" Cutter exclaimed. "We can take care of any stupid monster that happens to get in our way!"

"Don't be dumb, kid," Reynard snapped. "There's monsters out here that aren't so easy to kill—and we don't even know if it *is* a monster."

"You think it's a person?" I asked, surprised. "I thought the Tribes were all living in peace out here?"

"Nothing's ever completely peaceful," Reynard muttered darkly. "And we know Rodakis is out here, don't we? He might have left a trap behind him."

"That's a good point, but still . . . the last time I waited for the scouts to report back, I lost three days and got nothing back. Is this going to be like that time?"

"You never know, but I think—" Reynard cut himself off as shouts came from the edge of the village.

"Ikini! Ikini!"

Turem took off towards the cries. Reynard followed, gesturing for us to come as well.

"That's the name of the hunter that went missing," he said. "This might all be for nothing."

It didn't take long for us to get to the edge of the village. The other villagers had clustered a little way from the sharp break of cleared brush that indicated the start of the forest. As we drew closer, we could see why.

[Identification]: **Fungal Shambler – Threat: 16 – Properties: Infectious, Lacking Organs**

The humanoid figure that stumbled out of the forest looked a lot like a squirrel-kin. A squirrel-kin that had lost half of her fur, had her skin turned a pallid grey, and had grown some fleshy *extensions* from her torso and neck.

The conclusion was obvious, but Reynard confirmed it.

"That's Ikini," he said. "That's the missing hunter."

They didn't let us participate in the fight. Aside from us being honored guests, they had also noted the "infectious" property that the monster held. Precautions needed to be taken.

The fight itself was a bit of an anticlimax. Two . . . druids, I supposed, cast spells that grew vines around the humanoid, almost completely encasing it. While most of the village watched from a safe distance, an older deer-kin brought over a potion of some sort.

"Oh! I wonder what's in that," Felicia said, standing next to me. "I should compare notes with him."

"An antifungal potion, I'd imagine," I said, watching as the potion was handed over to a younger hunter. Soon, it was splashed on the immobilized shambler.

"Well, yeah, but what went into it? Does it keep for long, or was it freshly prepared just now? What ingredients did he use? Is it easier to make than the one I know?"

I got the impression that those were only the first on a long list of questions. "Be my guest," I said. "I don't think we'll be going anywhere soon."

> **Your party has killed a Fungal Shambler – your experience share is 16 XP.**

From the small startled jumps all around me, I guessed that everyone was getting a similar notification. "Huh. I guess we were close enough to count as participating after all."

That probably meant that we would have been in spore range if the hunters had just hacked it into a cloud of infectious spores. I was really glad they didn't do that.

I left Felicia to chase after the potion maker and made my way over to Reynard. Cloridan and Cutter trailed along.

"Where does this leave us?" I asked.

"It depends," he replied slowly, his attention still focused on Turem and Chief Urnmor, who were examining the body. The vines had disappeared now that the threat had gone, and the potion seemed to have washed away all the fungal parts. What was left was a corpse that looked as if it had been rotting for more than just the one night.

"It's possible," Reynard continued, "that Ikini was *really* unlucky and stumbled into a patch of really bad mushrooms."

"That can happen out here?" I asked uneasily. "Just . . . step on the wrong mushroom and get turned into a shambler?"

"You can't rule it out," he told me. "They clean out that species whenever they find it, but mushrooms are hard to eradicate."

I nodded. I knew that mushrooms were just the . . . fruit of a type of organism that grew mostly undetected and spread via spores that were too small to see. I'd never heard of anyone back home trying to eradicate a fungal species. Magic might make it possible. However, doing so in the Great Wild struck me as . . . ambitious.

"What's the other option?" I asked. "Or is it just one other option?"

Turem looked over at us from where he was standing over the corpse. "Myconid," he said. Reynard cursed.

"That. That's the other option," he said.

"And what's that?" I asked.

"A monster. The good news is that its spores aren't as infectious as the shambler fog. You'll only turn into a shambler if you get killed after being exposed."

All around us, the village was organizing itself in response to the news. Everyone had already armed themselves when the shambler arrived. Now they were forming small parties. Noncombatants were bringing supplies to the small knots of hunters that were forming up. Food, water, potions, and what looked like face masks.

"I guess the bad news is that a myconid is quite capable of killing you," I said.

"It is, but the really bad news is that there shouldn't be any around here. Put your packs someplace out of the way; there's going to be a council of war before they send the hunters out."

I sighed. Another meeting. This was starting to not feel like a holiday again.

At least five people were talking very loudly and quickly in a language I didn't want to let on I spoke. I looked over at Reynard, but he was ignoring them.

Despite knowing the language, it was difficult to tell what they were disagreeing about. They used a lot of what I assumed was hunter jargon and local terms. I gathered, though, that it was a combination of what size teams should be sent out, and how far they should range. Should they send out the maximum number of hunters to quickly intercept the myconids, or should they hold some in reserve in case a shambler slipped past the line and into the village?

I didn't have anything to contribute here. The one piece of advice I would have given them had already been followed. Parties had gone out already, sweeping just the nearby areas, so it wasn't the case that these guys were arguing over minor details while the village burned down.

The main reason I was there was to be kept in the loop when the reports from those parties started coming back. Which they now started to do. Each messenger that came in made the arguers more unhappy. From what they were saying, I gathered that the reports were coming back sooner, and in more numbers, than they would have liked.

Now Reynard started paying attention.

"They've made contact with myconid guardians at seven points, all north of here," he told us.

"That's the direction we're headed, right?" Cloridan asked.

"Close enough," Reynard agreed.

"So, about there not being any myconids around here," I said.

"There really shouldn't be." He glanced over at the arguers. "Myconids don't migrate. Myconid guardians exist to *guard* an immobile fungal . . . nest or growth or whatever you call it."

"And those take time to grow, so someone would have noticed it," I said.

"Right, so—"

Beginning Massed Combat: Outbreak Defense
Accumulated Experience: 0
Experience awarded based on contribution at the end of a defense.
Contribution: 0.000%

Everyone gave a little jerk and then stared at nothing. For a little longer than was called for.

"It's a dungeon break," I said.

"That's impossible," Reynard said, and there were murmurs of agreement from those in the room that spoke Latorran.

"Sure!" I said. "I wouldn't want to disagree with you guys. You're the experts. But *that* is what that notification is for. So the impossible just happened. And you know what else it means?"

If I'd followed proper dramatic imperative, I would have paused there. It would have made for a great moment, all of them staring at me in stupefaction while they worked out what I was talking about. But we didn't have time, so I just snapped it out.

"It means that the monsters have reached the village. We're under attack!"

I didn't wait to see what effect I'd had, but turned and headed out. My crew was right behind me. So was Reynard. I wasn't sure if it was because he believed me, or if he still wanted to argue about it.

"There isn't a dungeon around here to break!" he said. I didn't bother to answer him. I could already hear the screams.

Not, fortunately, the screams of noncombatants being torn to pieces. These were the screams of competent fighters realizing that something had gone very badly wrong and that they needed support. Now.

All around, beast-kin were fighting the barely humanoid forms of what must be—

> **[Identification]: Myconid Guardian – Threat: 18 – Properties: Infectious, Lacking Organs**

Right. Those. Reynard, to his credit, shut up. He could see what was going on just as well as I could. Maybe a little better.

"Reynard!" I yelled as we ran towards the front line. "Anything we need to know about these guys before we fight them?"

MYCONID MELEE

"o precision. Damage," Reynard said, his words getting chopped off by the need to breathe as he ran. "Vulnerable to blunt. Fire."

I scowled. We weren't *great* at blunt damage, and we'd left Janie behind. I missed her already. Still, it might be for the best. Vulnerable to fire probably meant a tendency to *catch* fire, and while Janie could control her burns, she might have trouble controlling a bunch of myconids running around on fire.

My Earth Magic was capable of blunt damage, but my accuracy was pretty abysmal, and would stay that way until I got my skill up. That thought was all I had time for before we reached the monsters.

My daggers were in my hands and they sliced through the pallid flesh of the myconid in front of me.

You have inflicted 112 damage!
You have inflicted 117 damage!

The monster didn't seem to notice. Attacking with both daggers had left them out of position to parry with. I tried to dodge, but the fungal arm slammed into me.

Dodging must have helped some because my armor absorbed the hit. The arm had felt so squashy as it hit me that I wouldn't be surprised if they had a negative damage bonus.

"Shouldn't you be casting illusions?" Reynard yelled at me, his blades swinging into his own opponent.

"They don't have eyes!" I yelled back, and it was true. These myconids really stretched the meaning of humanoid. They mostly had two arms, two legs, and a torso, but that was clearly a guideline rather than a hard rule. My target had three arms, and Kyle's had three legs. As for a head, they either had one big mushroom cap or a cluster of smaller ones.

Cloridan, normally our heavy hitter, wasn't exactly having a hard time against the guardians, but he was finding things more difficult. His daggers just made small cuts, no matter where he struck. He was able to avoid their attacks entirely, but their hits were so light it made little difference.

Kyle was doing the best out of our group. He hadn't brought his maul with him for this trip, so he was limited to slashing damage like the rest of us. His big heavy enchanted broadsword did a *lot* of slashing damage, though. He was taking down myconids with just three hits, compared to the seven or eight it was taking Cloridan. Cloridan *was* hitting at twice the rate, so it almost evened out, but Kyle still had the advantage.

Cutter was doing . . . all right. His swords had a high base damage, and he hit a lot, but he didn't have Kyle's strength or Cloridan's skills. He was whaling away at his opponents and showing every sign of having a good time. The myconids were hitting him, but he had heavier armor than I did, so I doubt he was feeling it.

Felicia was staying out of the fight, of course, hanging back to provide healing. We didn't seem to need it, so she moved further along the line, providing aid to the level threes and fours who were having a much harder time with the attackers.

With the five of us joining the fight, the villagers were able to form a defensive line against the intruders. Two druids managed to form a wall of vines that entangled the myconids that came near. They couldn't cover the whole front, but with the rest of the fighters covering the gap, I thought we had turned this fight around.

Then about a dozen lights floated out from behind the myconids. Fine golden dust floated down from them.

"Those will be spores!" Felicia called out from behind us. "They'll give status effects!"

Great. I took a break from whittling away at my opponent and cast Water Stream up in the air. Maximum dispersal, maximum spread, maximum velocity.

Just like the last time, water sprayed out like an upside-down fire extinguisher. There were shouts all around me from people getting soaked, but the droplets swept the spores out of the air around us. I couldn't cover everyone, but it looked as if the druids were on it with their own countermeasures. Felicia dashed off to cover a few people who had fallen to some spores that had slipped through the cracks.

Reynard also dropped out of melee combat and unslung his bow. "This water is going to ruin the string," he complained. Then in one smooth action, he put an arrow through one of the lights.

Whatever it *was*, it didn't like that and dropped like a stone. Further arrows followed.

Throughout all this, the myconid I'd started attacking kept trying to kill me, but I was able to keep fending it off while casting the spell. Score one more for silent and subtle casting. It felt a little odd being on the front line, but these monsters were easy enough for me to manage. And with so many attacking, everyone was needed.

I slashed at it again and again until finally . . .

You have inflicted 111 damage!
You have killed a Myconid Guardian. Contribution increased.

Huh. I don't think I got notifications for all those assists in the Talnier outbreak, I thought.

After that, it was just a slog. A desperate and dangerous slog for the lower-level villagers, but as the myconid numbers dwindled, the less capable could drop out and get the healing they needed. Eventually, it was over.

Outbreak Defense, Wave One completed.
Total Experience earned: 114,480
Your contribution: 7.3%
Awarded: 8,357 Experience
Next wave: Pending

Not bad for a morning's work, I thought. But it looked as though we weren't done yet.

"So does anyone still think that it's not a dungeon?" I asked everyone at the meeting. Chief Urnmor had gathered the leadership of the village to make some quick executive decisions. The two druids were the only ones I hadn't formally met. One was an owl-kin, introduced as Serenal. Her wing-arms were wrapped around her, covering her in a grey feathered cloak.

The other was a squirrel-kin called Nyer Fernshadow. He twitched with suppressed energy. During the fight, he'd been dashing around, and

I'd seen him earlier, bouncing with excitement. Given the seriousness of the current situation, he must be making an effort to sit still.

Turem was here too, of course, representing the hunters. From what I'd seen earlier, there wasn't a lot of agreement among the hunters. Having only one representative might not be the most democratic move, but at least it cut down on arguments.

In response to my question, there was a general reluctance among the beast-kin to meet my eyes. They didn't *want* to disagree with me, but . . .

"That's still impossible, Hammond," Reynard said. *He* was perfectly willing to disagree with me. "They don't get dungeons in the Wild, the mana is too calm."

"That's true," I agreed because it was. Latorran Theurges might sneer at the inefficiency of Tribal mana manipulation, but I thought the Tribes were leagues ahead in terms of controlling mana *safely*. They moved the mana the way it wanted to go, and it responded. It danced for them, moving across the land with nary a mana snarl or spawn point in sight.

The areas of the Kingdom that had been drained of mana were *mostly* safe, but it was trying to smooth over a wrinkled bedsheet. Every time you smoothed over one wrinkle, another popped up.

"It is impossible," I continued, "but it happened, so we have to work out *how* it happened."

Doubtful looks all around, but at least they weren't trying to find a way to disagree with me.

"Now, my Mana Sense doesn't go through trees," I said, "So I can't get a good idea of the mana in the area."

I pointed at the druids. "But you two, I bet you have some sort of tree sense, that can tell you what's going on? And even if you don't, then some of the people that go out patrolling must have Mana Sense."

There were nods around the table.

"And none of you noticed any disturbances in the mana?"

"There were no such reports," Chief Urnmor told me, while the druids looked at each other.

"No disturbance great enough to cause a dungeon," Serenal said. "And even if there was, a new dungeon would have no cause to break."

"True, so it clearly isn't a new dungeon," I said. "Have you done your mana sense thing since things started happening?"

"There hasn't been the time," she said. "The spell isn't difficult, but it takes time to examine a large area closely."

"Right, you're going to want to make that time," I told them. "You'll be looking for a dungeon that wasn't there yesterday but is today. Shouldn't be too hard to spot."

"Hammond," Reynard said wearily. "You haven't been doing this long enough to have special insight into how mana works. You're just spouting nonsense."

"Oh yeah? I've already got a theory about what happened," I said smugly. "It's not great news, but once it's confirmed, we'll at least know what's going on."

"You can't be serious," Reynard sighed. "There's no way that an old dungeon would have escaped notice all this time."

"What if it was underground?" I asked.

"All dungeons are underground," he replied, rolling his eyes. He managed to avoid adding "You idiot," so I gave him some points.

"They *go* underground," I clarified, "But they *start* on the surface and go down. What if a dungeon started way down, and went up?"

Reynard started to respond but realized he didn't have a response. He stopped mid-breath and looked over at the druids.

"Mana can travel through the ground," I explained. "Mana manipulation extends some way through solid material, but not far. Underneath our feet, there's just as much potential for a mana snarl as there is above ground."

"If that were true," Reynard said slowly, "we'd be getting old dungeons popping up all over."

"I don't know how it works," I admitted. "Maybe conditions on the surface are more conducive to mana snarls. We've got a lot up here messing with the mana, after all."

"Even so," Chief Urnmor mused, "our history is long. Even if underground dungeons are rare, we should have seen some in that time."

"It also might be that dungeons normally grow down, so we never see them," I said. "There could be endless volumes of deadly real estate, far below us."

"Normally?" Nyer asked.

"Someone might have changed its behavior," I said.

"That would take—" The druid cut himself off.

"I mean, I don't like it, and I admit it's unlikely, but you have to admit that it's *possible*," I said. "So check it out with your spell, and we can move on to figuring out what we are going to do about this."

Urnmor looked around the room. "Does anyone else have any theories about what is behind this?" he asked.

There were shakes of the head all around.

"Fine, then," he said. "Serenal, you do the spell, Nyer, you get back to growing defenses. If it takes an hour to finish the spell, we may well have another attack before we have any information."

"Should we bring the patrols in?" Turem asked.

"Yes. For now. Until we have more information about the mana flow, we need to go on the defensive. Make sure to divide everyone into shifts."

Urnmor sighed. "An hour isn't too long to say alert, but we might have to keep this up for much longer. If Serenal doesn't find Councillor Hammond's dungeon, then we're back to the start of the maze."

He looked at me. "I hope you enjoyed our hospitality, Councillor, because it looks like you will be enjoying it for a little while longer."

VİLLAGE DİPLOMACY

It was possible that this was all my fault. Not that I was blaming myself, but I was starting to appreciate that the attitude of King Alexandros was based on more than just prejudice. Crazy as it sounded, it was *possible* that some god had primed this dungeon to emerge in my path, either as a roadblock or as some way for me to improve my situation. No gain without pain, after all.

Or maybe they were doing it for laughs.

It was a scary thought, that my actions could be predicted that closely. Or even worse, that they *couldn't*, and whoever was responsible had who knew how many other roadblocks primed for where I *might* go.

The villagers were being pretty good about it. Even though one of their own had died, they hadn't brought it up with me. They hadn't even brought up my status as a Champion, even though I was pretty sure they knew. My best guess for *how* was Reynard blabbing to his hunter mates, but as long as they didn't ask, the whole thing could remain unspoken.

Still, even if no one was blaming me, I couldn't help but feel partially responsible. Between that and the fact that I couldn't go anywhere until it was fixed, I was happy to help.

"So, what is the goal here?" I asked the meeting.

"I'm not sure," Chief Urnmor admitted. "We're not familiar with dungeons, or how they work."

"Right now, the dungeon is in the middle of a break," Reynard said authoritatively. "That means it will pump out monsters until it runs out of mana. How long that takes depends on how big it is."

"Which depends on how much mana it has access to, and how much time it's had to grow," I said with a frown. "I think we can assume it doesn't have much experience, at least."

"What do you mean?" Urnmor asked. Reynard was giving me a puzzled look as well.

"Dungeons use mana to grow, but they get experience the same way we do," I said. "They get levels, and they get . . . perks as their levels increase. Things like spatial manipulation and extra monster types. My guess is that this dungeon won't have anything other than fungal monsters. Maybe some simple traps."

"That still gives it a wide variety to work with," Reynard said. "I think you can have a fungal version of most sorts of monsters."

"They'll all have the same weaknesses, though, won't they?"

"True," he agreed. "And they tend to be weaker than whatever they're copying."

"Right. So as I see it, there are three basic options. We can bottle it up and kill the monsters until they stop coming. Then you keep delving it regularly to keep it under control. That'd be the Kingdom approach."

I looked around to see how the Village Council was taking that idea. Not well, was what I judged.

"Or," I continued, "you can send a party down and reach the core. If we get there, I know how to stop the break."

"That's what you did in Talnier," Reynard put in. "Just what did you do?"

"Guild secret," I said smugly. "Pretty sure you're the last person they'd want to know."

He scowled, and I looked around at the rest of the meeting, who weren't looking very happy.

"Or, we could go ahead and destroy the core, and end the dungeon," I said. "Bearing in mind, that one will probably form again, given that the mana snarl is still down there."

"We should destroy it," Turem, the leader of the hunters, spoke up. There were some grunts of agreement around the table. Looking at me, he tried to explain. "I know your people see dungeons as a resource, but we don't want one so close to our settlement."

"You don't have to justify it to me," I said. "However you want to play it."

"We might be able to redirect the mana flow from the base of the dungeon so that it flows more smoothly," Serenal said thoughtfully. "We'd need to discuss it with—" The owl-kin stopped, suddenly startled by something. "Yoroly!" she exclaimed.

All around the table, the villagers erupted into a chorus of variations on "Yoroly! We should have—" while looking guilty.

"Who's Yoroly?" I asked.

Chief Urnmor winced. "Yoroly Willowshroud is our shaman," he said. "We really should have invited her."

Of course, nothing would do other than to immediately bring her in. And for some reason, I was the best person to do that.

"She's old," Serenal explained as she led me down the flower-lined path. "And quite eccentric. We really should have sent someone to check on her when the attack happened, but she doesn't live in the village proper."

Indeed, we were travelling past the outer ring of trees that I thought of as the village.

"Isn't that dangerous?" I asked.

"She has her wards, and she *is* level seven," Serenal said. "She's probably fine, and she doesn't like company."

"So no one likes her, is what I'm hearing."

"It's not a matter of *liking* her," Serenal said, with some frustration. "She's just difficult. If I went out to see her, she wouldn't leave without an explanation of what was going on. And when I told her, she'd insist on meeting you before going anywhere with you."

"So by bringing me in from the start . . ."

"Cuts through several layers of delay," Serenal sighed.

The path led us to a small clearing. Despite the open ground, the canopy overhead was completely grown over with foliage, leaving the forest as dark as I'd seen it during the day. Or at least it would have been if not for . . .

"Are those flowers glowing?" I asked.

[Identification]: Glowstone Blossom (mature)

"Yes, they're very pretty," Serenal said. "The nectar is an alchemical ingredient. You'll want to climb that tree over there."

She pointed at a lone tree house, about thirty meters up its tree.

"No lift?" I asked.

"There is one, but she keeps it at her level and won't let it down for visitors," she said. "If she likes you, she might let you go down on it."

"Right." I moved towards the tree. Serenal made no move to follow me. *Not a matter of liking her*, I thought. *Right.*

At least there was a ladder of sorts. At first, I thought that planks had been nailed to the tree, but on closer examination, I saw that ladder rungs had somehow been grown out of the trunk. Druid magic, probably.

I started to climb, my System-enhanced body making short work of the vertical distance. About halfway up, I caught a glimpse of a face looking down at me through the hole in the platform. It didn't look old.

She's probably got a granddaughter or some other kid looking after her, I thought to myself and kept climbing. I didn't see her when I got to the top.

The ladder led to an open platform that formed a ring around the tree. The actual house occupied the other half of the platform and presumably part of the tree as well.

"Hello?" I said walking around to what looked like the front door. "Elder Willowshroud?"

A cry came from inside the house. "Who's that talking? That you, girl, messing about?"

"No," I shouted back. "You've got a visitor!" I knocked loudly on the wooden door.

"Oh, you weren't lying were, you? You think I'm fooled that easy?"

The door was flung open, and an old squirrel-kin, her fur a mixture of white and grey, looked me up and down.

"Not even a convincing illusion," she sneered. "A human, here? Do better!"

That was a new one. I blinked in surprise and then reached out and flicked her on the forehead. She reeled back, allowing me entry into the house.

"A physical illusion? Girl, just what have you been playing at?"

"Rude," I told her, and then cast Blind. Then, because it was a little dark in here, I cast Light, sending it up to the ceiling and increasing the brightness until I could see the room clearly.

The old woman took to being blinded fairly calmly. Or maybe it just seemed that way since the spell blocked out sound. She didn't seem to have panicked, but she pulled out a knife and started swiping randomly around her. I made sure to stay out of reach.

There was another person, a young squirrel-kin girl, who was looking at me with frightened eyes.

"Is there a reason she thinks I'm an illusion?" I asked in a casual tone. There was a table and chairs, and I judged one of the chairs to be out of knife range for a little while. I sat down. "Are you some kind of budding Illusionist?"

The girl flicked her eyes at her master before responding. "Shamans can do anything, long as they're taught. But I can't—" She waved at me. "So I know you're real."

"Very wise," I said and cancelled the Blind spell.

"—and every misbegotten whore that claims to be your friend!" Yoroly yelled. She looked around wildly and fixed her gaze on me.

"You!" she exclaimed. "You're not an illusion!"

"Ah, progress." I deadpanned. "No. I'm a visitor. The village was attacked, your counsel is needed."

"You attacked the village?"

"No. I was in the village when it was attacked," I said patiently.

She eyed me with hostile intent. "You think I can't take you? You don't have my power!"

"I think you need to chant your spells, or you would have dispelled my Blind spell," I pointed out. "I'm not here to fight, but I don't think it would go well for you."

Just to be clear, I hadn't randomly started bullying old ladies for the fun of it. Charm had told me, as soon as I saw her, that the old woman responded positively to rudeness and direct opposition. Given how accommodating the rest of the village had been, I could see how they might not get along.

The old squirrel-kin glared at me for a moment more and then seemed to deflate. Only once she'd decided I wasn't a threat, or a victim, did she actually consider what I'd been saying. "Who died?" she demanded.

"Just one, so far. Ikini," I said, letting Memorize bring back a name I'd only heard once before. "A dungeon popped up, and they need your help to get rid of it."

"Don't be daft, human girl," Yoroly scoffed. "There's no way I'd let a dungeon get anywhere near . . ." She paused, glared at me again, and started chanting a spell. Charm didn't read her demeanor as hostile, so I let her.

Her eyes glazed over for about thirty seconds. Then her whole body jerked, her ears standing up straight. Then she was glaring at me again.

"There's a dungeon that just popped up!"

I rolled my eyes. "Nothing gets past you. Now that you're caught up, let's get you to the Council."

"I'm not done yet," Yoroly complained. "I still have more questions."

"You can ask them at the Council," I said. "Let's get going."

I looked over at the squirrel-kin girl.

"Bring your apprentice, too," I said. "If nothing else, she can check to make sure her family is all right."

Yoroly's eyes narrowed, but she nodded. Charm was telling me that she didn't *like* being told what to do, but she respected me for doing it. Weird.

"Get my bag, Luluti," she said. "We're going to the village."

She said it like we were going to Mount Doom or something, but Luluti just nodded and grabbed a leather satchel crammed with . . . junk. Yoroly herself grabbed a staff, a gnarled and twisted stick of wood, topped with a large green crystal. Curiosity got the better of me.

> **[Identification]: Staff of Shydaru – Quality: Perfect – Properties: Focus (Theurgy), Protection, Range Increase – Created by <dungeon lost>**

That's new, I thought. I wanted to ask what a focus was, but the basics seemed pretty clear, and I could wait to learn the details.

I got to take the lift down. I had to do the hauling, so it didn't feel like much of a privilege. We joined Serenal, who hadn't approached a step closer from where she'd left me.

"Oh good," she said with a brittle smile. "You managed to convince her to come."

She bowed to Yoroly. "I'm sure that now you've joined us, your wisdom will help everything go wonderfully."

Yoroly didn't pause, clumping her way along the path at a steady pace, about half the speed of what I would consider walking pace.

"Yeah, yeah, stick it up your butt, slut. I don't like it any more than you."

She kept going on to the village. Luluti, following along behind, shrugged as she drew even with the druid.

"Sorry," she said and walked on.

Serenal looked at me. "Thank you *so much* for convincing her."

ESCORT MISSION

I was never really into computer games back home, but I could hardly have avoided conversations about them. Now that I was living in a world that may or may not be one, I couldn't help but make the occasional comparison to what had been discussed back in those days.

Since this world wasn't an *actual* game, those discussions were a little less helpful than the already sparse guidance from the System help files. But I couldn't help harking back to those conversations, rants, and complaints.

One common topic to complain about, for example, was the escort mission. Now, it seemed, I was getting the chance to experience one for myself. All the classic ingredients seemed to be in place: Get an irascible, annoying, and physically less capable Elder to the bottom of the dungeon, where she could do . . . something that would make the problems go away.

At least I didn't have to worry about her getting stuck in a wall. Probably.

"Why *exactly* is her team going to be the one taking me down?" Yoroly was asking with irritation. It was a good question, and the villagers didn't seem to want to answer it.

"They're experienced delvers, Yoroly, they're the best suited for it." Chief Urnmor had said this before, but Yoroly wasn't buying it.

I wasn't exactly sure *why* they wanted us to do the delve. Feeling a little guilty, I hadn't protested the assignment. But there was a lot going unsaid around this table, and Yoroly was picking up on that, even if she didn't know what was being kept quiet.

I suspected that Yoroly wasn't up to date with the news. Specifically the news about the Champions having been summoned. So she wasn't in a position to interpret the significant looks the villagers were giving each other.

"She's an Illusionist," she continued. "I don't know if you've noticed, but mushrooms don't have eyes. She'll be useless, and her team is lower than her, and without any magic besides."

Not entirely true, but some people seemed to not count healing magic as proper magic. Felicia had Alchemy to fall back on, but that was a far cry from slinging spells.

The other thing that was going unsaid—and this was just speculation on my part—was that none of the village *wanted* to go with her. They were quite happy to leave her protection to the person without a history with her. Just to test my theory, I tried stirring the pot a little.

"I'm sure your magic will be helpful in there," I said brightly. "But it probably wouldn't hurt to have a druid down there with us."

"We're needed up here, to protect the village," Serenal said quickly, giving me a look that I struggled to interpret. Was that a *shut up you're ruining everything* glare? Or more of a *you can't endanger the village* glare?

It was hard to tell, but I thought it might be the former, so I let them continue the argument on their own. They were getting there. They had already dismissed another line of thought, that we should go down and clear the dungeon, and then bring Yoroly down.

That had been eliminated because they weren't sure if the dungeon would stay stable long enough for two trips, and because they thought the mana conduit would descend out of reach if it wasn't connected to a core.

I wasn't feeling too worried about it. The fact that the monsters had stopped suggested that the break was over. The previous breaks that I had witnessed had been a constant stream of monsters that lasted until they stopped. Talnier's dungeon had been an exception, but only because of how huge it was. The monsters literally couldn't get out in time before I reset it.

That probably meant that the dungeon had reverted to whatever was normal for it. That didn't mean it was going to be a cakewalk, and there was still a need to keep the village protected. There were probably myconids wandering around that had gone in a different direction and not run into the village.

Eventually, Yoroly was convinced, and we got to move on to the next step, a briefing from Felicia. She'd had a few hours to prepare, with the aid of the village herbalists.

"Don't waste my time, girly," Yoroly cut in before Felicia could start. "I've forgotten more about alchemy and herbs than you'll ever know."

"Great!" Felicia said brightly. "I'm sure we'd all appreciate it if a *real* expert were to explain how all these potions work!"

Yoroly glared at Felicia and grumbled something about having better things to do than give lectures. I smiled. Felicia had handled that exactly the way I'd advised her to. She moved on to the lecture.

"These are generic antifungal potions," she said, handing out three small bottles to each of us. Use them if you start to feel any effects, or if you see any growths coming off your skin.

"I'm not looking forward to that," I said, taking my allotment. Yoroly didn't say anything, but I noticed she took her share of the potions.

"I've got a few specific remedies for some of what we think might be down there, but dungeons have their own ecologies, so who knows what we'll find."

Felicia looked pretty excited at the thought of finding rare mushrooms. I tried not to let it bother me.

"Next up," she said, "we'll want to wear masks to protect our lungs. These are soaked in a potion that neutralizes most spores. We'll have to resoak them every hour."

What she handed out were little leather bags. Looking inside, I got a whiff of Old Spice and could see a wet rag that must have been the mask.

"Finally, we should all be carrying torches. I know we normally rely on Kandis's Light spell, but a torch will burn any spores that get close, greatly reducing the effect of them."

So I was going to be even more useless. Oh well.

Finally, it was time to leave. The village hunters had not been idle and had located the dungeon entrance. From her performance back in the hut, I got the impression that Yoroly could have led us right to it. However, she was happy to be led by the hunters, trudging along with the rest of us.

Happy to complain about it, anyway.

The entrance didn't look like much to normal sight. A dark hole between the roots of a particularly large tree. Looking at it with Mana Sense, though, there could be no doubt. The influx of mana was particularly noticeable against the normally calm flows.

"Was this tree always this big?" I asked the hunters. They shook their heads.

"Three days ago, it was half this size," one of them said.

An effect of the mana, or was it part of the dungeon? I poked my dagger into the bark. It seemed like a real tree, and not a fungus pretending to be one. I guess we'd find out after we killed the dungeon.

"Right," I said. "Masks on, light torches, we already covered the party order."

I tossed a Light spell down the hole. Just because we were carrying torches didn't mean we wanted to rely on them. They were, like, the second worst of all possible light sources? I mean, if you eliminated the silly ones like setting your own hand on fire.

Once we were prepared, Kyle was the first to go down into the not-so-dark hole. Felicia had to pass his shield down, as he needed one hand for his torch.

Reynard was next, then Cloridan, followed by Felicia. Then Yoroly, myself, and Cutter brought up the rear. Our line was long enough that it was worth another casting of Light to follow along behind us and keep the back of the line well lit.

When I dropped down, I found myself not in a tunnel exactly, but in a gap between slowly pulsating fungal tendrils. One large one formed the floor, and another large one of the walls, but the other wall and the ceiling were made up of smaller tendrils twisted together to form a flattish surface.

"Well, this isn't creepy at all," I said, and I promptly put my torch against the wall.

"Kandis!" Felicia shrieked in alarm. The wall itself had a much more muted reaction. It turned black and swelled up a bit, but there were no other changes.

"What if it had caught alight?" Felicia demanded.

"Better we find out now than during a fight, when someone has to drop their torch," I pointed out.

Felicia glowered at me. "I suppose that makes sense," she allowed. "But warn me next time!"

"What is this stuff, anyway?" Cutter asked. True to form, he started his investigation by stabbing it. I chose to use a different method.

> **[Identification]: Peridium Structural Element – Properties: Regeneration, Resistance**

"It regenerates," I murmured. Sure enough, the stab wounds Cutter inflicted closed as soon as he withdrew his blades. I looked over at the black spot I'd made. It remained unchanged. "Looks like fire stops it from growing back."

"It's not generally worth it to try cutting through a dungeon's walls," Kyle said. He was ever the traditionalist when it came to dungeons.

"Didn't Oakway have a spot you could smash through?" I asked.

"Yeah, *one* spot, in four levels," he replied. "You know how long some bonehead had to smash at the walls to find it?"

"Fair point," I admitted. It wasn't as if we were going to be reporting our findings to the Adventurers Guild. "Let's get going."

As we moved forward, we encountered our first spores. They were too small to see, but we could hear a faint hiss from our torches, and see the tiny sparks as they were incinerated. We made sure our masks were securely fastened and continued on.

The next obstacle was a minor one. Kyle cursed and swung as a small creature dropped down from the ceiling. Fortunately, a torch counted as a club as far as Kyle's skills were concerned.

The creature squealed as the lit tip connected with it and sent it flying into the tunnel wall.

[Identification]: Cavern Shroomling – Threat: 6 – Properties: Lack of Organs

The shroomling had enough hit points that it wasn't killed outright by the blow, but it *was* on fire. Before it could burn up, though, Cloridan stepped up and sliced it in half with his knife.

Your party has killed a Cavern Shroomling – your experience share is 5 XP.

I was surprised that I got as much as that from such a weak monster.

Cloridan looked down at his kill. "Not much of a threat, but they might swarm," he said.

Reynard unlimbered his bow. It was a bit awkward in the tunnel, but there was just about enough room to use it.

"Put the light farther forward and higher," he ordered me. "I'll shoot over Kyle's head before they can drop down."

I frowned at his tone, but it was a good idea, so I went with it. We started killing shroomlings. The little creatures didn't just drop down from the ceiling, but a lot of them did, which meant a lot of them died from an arrow before they could do anything. A few of them popped out of crevices to the side, out of Reynard's line of sight until they were in melee. They couldn't actually hurt Kyle, though, so he just let Cloridan take care of them. Close-in melee work was the Rogue's specialty.

Meanwhile, at the back of the line, Cutter was complaining that he didn't get to do anything.

"Settle down, you'll get your chance," I told him. "It's not like the little critters would be much of a challenge, anyway."

"I suppose so," he sighed.

"The tunnel's opening up!" Kyle called from the front. "Can you move the light forward?"

I couldn't really see what I was doing, but I willed the light to move forward about five meters farther ahead of Kyle. I could see him, at least, past the crowd that my party had turned into. His torch was flaring, burning up an even greater concentration of spores. It looked like it had a halo.

"What do you see?" I called back.

"It's actually quite beautiful," he said. "There's some new monsters, spore sprites. They're quite small and are flying around the cavern, dropping spores. The air is so thick with them you can see them glitter."

Something about Kyle's words was bothering me. "Hang on," I said, trying to figure out what it was. Lost in thought, I didn't realize that he didn't hear me.

He turned to Reynard. "Cover me, I'm going to look at those mounds," he said and dropped out of sight.

"Wait!" I called out. I was trying to get Memorize to help me, but I didn't know what I was trying to remember. Something about spores . . . dust? Coal dust! *Shit!*

"Come back!" I yelled, but if I was right, there probably wasn't time. Water? I didn't have a line of sight. Cloridan and Reynard were blocking the entrance. I couldn't see past them, but there was a gap in front of Felicia that I *could* target.

[Phantasmal Object].

Felicia jumped in surprise as the small wall sprung up in front of her. The explosion that followed wiped out whatever she was going to say.

EXPLOSION

Everything happened way too quickly for me to process, but some of the events were recorded in my log, so I could look at the time-stamps later.

The actual explosion wasn't recorded, but the spore sprites were the first to take the blast.

> **Your party has killed a Spore Sprite – your experience share is 6 XP.**

I got spammed by at least a dozen of these, but I didn't get a chance to read them. The next event was the obliteration of my Phantasmal wall. There was no notification for this, but I checked my logs later. Four milliseconds after the last of the sprite deaths, it logged its own destruction. It may not have lasted long, but I'm pretty sure it saved our lives by absorbing 540 points of damage.

Three milliseconds later, I took a hit-point loss. That involved a pop-up notification, so I got to see it.

> **You have taken 512 damage!**

I didn't get to see the next notification until I woke up. I must have been out before I hit the wall. Thank goodness for soft mushroom walls, I guess.

> **You have taken 51 damage!**
> **You have been stunned from massive damage.**

That was what I saw when I returned to consciousness. I groaned, and blinked it away, to see Cutter looking down at me. The citrusy taste of a standard healing potion was on my lips.

"What happened?" I asked.

"Big boom," he said, shrugging unhelpfully.

"Is . . . everyone all right?" I asked, stupidly. *I* wasn't all right. This potion had only given me back 100 hit points of the 561 that I'd lost. I wasn't even half healed.

"Is *Felicia* all right?" I corrected myself.

Cutter nodded. "I gave her a potion first," he said. "She's working on the squirrel."

That did sound as if he had his priorities right. I groaned again and got to my feet. Up ahead, I could see Felicia healing Yoroly. The end of the passageway was . . . much farther away than I remembered.

"Did you move me?" I asked Cutter.

"The explosion did," he explained. "Sent us all flying."

We trudged back up the passageway, catching sight of Kyle and Cloridan entering from the other end as we did. They both looked battered and more than a little singed. Looking around, I saw that the same was true for myself, and the walls around me.

Before joining them, we had to pass Felicia, who was just finishing up with Yoroly.

"Thanks," the shaman said brusquely, pulling her hand out of Felicia's. "See to yourself, though."

"Not yet," Felicia said, shaking her head. She turned to me. "Kandis is next."

"Are you sure? You look a little worse off than me," I asked.

"No," Felicia said, frowning. "I don't need hit points to heal. And . . . I won't have enough mana to heal everyone. Once I'm out, I'll be the most useless person here."

"Never that," I protested. I would have said more, but she started healing me, and having my aches and pains erased felt really good.

> **[Body Development] Level 4 acquired through use.**
> **For gaining a skill level, you have been awarded 1 XP.**

I blinked in surprise. Oh yeah, Body Development went up when you *healed* damage. You had to take it first, of course. I guess massive damage was good for something. Then I winced, because since it had gone up before I was fully healed, it meant that Felicia had more hit points to heal. I brought up a partial status.

> **[HP]: 765/960 (16/day)**
> **[Stamina]: 900/960 (16/min)**
> **[Mana]: 2530/2880 (48/hour)**

Yeah, I'd had 720 hit points, so that was an extra 240 that she had to heal.

"All done," she said and turned to Cutter.

"Now you," I insisted. "Don't make me turn Persuasion on you."

She rolled her eyes, but she did start healing herself. "The front line took a lot more damage than us, but they have more points," she told me. "Cloridan was behind your barrier, but Kyle and Reynard took over a thousand points of damage."

"Save Reynard for last," I told her. "Make him use up his potions."

"They're already on accelerated healing potions," she said. "Times five."

That was fine, I guessed, but it wasn't a replacement for healing. Healing acceleration was more cost-efficient for those with high strengths, but it took time. Kyle would get maybe two or three times as many points back with a potion that cost just five gold more. It would take him thirty hours to get the full effect, though.

With Felicia done with her report, Yoroly stepped up with her own demands.

"What was that barrier you cast—"

She stopped as I gave her a look. Just a look, but one with the full force of my Charisma behind it. She may have out-levelled me, but she clearly hadn't been prioritizing that ability. Whatever word she was going to address me with, be it "girl," "child," or the inaccurate "Illusionist," got stuck in her mouth. She paused, trying to come up with something more respectful.

"—Kandis" was what she eventually came up with.

I raised an eyebrow. I wasn't sure that we were on a first-name basis. In Australia, *everyone* is on a first-name basis, but there are exceptions. My bank, for example, has never referred to me by anything other than Ms. Hammond. That's pretty much it, though. Even the government refers to me as Miss Kandis Hammond, which isn't exactly a first-name basis, but it's a bit less formal.

I decided to allow it since Yoroly didn't have a last name, so I'd be unable to reciprocate.

"It's an illusion," I told her. "A solid illusion?"

"A solid illusion?" she said scornfully. "Do you think I'm crazy?"

I didn't want to argue with her, so I just conjured a Phantasmal cube and left it with her. It was too bad I couldn't flex by making it a Rubik's Cube, but I'd have to summon all the individual parts separately.

I bet I'd be able to do it in the dungeon.

For now, though, I left her with a solid cube and a lot of unanswered questions. If she was worth her salt at Theurgy, she could probably get most of her answers from studying it. I had more important things to do right now.

I joined Cloridan at the entrance to the next cavern.

"How are things?" I asked him.

"Well enough," he said. "I don't have as many hit points as these two, but I managed to stay conscious."

Right. That confirmed my suspicion from the last time I was knocked unconscious, that it was based on the proportion of the hit points lost. Kyle and Reynard had lost more than I had, but they had more than double my hit points.

"We've been keeping an eye out," Cloridan continued, "to see if the dungeon was going to make a move while we were down, but it's been quiet."

"Mhmn," I said noncommittally, looking past him and into the cavern. Kyle and Reynard were poking around through the debris, holding up light stones to see. One of the lumps moved, and Reynard skewered it.

Your party has killed a Fungal Mimic – your experience share is 8 XP.

"More than just the sprites then," I commented.

"There were a few of those, but they were all stunned by the blast," he said. "We're picking up a few cores, but the sprites were obliterated."

I did some quick calculations. Ten gold each on potions for Felicia and myself. Fifteen gold for the potions that Cloridan and Kyle had taken. We were in the hole for fifty gold, and Felicia was tapped out, or was about to be. It was going to be mostly potions from here on in.

I looked around at the ashes that were left of the room. There probably weren't a lot of alchemical recipes that called for fungal ashes. We might be taking a loss on this delve.

Looking at the lightstones that the others were carrying made me realize that my own lights had gone out. Frowning at my lapse, I quickly cast a small light behind me in the tunnel, and a much brighter one to fly up and illuminate the cavern.

It wasn't much to look at now. The floor sloped down in a bowl, though not as steeply as the dome of the ceiling. Whatever sprites or fungal growths that were there before were now shattered and burned, leaving only unidentifiable lumps behind. The rest of the party caught up with us, and we descended into the cavern.

"You shouted something before it all . . . happened," Reynard said. "Do you know what went wrong?"

"It was probably a deliberate trap," I explained. "When you get a fine powder suspended in the air, it can burn really quickly. If there's enough of it, you get . . ."

I gestured around the cavern.

"I've never heard of that," Kyle said.

I shrugged. "Conditions have to be just right," I said. "And most adventurers get light stones as quickly as they can."

That was because torches were a pain. They didn't last long, they smoked, and they went out when you dropped them. Light stones were cheap for magic items, and they were in high demand for parties that didn't have someone to cast Light.

"We only got torches because we were expecting to burn some mushrooms," I added.

"This is my fault," Felicia said. "I knew that the torches would burn the spores, I should have . . ."

"You weren't to know," I insisted. "That sort of conflagration, you can't imagine it, if you don't already know it's possible."

"Actually . . ." Kyle said, trailing off as he looked thoughtful. "Is something wrong here?"

"What do you mean?" Felicia asked.

"It's not like a dungeon to take out its monsters with a trap meant for us," he said. "It's . . ."

"Counterproductive," I finished for him. "Yeah, I don't think this is the dungeon's idea."

"What else could it be, other than the dungeon?" Yoroly asked.

"We've seen it before," I said. "Dungeons acting strangely. This one was already strange, in how it popped up in your territory, but it looks like that wasn't the end of it."

"But what could influence a dungeon?" Yoroly objected.

"A god," Reynard answered. I scowled at him. He shrugged unconcernedly. "She was going to figure it out eventually."

"Yeah, yeah," I grumbled. "A god," I agreed, addressing Yoroly. "Giving things a little nudge."

"But why would a god . . ." she paused, making the connections. "You're a Servant?"

I raised an eyebrow. "That's a new one," I said. "Normally, it's Chosen or Champion."

"Other countries have other terms," Reynard explained, watching with amusement as Yoroly started fuming.

"Why didn't those pups *tell* me!" she screeched.

"This may come as a shock," I said, "but I don't think they *like* you very much."

She glared at me. "Bunch of ingrates, the lot of them. You're serious, though? The lot of you have been called, the god's game is running rough-shod over everything?"

"Pretty much," I agreed. "If that makes you want to turn back . . ."

She scowled. "I wish I could. But I can't let a dungeon spawn here. We've got to kill it."

I sighed. "Yeah, that's about how it normally turns out."

We pushed on. Fearing more explosive caverns, I took point, or at least my Phantasmal Emissary did, carrying a lit torch. It seemed that I'd finally found a way for my illusions to do damage. I wondered if it was worth developing some kind of fuel-air bomb that my emissary could carry, but I kept it to myself.

"Don't tell Janie that I'm setting off bigger fireballs than her," I told the group.

"No fear of that," Cloridan said. "The maniac would only take it as a challenge."

It turned out that remote detonating someone else's bomb didn't give you credit for the kills unless you were in the blast radius. I got no notifications for the sprites killed in the explosions. All we got was the paltry contribution from finishing off the mimics.

The amounts were so low that it wasn't worth bothering about, though. After clearing three more chambers, we finally came to one with a scorched but still intact chest.

"Was this the boss chamber then?" I asked.

"Probably," Cloridan said, going over to inspect the chest.

"Well, stay alert. I'm guessing whoever is responsible has got a new surprise for the second level."

DEMON

The second floor went back to the basics. The layout was a bit more dungeon-like, with passageways linking small chambers with monsters for us to fight. Mostly myconid guardians, which were a hard fight for Felicia and me. With Kyle, Cloridan, Reynard, and Cutter facing the brunt of the fighting, we managed to maintain a secure perimeter for Yoroly, who was significantly worse than me when it came to fighting.

She wasn't completely useless, as she kept herself alert and at the center of our formation. After so much practice, fighting with one or two of us invisible, we moved together like a well-oiled machine. She managed to fit in with us and even managed to pick up things that we missed.

"Ware! Cutter's left!" she cried out now. I glanced over to see a section of the fungal wall split off and lurch towards us.

[Identification]: Lurking Moldbeast – Threat: 20 – Properties: Colony Organism

---

What the fuck is a colony organism? was all that I had time to wonder before Cutter whirled to face the thing and sliced it in two.

That was less impressive than it sounded. The thing had no bones, and its flesh offered even less resistance than the myconid guardians we were already facing. Just by dashing towards it, under its slowly swinging arms, he managed to combine a charge with a slash and cut through its belly entirely.

That charge took him out of our formation, but we were able to compensate. Kyle and I took a half step closer to each other, covering the gap until Cutter could make his way back.

The only problem with that was that the moldbeast wasn't dead. In fact, it had split in two. Half of it attacked Cutter as he was recovering from his charge, forming an arm out of what had been its lower body.

The other half lunged at me. I blinked.

> **[Identification]: Lurking Moldbeast – Threat: 15 – Properties: Colony Spawn**

Threat fifteen. That *wouldn't* have been a problem, except that I was already fighting a Threat *eighteen* myconid guardian. I blocked its attack with my dagger. It wasn't the same as stabbing it, but the dagger sank into the soft flesh of its moldy arm, and it jerked it back with a soft, high-pitched hiss that might have indicated pain.

Forced on the defensive, I blocked a blow from the myconid guardian and glanced over at Cutter's fight. He was now facing two smaller moldbeasts . . .

> **[Identification]: Lurking Moldbeast – Threat: 12 – Properties: Colony Core**
> **[Identification]: Lurking Moldbeast – Threat: 12 – Properties: Colony Spawn**

"The one on your left!" I called out. "Use Identify!"

The hesitation left him, and he stabbed out with both blades. Of course, this might mean it just split again . . . nope. Was two splits the limit, or did you have a chance of killing it each time? Hard to say. But when he killed the core, the spawn all dropped dead.

Cutter made his way back into formation, and not long after that, the room was cleared. We went over what had happened, and I shared my theories about how the colony organisms might work. No one had any better ideas.

We pressed on, this time keeping an eye on the walls with Identify, to see if we could get a warning about the next lurking moldbeast. It seemed, though, that they were invisible, or at least part of the standard fungal tissue that made up the walls until they started to move.

Further experimentation showed that the colony spawns could be divided many times, slowly shrinking their threat level with each division. Colony cores could be killed, but the jury was still out on whether it was after a set number of divisions or random chance each time.

By now, we thought we were getting close to the end of the floor.

"Do you think there will be a third floor?" Felicia asked.

"The village got attacked by the myconid guardians that are on this floor," I said. "I didn't see any fungal trolls back then."

"There were a few," Kyle told me. "Not many, and they look pretty much the same."

"I guess I missed them," I admitted. Fungal trolls, despite the name, were just bigger guardians, at least as far as we could tell. I suppose being bigger made them more troll-like, but they were only vaguely humanoid in the first place.

"Anyway," Kyle said. "If there was another floor, I would have expected to see some monsters from that floor in the attack. So I think it's two floors only."

"Enough chatter," Reynard called back from the front of the group. "I think we're at the boss chamber."

We paused to change out our protective masks, but that was about all the preparation that we could do. The passageway ended in membrane, thin enough for us to sense light and movement on the other side.

"If this is sealed off because it's filled with spores again . . ."

"We'll run and light a torch," Cloridan said. "Dungeon would be pretty dumb to put its final boss in a blow-up room, though."

With a quick swipe of his blade, Cloridan cut through the membrane. Behind it was a large room. Not as large as the "blow-up" chambers, but bigger than the cells we'd been fighting in so far on this level.

At the far end of the room, standing on a raised platform was . . .

[Identification]: Fungal Troll Champion – Threat: 25 – Properties: Fungal Regeneration

---

"Not sure what fungal regeneration means," I commented. "Maybe he needs to absorb fungal monsters to heal?"

"He's waiting for us," Kyle said. "Big room like this, he's probably got minions set to attack us."

"Standard formation then?" I asked, and everyone agreed. We started moving carefully forward, waiting for the first minion to make its appearance. Reynard put a few arrows in the troll as we approached, but arrows weren't terribly effective against fungi. They went straight through, doing minimal damage. The fungal troll champion roared, in fury or pain, but stayed where he was. The holes were so small that we couldn't tell if he was regenerating or not.

Then the ambush started. Lurking moldbeasts started folding themselves out of the floor, and the fight was on.

I think there were five of them to start with, then ten, and then I lost count, too busy fighting. I focused on the dregs, the ones left after a split or two. If you didn't get the core, you could be left with lots of little beasts. Easy to kill, even for me, but too dangerous to be ignored. Felicia made herself useful, calling out the cores as quickly as she could Identify them.

"Cutter! The bigger one, on your right! Kyle! The one at the back!"

All the while, we were slowly making our way over to the troll, who was waiting for us eagerly. I could hear his excited hoots coming closer as I stepped backwards on Kyle's call.

The frontline had the harder job, no question, pressing forward through the scrum of fungal monstrosities. But it was no milk run being in the back, having to step backward every time Kyle called, "Push!"

Still, step by step, we were pushing forward. It seemed as if there was an endless supply of moldbeasts, and it sounded as though the front line had engaged some fungal trolls, but we were getting there.

When I saw the demon, I didn't know what to make of it. Identify was on the case, of course, my thought of *what is that* instantly answered.

Warning! Demon Detected!
[Identification]: Vingt Possessor – Threat: Unknown – Properties:
Unknown
Warning! Demon Detected!

"Demon!" I called out, almost by reflex, my eyes still fixed on the thing. I didn't know what else to do right away. It was out of the reach of my dagger, and while it didn't look like much, the red warning labels on Identify didn't encourage me to approach it.

Should I try an Iron Dart?

It looked like a worm, a big one. Too big to be called a worm back on Earth, but I'd long left that prejudice behind. It was about sixty centimeters long, and ten wide. Grey-colored flesh, like most of the creatures around here. No visible eyes. It was wiggling along, about five meters behind the two Moldbeasts I was fighting.

There wasn't a lot of reaction to my warning, what with us fighting for our lives and all. I heard a gasp from Felicia behind me and a hiss that had to come from Yoroly.

From the front came an alarmed "What!" from Kyle.

Cloridan was still facing forward, but he was next to me on our circle. He gave me a "Where?" but I don't think he could disengage to get a look.

Cutter was facing backward, like me. He saw it. But now it was doing something, scrunching itself up into half its length.

"I think it's going to—" I started to say, but I was interrupted by the creature, as it sprang forward. Fast. Towards me. Too fast to dodge or parry. It seemed as though I froze as time slowed down, the worm growing larger as it headed straight for me

It was too fast for me to dodge. Other people had higher Agility.

My eyes were fixed on the demon, so the first thing I sensed was the collision as Cutter knocked me out of the way. Then I was falling, and Cutter was in the way of the thing. He reached out with his swords, but the monster twisted between them, impossibly agile.

Then I was on the ground, and a moldbeast was pawing at me. It was trying to kill me, but more importantly, it was blocking my view.

By the time I killed the beast and got to my feet, Cutter was lying face down, and the worm was nowhere to be seen.

"Cutter!" I cried out.

"Wait!" Felicia called out, as I went to approach him. "What happened to the demon?"

I killed another baby moldbeast as I considered the question. The worm had hit him in the front, and he was lying face down, so . . . it must be under him?

The fungal flesh that we stood on was broadly flat. There were undulating curves, but no crevices or crannies for the thing to hide in. It must be underneath him, or . . .

"Cover me," I told Cloridan. Knowing that he would, I sheathed one of my daggers and used Phantasmal Object to summon a pole with a flat hook on the end.

Gingerly, I took a step closer to Cutter and poked the pole under him. Straining with the poor leverage, I managed to roll him over.

There was no sign of the demon.

"He's still alive," Felicia said. "He doesn't register as injured to my Diagnosis spell."

"But he's . . . where is it? Where is it!" I yelled.

"Ware!" Kyle's voice came from behind me. "The champions attacking!"

Then it was just fighting. Hard fighting. We fell back around Cutter so that Felicia could see what she could do. Now our perimeter was only four people, with me being the weakest, so we all had our work cut out for us. Kyle and Reynard faced the champion, while Cloridan helped me finish off the moldbeasts.

The notification finally came.

> **You have cleared the second level of the Myconid Maze for the first time!**
> **You have been awarded 4,000 experience.**
> **Your party is the first to clear the second level of the Myconid Maze!**
> **You have been awarded 4,000 experience.**

A chest rose from the floor of the raised platform that the champion had been standing on. I ignored it for now. The core, now clearly visible from behind it, was much more interesting.

"Yoroly, can you move the mana stream from here?" I asked.

Yoroly, staring at Felicia as she ministered to Cutter, jumped and looked at me.

"Ah . . . no, not while the core has a grip on it," she said.

I nodded. Looking at Cutter, I tried Identify. No result. *He's still a person, not a corpse,* I thought. *Hold on to that.*

"How long will it take you?" I asked.

She shrugged. "At least five minutes, probably more like fifteen," she replied.

"All right," I said. "Kyle, Cloridan, and Felicia, you take Cutter back to the surface. We'll wait here, and when enough time has passed, we'll kill the core."

Kyle, standing protectively over Felicia, nodded. So did Cloridan, who was looting the chest.

"Why me?" Reynard asked.

"Your bow," I answered. "It's the best way to kill the core without getting mana near it, or touching it."

He nodded. "And your role?"

I sighed. "This place doesn't have spatial manipulation to collapse, but these walls might not last long after the dungeon goes. I've got

Earth Magic; I'm pretty new at it, but I might be able to get us out if it collapses."

"Kandis . . ." Felicia said.

"Go on," I told her. "Get out of here. There has to be some way to save Cutter, and you need to find it. I'll finish the mission."

DEMON HUNTERS

Reynard's arrow hit the crystal dead on, shattering it instantly.

Dungeon core has been destroyed.
Five minutes before external construct unravels.

I conjured up what I hoped would be half of a survival capsule. Flat bottomed, with curved raised sides, it was just big enough for one person to sit in. That was as big as I could manage with Phantasmal Object.

"Here," I told Yoroly. "Get into that before you start messing with the mana."

As she did so, I started creating shells for Reynard and myself.

"I thought you were going to use Earth Magic," he said, eyeing the illusions.

"There's no earth around for me to work with, not until this fungus dissolves," I explained. "Hopefully these will keep us alive until that's done with."

"How?" he asked.

I answered him by conjuring the rest of Yoroly's capsule. A roof that rested on top. Doing it that way meant that I could build something bigger than my object limit. And it meant that there were two spells that had to fail once it started taking damage.

"You can run instead," I said. "You've done your part."

He grimaced. "Never let it be said that I left two women to face an uncertain fate alone."

I raised an eyebrow. Chivalry from a criminal? I didn't say anything, though. I just conjured his roof once he got in, and then added my own. Then we waited.

One minute before external construct unravels.

It started with a hissing sound. All around us, bits of fungal matter were dissolving into a fine silvery dust.

External construct has failed.

Our capsules settled slightly as the gentle undulations of the previous surface dissolved. The dust seemed frictionless but heavy. As it fell from the ceiling, the level of the floor started to rise.

I started to worry about our capsules. I hadn't thought to seal them; people would need to exit them afterwards. The hissing sound grew louder, coming from the entrance.

As dust started to pour in from the entryway, I realized what it was. The upper level. It was all turning into dust and it was all flowing down to here.

I *really* started to worry at that point, but even as the dust poured in, the level of it down here seemed to rise only slightly. The dust wasn't the end product, I realized. It was decomposing into . . . well, not nothing. Undirected mana was rising from the floor around me. It floated freely until it started getting sucked into the structure that Yoroly was constructing.

Before long, our capsules were sitting on bare earth, in a much bigger cavern than we'd been in before. The roof . . . seemed stable.

"I'm done," Yoroly announced. "Let's get out of here before something falls."

I dismissed the capsules and we started to move. Climbing out of the new cavern complex was a little harder than getting in had been. I managed, thanks to my climbing skill. I was a little worried about Yoroly, but she scampered up the walls like, uh . . . a squirrel.

I wonder if that's racist? I thought to myself.

We exited the cavern and reunited with my friends. They hadn't gone far and had set up a makeshift campsite to better tend to Cutter.

"How is he?" was the first question I asked.

"Still unchanged," Felicia said. "What kind of demon was it?"

I hesitated, not wanting to say it. I *knew* where the demon had gone. "A vingt possessor," I finally said.

Felicia's face fell.

"You know of it?" I asked.

"No . . . but the name doesn't leave much doubt, does it?" she replied.

Yoroly was staring fixedly at Cutter's recumbent form.

"His mana is strange," she stated. "And . . . it doesn't respond to me."

"Is that something you can do? Affect other people's mana?" I asked.

Now that I looked for myself, Cutter's mana was strange. Normally, Mana Sense didn't give much information on people. They weren't impervious to mana, but they seemed to be clouded over. *Affecting* that clouded mana wasn't something I could do with a spell. Spells like Phantom World that could be considered a mental illusion were constructed in the air, and then . . . inserted into the body of the target.

I suppose a spell like Iron Dart worked the same way, only with a physical component.

Anyway, while Cutter still had that cloudy body, it wasn't following the shape of his physical body. It was misshapen and moving independently, twisting and writhing as we watched.

"That's . . . not normal," I admitted. "Does anyone know about cases like this? About demons just *wandering around* in a dungeon?"

A chorus of noes came from all around. Yoroly went into more detail.

"This is . . . unprecedented in my lifetime at least. There are stories. The System hates demons, they say, and creates quests for heroes to hunt them down. It is only when the heroes fail that the gods step in."

"Those are the ones that we hear about," Kyle agreed. "When the demons get out of control, beyond what mortals can handle . . ."

"The System gives out quests?" I asked, surprised. Then I considered it further. "I suppose the dungeon break events are sort of like that. So why didn't we get a quest notification?"

"Because you do not qualify."

The unknown voice came from behind me. I whirled around, one hand going for my dagger.

Standing there were two elves, a man and a woman. They must have stepped out from behind a tree, because no one, not even those in the group that were facing that way, had sensed their approach.

"Peace, friend," said the male, holding his empty hands up. "We do not come as enemies."

"Elves . . ." I said, dumbly. "They don't let you out of the Grove until . . ."

For just a second, the pair stopped holding back their aura. I—we all—flinched at the feel of it. The only aura I'd felt that was that strong was the King's.

"We're not runaways," the man said easily. "I think you might be able to help us with a quest that we're on. Have you encountered any demons?"

"Uh . . ." I stared at the man, waiting for my brain to catch up. He was a good-looking man—er, elf. High cheekbones, long blond hair, brilliant green eyes. His clothes, that is his armor, were stylish, in a way that armor normally wasn't. Leather sagged, needed tightening, and then got bunched up. It never fit right. This . . . did.

> **[Identification]: Golden Tsunti Leather Armor – Quality: Perfect – Properties: Comfortable, Temperature Control, Enhanced Protection, Weightless**

I swallowed. Dungeons could make perfect items, but for equipment the cost was prohibitive, so they rarely did. This must be the result of the peerless crafters that the Elven Grove was supposed to have. All that time to practice their skills . . .

I tried to focus on the question at hand. They were demon hunters, and we had a demon problem. The question was, would they help us, or would they just kill Cutter?

The elf waited patiently for me to respond as if he had all the time in the world. I suppose that he did.

"You already know that we did," I finally said. He nodded.

"We heard you speaking as we approached. I heard you mention the name of the fiend, a demon that we have been chasing for quite some time. Shall I tell you of it?"

"Do you know how to extract one?" I asked. He shook his head, sadly.

"The vingt possessor is a parasitic type that only infects humans. There are variants that infect other species. Once it enters the host via the mouth or . . . another orifice, it sheds its physical form and becomes a liquid that coats the inside of the host's lungs and digestive tract.

"We can't cut it out?" I asked. The elf shook his head.

"I'm afraid your friend is already dead. The creature maintains the physical process of life, but air no longer enters his bloodstream. Oxygen has ceased flowing to his brain."

"No," I protested. "He's still breathing! He's still warm. The System doesn't show him as a corpse!"

"Possessors are made to deceive the [Status]," the elf said. "And the victim's loved ones as well. In 24 hours, the possessor will have consumed your friend's mind and memories, and it will wake up. As far as you can tell, it will be your friend.

"It is not. It will be a broodmare for creating more possessors."

"No." I stepped protectively in front of Cutter. "I won't let you kill him."

"He is already dead," the elf said. "And you can't stop us. We can wait a little while, for you to come to terms with this, but the body must be burnt. Consumed in fire to destroy every last trace of the demon."

"He's still alive, though!" Felicia protested. "My spell, Diagnosis, tells me that he's still alive."

The elf shook his head. "Your spell depends on the Status, and the Status is being fooled. Perhaps this will show you—"

He stepped to the side suddenly, and I felt the sensation of something moving past me. Fast. Too fast to see, let alone to stop. When I turned to see where it went, I saw the small throwing dagger embedded in Cutter's neck.

"No!" I cried out.

"Pull the dagger out!" Felicia said urgently. "I still have some mana, enough to stop the . . . bleeding?"

She stopped, as confused as me. I had pulled out the dagger, but instead of blood spurting out, a blue-black liquid was oozing out slowly. The elf spoke again.

"His heart seems to beat, but it does not pump blood. The lungs do not provide the breath of life, so the blood becomes dark and cold. And yet the flesh seems warm, heated by the demon. He is dead, children."

"You ass!" I threw the dagger back at him, as hard as I could. He caught it out of the air, as unconcerned as if I had passed it back to him.

"My companion and I will prepare a pyre. One has to take care, setting a large fire in the woods. Take this time to say goodbye, make your peace with the unfairness of it all."

They moved back, to give us the appearance of privacy. I didn't doubt that they could hear every word we said, though.

"I think he's right," Felicia said. "The way that blood moved, it's just . . ."

"It should have been me," Cloridan said. "Why'd I bother teaching the kid, if he was just going to end up like this?"

Kyle didn't say anything, just put his arm around Felicia.

"It was *supposed* to be me," I said. "The damn thing was aiming right for me, and Cutter just . . . This was an assassination attempt, and Cutter took the bullet for me."

"You think the gods set this up?" Yoroly asked.

"One of them, at least. Maybe more, working together. I don't know . . . which, though."

I stared morosely at Cutter's body.

"They can all go to hell, as far as I'm concerned."

The elves set up the pyre at what had been the entrance of the dungeon. The bare earth made for a good firebreak. They didn't bother doing any further damage to Cutter; they just bowed respectfully to us and then wrapped him up in the groundsheet we'd placed him on. Lifting him easily, they took him down to the cave.

I wanted to stop them, but I knew that I couldn't. Instead, we just followed them.

"Are there prayers for the dead that anyone would say?" he said, once the body was in place.

"The gods can fuck right off," I said bitterly. Yoroly gave me an alarmed look, but no one else said anything. The elf nodded.

"This man was young, but he fought for others. He sacrificed his life, so that another might live. He was brave. He lived well, with the years that he had. Many humans of twice or three times his age could not say as much. Many elves, with ten times his years, could not say the same."

He put a small wand against the stacked wood, and flames licked out.

"He now makes one final sacrifice to save others."

The smoke that came off the pyre was black and thick, choking us. We stayed close by as long as we could, but we eventually had to flee the cave. We waited at the entrance, watching the smoke roll up, until the fire was done.

PEP TALK

Seems like someone needs to vent a little."

I jerked at the sound of my voice, but as I was about to whirl around, I saw that everything in front of me—my friends, the elves, the smoke—had all frozen. I knew what this was. I knew who was speaking to me. So I controlled my turn, giving the person behind me a measured glare as he came within my line of sight.

"You," I said coldly.

"Me," Fyskel replied, perched jauntily on a weathered stump that had not, as far as I could remember, been there a minute ago.

"Vent?" I asked. "Cutter is dead because of your stupid game, because one of your lot was gunning for *me*."

I hadn't been expecting sympathy from him. I would have assumed it was a lie if he'd tried to express it. Watching his face never change from its normal expression of cool amusement, though, was a little infuriating.

"Don't take it too personally," he said. "Everybody dies."

He glanced over at the frozen bodies of the two demon hunters. "Even elves," he added. "Agelessness is all very well, and it pissed Ashmor off no end. But it's a cheap hack and appallingly fragile."

"Cutter didn't die of old age," I retorted. "He was deliberately killed, by something *you* aren't supposed to tolerate."

"The demon, you mean?" Fyskel gave a slight frown. "That's why I'm here."

"Except you're *not* here, are you?" I asked rhetorically. "This is a memory that you haven't given me yet."

"That depends on what you mean by *here*," Fyskel said, switching to a sunny grin.

"What do *you* mean by here?" I shot back. Fyskel just grinned, and didn't reply.

I thought about it. "If *here* is a memory, then *you* being here means you're in my head. *That's* not creepy at all. What does the demon have to do with that?"

Fyskel shrugged. "Try not to let it bother you," he suggested smugly. "For one thing, if I'm in here, the others can't be, not at least without me knowing."

I scowled. "I don't want any of you trudging through here, leaving footprints all over the place like my brain was a hotel lobby."

He laughed, annoyingly. "I'm sure you don't," he chuckled. "But we were talking about the demon."

"You haven't said *anything* about the demon."

"Allow me to rectify that, then. Demons have gotten better at hiding from us over the years. Vingt possessors, for example, are entirely unde-tectable once in a person."

"Which means you *can* detect them when they're wiggling about as worms."

"Correct. Normally we let the System handle them, and it was doing its job, sending those elves after it. None of our concern. But we definitely *should* have noticed it once you entered the dungeon."

"Because I'm one of your little game pieces."

"Aww, not at all," Fyskel crooned condescendingly. "You're a big, grown-up game piece now!"

I gave him the finger, and he laughed.

"Where was I? Oh, yes. The fact that we didn't means that its presence was concealed by one of our own."

"I figured out that much on my own," I said sourly. "My money is on Ashmor."

"Mmn, maybe. The problem with that is, I don't think he wants you dead."

I raised a doubting eyebrow.

"Allow me to clarify," he said hastily. "While he does want you dead, there are some things he wants you to do *before* you die."

"But who else of your colleagues are dumb enough to mess with demons?" I asked.

His eyes twinkled. Literally twinkled. I don't know if he was manipu-lating the light source, or moving his head infinitesimally, or if it was just an illusion.

"Oh. *You* would," I said. Then I realized that wasn't bad *enough*. I sighed. "You all would, wouldn't you?"

"Given the right motivation, the right set of circumstances . . . yes," Fyskel said. "Demons are more complex than you've been given to understand so far. They may be anathema to the System, but we gods are not the System."

"Well, isn't that just fucking terrifying. Does that mean the elven portal is real, then? Is that where the demons come from?"

"The map was real," Fyskel confirmed. "Telling you anything more than that would compromise my neutral stance."

"Was Ashmor lying, then? About ending the world if I cracked the barrier?"

"Not lying, but the truth is considerably more complicated." Fyskel paused, a thoughtful look on his face. "Cracking the barrier can be like breaking an egg, but it need not be. There are other ways of penetrating either an eggshell or a dimensional barrier."

"So it is possible to go back," I pressed.

He shrugged. "Getting past the barrier is only the first of many obstacles in the way of that goal. I couldn't say if the body you are in is even viable outside the domain of the System."

I glared at him, but he was entirely impervious to my stare. The truth was that I had too many ties here to think about going back. If they weren't actually real, then maybe. But they *felt* real. He knew all of that, of course, even if he didn't bother to acknowledge it. With a sigh, I returned to the subject at hand.

"So who *does* want to kill me?"

"Hmm, don't be too hasty," Fyskel cautioned. "I haven't eliminated Ashmor as a suspect."

"But . . . no motive?"

"You should consider the possibility that Cutter was the target all along," Fyskel said.

"What? Why would he want to kill Cutter? And how would he . . . ?"

"It's always wise, when a god's plot is foiled by accident, to wonder if the eventual result was what the god wanted from the beginning. That's how we work."

He smiled apologetically. "We try so many things and we are opposed by our peers in so much of what we do, that it's only the most unlikely gambits that can play out to the end."

"That's insane . . . why would he want Cutter dead?"

"For an emotional effect on you," Fyskel replied promptly. "It *has* had an effect which I'm evaluating now . . . in detail."

Presumably, that meant that he was rifling through my thoughts like a burglar while he was talking to me. The idea of it made me feel sick, but there wasn't anything I could do about it.

"So what other gods want me dead?" I asked instead.

"Hard to say . . . there are a number who *don't* want you to do what Ashmor wants."

"We're talking about me summoning demons, right? What makes them think that I want to do *that*?"

"It *is* unlikely," Fyskel agreed. "The sheer improbability of it is why enough of us agreed to let Ashmor give you the knowledge of how to do it. There might be some, though, who don't like those already favorable odds."

"So they'd just bump me off early, just to be sure?" I shivered at the thought.

"Perhaps," Fyskel said. "If so, they would be incentivized to make it *look* like Ashmor was responsible. Bringing demons into the Game is a violation of the rules."

"So that's why you're here," I said, finally realizing. "There might have been cheating, and you're the referee. You're looking for evidence."

"Not that there's any to be found, in any of your group's memories. And the dungeon is a lost cause now. They're annoyingly separate from the rest of the continuum."

So gods aren't infallible, I thought to myself. Of course, my thoughts were probably an open book to Fyskel right now.

"Hey," I said aloud. "This way that you're talking to me . . . can the other gods read this memory and know what you've told me?"

"Never say never," Fyskel cautioned me. "What one god can do, another can overcome. They should find it very difficult, however."

"What you were saying, about one of the other gods cheating, you wouldn't have said that if they could overhear it . . . or find out about it later."

"It would compromise my investigation," Fyskel agreed.

"So is there anything else you want to tell me that won't be overheard?" I asked.

"So many things . . . but I'm afraid that doing so would be a violation of my neutrality," Fyskel said. He gave me another grin, then vanished.

I stumbled as my perception suddenly changed. I'd been moving about in the memory, but now I had returned to where I'd started.

"Dammit, Fyskel," I muttered.

One of the elves looked over at me. "You would invoke the attention of that one?" he asked. I'd spoken under my breath, but that probably didn't matter. At their level, they could probably hear a pin drop at fifty meters.

"Not willingly," I said. "I just had a visit."

That got me looks from just about everyone. The elves looked at me in surprise—I guess gods didn't just talk to anyone, and they might have expected themselves to be the ones addressed. My team was looking at me, surprised that I'd mentioned it in front of strangers. Yoroly was giving me a fearful look, moving her fingers in complicated gestures. They were probably a ward against evil, and they probably worked as well as the ones back home.

Only Reynard seemed unsurprised by the revelation. He was either beyond caring about my random antics or giving a good impression of it.

"He didn't speak to anyone else?" I asked wryly. "What are the odds."

The two elves looked at each other. The male one stepped forward.

"We were going to leave you to go your own way, now that our task has been completed," he said. "Now, though, I think that introductions are in order."

"Oh, now you want to chat and make friends?" I asked harshly, in exactly the sort of way that Charm didn't want me to. I knew that this wasn't the ideal approach. This pair could probably kill us all without raising a sweat. Part of me didn't care, though.

The elf bowed his head. "I apologize. We have not met under the best of circumstances. I am Morthanial, and this is Culathidae. We bear you no ill will, and hope that you can return the favor."

I took a deep breath and tried to remember what Yoda said about letting go of anger. Was it that it led to fear? Or was it the mind killer? Memorize couldn't help me when I hadn't been paying attention in the first place.

In the end, I just stopped listening to the part of me that wanted to scream in their faces and just turned Charm back on. The looks of surprise were somewhat gratifying. Only a little, though. Unlike most people, my skill didn't overwhelm them, it merely matched their own totals.

I can't imagine they were used to that, coming from a human. Especially at their level. So I took what gratification I could as I introduced my companions. Once that was done, both of the elves bowed.

"Well met," Morthanial said, continuing to do most of the talking. "It seems that most of you are far from home, as are we. I have many questions, about you, this dungeon, and what business Fyskel has with you. Are you agreeable to answering any of them?"

"We're not all far away from home," I replied, glancing at Yoroly. "And her village is waiting to hear back from us."

"Hmmph! Bunch of arseholes, let them wait," Yoroly snorted.

"Yeah, no, I don't think we'll be doing that," I answered. "We should go back—wait. Are there any more demons running around?"

"The System would have a quest for us if there were," Morthanial assured me. "If there is one in the Wild, then some other hunter is closer to it than we."

"All right then," I said, breathing a sigh of relief. "Then how about we go back to the village and let them know what's going on. Then we can fill each other in."

Morthanial cocked his head to the side, considering. Then he nodded. "The Tribes have no objections to our passage. We pass through at speed, interacting as little as possible. With the need for urgency passed it would be . . . politic, to meet with the nearest Tribe and break bread with them."

"Great," I said. "And on the way, I can tell you something that will answer at least a few of those questions. The village already worked it out, those that followed the news, anyway."

I took a breath. It felt weird to just say it, after all that time hiding it. But I was level six now. If I wasn't a power just yet, I wasn't someone who could be just pushed around.

"I'm one of the Chosen of the Gods," I said.

MELANCHOLY

There was a feast. *Of course* there was a feast. The village had just been saved, the dungeon was dealt with, and the Champion of Whoever was partly responsible. There were two *new* guests, high-level elves! A feast had been pretty much guaranteed even before the news of demons had been added. There were demons! That had been defeated!

I was not in the mood—none of us were, really. Even the elves seemed cool on the idea. They had planned to disappear back into the Grove with no one the wiser but had stayed to talk with me some more. That made them guests of honor at the feast, and everyone in the village seemed to want their moment to chat with a level eight.

From a distance, it seemed that their well-developed Charm skill was being put to good use, deflecting and distracting attention, sending people away without getting them mad. It would take them a while to get through the whole crowd, though. For which I was grateful.

Yeah, I wasn't in the mood to talk to them, either. I was still thinking about Cutter. The rest of the group were handling it in their own ways. Felicia was particularly distraught, and Kyle was being a rock for her. They had withdrawn from the feast as quickly as they could. Cloridan had withdrawn in another way, hitting the booze harder than he had for a while. He'd fallen in with Reynard and his group of hunter friends, who were all drinking heavily.

It wasn't like the feast didn't have an undercurrent of sadness. The villagers had lost one of their own, and they hadn't been anything less than respectful at the news of Cutter's death. Toasts were given to the fallen, and expressions of deep sorrow were made. I won't say it grated on me, but I did get tired of it. I wanted to go home. Home to Sydney, of course, but Talnier would do in a pinch.

Looking for a quiet place to enjoy a private drink, I should have realized that I wasn't the only one who wanted to get away. Walking around the curve of a tree trunk, I almost stumbled over Yoroly.

She was sitting on the edge of a platform that overlooked . . . darkness. It wasn't entirely black; there were some specks of light down below. They must have been luminous flowers, but from here they were just tiny points of light. Like looking down on the stars. Yoroly looked over her shoulder as I approached.

"You," she said. From anyone else, I'd say her tone was sour, but from her, it sounded pretty neutral.

"Me," I agreed. I sat down next to her. Unlike her, I made sure that I was sitting next to the railing support, which I put an arm around. It was a long drop into darkness. "Not enjoying the fruits of your labor? You were the one who fixed the problem, after all."

"Bah!" Yoroly snorted. "I hate them, and they hate me. It's simpler for everybody if we keep any foolish notions of respect or gratitude out of it."

"You did risk your life to save them," I pointed out. I wasn't sure where I was going with this; the simple statement seemed quite likely to provoke her.

"I'm too old to find another village at this point," she said. "It's too late to change, we're stuck with each other."

She sounded almost smug as she gave that pronouncement.

"That being the case, it seems to me you'd want to build some bridges with the rest of the village. Unless you like being alone."

"Of course I like being alone!" she said incredulously. "I tolerate the brat because she cleans the place, but I could give two figs for the rest of them."

"You're not worried they'll throw you out?"

"They wouldn't dare," she said, and this time she was definitely smug. "Especially not after today. They know how much they need me. What about you, though?"

"What about me?" I asked glumly.

"You're a Champion," she pointed out. "You're a big important muckety-muck from the Kingdom. You've got elves hanging on to talk to *you*, instead of the other way round."

"I didn't want any of that, though," I said. "I may have worked towards some of it, but that was just because Talnier was being ruled so *incompetently*. Someone needed to step up—once things have settled down, I can be replaced."

"Yeah, that's *exactly* how it always works," Yoroly said sarcastically. "No one is ever interested in important people, and they always get to go off and retire as soon as they like. How'd you get away from the feast, though?"

I shrugged. "Just about everybody got meeting me out of their system at the last feast —the one you weren't invited to—and the elves are stealing all the attention."

Yoroly opened her mouth to reply, but we were interrupted.

"I don't believe that 'stealing' is the appropriate word to use when the attention is unwanted."

The words came from behind me, spoken in dulcet tones in a female voice. I hadn't heard her speak until now, but I knew before I looked over my shoulder that I'd see the elven lady, Culathidae, standing there.

"I guess I didn't slip away entirely unnoticed," I said.

"We are very observant," she agreed, stepping closer to the edge of the platform to put herself more easily in view. "This is a more pleasant place to converse than a forest trail, but we had hoped for a private conversation, rather than a public spectacle."

"I should go, then," Yoroly groused.

"There is no need, Mistress Theurge. When I said private, I meant merely quiet. I do not expect Lady Kandis to divulge any of her secrets."

I sighed. "Why are you here?" I asked. "I thought that Morthanial was the one who did all the talking."

She shrugged. "We have worked together for many years and long ago established who was most suited for which roles. He is, as you say, doing most of the talking, freeing me to talk to you."

"Lucky me. So what did you want to ask me about?"

"I am interested in whatever you are willing to talk about," Culathidae said. "Whatever interests a Chosen is an insight into the mind of the god that chose her. Such insights are keenly sought by my nation. To start with, though, what brings you to the Great Wild?"

"A few things," I said carefully. "I was told by a Council member that if I showed up, I might be able to help them with a problem that they weren't willing to tell me about."

"Elders!" Yoroly snorted. "Can't decide on a tea blend without three hours of discussion and four hours of sulking from the losers."

"I don't think that's a bad thing," Culathidae said, looking at her. "Passions run high in the beast-folk, and in days gone by the tribes would have settled things with knives, rather than words."

"They still run high," Yoroly replied, giving the words a sarcastic edge. "Even among the Elders, who should know better, no one can say anything approaching the truth, just in case it offends someone."

"I am surprised that you do not fill that role yourself," Culathidae said.

"Bah! I am older than this village's representative," Yoroly admitted. "And a damn sight smarter, too. That's why I didn't want anything to do with the job."

"You've worked hard not to get it," I said with amusement.

"Don't think it was that easy! Remember, the job of the representative is to *leave*. There was some that wanted me to take it, regardless of what I wanted."

"I am glad that you have found a place in your village that suits both you and the greater Tribe," Culathidae said smoothly.

Yoroly glared at her. The constant politeness was getting on her nerves. What's more, I think that Culathidae knew it. She turned back to me.

"So you are only travelling to the Tribal Gather?" she asked.

"Well, it depends on what this mysterious problem is," I hedged. "And having come all this way, it would be a shame not to press a bit farther and see the Grove."

She nodded. "It is a sight to see, and not one vouchsafed to most mortals." Ignoring the effect that word had on Yoroly and me, she blithely continued speaking.

"You will not find our border as easy to cross as that of the Tribes, however. It would be easiest if an invitation were to be extended. I could arrange for someone to contact you at the Gather?"

"That would be useful," I said. "This invitation would be coming from your government?"

"The Administratum, yes. I am reasonably confident that one would be extended to a Chosen. It would help if there was a particular task you wished to accomplish?"

Don't mention the portal, I told myself. "I've had a few hints," I said carefully, Charm doing its best to make sure I didn't give anything away. "I did have some well wishes to pass on to someone's sister."

"From a runaway? Best not to mention that to the Administratum. I shall tell them that you wish to visit on Chosen business."

"You're not concerned with . . . runaways?" I asked.

She shook her head. "They are not a part of my duty," she told me. "If there was one in front of me . . . I would be rewarded if I brought them in, but I doubt that it would be worth my trouble."

"He wasn't lying when he told me there were hunters, though, was he?"

"There are hunters," she confirmed. "There are not many, though, and they move slowly. To allay concerns from the mortal nations, they make sure to submit to whatever border controls that are in place. The Great Wild is one of the few places where we can move freely."

"A courtesy that is not returned," Yoroly put in.

Culathidae inclined her head. "It is not up to me, of course," she said. "I will merely note that, as we have seen very recently, the world is not fair."

We left early, despite Cloridan's aching head. Felicity gave him something that, while it didn't stop him from complaining, seemed to give him enough energy to put one boot in front of the other.

"Where are we headed next?" I asked Reynard.

"Singing Feather Haven," he said. "Don't look at me like that, I didn't choose the name. Bunch of birds living there."

"Bird-kin, you mean," I said.

"And birds. You don't get cats living with cat-kin, and most of the other types are the same, but birds seem to get along with bird-kin just fine."

He looked back at me. He was leading the way, but he was far more at ease in this terrain than any of us and could afford to take his eyes off the ground.

"I hope this delay isn't too disruptive to your plans."

I shrugged. "It just means we'll be longer getting back. I can send word back to Talnier when we get to the Gather that we've been delayed."

He nodded and looked back to the path, seemingly reassured.

"Do you think it's disrupted any of your mistress's plans?" I asked.

If the question bothered him, he didn't show it. "If she has any, she didn't tell me," he said. "I wouldn't rule it out, but her ability to arrange things out here has gotten to be limited."

Is it, though? I wondered. She had Reynard; how many others did she have? How many more of those amulets were there? Reflexively, I checked his. It was still disconnected from wherever it was getting controlled from.

"If you're keeping an eye on me," I asked, "just how are you getting word back to the Countess?"

"I had some contacts in Talnier," he told me. "I'm sure you'll forgive me if I don't tell you who they are. I assume I'll be contacted at the Gather. It's a big place; it wouldn't be surprising if she had agents there."

That might be true. She could be relying on the link that I had severed, but she might have agents out here already. One of them could replace the amulet instead of sending him back to get it reconnected. I'd have to watch out for that.

"Come on," Reynard said. "Let's pick up the pace; I want to be drinking nectar by nightfall."

LOOSE TONGUES

Singing Feather Haven was not a treetop village, despite being populated by different strains of bird-folk. Given that bird-kin couldn't *fly*, that made sense, but I was still surprised. I suppose that it was the influence of the squirrel-kin in Mossridge Gather who put so many of their buildings in the trees. Climbing *was* something they shared with their nominal cousins.

The village was built in a wide clearing. I don't know if it was due to the soil not being suitable or if the village had cleared out the trees long ago. Seeing the evening sky was a huge relief after clambering over roots in semi-darkness for an entire day. The village itself was comprised of small wooden buildings with thatched roofs. It could have been a particularly picturesque English village, if it weren't for the flowers.

They were everywhere, and not neatly contained in pots and carefully tilled gardens. They grew on climbing vines that covered the houses, on what were either large shrubs or small trees, and they covered every unused piece of ground. Different kinds of flowers, a huge variety of blossoms.

It looked fantastic . . . and then I remembered it was winter. It wasn't that cold, but weren't flowers supposed to bloom in the spring?

"Hang on a minute," I said, pausing and frowning. Reynard waved me on.

"Just keep walking, it will become clear in a minute," he said.

I did as he said, and as I did, I could feel the temperature rising. Just a few steps and the chill of the winter air was gone. I started thinking of losing a few clothing items.

"It's a natural effect of . . . one of the flowers," he told me. "I forget which. It's a small effect on its own, but when there's as many as there are here, it's springtime all year round."

"It's really nice," I said, not sure if I was talking about the temperature effect or the village in general. Thus far, the villages we'd seen all seemed to be competing for the title of "Most Magical Fantasy Village." The houses all looked adorable, and I could tell from the scents wafting towards us as we approached that this place was going to be a delightfully aromatic stopover.

"Birds aren't noted for their sense of smell," Reynard observed. "Some of the more sensitive Tribes find this place a bit much." He pushed on ahead, leading us towards a group of villagers that was already forming in the main square.

Villages in the Great Wild worked a little differently from the villages in the Kingdom, I was learning. "Tribal" was a term that got slapped on most of the organization here, and it wasn't meant as a synonym for primitive.

Everything here was family-based, rather than the more commercially orientated setup I was used to. You couldn't walk into a village, stay a night at an inn, and then wander out again. You were a guest of the whole village. At least, you *needed* to be a guest of the village, if you wanted to stay. They didn't let just any freeloader show up.

Reynard wasn't just leading me from village to village. His recommendation of my group as decent people was what opened the doors. Naturally, as guests, we couldn't be expected to pay for food and accommodation. Equally naturally, we couldn't allow the burden of hosting us to go uncompensated.

Negotiating that little social dance was a form of bargaining that I hadn't encountered, where the object was to pay *more* than the other party would allow. Again, Reynard handled it. I watched. His performance was good enough, as these things went. Now that I'd seen it a few times, I could probably manage to do it better, even with the handicap of not being known to these people.

It didn't take long to get it all sorted out. There would be a feast to welcome us, and we would pay for a portion of it. Quarters would be made ready for us in some spare houses that the village maintained for just such an occasion.

"What happens if one side gains the advantage in that little reverse bargain?" I asked Reynard when they were done.

He shrugged. "I've never tried . . . it's always gone the same way in each village; after a while you get used to knowing how it's going to turn out."

He thought about it. "I suppose that if you paid too much money, the village leader would owe you a debt of honor. Not the friendliest thing to do, but if you had something you wanted him to give you in return . . ."

"Seems a bit of a roundabout way of doing things," I said disparagingly. I didn't mind paying a bit extra if it was going to make people feel grateful, but if all they felt was burdened, then no thanks. I turned my attention to other matters. "Are we going to have a feast every night on this trip? It's getting a little old."

Reynard snorted. "It's two days to the next village, so you'll get a break when we camp. But yeah, you're kind of a big deal. They're going to want to show off for you."

"Hmmmp," I muttered. "I might be *more* impressed by a quiet, private dinner."

Reynard chuckled again. "Trust me, you don't want to miss *this* feast."

"Why not?"

"Because this village's specialty is honey mead," he said. "All of the trade done with it is locked up with other Tribes, so the only way to get a taste is to be a guest."

I narrowed my eyes. "That wouldn't be the reason it's on our itinerary, is it? Cloridan might appreciate the chance to get drunk, but I don't have unlimited time here."

"It's on the way, trust me," he assured me. "It's useful in other ways as well. Since they have such good trade relations, they get news a lot faster than most villages. Breaking out the mead might help convince some of them to share that news."

"If you say so," I said. "I'd better let Cloridan know he's getting drunk with a purpose."

I had to admit that I had my doubts about the honey mead. The commercial versions I'd had back home had been . . . nice enough in their own way, but nothing to write home about. I'd known a few people who had raved about the special home-brewed mead that they'd gotten from some friend, but that was an urban legend as far as I was concerned.

This made me think that they were telling the truth. Sweet but not cloying, it had a richness and bite to it that I wasn't used to experiencing. And the aroma! It wasn't any particular flower that I could detect, but the floral bouquet was exquisite.

I had to watch my consumption very carefully. In this world, both taste and potency were linked to the Crafting total of the brewer or vintner.

Alcohol content had *something* to do with it, but a single well-crafted beer could put a strong man in his cups. This was . . .

> **[Identification]: Celestial Nectar Mead – Quality: Perfect – Properties: Intoxicating**

This was the good stuff, I guessed. The rest of the night was a bit blurred. My level gave me some protection against the effects, but my Strength was lacking. I spent most of the feast talking with the village leader. I did ask about rumors of humans travelling in the forest, but most of my night was spent seeing if there was a way to unlock a trade deal.

That was some good stuff, I thought to myself when I woke up in the morning. I winced in anticipation of the hangover. I *may* have overindulged; it was difficult not to when the mead was flowing so freely.

The hangover . . . had failed to materialize. Very good stuff.

I got dressed and headed out for breakfast. It was also a communal affair, perhaps in our honor, but it was much less formal than the feast. People were just picking up some flatbread wrapped around honey and cheese. Some of the villagers were sporting obvious hangovers.

Not hangover-free then, just less, I noted. Still worth getting a shipment.

I hadn't had much luck with the mayor, but there had to be a way. Maybe the Elder at the Gathering would be more disposed towards trading with humans.

Because of the decentralized, flat command structure of the Tribes, I couldn't get a straight answer about who was responsible for making decisions about trading the mead. Was it the ones who made it, the mayor, or the Elder? No one thus far was prepared to say. I did, at least, get the name of their Elder. Once I reached the capital, I could sound him out, at least determine what faction he was in.

Reynard was the second to last to show up to breakfast. He was one of the ones showing signs of overindulgence, but he seemed alert enough.

"Ready to go?" he asked. I nodded. We hadn't unpacked much, so packing had been quickly accomplished.

"As soon as Cloridan gets up," I said. "Did you hear anything interesting?"

"He wasn't far behind me," he said, picking up his own wrapped flatbread. "And yeah. I did hear something."

He chewed on his breakfast for a bit before continuing. "There's a rumor about a bunch of armed humans hanging around Hidden Hollow."

"Another village, I presume." He nodded in response. "Is it near here?"

"Nowhere near," he told me. "Five days travel? And I've never been there. Hidden Hollow isn't friendly towards outsiders."

"You mean humans? Or the other Tribes?" I asked.

Reynard started to answer, but then stopped. "I'm not sure," he admitted and called one of the villagers over. As he asked the bird-kin the same question, I noticed Cloridan stagger over. I pointed at the breakfast table and made running motions.

Meanwhile, the villager had had a chance to think about the question. Based on the red and black feathers in his hair, I thought he might be a robin-kin.

"Hidden Hollow?" he said slowly. "That's badger clan. Tight-knit group, standoffish. I wouldn't call them unfriendly, though."

"What about to humans?" Reynard asked.

"Oh, they don't like humans. At least not humans from your Kingdom. They might make an exception for Tribal humans, I'm not sure."

"And yet, they're hosting a bunch of humans?" I asked doubtfully.

"Oh, I heard that rumor too!" the beast-kin said. "Weird isn't it? I never would have thought it of them. Worrying, too, I suppose."

"Why worrying?" Reynard asked.

"Oh, any time a Tribe does something out of character, there has to be a *reason* for it," the villager explained. "For a whole village to change like that, the reason has to be pretty big, big enough to affect other villages."

He frowned for a moment before his face cleared. "But I suppose that's the sort of thing that the Elders have to worry about! Not our business!" He wandered off to get another helping. Reynard shook his head at the beast-kin's back.

"I suppose it's not that different from an ordinary townsfolk leaving bigger questions for their lord, but it still seems strange to not care about the bigger picture."

"That's an adventurer's viewpoint, all right," I said lightly. "But do you get to say that when you've left all *your* big-picture concerns to your patron?"

He gave me a sour look. "I get *paid* to do that," he said. "Speaking of, do you want to detour to check out these rumors?"

I didn't have to think about it.

"No," I said. "We're not here to find Hector. We're here to ask for help catching him. We can get Tinidan to update Talnier when we get to the Gathering Place."

I could beat Hector in any sort of social situation, but out here in the forest, his own strengths came into play. If I did confront him in this forest, it would be with the backing of half the Tribes. Actually, strike that, never mind *backing*. I'd need them out front, to do the actual stabbing.

I looked at Felicia and Kyle, standing ready to go, and at Cloridan, hurriedly consuming his flatbread. Yoroly had stayed with her village, and the elves had gone back to the Grove.

"Let's get going," I said. "We've got a lot of ground to cover before we can get to the real work."

WAYLAİD

The attack came in the middle of the night, during Felicia and Kyle's watch. We were standing watch in pairs, partly because I didn't trust Reynard to stand watch alone, and also because four eyes were better than two.

Cloridan took his watch alone. His partner had been Cutter.

I don't know if they chose to attack during Felicia's watch, or if they just attacked us when they found us. "Eliminate the Healer first" was a pretty common tactic. Did they shoot at Felicia first because she was a Healer, or because she was on watch? Or did they wait until they could fulfill two objectives with one attack?

All I knew was that I woke up to her screaming. When I wriggled out of my tent, the first thing I saw was Felicia with an arrow in her.

"Felicia!" I shouted. Then I berated myself for wasting time. Kyle was standing over Felicia, and I could see a few arrows stuck in his shield. Another arrow was sticking out of his thigh. I couldn't see any attackers, but in the forest at night, visibility didn't extend farther than the clearing we were in.

"Eyes!" I called out. Following my own instruction, I closed my eyes and cast Light at maximum brightness, about twenty feet over our campfire. Slitting my eyes against the glare, I opened them again and tried to find the rest of our party.

Reynard was there, looking a lot more alert and ready than I felt. He had his bow out, ready to fire back at wherever the arrows were coming from. My light seemed to have caused a pause in the assault, so he was stuck looking for targets.

Cloridan had his back to a tree. A single arrow was stuck in the roots near his feet. He seemed to have an idea where the attackers were, but he was pinned down.

"Go!" I shouted, casting Greater Invisibility on him. Only I could see that he nodded and slipped out from behind his cover. I dashed over to Felicia. It was the safest place; Kyle could cover us both with his shield.

"I can't help her!" he exclaimed. "I've got to keep this . . ."

"I've got it," I assured him. Hopefully, that was true. Felicia hadn't needed help healing when we were in the dungeons.

Right now, she was breathing heavily. One hand was on the arrow, the other was fumbling for her dagger.

"Barbed . . ." she gasped. "Need to get it out before . . ."

I nodded and pulled out my own dagger. Hopefully Weapon Mastery covered impromptu surgery, because I wasn't sure I could do this unassisted. There was a slit on either side of the arrow entry point, indicating where the blades of the arrowhead had sunk in. I went to slip my dagger in and cut the arrow free, but Felicia stopped me.

"Wait . . ." she said. Then, "Pain Relief." She cast the spell and instantly relaxed.

You didn't cast that before now? I thought, but went to work without saying anything. It wasn't pretty, but I got it out pretty quickly. Felicia grabbed for the arrow as I drew it out, and looked at the head.

"Poison," she said. I got out one of the alchemical antidotes and gave it to her even as she cast her healing. As I watched, her wound started to close up.

Throughout all of this, we were uninterrupted by arrows.

"I think they've gone," Kyle said, still maintaining a vigilant watch against the darkness.

"No deaths," I said, "So no notifications. If it's an Intrigue, it must be only the opening salvo, so there's no notification for that either."

Felicia finished healing herself and moved over to repeat the process on Kyle. His arrow was stuck in his armor, not his flesh. It had cut him, but not deeply, and she was able to easily heal it. He got an antidote potion as well.

It took a few moments more of us standing around nervously before Cloridan emerged from the forest and waved at me. I cancelled the invisibility spell.

"I think I found where they were shooting from," he said. "You want to take a look?" he asked Reynard.

"Sure," the Ranger said. Glancing at me for permission, he headed off with Cloridan.

"You can, uh, probably turn that down now," Kyle said, pointing at my Light spell.

"Oh yeah," I agreed. I kept the spell on, but I turned the light down until it was just enough to light up our clearing. "I wonder if we should have camped with it on?"

"It would have made it difficult to sleep," Felicia pointed out, "And possibly attracted beasts."

"Good point," I agreed. We maintained a watchful silence until the boys came back.

"There were three of them, and they were Tribals," Reynard said without preamble. "That's about all I can tell."

"I could have guessed that much from the arrows," Kyle said.

"Can they tell us anything?" I asked, glancing at one of them.

> **[Identification]: Tribal War Arrow – Quality: Excellent – Properties: Accurate, Poisoned**

"Not much," I concluded.

"War arrows," Reynard said. "This wasn't a random encounter. They don't use those arrows for hunting."

"More allies of Hector?" I asked.

"Hidden Hollow is a fair way away, but they could have sent out hunting parties," he said. "We might be able to get these arrows identified at the Gathering."

"We already did, though?" I asked.

"Specialist crafters will get more information from an Identify on things within their specialty," he told me. "Or they might have just seen this design before."

I nodded my understanding. "Can you track them?" I asked.

"I *could*," Reynard said. "They weren't so good as to leave *no* tracks, and they're not far ahead. I don't think that's a good idea, though."

"Why not?"

"They're good enough at woodcraft that they might be able to lose me at some point. And following someone who knows you might be following them is just asking to be led into a trap or an ambush."

"Right, that sounds bad. What are we going to do, then?"

"Anybody feel like going back to bed?" Reynard asked. There were rueful chuckles all around. "It's only a few hours until dawn. We might as well get a head start on tomorrow's travel."

The inhabitants of Mistwood Enclave, the next village we arrived at, were very interested to hear about the attack on us. Interested, angered, and alarmed. They assured me that patrols would be sent out, and that we would be safe here.

Unfortunately, that was about all the help they could give.

"I doubt these criminals will set hoof in our territory," the Chief told me. "But the forest is wide, and there are many routes to travel that do not pass through us. I wish I could say that I could trample these miscreants for you, but a successful outcome is unlikely."

I smiled and nodded. I'd already come to terms with the lack of control that the Tribes exerted on their territory. I let Charm handle the same sort of meet-and-greet ritual that we'd seen at the other villages. There was a more important question in my mind that I needed to get Felicia in a Privacy bubble to answer.

"What are these people?" I asked her when I finally got the chance. "Are they centaurs and satyrs?"

"I don't think so," Felicia said. "I don't know what those are. They're deer-kin and pony-kin. The deer-kin are—"

"The ones with two legs, I get it," I said. "Though why they have two legs, and the . . . pony-kin have four . . ."

Felicia shrugged. "That's just how pony-kin are," she said.

"Right," I said. Answers reached, I dismissed the bubble and we rejoined the party.

The inhabitants of Mistwood did look a lot like those old Greek legends, but there were some important differences. For one thing, they were fully clothed, which came as a great relief for me once I'd remembered how the Greeks had depicted them.

Aside from the clothes, the deer-kin looked identical to how satyrs were generally depicted. Furry legs with hooves, and horns. The pony-kin, though . . . technically, they looked like centaurs. Human upper half, horse (pony) lower half. Centaurs, though, were huge. As big as a man riding on a horse, which is where the idea came from as far as I knew. The pony-kin . . . were not. All up, they were only as tall as a man, perhaps a little shorter on average. Their horse body was appropriately sized, about three or four feet off the ground. They looked . . . cute. Especially because they were clothed, including the bottom half.

They looked appropriately fierce, though, when they were talking about finding whoever was engaging in banditry nearby. I approved.

Naturally, they held a feast to welcome us. As before, Reynard negotiated for us to pay a portion of the cost.

"Not going to complain about feasting this time, I'll wager," Reynard snarked at me when it was announced.

"I do prefer it to an arrow in the night," I admitted. "This is the last stop before the Gather, though, right? Do you think we'll have to worry about any more ambushes?"

"Worry about, yes. But I think it will be fine. I'll let their hunters know our route out and they'll sweep it before we go through. It should stop anyone from setting up an ambush."

"Unless these were the ones who ambushed us." It was a bit paranoid to think that, but getting shot at in the night will do that to you.

"It wasn't," he assured me. "They weren't familiar with the arrows that we collected." He held up a hand to forestall me as I took a breath. "*Part* of that was for them to show me the arrows they *do* use. They're not alike."

I nodded and wiped away one layer of the suspicions that had been building up. Coming from Reynard, the information was suspect, but it checked out. Had the village wanted me dead, they would have turned me away when I arrived—or shot me dead at the entrance. Attacking me after welcoming me in would be a much bigger breach of . . . their honor, I guess the term was.

The feast went ahead. The main difference in the food was that it was lighter on the meat. Lots of fruits and leafy greens. They *did* eat meat, just less of it. How that tracked with their presumed origins, I didn't know.

I was distracted from thoughts of pony-kin evolution by the post-feast entertainment. Which was dancing. Lots of loud, rhythmic dancing.

The houses in Mistwood Enclave were all on the ground. No tree-climbing for hoofed villagers. They were pretty nimble, so they could probably have managed it, but they clearly preferred it on the ground. The feast had been held in a long hall with a wooden floor. Once the dishes had been cleared away, they started clearing away the tables, to make room for the performance.

I got to stay where I was; the head table remained after the others were removed, looking over the dancers. About half the village was on the floor, the other half crammed around the sides of the room. Then they started to dance.

The style of it reminded me of Riverdance, but it was also a little bit like tap. The stomp of their hooves on the floor was about halfway between the *thud* of a foot and the *clickity-click* of a tap shoe. I quickly realized that the point of it was less about the movements, and more about the intricate patterns of hoofbeats that resulted.

I was impressed. It was impressive. I paid close attention, intending to show an illusion of it to people when I got back to Talnier. The energy of it all was intoxicating, and I got swept up in the rhythms.

It was just as well that it was a performance and not something I was expected (or able) to join in. I yelled my approval with the rest of the onlookers and congratulated the dance leaders. There was a bit of min-gling, making sure everyone got a chance to shake hands with the Chosen. Then bed. It was a big day tomorrow. We'd finally reach the Gathering Place.

They made doors sturdy in Talnier. They needed to. Talnier had more than its fair share of adventurers and they tended to have higher levels than most ordinary townsfolk. You needed good, mana-enriched wood. You needed a craftsman with as high a skill as you could find, as high a Finesse as you could find, and as high a level as you could find. Otherwise, your door was likely to be accidentally broken.

It meant that the door put up a modicum of resistance when Koenig put his axe through it.

"Down on the floor if you want to live!" he yelled. "Face to the ground!"

Most of the suspects thought to be in this building were noncombatants. There were a few adventurers, but no mages that they knew about. That fit with the caution of their adversary—mages could see magic being cast, even if they didn't know what it was.

"Eyes down!" he yelled again, rushing into the room. It was a basic precaution against mages. Some mages could cast without words, and some without gestures, but very few could cast offensive magic without looking at their target. Yelling only accomplished so much. It was very hard for someone to *not* look at the large shouting man threatening to kill them. But everyone who managed it was someone that Koenig didn't have to worry about casting a spell at him.

He hadn't worried about someone *physically* attacking him since he'd achieved level six. Most people, adventurers or not, only reached those giddying heights towards the end of their lives. The physical body *behind* their enhanced abilities was starting to falter. Not so for Koenig. He still had ten years, he estimated, before he started to lose his condition.

Probably enough time to reach level seven, if he worked at it. He had less time for delving nowadays.

It didn't seem anyone here was going to put up a fight. Most of them were cowering, defeated before the fight had begun. A few of them—adventurers—were tensed, waiting for a chance to run or fight. That was just habit on their part, though. Those were the ones who *knew* him, at least by reputation. They knew they didn't stand a chance at either.

Koenig glared around the room, keeping them all in place with his Intimidation. There was no point in interrogating these victims yet. Given time, they might be able to convince them that they *were* victims, but first he would have to find . . .

Ah, there it was. Koenig stepped over and reached for the amulet hanging on the wall. Before he could grab it, though, a dagger flashed into his field of vision and bisected it, burying itself in the wall.

"Hey! That's mine!" he roared, turning to look where the dagger had come from. His deputy, Nadine Lagacé, was giving him a sour look. Anybody who had been looking—and he had been—would have told you that she wasn't there a moment before.

"Think about what you just said, Chief," she said in an unimpressed tone.

Koenig's eyes narrowed as he tried to work out her meaning. What was wrong with what he'd just said? The amulet *was* his, it was . . . wait. Wasn't it the object that they were here for? The object they were looking to find? It was . . .

"Dammit," he said, looking down at his own amulet, the one provided by Lady Kandis. It was glowing red, a sign that his mind had been altered. Green meant that it was fending off an attack; it turned blue if the attack penetrated. Once the attack was over, the amulet turned red and stayed that way until it touched an amulet that wasn't lit.

Nadine's amulet was unlit. Their enemy had been unable to target her behind her Stealth skill. Koenig sighed and held his amulet out for a reset.

"Oh, no," Nadine said, smirking. "You know the procedure. You need to get checked out before we reset you."

Koenig groaned. Getting checked out was so tedious. He would have to go over all his mission-critical memories and figure out which ones had been changed.

"At least this bunch is clear," he said hopefully. Nadine shook her head.

"It will be, once you've searched all of them," she said. "Don't miss any-one," she added, fading into the background as he watched. At her level of skill, Stealth was almost as good as invisibility, and Perception had never been one of his strong skills.

Koenig sighed again. It was a pain, but the enemy *might* have started putting more than one amulet in a cell. He started with the adventurers. Naturally, he disarmed them first, but what he was really checking for was more amulets. Nadine, he assumed, kept a watch over him to make sure he didn't miss anything.

Once they were cleared, he could hand them over to the guards waiting outside.

"The town guard appreciates the Guild's assistance in this matter," their sergeant said formally once he was done.

"You'd better," Koenig said without heat. He held up his still-glowing amulet. The guard stiffened.

"Are you all right?" he asked cautiously. He knew what the light meant.

"I think so," Koenig said. "Nadine stopped it before they could make many changes."

The sergeant nodded slowly. Lady Kandis hadn't been able to provide enough amulets for everyone, which was why Koenig was the one smashing down doors and attracting attention. Not that the amulets were enough to *stop* the magic of their adversary, but they did slow it down, and they *did* alert the rest of them.

Koenig knew that his red light would go in the sergeant's report, which would be cross-referenced with *Nadine's* report and matched with Koenig's eventual memory-checking session. All part of the procedures dreamed up by Lady Kandis. Tedious, but they just might work.

"At least you got to do the exciting bit," the sergeant ventured. Koenig snorted in response. Kicking in the door had been a moment of fun, but no one inside had put up any kind of a fight.

According to the records Koenig had read, Mind Mages would normally wield their victims like puppets, forcing them to fight without regard for themselves. It made for a dangerous fight, particularly when the Guild had been trying to keep the victims alive.

This one, who might or might not be the Countess Rankin, did things differently. Koenig was fairly sure that this lot, once they'd been tediously interviewed and processed, would probably turn out to have some memory planted which led them to group up and hide in this safehouse.

And that was it. Some of them would go out, carrying the amulet to meet with others who could be influenced in turn. They did weapon training in the backyard. But mostly, they waited. Not knowing what they were waiting for, which was fresh orders from their master, transmitted through the amulet.

As adversaries went, the Countess—or whoever—was proving to be as boring as she was careful.

"If you're looking for excitement, you could always join the Guild," he said. "Now, if you'll excuse me, I've got to get escorted back by my minder."

He stepped back inside to find Nadine, fully visible, staring at the two halves of the amulet. Reflexively, his eyes flicked to her unlit amulet.

"It's busted, right?" he asked. Dungeon artifacts were tough, but between Nadine's skills and the enchantments on her throwing knives, the amulet hadn't stood a chance.

"Just two inert lumps of silversteel," Nadine agreed. "You get to take it back, of course."

"Of course," Koenig agreed. Procedure. Dungeon artifacts could be tricky, and this one was already faking its Identification tag. Best that it only be handled by someone already compromised.

"How many of them do you think there are?" Nadine wondered.

Koenig shook his head.

"It might not be a number," he said. "If it *is* the Countess, and she's using her dungeon to make them, then she can make as many as she needs, as long as she stays put. The hard part would be getting them into town."

They were already checking for them at the gates, and Koenig had heard that Anchorbury was instituting a similar procedure. Naturally, those carrying them didn't know they were doing so.

"Isn't she cut off from her dungeon, though? I heard that she lost it after the Oakway debacle."

"I don't know what the situation is there, right now," Koenig admitted. "I passed our suspicions up to leadership, of course. It could be that she lost administrative control, but they didn't think to deny her access to the dungeon itself."

"Why would that matter?" Nadine asked. Then her expression changed, as she answered her own question. Her voice dropped to nearly nothing. "You think she's a *Dungeon Master*?" she whispered intensely.

Koenig cast about with his own senses. The guards had left, leaving them alone in the house. Nadine was better at sensing than he was, but it would be remiss of him not to check.

"Maybe," he whispered back. "Or maybe she's just the puppet of a Dungeon Thrall."

The two terms were some of the deepest-held secrets of the Guild. Having a noble *know* about them was a disaster, only slightly allayed by the possibility that the Countess was a secretive psychopath who hadn't *told* any of her peers.

As an organization, the Guild strove for egalitarianism. Dungeon Masters were the antithesis of that, which was why they were forbidden, and knowledge of them was actively suppressed. Lady Kandis was an extraordinary exception, finding out about it on her own. Normally, someone who did that would be co-opted into the higher levels of the Guild, or killed, but Lady Kandis was exceptional in more than one sense.

She was, on her own, a surprisingly effective force for egalitarianism. Even before her nature as a Champion had come out, Koenig had been reluctant to snuff her out. The benefits of not doing so were now becoming apparent. In this small town, Lady Kandis had erased noble privileges that had been built up over decades. The King was openly questioning whether he should use Talnier as an example.

It was no surprise that the nobles were fighting back, but this . . . this subtle infiltration was a surprise. Koenig hadn't thought the nobles capable of it. Perhaps they weren't.

"A Dungeon Thrall?" Nadine whispered. "How would that work?"

"It's possible that the Countess isn't the one with the Mind Magic," Koenig murmured. "If a Dungeon Thrall had the skill, it would be available to the dungeon."

Koenig didn't think he'd need to say more than that, and he could see Nadine taking in the possibilities. In some ways, thralldom was an even more tempting state than Dungeon Master. Having your soul absorbed by the dungeon did forever limit your ambitions to the space enclosed by it. But.

Immortality was a hell of a consolation prize.

If the Guild had allowed it, had allowed the possibility to even be known, adventurers or their dependents would have been lining up for it. The critically injured, the broken, the aged, they would have all jumped at the chance to lose their physical bodies.

The Guild knew the other part of the secret, though. Immortal you might be, but you would change. The implacable hostility to mortal kind would seep into you, and you would become a much greater threat to anyone delving into your domain.

Dungeons had rules, but intelligent, malevolent thralls could bend or break those rules. The Guild hid the knowledge as best they could, but people did get absorbed, either deliberately or by accident. When that happened, the only recourse was to destroy the core.

"Another possibility is that the local Guild Master is compromised," he said. "That's going to be Guild Master Voight's main concern."

Nadine nodded in understanding. "She did it with Reynard," she agreed.

"Exactly. Investigations, as they say, are proceeding. Now let's get back to headquarters. I've got an extremely tedious interview to get through."

THE GATHERING

My first impression of the beast-kin city was that . . . it wasn't one. Certainly not by my standards: There wasn't a skyscraper to be seen unless you counted the trees, which I didn't, no matter how many people they had living in them.

Even by more local standards, I had a hard time seeing how it would qualify. There was no wall, which was a requirement for any Latorran settlement. No densely packed housing, no cobbled streets, no *smell*.

Granted, Latorran settlements didn't smell as bad as I'd been expecting from my knowledge of old-timey hygiene. The main difference was the lack of horses. Latora did have them, but they relied on carts much less, since a couple of men could carry almost as much, faster. Men, mostly, didn't shit in the street, so there was much less manure sitting in the open air. Not *none*, not an acceptable amount, but less.

The Gathering Place—that was another thing it didn't have, a *name*—didn't have that. There were no streets for carts, no horses to shit on them. It must have been hell for industry, but I supposed that men—or beast-kin—could manage travelling over the root-covered forest floor just fine.

There were a few things that distinguished this place from the other villages I'd passed through. Size, for one. It was difficult to tell in the dim light, and with all the trees in the way, but the villages had been small clusters of dwellings huddled together around a central point. You might not have been able to see the entire settlement, but only because your line of sight was blocked. This settlement extended . . . I don't know how far, but we were nowhere near the central grove.

There was also an increase in density. Unlike the villages, there wasn't the same consensus on what sort of houses to build. I saw doors leading into subterranean burrows, tree houses, and regular stone buildings, all jumbled up together. The trees were on the large side here, and people made the most of it, stacking dwellings against the trunk. It wasn't apartment-building dense, but it held a lot more people than the villages could boast.

So I didn't doubt that we were in a city, that we'd reached our destination. It just turned out that our destination was a little vaguer than I'd originally thought.

"With no walls, there's no gate," I mused aloud. "With no gate, how do we know we've arrived? How do *they* know we've arrived?"

International delegates at home never had this problem, I surmised. Everything was arranged in advance, from the hotel they stayed at to their itinerary. They would be met as soon as they entered the country and shadowed every step of the way, by the media if no one else.

"Someone will be watching," Reynard said. He waved vaguely in the direction we were going. "Just keep heading towards the center and someone will come and find you."

It seemed awfully lackadaisical to me, but it turned out to work that way. Barely five hundred meters of travel later, we ran into someone who was waiting for us. The long ears poking out of her blonde hair made her one of the easier types to identify.

"Greetings, La—Councillor Hammond," she said politely, bowing. "Welcome to the Place of the Gathering. My name is Lira. I, uh—if it pleases you, I am to be your guide."

"Just Kandis is fine," I said easily. "Do you work for Elder Tinidan, then?"

She bowed again. "Yes, I have that honor. I am filling in for Anas as an apprentice in his absence."

I nodded. Anas was, of course, in Talnier, serving as the Tribe's voice to the Council. I was under the impression that meant he had graduated from his apprenticeship, but perhaps they were holding off on declaring the arrangement permanent.

"Are you always so formal here?" I asked. Lira froze, and I watched her ears flicking while she tried to work out how to answer my question.

That probably had something to do with the fact that I already knew the answer, and it was no. Charm kept me informed of the local etiquette, and this wasn't part of it.

"I thought . . . I mean, aren't people from Latora supposed to be super strict about titles and forms of address?"

I raised an eyebrow. "Nobles, maybe. But we're all commoners here. Can't you focus on Charm, let it tell you what sort of formalities we expect?"

The rabbit-girl's ears drooped. "I, uh, don't have Charm," she admitted.

I sighed. This was *why* the Tribes hadn't been recognized as a state. It wasn't that they were unfriendly; they were just very, very bad at diplomacy.

"Elder Tinidan *is* a diplomat, yes?" I asked. I wasn't sure. He might have just been the only Elder willing to talk to us.

She nodded, so that was one question answered.

"So you're an apprentice to a diplomat, and you don't have Charm? What are you learning?"

"I was gonna get it, but I wasn't supposed to be the apprentice! I was gonna be a hunter until Anas skived off—"

I held up a hand to stop the sudden flood of words. I couldn't actually hear accents; the perfectly clear translation tended to overwrite what I was hearing. Nevertheless, I was getting the impression that she'd slipped into a particularly thick one.

"Enough," I said. "It's none of my business, though I would advise you to get the skill as soon as you can. Maybe pick it up through demonstrated expertise? It can't be that hard to be charming."

"I thought I was," Lira said. "With all the fancy talk, I mean."

"That wasn't charming," I told her. "That was just stiff and formal, and on you, it was a bit off-putting. Now, has Tinidan arranged some place for us to stay?"

"Oh!" she said, her ears perking up. "Yes, he did! I'm supposed to take you there! Follow me!"

She turned and took a few steps before halting.

"Oh!" she said again. "I'm supposed to say what a welcome surprise it is to see you here, and to apologize that these lodgings were only arranged at the last minute."

"That's only to be expected," I said mildly, refraining from rolling my eyes. "After all, Elder Tinidan had no idea we were coming."

"Yeah!" the rabbit-girl said, nodding. She turned again and led us to our lodgings.

"My apologies for the runaround," Tinidan said. He'd shown up after we'd been fed and bathed, putting me in a much better mood. Also improving my mood was the very fine berry brandy that he'd brought for us to have this discussion over.

We had retired to a private room equipped with two comfortable chairs that I could sink into. It was all very private and cozy. Had we been on Earth, one of us would have been smoking a cigar as we hashed out the details of our secret dealings.

He started by asking about my trip, and then he shared the news from Talnier. Mind control was a nasty business, but they seemed to have it well in hand. Then he'd moved on to the apologies.

"It wasn't that bad," I admitted. I wasn't angry at Tinidan, but I was a bit frustrated at the hoops I had to jump through dealing with the Tribes. This was not, I felt, an uncommon feeling. "Once we managed to find a guide, we had an easy enough trip that I don't think an official invitation would have helped much. Maybe with the attack."

I was also leaving off the dungeon break, but it wasn't like an official invitation would have helped with that. Tinidan frowned when I mentioned the attack.

"I'd like to promise that the perpetrators will be punished, but I fear that the Council will take the stance that outside of a village's territory, there is little that can be done."

"Reynard and Cloridan are checking with Reynard's contacts to see if we can identify the village responsible," I said. Cloridan didn't have Reynard's contacts, but he knew what to look for if anyone tried to contact him in secret. And I didn't trust Reynard.

"It's useful to know who's shooting at you, but I fear it will make little difference to the Council," Tinidan said. "Since they don't see you as a delegate, it will just be two private groups fighting on unoccupied land."

"That's what the villagers said," I agreed. "But we'll check it out anyway. Getting back to the runaround, the hard part was my heading out here at all, given the lack of information."

"I apologize for that as well," Tinidan said. "Unfortunately, with the Council divided, I can't promise anything, or even reveal some of the things that you want to know."

I sighed. "It's a real quaint system you've got here, Tinidan."

He shrugged and glanced fondly at his staff. He hadn't brought it with him to Talnier; it was a gnarled and intricately carved piece of wood, with nine rings hanging off it. They were also intricately carved. I started to ask about it, but wondering brought its own answer.

[Identification]: Council Speaker's Staff – Quality: Excellent – Nine Tokens

"I didn't think you were on the Council?" I asked.

"All the Elders are on the Council," he told me. "But most don't attend."

He nodded at the staff. "The nine rings are tokens from nine Elders who trust me to attend in their stead."

"Like proxy votes," I said.

"Not exactly. Almost all decisions are by consensus, so it matters little how many votes one has."

And just when I thought they'd managed to institute something workable.

"So they're a status symbol?"

"Perhaps. A symbol of how much I am trusted by my peers."

"So how many *do* show up on the Council?"

"About a hundred, give or take," Tinidan replied. "Not a very wieldy number, so there is a smaller group. The Nine."

"Are they an executive? I mean, do they handle things when there's a need for quick decision making?" I noted to myself that the Tribe's allergy to naming things even extended to this sub-council. "The Nine" for a nine-person group—astounding.

"They are empowered to make some decisions," he agreed. "Not many, though. They mainly determine the agenda for the main Council meetings. You'll need to meet with them before you meet with the main Council."

I groaned inwardly as my hopes of getting a quick answer were dashed. Charm kept it all on the inside, though I did allow my smile to become a bit more strained.

"Can you at least tell me something about the task that you had Anas allude to?"

"I can't, I'm afraid. The Nine will likely ask you to intervene when you meet them, but I'm not authorized to tell you anything about it. However"—he held up a hand to interrupt me before I spoke—"you should be able to work it out from what you've told me about your trip."

I narrowed my eyes. There were three major incidents during my trip through the Wild. The attack was on me. Unless the Nine wanted me dead, that couldn't be the reason they would like me here. The dungeon break was more likely, but it had happened after I'd left. None of the villagers had heard of something like that happening before. That left . . .

"The demons," I said flatly. "You're concerned that demons are escaping from the elven lands."

"I can't confirm that, of course," Tinidan said smugly, "But it is a conclusion one might easily draw."

"Why do they want me involved?" I asked. "The demon I saw was taken out by elf hunters—I don't know if I could have beaten it."

"It's not that we doubt their capability," Tinidan said slowly. "But the Council is in a delicate position. Our relationship with the Grove is good, but elves are . . . standoffish and prickly about maintaining their border."

"Unlike you guys," I noted.

"Indeed. Over the last century or so, there have been a few demon incursions, and we have been grateful to the hunters for their prompt handling of the matter. However, in recent months, the number of incursions has greatly increased."

"Increased by how much?"

"For much of the last hundred years, we could expect to see a demon perhaps once every five to ten years," he told me. "Your sighting is the third in as many months."

"And the elves haven't said anything about it?"

"Nothing at all. They are known to be more . . . forthcoming towards Champions."

"And you didn't send Kaito because . . ."

Tinidan smiled wryly. "I'm afraid that's your fault, not that I blame you. When you reached level six so quickly, Lady Washiyama became obsessed with catching up to you. A diplomatic mission didn't promise huge experience gains, so . . ."

"I see," I said, with no expression on my face. *Sorry, not sorry*, I said to myself. "So how do you suggest I approach the Council—sorry, the Nine?"

"You have requests to make—make them," he said. "Coming as a supplicant will enhance their opinions of themselves. They will probably put you off or deny you, but they *should* see the opportunity this brings them and ask you to visit the elves in return."

"Should?" I asked. Tinidan sighed.

"The Nine is comprised of the most popular and the most egotistical of all the Elders," he said. "There are no guarantees, but if they don't think it's their idea, they'll never agree to it."

COUNCIL OF NINE

When Tinidan had told me that he was taking me before the Nine, I had imagined some kind of conference table situation. Maybe they'd all be sitting along one side of a long table, and I'd be facing them, either on the other side of the table or standing all on my own. Perhaps I'd be standing at the focus of a horseshoe-shaped table, getting interrogated from all sides.

Some scene from a *Star Trek* episode sprang to mind, with me in a sunken pit, surrounded by accusers. It would take some magic to get the lighting right—a single spotlight shining on me, while the Nine were in shadow—but I could make it work, so I supposed they could manage it.

Thinking like that showed that I hadn't entirely grasped the Tribe's dislike of formality and professionalism. What Tinidan took me to was a lunch. No, not even that.

Looking around the open-air gathering, I realized that I was looking at something familiar: a barbeque. Two older beast-kin were flipping steaks on a hot plate. One of them was some kind of cat and the other had scales. Cooked meat was being piled up to be taken by whoever needed it.

A long table was piled high with salads, fruits, and nuts. Another table groaned under the weight of a selection of wine casks. Everyone was wandering around talking to one another, cup and plate in hand. Everyone was—there were a lot more than nine people here. The others must have been other petitioners, wives, children . . . grandchildren.

"This is how the Nine handle their duties, is it?" I said. Charm kept a polite smile on my face and the tremor out of my voice, but Tinidan must have known that it was there.

"Yes . . . I gather it takes some getting used to, for outsiders."

A genuine smile twisted my lips at the thought of . . . oh, any noble that I'd met having their self-importance and dignity challenged by having to deal with this. Even the elves I'd met recently had been excessively formal. They might have skills to save them from dealing with this, but I doubted that they would want to develop them.

"It's no problem, Elder," I said. "Where I come from can be equally informal."

That was true enough if you were talking about your local footie club association, rather than a branch of government.

This is why no one takes you seriously, I lectured from the safety of my head. How can they when your executive council has all the gravitas of a sausage sizzle?

"So, you promised me some introductions?" I said aloud. "If it's not too rude, I'd appreciate notes on who is what race. I still have difficulty telling."

Tinidan nodded. "It's no problem," he assured me. "Most of the Nine will be eager to meet you."

There was that celebrity status again. "Lead on," I said, and he did so.

Fortunately, I had Memorize to handle all the names and faces that were thrown at me. The two meat grillers were, of course, of the Nine. They were Faelan Whisperwind, a panther-kin, and Riven Stormcoil, a snake-kin. They greeted me jovially while piling meat on my plate.

As Tinidan took me around, I started to get a feel for how things worked. Most of the people here were related to one of the Elders. There were a few petitioners, a few aides, or people like Tinidan who worked for the Council in some capacity. Mostly, though, it was family. And the family was a part of the politics.

My Intrigue skill started to perk up, feeding me information. There were factions here. Most of the children of the Elders were fully grown. The few kids I saw running around always turned out to be grandchildren (or great-grandchildren). Some of the next generation were working as aides, some of them belonged to factions . . . not always the same faction as their parents.

Intrigue took in half-overheard conversations, noted who was looking at whom, and gave me a sense of what their body language was saying. It didn't tell me what the faction's policy was, but there were other ways of finding that out.

Asking Tinidan, for one. He was reluctant to spill the details of his nation's internal divisions, but there were a few things he didn't mind sharing.

"Under other circumstances, I wouldn't bother introducing you to this one," he said as we made our way towards a lynx-kin with snow-white hair and ears. "But I don't want her to claim that we've snubbed her."

"Hostile?" I asked softly, though probably not quietly enough, given the size of those ears. There were a lot of conversations going on, though.

"Yes," he said shortly. There wasn't much there, but it was useful information. Vesper Frostpaw, as she was shortly introduced as, was the singular Elder in her faction. There were some other people here who looked to her, but none of them were part of the Nine.

There were two *pairs* of Elders who looked at her with disdain. The two pairs were standoffish to each other, so I took them to be two separate factions that opposed her while maintaining their own disagreement. Tinidan deferred to one of those factions, so I tagged that one as being in favor of trade and diplomacy. Where that left the other one, I didn't know, but they were hopefully not as hostile as Vesper.

"Ah, the human," she said at my approach. "Here to cut down the trees and drive out the Goddess."

I raised an eyebrow and patted at my clothes. "I must have forgotten to bring my axe."

She grimaced at me. I had Charm running at full blast, of course. Her own total was quite respectable, but mine was higher. Not enough to win her over, not when she wanted to dislike me so strongly. But it must have felt quite uncomfortable, holding on to her grudge so strongly.

"Do you really think that was why I was here?" I asked, genuinely curious. "I get that there's a history between the Tribes and the Kingdom, but I'm not from around here, you know?"

Now that my little secret was out, I'd be damned if I didn't wring every bit of advantage out of it.

"I got on quite well with Lady Kaito, and a lot of the beast-kin living in Talnier," I added.

Mentioning Kaito gave her pause, but she skipped over it and focused on the other beast-kin that I mentioned.

"Traitors to the Way," she growled, with a dismissive tone that told me I wasn't going to get anywhere arguing the point. "Why are you here, then, human?"

"You know, I don't think I'll get very far talking about my hunt for a human criminal in your territory," I said. "I don't suppose you're associated with Hidden Hollow?"

She didn't answer, but she smirked, which was as good as a treatise to Intrigue.

"Fine, then," I continued. "Then let's go with my greater purpose, which is to promote ties and trade between the Tribal nation and my town of Talnier. In the hopes of setting an example that the rest of the nation can follow."

"Fine words, when what you mean is to take our goods and replace them with cold metal coins. What good are such worthless things?"

"Most of your goods are grown or made by you," I patiently explained. "In time, you'll have more goods *and* you'll have the coins. Which can be exchanged for goods produced by *us.*"

Do I really have to explain how trade works? I thought to myself incredulously. Actually, though, it didn't matter what I said. I wasn't trying to persuade her of anything, which was for the best as I sensed her Persuade skill was a good bit higher than mine. We were even on levels, but my Charisma *might* even the totals.

What *I* was trying to do was to get her, and everyone listening, to *like* me. To make me seem like the reasonable one. My words, and the tone of my voice, extended out to enfold us all in a friendly embrace. It made her seem shrill and argumentative.

I'm just explaining how trade makes us all prosperous, my tone said. Who could argue with prosperity for everyone?

Vesper recognized a losing battle when she saw one, so she elected to cut her losses and leave the field.

"Fine," she said, grimacing. "I don't need to hear any more."

I bowed. "A pleasure meeting you, Elder," I said. I backed off, giving her the space, and some semblance of a win. I wanted to be liked, after all.

To say, as I went around meeting everyone, that they were putty in my hands would be an exaggeration. I *was* charming, possibly more charming than they'd ever seen. I schmoozed, I smarmed, and I flattered.

As I'd discussed with Tinidan, I mentioned that I was here to get help finding Hector, but I didn't discuss any details. That would have moved the discussion out of light social chatter, the domain of Charm, and into more serious topics. That was the domain of Persuade and Bargain. I steered well clear of them, not just because this was an informal lunch, but because I got the impression that was much shakier ground.

Vesper wasn't the only one here to favor Persuasion over Charm. Convincing their peers of a course of action was what these Council members did all day. Naturally, they had the skill for it. Like Vesper, my Charisma made up for my lack of skill, but it was a close thing, and I wouldn't know who was better until one of us won.

"That went well, I thought," Tinidan said once we'd done the rounds. We'd covered all the members of the Nine. Most of them had introduced me to at least one family member, and we'd also gotten to a few of the petitioners and attendants as well.

"Yes," I said doubtfully. "But . . . Thorn Emberstripe is waiting for something."

Tinidan looked warily over at the tiger-kin. Thorn had grown so old that you could barely tell his sub-species. The orange and black striped hair that his descendants were wearing had faded to slightly lighter and darker greys.

It was his body language that had given away that he was tensely waiting for something—or someone, perhaps a guest—important, but that wasn't why I'd pointed him out. He was part of the other two-person faction that opposed both Vesper and Tinidan's group, so I was hoping Tinidan would let a detail slip. I was not disappointed.

"What are the Isolationists planning?" he wondered aloud. Then he looked at me guiltily. I smiled innocently.

"We're about to find out," I said. "Look."

Thorn was talking to a much younger tiger-kin. Well, the youngster was whispering into his Elder's ear, but that surely counted. Report given, the aide was clapped on the back and given some kind of instruction. He headed for the entrance.

It was only a few moments more before someone came in, escorted by two tiger-kin.

"Another human?" Tinidan asked incredulously. "Where did he come from?"

I scrutinized the man as best I could from the distance we were at. He didn't *look* like he was from the kingdom. The clothes were wrong.

"I guess we'll have to find out," I said, starting to head closer. "Is there any etiquette I have to be aware of?"

This was mostly a question to keep Tinidan's brain busy while I got a few steps ahead. It had occurred to me that he might want to keep me separate from whatever the Isolationists were planning. I'd already felt out the local etiquette using Charm. The entirety of it, translated into Australian vernacular, would be: "No worries, mate."

"Um, don't get into any shoving matches." Tinidan replied, belatedly catching up with me. "Or, uh, any kind of physical altercation."

"Got it," I said, as I stepped into what I was starting to think of as "social range."

Thorn turned to greet me. "Ah, Councillor Hammond, just the person I wanted to start with!" he exclaimed. He seemed just as friendly as he had when I'd been introduced to him earlier.

"May I present Borys Borkowski, Champion of the Storm."

CHAMPION OF THE STORM

Borys looked as surprised to see me as I was to see him. My trip had been low profile, but I wasn't trying to keep it a secret. Tinidan must have made some arrangements to keep my arrival low-key because most of the Nine members I'd met seemed to think that I'd popped up out of nowhere.

By the same token, the fact that Borys had caught *Tinidan* by surprise meant that Tinidan wasn't the only one who could make secret accommodations. It was a timely reminder that while the Tribal Council might act as though they were just a local Rotary club, they were, in fact, a government staffed by the most experienced politicians they had.

Borys looked down at me. He didn't have any choice in the matter, he was a full head taller than me. He had blond hair, blue eyes, and a fairly handsome, European-looking facial structure. He wasn't wearing armor, but he had a large sword strapped to his back. Another smaller sword was on his hip, and his short sleeves didn't conceal the two dagger-sized scabbards strapped to his arms.

He looked . . . *hard.* Not just in the sense that he was tall, broad, and well-muscled, although he was all of those.

I'd lost a lot of softness since coming here. In my muscles, sure. Training enough hours to get my physical skills up had resulted in a package that an exercise junkie wouldn't sneer at. The point of the training had been the numbers, but they also conditioned the body beneath that. But I'd also been through some terrifying life-or-death scrapes. I'd learned how to kill and skin monsters. I hadn't killed anyone with my own hands, but I'd watched people die in horrible ways, knowing that I was at least partly to blame.

Even without the System, I was fairly confident I could take my former self in a fight.

Borys looked to have taken that to the next level. He looked dangerous, like a killer. It wasn't in his demeanor—he was being as charming and affable as the situation called for. Part of it was in his aura. He was the same level as me, if I was any judge, but he had the sharpest aura I'd ever felt. It reminded me of Liam Warner's back from my first days in Oakway.

The other part of it was in his eyes and the way he moved. It was the almost imperceptible scars on his hands and forearms. And on his face?

What the? My Perception sometimes surprised me by pointing out details I couldn't normally see. Borys was covered in small scars, crisscrossing across every visible part of his body.

What's up with that? I wondered, but now wasn't the time to bring it up. He seemed fine with whatever it was, but he'd clearly gone through a lot of pain to get where he was.

Borys was looking right back at me, and I could tell that he liked what he saw. It wasn't an uncommon reaction, if I do say so myself. His control over it was less common, and a point in his favor.

"This is a surprise," he said in a slow, deep voice. "I had heard that you were level six."

"I hadn't realized that rumors about me had spread so far, but that's correct," I said.

He looked at me doubtfully, and I realized that he was feeling out my aura. I hadn't mastered suppressing it yet, but I was able to consistently keep it to about the same as a level five's.

"Has no one told you about suppressing auras?" I asked. "It keeps the people around you less nervous."

To give weight to my words, I released my control momentarily. Borys's eyes widened as he took in my actual level. Since he was checking me out, I chose to do the same to him, with all my skills.

Just about all the skills had an information-gathering component. They were mediated by your Inteligence Ability and tended towards the very specific. Weapon Master told you how good your opponent was with that weapon, for example. All of my weapon skills gave me the same answer when pointed at Borys: *Better than you.*

It was a different story when it came to social skills, though.

Shouldn't have used Charisma as your dump stat, Borys, I thought gleefully. I shouldn't get too cocky; he clearly outclassed me physically. But none of that mattered if he didn't want to fight me.

And he wouldn't. I kept it light, to start with. The same level of Charm that I'd been using with the Elders here. Just light, friendly touches. Bullying people with social skills was still bullying, and it tended to provoke an unfriendly reaction once it was over.

The Elders, I realized, were in a similar situation. They didn't have my Charisma but they had social skills and levels. They could probably convince Borys to do anything they wanted. As if he was their personal enforcer.

Had it been that way with Kaito, too? Kaito had decent Charisma but they hadn't at the start, and they'd been a lower level as well. I started to wonder if this monster hunting trip had been an excuse to get themselves out of the Council's reach . . .

And now here they were, with a new Chosen. Two of them, even, although I didn't have any intention of being a pawn. I glanced over at Thorn, who was starting to look as though he'd realized his mistake. He hadn't planned on bringing Borys to this meeting, but he'd sent for Borys to counter my appearance. Introducing him to me had been showing off, but now he was realizing that I could negate his influence over Borys.

"I didn't know such a thing was possible," Borys said, talking about my suppression. "Or desirable. Isn't it better to show your strength?"

"There's a time and place for it," I explained. "In most social situations, you don't want to put the other guests on edge."

I looked over at Thorn inquisitively. "I'd wager most of the Elders here are suppressing at least one level, yes?"

Thorn got a sour look on his face, but he nodded.

"I can't tell," I assured him. "I'm not that good at it, but . . . actually, your presence is giving the game away."

"How so?" Borys asked.

"They're not reacting to your aura the same way that someone of their apparent level should," I explained. "I'm sure you remember how it felt around people with a much higher level than you."

Borys nodded. "Intimidating, almost painfully so, sometimes." His face fell. "I've been intimidating the weak since I got this level and I didn't even realize it."

"I'm sure they're used to it," I told him. "It's not a universally followed courtesy. The opposite, if anything."

He nodded. "Can you show me how to do this?" he asked.

"I—" I started, but I was interrupted.

"Actually, there are a lot of people that are waiting to meet you," Thorn said quickly.

"Oh, you can't steal him away that quickly," I said. I smiled, but there was steel in it. Affable friendliness wasn't the only setting that Charm had. "We haven't had a chance to catch up, or even say what countries we came from."

"Poland," Borys said eagerly.

"It's been a while since you spoke to someone who knew what that meant, eh?" I replied in Polish. "I'm from Australia."

"So far away, and yet so close," he said in English.

Thorn's ear twitched, and Charm let me know that was a tell. I was stealing his weapon!

It was tempting to continue, but I was here to make friends with the Council, not enemies. Whatever it was that they planned for Borys to do, I could probably intervene if I felt it was necessary. I'd gotten my foot in the door; I could come back to it if I felt what they were doing was wrong.

"We'll talk later," I said. "You can probably get someone else to show you how to suppress your aura. It seems like a common skill around here."

I looked at Thorn. "I'll let you get to it," I said. "I'm sure you're eager to have him meet the *right* people."

Thorn blinked, unsure of what I was implying with my tone. That was the beauty of tone, though. I implied there was something significant without saying what it was. To Thorn, it was just confusing, but he wasn't the intended audience for the emphasized word.

To Borys, it implied that *I* knew something that Thorn *also* knew, but that Borys did not. It set up a doubt. It wouldn't stop Thorn or any of the others from manipulating Borys with Persuasion but it would leave a key in the door for when I wanted to bring the whole edifice down.

Borys gave me a slight bow. "It was nice to meet you, Champion Hammond," he said.

"Just Kandis is fine," I told him. "It was nice to meet you, too."

I watched them go as Tinidan appeared by my side. He hadn't gone anywhere, he'd just faded into the crowd while we talked. Thorn hadn't been interested in introducing him to Borys, which tracked. I doubted he wanted Borys to know anyone in the opposing faction.

"So what was that all about?" I asked him.

"I have no idea, I was going to ask you," he said. "Champions are guided by the gods, are they not?"

"Subtly," I said. "King Alexandros wasn't at all pleased to have three Champions showing up in his capital, but you guys invited two of us here without telling anyone. Have the gods been talking to you?"

"Not . . . not as far as I'm aware," Tinidan said. "Now that you mention it, some of the decisions I made . . . they still seem like the right ones. But you're right, they have led to this situation, which is not . . ."

"Optimal," I finished for him. "After all, the plan is to get us out to the Elven Grove as soon as you can, right?"

"To get *you* out there," Tinidan said. "I'm not sure if that is Thorn's plan. Borys is a fighter, not a diplomat."

"My experience," I said slowly, "with mortal rulers throwing Champions at the problems they have, is that they don't worry too much about the abilities or level of the Champion in question. They figure that the gods will sort it out, one way or another."

"That is how the stories go," Tinidan agreed. "And hasn't it worked out that way for you so far?"

"So far," I admitted. "But that's just a trend. And whether it's oil futures or Bixby Babies, there's only one thing you need to know about trends."

"What?" Tinidan asked, probably about the Bixby Babies as much as any wisdom I had to share.

"They keep going until they can't anymore, and then they stop," I said.

"Isn't that just a truism?"

"One that people forget," I said. "People think that just because something has happened in the past, it will happen in the future. In reality, it will keep happening until the *reason* for it happening stops, and then *it* will stop."

I gave him a sour look. "Me living is the *it* in this scenario, if you weren't clear," I said. "So I do wish that gods and men weren't so cavalier about risking my life."

"I understand," Tinidan told me. "But it is the same for all of us. We live until we cannot, and then we die. Was that not so in your world?"

"We were only doing a little better than you were, I'd say," I admitted. "But you have gods and magic. Immortal elves and who knows what else. I'd like to think we can do a little better than threescore years and ten."

Investigations

The Champion of Storms?" Felicia exclaimed.

"Don't get too excited," I told her with a smile. "I'll start to think that you're going to leave me for a Champion with rock-hard abs. Or worse, that you're going to leave *Kyle*."

"Don't be silly!" she insisted, blushing a bit. "I would never! It's just . . . well, the stories about the Champion of Storms are so much more exciting than the others."

"All of them, or just the last one?" I asked.

"All of them," Kyle confirmed. "Rakaro likes direct, overwhelming force, and his champions embody that. Lots of fight scenes in his stories."

"I can't claim the current one bucks the trend," I admitted. "He looks like he's been training, or fighting, very hard for a long time."

"Probably both," Kyle said. "He's level six as well?"

"Yeah, and as far as I know he hasn't been the beneficiary of a hacked dungeon run," I said. "All hard work, I guess."

"Did he say why he was here?" Cloridan asked.

"He's here because he was invited—by the isolationist faction, if Tinidan's slip is to be believed. I'm sure he has his own agenda, but he didn't say what it was. How did your investigations go?"

"They were troubled," Cloridan told me. "That is, they went well, but the implications are troubling."

"Par for the course," I muttered. "Let's have it then."

I'd sent everyone out together while I dealt with the Nine. Reynard because he knew the town and could find the people we needed. Cloridan because I didn't trust Reynard and he had a nose for sniffing out unsavory types. Felicia and Kyle were there to back Cloridan up.

"First of all," Cloridan said, "we found someone who could identify the arrows. Hidden Hollow, as we suspected."

"Noted," I said. I needed to find out who the Elder that represented that village was, whether they were here directly or had passed their proxy on. If they had handed their token to another Elder, I'd have to be at least a little suspicious of everyone else he held a token for.

Tinidan probably wouldn't want to tell me that, but there had to be someone in the city who kept track of these things. Perhaps Lira would know, or be able to find out.

"So what's the bad news?" I asked. Identifying the would-be assassins hardly rated as troubling news.

"One of the people we talked to asked about Reynard's amulet," Cloridan said. "He said he'd seen it being worn by others."

"That is troubling," I said quietly. "Has everyone still got *their* amulets?"

Everyone pulled out their defensive amulets for inspection, while I started activating Mana Sense and cast Dispel Image. None of the amulets showed any signs of mental intrusion. No one had suspicious invisible mana lines leading south. I relaxed a bit.

Not completely. As the one with the highest Soul, Felicia held the control that could reset the other amulets. We were betting that she had the best chance of resisting any mental magic that was used on her . . . but we hadn't had a chance to test whether that would be enough.

"What's the story with those amulets, anyway?" Reynard asked. He was sitting a little apart from the others as they made their reports. We all looked at him, and he shifted uncomfortably.

"I mean, I know that the Countess provides them," he said. "And I know they're magical. But what do they do?"

"What did the Countess tell you?" I asked.

He shrugged. "Just that I should wear it as long as I was working for her, and that I should always keep it visible. I kind of got the idea that it was what broke my geas, but she never actually said that."

"You didn't have in Oakway, did you?" I asked. Thinking back, he hadn't been wearing it.

"No?" he said. "My geas was broken before then, though, I . . ." He paused. "When *did* I get it?"

"If you don't remember, then I certainly can't tell you," I said wryly. "But moving on . . . have you been contacted by any of the Countess's . . . people since leaving Talnier?"

"No," he said shortly.

"Did that surprise you?" I asked.

"It did," he agreed, speaking carefully. "What's the point of keeping an eye on you if I can't report on what you're doing?"

"And," I added, "they could have passed on new orders, orders to break your deal and betray me."

"The thought crossed my mind that it was a possibility," he said. "Can't say I would have liked it—and she told me straight out she wouldn't. But she's the boss."

"Quite," I said coldly. "We have a pretty good idea now what the amulet does from seeing it in action in Talnier. It forms a long-distance link, allowing someone on the other end to use Mind Magic on anyone within range of the thing."

He looked at me in surprise and then looked down at his amulet. "And you let me get close to you?" he asked.

"I chopped it off," I told him. "I broke the link. It can be reestablished, but only by reuniting it with the other end."

He nodded slowly. "That explains a lot of stuff. She could get what she needed by reading my mind, and give me orders the same way."

"Alas, you've been cut out of that loop," I said.

He nodded again. "If you're expecting me to turn on her ladyship because she uses Mind Magic, you can think again. I threw in with her, and she's not the sort that takes breaking up easy."

"It doesn't matter," I said. "Without a link to give you orders, you're no more untrustworthy than any ex-Guild oathbreaker."

He chuckled at that but stopped when he realized something. "That's what's got you all heated up about those amulets. If her ladyship has got people out here, they can get to me."

"Or to me," I said. "There's no obvious reason why they wouldn't act directly."

He nodded amiably. "So those amulets are protection against Mind Magic," he said. I nodded, choosing not to tell him that they were mostly ineffective. "So how did she get them out here?"

He paused in thought for a moment and then answered himself. "Hector. That's why he was acting strangely. She got to him, and then he took a bunch of amulets out with him."

"You were probably the one that brought all the amulets into the town in the first place, you know," I said sharply.

"No, I never . . . ah, but I might not remember if I did, eh?"

"Probably not," I agreed. "It doesn't matter, though. There were any number of ways they could be smuggled in. We weren't checking for them at the gates."

Weren't. We are now, I added to myself.

"So, are you going to throw me out?" Reynard asked.

"You don't seem very concerned at the prospect," I said.

"This is a nice place, but I've got friends I can stay with," he replied easily. "Got a trade, can make some money if I need it. I could head back to Talnier and get my link established again. I've got options."

"I'm sure you do," I agreed. "But I intend to hold you to the deal we made, at least for now."

"As you like," he said easily. "You're the boss. Gonna give me one of those protection amulets?"

"No," I told him. Not that I had any to spare; they'd all stayed in Talnier. "I don't plan on giving the enemy a copy of my defenses. We should be fine as long as we keep you away from amulets."

I didn't mention that, given a little time, I should be able to kill any amulets that I saw. He didn't need to know.

"Anyway," I told the group. "Our main concern is the people that the amulets have already affected. It's not limited to the person who carries it, and we still don't know what the goal is."

"Should we let Tinidan or the Council know that there's Mind Magic about?" Kyle asked. "They might have customs for dealing with it," he added doubtfully.

"Not a bad idea," I said. "They may look—and act—like a herd of cats, but they can be surprisingly sophisticated when they want to be."

"Mind Magic!" Lira said in shock. Her ears flicked back and forth in agitation. "That's a very serious accusation!"

"I'm sure," I said. "I don't make it lightly. Anyone wearing an amulet like this one could be a source of it."

"Then he's—"

"This one is broken," I assured her. "But others have been seen about the place."

"Who? Where?"

"Our guy didn't know," Cloridan said. "Out of towner."

"Was he a badger-kin?" I asked. Hidden Hollow was supposed to be mainly that type.

"No, he never got a clear look, but he thought they were some kind of cat," Cloridan said. "They had a hood up, which made wearing the amulet openly all the more obvious."

"Is that all?" Lira asked anxiously. "I will take this to Master Tinidan immediately!"

"Wait, before you go," I said. "Is there some kind of register of who is the representative of which villages?"

"Of course!" Lira replied, hopping impatiently from one foot to another.

"Is it open to the public? Or can you look something up for me?"

"I can take you there, first thing in the morning," she assured me, "But now, I have to go!"

I let her go with a nod.

"Do you think it will help?" Kyle asked.

"It can't hurt," I replied. "Mind Magic works best when you're not expecting it. If you are, then mages can see it going on, at least."

"So what do we do now?" Felicia asked.

"Now? We keep an eye on Reynard, we watch out for anyone suspicious, and we let the Council do its job."

The four of us kept a watch that night, despite the supposed safety of the room. We didn't want Reynard sneaking out to try and make contact with whoever was out there, and we weren't confident that the rooms were as safe as they appeared. Morning arrived without incident, though, and Lira arrived as we were eating breakfast.

"There's been no news," she said in response to our enquiries. "People are asking around about the amulets and the priests have been alerted."

"Priests?" I asked.

"Priests of Naldyna have protections against Mind Magic," she explained. "I think most priests do. Plus, they have a high Soul requirement."

"Is that true?" I asked the others.

"I never heard of it," Kyle answered. "But religion . . . isn't as important back home as it is here."

"Tonet could have mentioned something," I muttered. "She's supposed to be a priestess *and* she's involved in the defense."

"If there's just the one of her, maybe she didn't want to do all the work?" Lira suggested. "Naldyna is very big on self-reliance."

"We should have gotten the other temples more involved," I said.

"I dunno if that would have worked," Kyle said. "They don't like getting involved in politics."

"Naldyna being the exception," I said.

"I think that's more *Tonet* being the exception," Cloridan put in. "She's always had an agenda, and I don't think it's always lined up with the Council, Naldyna, or even Kaito."

"She did what Kaito told her to do," I objected.

"Yeah, but she was doing her own thing, before and after that," Cloridan pointed out. "Just as she worked with you, after she worked against you."

"She's probably acting in line with some faction of the Council," I mused. "I should probably try to find out which. I don't suppose you know, Lira?"

"That sounds like the kind of thing Master would know," she admitted. "But . . . uh, I don't think he wants to tell you that."

"He probably doesn't want us to know who's representing Hidden Hollow either," I said. "Are you still going to show us the register?"

"Yeah," Lira said. One of her ears drooped. "You're right, but knowing who speaks for whom is public knowledge. It *has* to be or people couldn't trust what they were hearing. So he doesn't want me to, but he won't stop me."

"Nicely put," I told her. "Let's get going. And if there's anything else that your civics lessons tell you that we need to know, please speak up."

POLITICS

Our first stop was the political registrar. Lira was happy to tell us all about it, but what it amounted to was a room full of lists.

"It takes a lot of work to keep it up to date," she told us. "But every time an Elder wants to reassign their proxy, they need to come here with the other Elders involved."

Her youthful enthusiasm made it seem that all three Elders would just show up out of a pure desire to make sure that every village got the representation they wanted. I didn't have the heart to ask what would happen if an Elder didn't *want* to give up their proxy. I was sure there must be some procedure but it wasn't relevant to today.

What was relevant was what we'd come for, the name of the Elder representing Hidden Hollow. I let Lira do the honors. She seemed familiar with what books to look up, though her reading speed left a lot to be desired. It was barely superhuman. I got the answer a second before she did, looking over her shoulder once she'd found the right page, but I let her make the announcement.

"It's Vesper Frostpaw of Snowfall's Embrace," she told us. "That's to the west, up in the mountains," she added.

"One of the Nine," I said mildly. "We met her yesterday. What faction would she be in, do you know?"

Both of her ears drooped. "I'm not supposed to talk about factions," she said guiltily. "And she's . . . I'm especially not supposed to talk about her faction."

"That's fine," I told her. "I'm getting the picture anyway. She was opposed to the isolationist faction—"

"How do you know—" Lira interjected, before snapping her mouth shut. She must have realized that she was giving too much away.

"Tinidan let it slip," I explained, and she sniffed in exasperation.

"How am I supposed to keep quiet if Master can't?" she protested.

"It's completely unfair," I agreed. It *was* more than a little unfair for Tinidan to expect her to keep secrets from me. The girl was an easily opened book to skills like Persuasion and Intrigue, and the two skills were itching for a chance to crack her open. She liked me, and she was assigned to help me. Give me five minutes and a cup of coffee and she'd be spilling her deepest, darkest secrets.

There were two reasons I didn't. Three if you counted a lack of coffee to bond over. The first was that it was rude. Tinidan and Lira were my allies, hopefully for the longer term. There wasn't anything to gain by antagonizing them.

The second reason was that Tinidan must have known I had that capacity. He didn't want me to understand the local politics, but he couldn't have been that concerned about it. Not if he was leaving his apprentice in my hands. The other possibility was that he'd fed her some misleading information to poison anything I got from her. She was new to this; she probably didn't know enough on her own to verify what she'd been told.

The other other reason was that I didn't need to.

"She was also quite hostile to Tinidan," I continued. "Who, let us say, seems to belong to the Trading faction."

The look on Lira's face told me I hadn't gotten the name right, but it was close enough.

"Now, opposed to both isolation and trade and connected to a distinctly hostile village makes me think that we've found the faction that wants war. Shall we call them the militant faction?"

Lira's nose twitched. If that was a tell, it was adorable.

"Did—did you want to watch a Council session?" she asked, desperately changing the subject.

"Sure," I said. That was three of the four factions I'd seen identified. It was hard to imagine what position the final faction held. Perhaps it was just concerned with maintaining the status quo?

There was a hushed quiet even before we got near the Grove. Lira cautioned us to maintain a respectful bearing.

"It's a holy place, as well as our most important institution," she said. We all nodded in agreement. This time I had the whole gang with me—I think in hopes that we'd run into Borys again.

As we approached, I noted several priests. At least, they were wearing the same robes that Tonet wore.

"There's not normally this many priests," Lira said, "But we're on alert because of the Mind Magic."

The Grove was a large clearing around a truly massive tree. Its branches must have blocked the light for a hundred meters around its trunk, leaving a space where no other trees could grow. I didn't know the species, but Identify was on the case.

> **[Identification]: Blessed Oak – Properties: Protection, Blessing, Immortal**

I raised an eyebrow. That was a short but quite spectacular set of benefits. Must be on Ashmor's hit list, I speculated. But then, it must also get special attention from Naldyna, so I guessed it evened out.

Around the massive trunk was a raised platform, supporting several posts with placards and baskets. I looked at Lira for an explanation.

"When a proposition is put before Council," she murmured. "It goes up on a post, and members can put a token in the basket to register their disapproval."

"Is this one of their proxy tokens, or is this a different token?" I asked softly.

"A different one; it basically just has their name carved in it," she said. "So that those in favor of the proposal know who they need to convince to let it go forward."

"Can't you just take someone's name out?" Cloridan asked.

"Well, you can, but it doesn't mean anything," Lira replied. "Once the basket is empty, you can take your proposal to the floor, and everyone votes on it. That's the vote that counts, not the basket."

"The basket is just to coordinate the negotiations," I said. I looked out over the rest of the Grove. It was dotted with comfortable chairs and tables, in small groups mostly arranged to give them a view of the tree. Various beast-kin were sitting in the chairs, wandering between groups, or walking up to the tree to examine the baskets.

"What happens when it rains?" I asked, looking at all of the expensive chairs.

"Oh, it doesn't," Lira replied. "Rain, wind, snow, fire, insects, or beasts, none of them can disturb the Grove."

"Is that what Protection does?" I asked. "It's pretty powerful; too bad it doesn't protect against Mind Magic."

"Um . . . it might? I'm not sure about the rarer protections. I know it doesn't stop *violence*, but other things I'm not sure about."

Other things? I reached out with my Shadow Magic senses, since trying to lob a water ball might be taken the wrong way. Sure enough, just ahead of me was a region where, despite all of the shaded areas, my senses told me that there were no shadows. Ironically, the Grove that anyone could walk into was protected from Shadow Walking.

"It's not very exciting," Felicia complained.

"Sometimes there are speeches," Lira said defensively. "But most of the time they're just talking."

"When democracy gets exciting, something has gone very wrong," I said. This was a democracy, even if it was a form I hadn't heard of before. I supposed there were worse forms of government, though none of them sprang to mind.

A thought occurred to me.

"What happens if an Elder isn't present for a vote?" I asked. "If they show up late to vote against, does that break the consensus?"

Lira shook her head, "Overturning a vote requires a new vote," she said. "If you miss it, or if your proxy holder votes against your interest and you take your proxy away, you have to call a new vote and get it overturned. It doesn't happen often."

I nodded in understanding. There would have to be exceptional circumstances for every Councillor to change their vote at the request of a single voter. It underscored the importance of attending votes and cast fresh light on the proxy system. I'd been thinking of it as a hierarchy, but there might also be groups of Elders that trusted each other, taking turns attending so that no single one of them was unduly inconvenienced.

Having more than one vote didn't mean that much when it only took one vote to derail a proposal.

"Is Tinidan here now?" I asked.

Lira nodded. "He should be canvassing opinions about how to word your request," she said, looking around the Grove. After a moment, she pointed. "There!"

My instinct told me that I shouldn't be able to recognize Tinidan, more than a hundred meters away in the dappled shade of the Grove. Instinct was wrong, and I picked him out easily. He had apparently noticed us as well, and soon started heading our way.

"Good news," he said, as he approached closely enough to address us in the hushed tone that everyone seemed to use around the Grove. "The Nine have agreed to post your request for a vote."

"Is it really my request when I haven't even seen the wording of it?" I asked skeptically.

"Oh, that doesn't matter, the request has no chance of passing."

"Is that why Elder Vesper let it through?" I asked. "I can't imagine the militant faction is ever going to let it succeed."

Tinidan glared disapprovingly at Lira.

"I didn't tell her!" she protested. "You were the one who told her about the Isolationists!"

He cleared his throat, embarrassed. "Yes, well, you are broadly correct."

"So how does this help us?" I asked.

"This opens negotiations," Tinidan explained. "You don't actually want a resolution from the Council."

"I don't?"

"No, you want to find your rogue Captain. Now, a Council resolution is one way of achieving that, but as long as he has the support of a single village, you will never get that resolution." Tinidan leaned in, warming to his pitch.

"But there are other ways," I said.

"Yes! You see, I—" Tinidan broke off suddenly. "Actually, we shouldn't be having this conversation in the open."

I shrugged and cast Privacy. "Is this better?"

He jumped as the rustling of leaves and the murmur of other people's conversations was suddenly cut off.

"It's . . . a little unconventional, but I really shouldn't be leaving the Grove right now. I'm sure it will be fine."

"So the other way . . . or ways?"

"Yes! As I was saying . . . if a village, or better yet a coalition of villages, chooses to go after this Hector and deliver him to you, then this would be simply a conflict between villages."

I frowned. "I thought that you—that everyone in the Wild—forbade inter-Tribal conflict."

"It's discouraged, certainly," Tinidan allowed, "But it can never be eliminated entirely. The Council mechanism doesn't work well for disputes between villages."

I looked at him speculatively, and he quickly clarified. "That said, my faction isn't well placed to threaten Hidden Hollow. We don't have the numbers or the warlike inclination."

"So if you're not going to threaten them . . ."

He smiled. "There are many Council members who want something done about this demon issue, *and* many of them think that the best person to do it is a Champion."

"So if we make clear that Hector is our price for intervening . . ."

"Then they become interested in acquiring him as a bargaining chip and start to form a coalition, stretching across the main factions to do so."

"I see," I said slowly. It seemed that the Tribes did use majority rule for some things after all. "So all I have to do now is wait for an offer from someone. It won't come through the Council?"

"No," Tinidan said. "It may come through me, or they may approach you directly. Accept the Council mission in return for having Hector handed over."

"Huh. And how does Borys fit into this?"

"I'm not sure," Tinidan admitted. "Most likely, Elder Thorne had the same idea that we did and just wants something of his own. I doubt it is at all connected to you. Assuming that his goal isn't in direct opposition to ours, we'll be pushing for the Council to send you both, and pay both rewards. Two Champions are better than one, after all."

"Will Borys be posting his own request, then?"

"He may do; we'll certainly be looking out for it." Tinidan looked thoughtful. "Or he may send it through other channels. We'll find out soon enough."

"All right," I said. "I guess I'd better let you get back to work."

"Ask Lira to show you around," he suggested. "There are many fine sights to see."

MARKET

I had Lira take us shopping. If politics was going to make us wait, then commerce could fill in the gap.

"I heard that the Tribes were the best place to get leather armor," I commented as we browsed through the open—or at least covered only by trees—air market. "Can I hope that this market is the best place to get some?"

Leather was an inadequate term for what we were speaking of, but it was all I had. The Great Wild was home to many dangerous beasts of a wildly diverse nature. From time to time, a tribesman would kill one of those beasts. Sometimes for food or resources, sometimes because it had become dangerous. Whatever the reason, the hide of a magical monster was almost always excellent armor.

Dungeons produced a similar bounty, but they had less variety, and to get to the good beasts, you had to go through each level in turn. Here, they were wandering around, ripe for ambushing. The greater availability of legendary hides led to more craftsmen of legendary skill, and a comparative advantage was formed.

At least that was the theory. Getting the armor out of the Great Wild had proved difficult. I did need new armor, but I was also hoping to make some contacts here that could help me establish a basis for trade.

"Eh, the stuff they have here isn't *bad*, but—" Lira cut herself off, guiltily.

"But what?" I asked mildly.

"Uh, it's fine, really," she said. "There are some great craftsmen here, and there's armor sets that have come in with traders . . ."

She trailed off under my inquiring gaze. It wasn't so much that she was lying, that much was obvious. The interesting thing was that it looked like praising the craftsmen here was causing her physical pain.

The silence stretched out long enough to become awkward.

"Look," I said. "I'm sure you're not supposed to disparage the traders here, but if you keep that up, you're going to do yourself an injury. Why don't you just tell me?"

She looked at me warily, and I wondered if my expression hadn't translated well.

"You won't tell?" she asked.

"I won't. What's wrong with the armor here?"

"It's just—you *can't* buy armor that way!" she burst out.

I raised an eyebrow. "Since I've never heard of another way, I assume you mean shouldn't?"

Lira rolled her eyes. "Fine, *shouldn't*. Buying armor off the shelf, you're lucky if it matches your fighting style. It's not going to mesh with your mana, it won't have the right effects, the enchantments will—"

"Hold on," I interrupted. "How *do* you buy armor?"

"Well . . ." Lira had to stop and organize her thoughts. "First you decide what sort of armor you need, what enchantments and natural abilities it needs."

"Wait, enchantments? I thought you couldn't enchant leather."

You could enchant mundane steel. Doing so degraded both the steel and the enchantment, so it wasn't a good idea, but it could be done. Leather, no. The few tests I'd done trying to engrave leather invariably caused it to catch fire. You *could* paint a rune in engraving dust mixed with glue. That would work—briefly. The rune had to be stiff, and leather was not. And the mixture of dust and glue had all the sticking power of warm spit, which was to say, not a lot. Your rune would pop off the minute you put the armor on.

"You can," Lira insisted, "if the skin is magical enough. And the magic of the skin has to match with the kind of enchantment you're trying to instill."

I narrowed my eyes. I'd yet to work out why runes needed different types of powdered gemstone mixed in with the gold dust to work. Matching the type of magic was as good a reason as any.

"How do they engrave the runes, then?" I asked.

"I dunno, I'm not an Enchanter, and I've never been able to afford a set of proper armor. But I asked around because I want to get something good one day."

"Getting back to the process," I suggested.

"Oh, right. So you start with the enchantment, which means starting with the Enchanter. He can tell you what sort of skin you need."

"Which you take to the craftsman," I said.

"Well, yeah, but it's not that simple. You have to find the skin in the first place. Good skin is hard to find, and depending on what you need, you might have to hunt the beast for it. Then, not all craftsmen work with all the types of skin. Not all of them will make the kind of armor you're looking for. So you need to find the right craftsman."

"Sounds complicated," I admitted. "So the stuff here . . ."

"Mostly, it's either unenchanted sets made out of whatever type of skin was handy, or it's enchanted with whatever seemed to suit the material. It's not designed for the wearer."

"I see. Thank you for explaining all that," I said. "However, since I don't have the time to go through all that, how about we take a look at what's on the shelves and see if there's anything I like?"

"I suppose we can do that," Lira said reluctantly. "You'll be lucky to find what you want, though."

"I'm starting to realize," I said, "that luck, good or bad, isn't something I need to worry about. When the gods have their thumbs on the scale, the odds are meaningless."

Lira frowned. "You think your patron has arranged for the perfect set of armor to be waiting for you?"

"Maybe, maybe not," I said. "Maybe Ashmor has arranged for the building to be dragged into the pits of hell."

Lira looked confused.

"Sorry, it's an expression from back home," I said. "The point is, you can't—I can't let the odds of something get to me. I just have to try to be ready for whatever happens."

"You can't be ready for everything," she objected.

"True. But right now, I'm ready to find some nice armor."

With that, we went looking.

"This guy is probably your best bet," Lira told us as we entered the shop. "He's an Enchanter who does his own crafting."

"Come to pester me again, brat?" The gruff voice that spoke came from a grizzled old lion-kin sitting behind a workbench at the back of the store. He was holding a piece of leather in his hands.

"Nuh-uh, old man, I brought customers!" Lira crowed.

"Brought a horde of gawkers, more like." The old man looked over at us with a jaundiced eye. "The men are dressed in metal, they're not going to want to buy from me. And who dresses women for combat?"

"*You* do, or have you gone senile and forgotten?"

"Bah!" Addressing us, the man was less gruff, but only a little. "Is the lying whelp telling the truth this time? Are the pair of you potential buyers?"

I looked over at Felicia and she shook her head. "I don't think so," she said. "I'm not as adventurous as you, and I don't think I could wear . . . what you do, or what those others did."

"I'm fairly sure that the leather crop top isn't required," I said dryly. "Kaito's crew had other priorities in mind than maximum protection."

"Even so," Felicia said, blushing. "I don't want to abandon propriety."

"A skirt isn't any harder to make," the lion-kin said. "Easier, even."

Lira snorted. "How do you even fight in that?" she asked scornfully.

"Not important right now," I said. "But we probably won't have time for you to make something, so unless you have an armored dress in stock, I'm going to be the only customer. The name is Kandis, by the way."

"Voss," he replied. "Since the brat wouldn't have thought to give you my name."

"I was gonna!" Lira protested. The storekeeper ignored her.

"So, what are you looking for . . . Kandis?" he asked.

I shrugged. "I'm pretty new to enchanted leather," I said. "Why don't you show me what you've got that you think will fit, and we'll see if there's anything I like."

"Fine," he said and started pulling pieces off the shelves and laying them on the table. As he did so, I felt his Bargain skill start to engage.

"Damn you, brat," he said without heat. "You've brought me a customer who'll take me for every penny."

"If you believed that, you wouldn't be selling at all," I pointed out.

"Yeah, yeah," he muttered. "You don't have the Armor skill, I take it."

"I do not," I said. There were lots of people who thought I had more skills than was possible, but I didn't have *every* skill.

"Well, these are light enough to use without a penalty. *These* will penalize you, but only by one."

"That's minus one to Agility and Finesse, right?" I'd looked into the penalties a long time ago.

"*And* spellcasting," he said. I wasn't sure if that applied to me, as I didn't need to make gestures. I'd never bothered to test it, though.

I checked out the first group. There were only two pieces of main body armor there; the rest were smaller pieces. First up were a pair of gauntlets. They looked like normal leather that had been dyed somehow with a fractal pattern in light blue.

> **[Identification]: Frostbloomed Leather Gauntlets – Quality: Excellent - Properties: Resistance to Cold, Enchanted: Freezing Grip – Protection: 102**

Already I was looking at a protection much higher than the measly 68 that my current "Great" leather afforded. That didn't mean much when it only covered the hands, but protection from cold and a damaging attack sounded pretty great.

"Is the Freezing Grip on all the time?" I asked. Voss shook his head.

"All of the enchantments can be activated or not. The basic properties are on all the time, though."

"It might be worthwhile for the rest of you to check these out as well," I said to my group. "Any of us can wear gauntlets without changing our basic armor."

That was almost true. Kyle had silversteel covering his gauntlets to match the rest of his armor. I gave him an Identify, to compare with what we were looking at, and instantly regretted it.

> **[Identification]: Silversteel Partial Plate – Quality: Great – Properties: Corrosion Resistance, Enchanted: Protection – Protection: 1,080**

In fairness, as the team's bulwark, he needed all the armor we could give him. The heaviest, the strongest, and the most enchanted. The team started checking out the smaller pieces, while I turned my attention to the larger items.

> **[Identification]: Shadowhide Longcoat – Quality: Excellent – Properties: +1 Agility, +2 Stealth, Enchantment: +1 Shadow Magic – Protection: 203**
>
> **[Identification]: Venomhide Gilet – Quality: Perfect - Properties: Venom Immunity, Enchanted: Poison Touch – Protection : 356**

A gilet, apparently, was a protective vest that extended down to cover my thighs. Both of them were significant upgrades in protection. And the shadowhide longcoat . . .

"How do you enchant skill bonuses?" I asked incredulously. I started going over the coat to see how it was done.

"The animal has to have it as a natural ability," Voss grunted. "And you need the right runes, of course."

"Of course," I said absently. Looking at the coat with Mana Sense, I couldn't see any runes, but there were some anomalous patterns in the mana around the coat. The naturally magical material had been changed, in some way, to make it more conductive to mana. I felt Enchant perk up, telling me not how it was done, but how I could do the same. I'd need a different tool from my engraver, something . . .

I broke off from my trance. This wasn't the time; I had other magical gear to check out.

> **[Identification]: Griffin Skyleather Gauntlets – Quality: Excellent – Properties: +1 Agility, +1 Acrobatics, Enchantment: +1 Wind Magic – Protection: 203**

Another tempting item. Finally a chance for some Wind Magic! But . . .

"The Agility modifiers, they don't stack, do they?" I asked Voss.

"Nope," he agreed. I grimaced. I was already getting plus one Agility from my dagger. That made the shadowhide and these gloves less appealing. Although this might be a chance to upgrade my weapons . . . I moved on.

> **[Identification]: Phoenix Emberskin Boots – Quality: Perfect – Properties: Fire Resistance, Enchantment: Fire Absorption – Protection: 255**

Dappled in different shades of red, and stubbled with little nubs where the feathers had been, the phoenix emberskin boots weren't the most attractive shoes I'd ever seen. But Fire Resistance might make them worth it.

That was all of the unencumbering armor. But I took a quick look at the other pieces.

[Identification]: Thunderdrake Scaled Jacket – Quality: Excellent – Properties: Electrical Resistance, Enchanted: Static Charge – Protection: 305
[Identification]: Basilisk Scaleskin Coif – Quality: Excellent – Properties: Immune to Petrification, Enchanted: Protection – Protection: 610
[Identification]: Manticore Bloodscale Trousers – Quality: Excellent – Properties: Resistance to Poison, Venom, Enchanted: +1 Agility, +2 Acrobatics – Protection: 305

All of these pieces were of scaled leather, which was to say that they had been taken from a beast with protective scales, and whatever process they had treated the leather with, it had left the scales on. That made the result heavier, stiffer, and more protective.

"Hmm," I pondered. "I do like that shadowhide coat . . . but I'm starting to see what you mean about getting your armor custom-made."

"There are some other places I can take you," Lira suggested. "You don't want to just buy the first piece you see."

"Traitorous brat! You'd take her to see someone else?" Voss growled unconvincingly.

"Course I would! Just count yourself lucky that you were first!" she replied cheekily.

"Uh, Kandis?" Cloridan interrupted from the door. "You might want to take a look at this . . . something's happening outside."

Treetop Terrorism

W hat is it?" I asked, standing on the platform outside of Voss's shop. There wasn't exactly a street to look down, but there was a view.

The . . . let's say *eclectic* style of Tribal construction meant that there wasn't anything like the grid of paved streets that I was used to. There *was* a sort of order, but it was the kind of order that you needed a mathematician to stare blindly at for a few hours before having an epiphany and writing lots of equations on a glass wall.

Most of the businesses—or homes; zoning was not any kind of a thing here—were built onto the trees. They were large trees, and widely spaced, so there was plenty of room at ground level to travel in any direction you wanted. Except for the *other* buildings.

Unlike the trees, which grew wherever it was that they wanted, the freestanding structures did exhibit an overall plan. Someone had clearly decided where things could be built. They blocked off routes in key areas, funnelling the foot traffic into streams that might, if you were shortsighted and missing your glasses, look like roads.

Many of these roads ran towards the Blessed Oak, and from where I was standing I had an excellent view that stretched all the way to the ceremonial gate that granted access to the Gathering Place. Since it was dimly lit and far away, I doubt I could have made out much with my old eyes, but my enhanced vision made it clear and bright.

Cloridan was pointing out three people, clad in matching dark hooded cloaks, that had been accosted by a pair of . . . raccoon-kin, going by their striped hair. They might have been guards, but it was hard for me to tell. Say what you like about military and police uniforms, but the more ridiculous they were, the easier it was to tell them apart from regular folks. Individualism had its benefits, but the Tribes took it a little too far.

"What about it?" I asked.

"It's not the argument itself," Cloridan said. "It's more the fact that those aren't the only ones."

He pointed out three more locations on the forest floor below. At each, there was another group of three people, all dressed in identical hooded cloaks. Two of them seemed to be paying attention to the argument; the other group was further ahead and didn't seem to have noticed.

What was I just thinking about individualism in the Tribes? I thought to myself uneasily. *I guess they can dress alike if they want to. Unless . . .*

"Lira, do you recognize those hooded cloaks? Are they a uniform or something?"

Lira stepped up next to me and looked down at the arguing group. "No idea," she said. "I wonder why they're arguing with the guards?"

"Those are guards? How can you tell?" I asked, but she just gave me a look, confused that I couldn't tell the obvious.

I sighed in frustration. "Well, it does look troubling, but is there something we should do? It seems like the guards are already aware of some of whatever it is."

"I dunno," Clordidan said. "It just seems like . . . trouble."

"There are two Champions in town right now; not every piece of trouble has my name on it," I said. "We should just—" I paused because the situation down below had taken a turn for the worse.

One of the cloaked figures had stabbed one of the guards. The other guard was struggling with another one of the cloaked figures. It looked as if he'd grabbed the weapon before he could be impaled by it.

"Oh no," I said. "That doesn't look good. What are we supposed to do in a situation like this, Lira?"

I wasn't exactly trained as a diplomat, but I was fairly sure that I shouldn't be getting into fights, even to save lives belonging to the state I was visiting. On the other hand, I was a Champion, and we were sort of supposed to stick our noses into other people's business. That was supposed to be on behalf of the gods, but King Alexandros had shown a distressing enthusiasm for having me handle his problems.

"I . . . I'm not sure," Lira admitted. "My training didn't cover this, but generally I think we should help. It's the right thing to do."

Sure enough, while a lot of the closest individuals were screaming and running away from the sudden bloodshed, a few more civic (or martially) minded townsfolk were running towards the sudden conflict. Or were they guards? I still couldn't tell.

Helping was all very well, but I wasn't going to charge into the middle of a fight I knew nothing about. That was Cloridan's job.

"Cloridan," I said. "Use your own initiative as best you can. Improved Invisibility." I cast the spell aloud so that Lira could see that I wasn't disintegrating him or something. Cloridan nodded, but only I could see that. I was also the only one who could see him vault over the rail to the ground below. Hopefully, he would be a big problem for the right person.

"Let's take the normal way down," I said to the rest of the group. It wasn't an impossible jump for Felicia and me, but it would be a hard one. "But first . . ."

There were a few things more I had to do. The automatic aiming didn't help as much as I'd like for this one. It let me put the source where I liked, but I had to point the cone . . .

"Light," I said, casting the spell at a longer range than I ever had before. Like a spotlight turning on, the two guards and three cultists were suddenly illuminated in bright white light. As a combat distraction, it was a wash, as none of the combatants were expecting it, and they *all* froze for a second. Not that it would have helped. The guards were clearly on the losing side of that conflict. It was just a matter of whether they would die before the reinforcements arrived.

That wasn't why I cast the spell, though. The people on the ground didn't seem to be aware of what Cloridan had noticed, so it fell on me to point it out.

"Light. Light. Light." I don't think I'd ever had the need to cast that spell four times in a row before. Three new spotlights appeared, attracting attention to the other three groups of hooded figures. It was possible that Lira had missed the latest Tribal fashion trend, but I felt pretty sure about assuming the other three groups were up to no good.

They froze for a second as well and then made a dash for it. In theory, I could have tracked them with the Light spell until they went out of range, but controlling four lights was hard. Two of the groups split up, which made it even harder. Attention had been directed to the cloaks, however, which was my goal. People were pointing and shouting at the running figures, which was good enough, I thought.

"Let's get down there," I said. Lira, who had been hopping impatiently from one foot to the other, made a dash for the stairs.

"Wait, Lira, do you have a weapon?" I asked.

Lira froze. Then she spun around to look at me, attempting to use the movement to disguise the way she brought her right hand forward, away from where it had been reaching behind her back.

"No, ma'am," she said guiltily. "As an apprentice diplomat, I can't be carrying weapons, as that might be seen as a threat to you."

She had clearly Memorized that line, as it was delivered with entirely different cadences than her normal speech.

"That's a little inconvenient," I said dryly. "Why don't you use that one hidden behind your back, and if anyone asks, you can say I gave it to you."

"Yes'm," Lira mumbled, half chagrined, half elated.

"And stay close," I told her. "I'm not sure if you're bodyguarding me or if I'm babysitting you, but we can't do either if you get too far away.

"Yes'm," Lira mumbled again.

I looked around to make sure we were ready to go. Kyle had unlimbered his shield and was standing protectively close to Felicia. Reynard was . . . there. Standing quietly in the background, as he'd been doing all day. I wanted to tell him to stay back, but he was safest where we could keep an eye on him.

As long as he was with us, we should be able to tell when he received new orders, or new memories. Since I didn't fancy getting sniped by that bow of his, he was safest where we could see him.

With a wry grin that told me he knew exactly what I was thinking, Reynard turned and led the way.

By the time we got close to the first fight, the guards were down. The mysterious cloaked figures were still there, though, accosted by an angry group of beast-kin. The odds had been reversed—the three figures were surrounded by five armed and armored Tribe members. Three more beast-kin, apparently unarmed, were hanging back from the fray offering shouts of encouragement.

Still not knowing what was going on, my goal was to get Felicia close enough to try healing the guards. Before that could happen, though, the situation changed, again.

One of the figures barked an order, and as one, they all tore off their cloaks. Revealed beneath was . . .

"Hector?" I exclaimed in surprise. It wasn't Hector. It *was* some of his men, though. The uniforms were distinctive.

"Humans?" One of the opposing beast-kin shouted in surprise. Another one seemed to have a better idea of what he was looking at.

"Latorrans," he growled. "Your kind aren't welcome here,"

"We go where we will, dog," the leader declared. Inaccurately, I thought. The one who'd spoken was a stoat-kin. Probably. "Out of our way before we strike you down." All three of them had been wielding daggers, but now they drew out swords into their other hand.

"Hey! There's more of them!" One of the three hangers-back pointed in our direction. Hostile looks were directed our way.

"None of that," I said quickly. "Lira, take the front. Improved Blind!"

I cast the spell aloud because I wanted the beast-kin to associate my casting a spell with the black sphere that appeared around the human soldier's head. The leader of the group dropped his weapons and clutched at his head uselessly. He might have been saying something, but no one could tell.

"Ahhh, guys, guys, these humans are guests of the Council!" Lira said hastily, holding her palms out in a gesture of peace.

"Blind."

"They're good guys, here to warn us about *these* bad guys!" she continued urgently.

The one remaining soldier looked at me angrily, but he couldn't turn his back on the beast-kin in front of him, and he couldn't get through the beast-kin between him and me. There was only one way this could go.

"Blind."

That was the human threat wrapped up. The forest floor was too tangled with roots to walk on without vision, let alone fight. That just left the rapidly escalating beast-kin threat.

"It's true," I said, stepping behind Lira and putting my hand on her shoulder. I resisted the urge to scratch her behind her long ears. "These soldiers are criminals in Latora, who fled justice by coming here. My companions and I have come to beg the aid of the Council in apprehending them."

I had Charm cranked up to full, of course, and under the circumstances felt it was appropriate to use Persuasion. I was relieved to see that there wasn't anyone here who could resist it.

> **You have defeated a group led by Ashrad in a Tier 2 Social Contest! You have earned 104 XP.**

I blinked at the tier two. Tensions must have been higher than I thought.

"Well, you seem to be all right," Ashrad admitted. "What should we do with these guys?"

"Capture them and bring them before the Council," I ordered. They were naturally inclined to follow such an order, so it was an easy ask. "Then we should head to the Blessed Oak. I fear that there are more of these groups."

Faces grim, the beast-kin agreed and swiftly secured the captives.

Your party has defeated Daniel Furst! You have earned 12 XP.
Your party has defeated Lucas Lemann! You have earned 12 XP.
Your party has defeated Tobias Wurfel! You have earned 12 XP.

Given how many people I was sharing it with, I was surprised it was that high.

"Come on," I told my impromptu group. "There isn't a moment to lose."

FLAMESTRIKE

We ran towards the Blessed Oak, the center of the Tribes' culture, governance, and religion. "Ran" would be the wrong word, though. More like skipped. Not out of any feelings of joy, but because it was easier to skip over the gaps between the roots than to climb over them every time.

The noncombatant beast-kin from before had agreed to take care of the prisoners after I'd carefully checked them for mind-control amulets. They would follow more slowly, hopefully not showing up until the fight was over.

Four of the fighting beast-kin had insisted on following me, to try and stop whatever was going on. I thought that they were more motivated by a civic duty to help than they were by their lack of trust in a stranger who wanted to get involved. But both motivations pushed them in the same direction, so it was hard to tell.

We did pause, briefly, to let Felicia heal two beast-kin we found on the way. We found one human body, dead, with dagger wounds in his back.

"Do you think that was Cloridan?" Felicia asked. The corpse was right next to the rat-kin she was healing.

"Maybe," I said. I hadn't seen Cloridan since he jumped over the railing and I was starting to worry. I could put together a story that had Cloridan saving the guy Felicia was healing by stabbing the soldier, but it was just a story.

Lira was hopping impatiently from one foot to the other again.

"We've got to get going," she said urgently. "Who knows what could be going on!"

"Just enough healing to stop the bleeding," Felicia insisted. I'd thought about leaving her behind to finish, but then Kyle would have stayed with her. That would have left me with Lira and a bunch of people I didn't trust. Starting with, and most especially, Reynard. Lira's job was to stay with me, of course, and the four beast-kin weren't going to leave me to get up to mischief. So we all stayed while Felicia healed.

"Done," she said, and we were off again.

As we got closer to the Oak, we could see that the twelve men that we'd noticed were not the full extent of the incursion. Hooded figures had converged on the Tree from all directions, and they were now fighting with a ragtag group of beast-kin that had sprung up to resist them.

It wasn't clear to me what Hector was trying to accomplish. It *was* Hector; I was pretty sure that was him leading the troops. Right now, it looked as though they were winning, but that was an impression as false as any of my illusions.

Fully armed and armored, Hector's troops were more than a match for any of the hastily assembled Rangers, foresters, and priests that they were fighting. Forming up into a . . . fighting wedge? Was that the term? Whatever the name was, it synergized with their fighting style, letting them press forward against the same or even greater numbers of troops.

But they couldn't fight everybody. Beast-kin were pouring out of the forest, joining the fight to protect their home without question. Eventually, numbers would tell.

And now there were archers joining the fray. This was how beast-kin preferred to fight, sniping from hidden shadows.

"About time," Lira sniffed. "How long does it take them to get set up?" She looked at me. "Are we joining in?"

"Give me a minute," I said. The four beast-kin we'd gathered were also holding back, looking to me for guidance. Though they'd no doubt deny it if asked.

I used Mana Sense on the conflict in front of me, trying to determine if there were any of the Countess's amulets at work, but it was too chaotic to be sure. I thought there might be two, neither of which was being worn by Hector. The currents were too twisted to tell me who they were being worn by.

"There might be some mind-control amulets in there," I told my group. Was that Hector's plan? Get the amulets in range of the Council? They were surely being evacuated now, though . . .

As it turned out, Hector had a different plan. In response to the arrows peppering his troops, about half a dozen grenades were thrown out.

To someone like me, whose experience of grenades was watching a few World War II movies, a thrown grenade implies a lazy arc. The hero tosses it over the wall the enemy is hiding behind and flicks away incoming ones, causing them to detonate just out of range. Has there ever been a movie grenade that *didn't* go off close enough for the blast to ruffle the hero's hair?

With a soldier of eight times normal strength, though, a grenade gets thrown like a rocket, flung on a flat, rising trajectory that impacts the upper trunks of nearby trees and explodes into flame.

I felt a shiver run through me as I recognized the same potion that Hector had used on *me*. This wasn't a forest that caught fire easily, not like back home, but it wasn't immune to alchemical fire.

Flames bloomed in the treetops all around the conflict. I wasn't sure what the goal was, unless it was indiscriminate destruction. To deny a place for archers to snipe? To keep the Tribes too busy fighting fires to fight humans?

"Don't worry!" Lira called out to me. We weren't in the fight, but she still needed to yell. The roar of the fires all around, the shouts of those fighting, and the screams of those just trying to get away made it necessary. "The Blessed Oak's protection won't allow it to be harmed by fire."

That was all very well, but the tree's protection didn't seem to extend to us, or the trees around us. We pushed forward, and I conjured a Water Stream to douse the nearest fire. It was only a drop in the bucket against such a volume of intense flame, but I wasn't the only one with that spell. I cast another one ahead of us, this one tuned for a wide dispersal so that we were walking into a fine mist. It would get us damp, but I had a feeling that we'd welcome that shortly.

We weren't trying to join the melee. Hector's formation had left a lot of beast-kin fallen behind them, and not all of them were dead. Felicia wanted to do what she could for them, and that did seem like the most non-offensive way we could contribute. I did have the idea, if we got close enough, of blinding Hector with that spell, but for the moment he was out of range and I lacked a good line of sight.

I glanced over at Reynard who was walking next to us, looking out for incoming attacks but otherwise unconcerned. He hadn't even drawn his bow.

"Not going to join in?" I asked.

He looked at me sardonically. "My orders are to protect you," he said. "It's hard to be sure, but I *think* these guys are working for my lady. I'd have a hard time justifying attacking them."

"And I'm supposed to believe that you're not going to join them?" I asked skeptically.

He shrugged. "Believe what you like. The lady doesn't appreciate initiative, so I'll stick with what I know. You want me to hang back . . ."

I scowled. "No, stay here where—"

"Ware!" Kyle called out. He didn't wait for us to respond, but quickly moved his shield to cover me. There was the sound of an impact and a shriek of tortured metal, way too close to my head for comfort.

"What the?" I exclaimed. There was a hole in the underside of Kyle's shield, with what had been the sharp point of an arrow poking through it. I blinked, shocked.

I wasn't an SCA nut by any means, but I was pretty sure that shields back home were mostly wood. Maybe sometimes they were edged with metal, maybe sometimes they were covered by a thin layer of metal, but mostly wood. People had to carry them around all day, after all.

That wasn't how shields were here. Kyle's shield was a plate of metal, too heavy for me to lift. I could *support* it, if one edge was on the ground and it wasn't tilted too far. It was heavy.

It was also crafted and enchanted for additional defensive strength. I could—well, Cloridan could—stab through an ingot of steel with my darksteel dagger. It just skittered off Kyle's shield.

So to see something put a hole in it was a bit of a shock. I froze up for a second, long enough for Kyle to grab and reposition me closer to Felicia so that he could protect us both from whatever else was coming from that direction. Felicia's eyes had widened with shock, but she kept healing the fallen cat-kin that she'd been working on.

Lira actually reacted before I did. "You idiots!" she yelled at the top of her voice. "They're *guests of the Council*, not enemies!"

Another arrow whizzed by. I was pretty sure it was aimed at us, but with Kyle on alert from that direction, we were harder to hit now.

"Don't waste your breath," Reynard told Lira. "It's another Hidden Hollow arrow."

She stared at him. "You mean they're targeting her deliberately?"

"Seems like it," he said. "They must be working with Hector's crew."

"This is outrageous!" Lira exclaimed. "Taking part in an attack on the tree . . . the Council will never stand for it!"

"That'll be great for the next council meeting," I said, finally getting myself together. "For now, though, if they're after me, I should just take myself out of the equation. Greater Invisibility."

"Wow, I can't smell you or *anything*," Lira said, forgetting outrage instantly.

Another arrow caromed off of Kyle's pauldron. A better shot, but still not enough to get past his defense.

"They're still firing," he reported.

"They probably don't know that she's invisible yet," Reynard said wryly. "Too easy to hide behind you."

Kyle had the grace to look embarrassed for me. "Well, when Felicia's finished we can—"

Lira screamed in horror.

"What are they doing? Why would they—"

She was staring, not at the bodies around us or the conflict ahead, but beyond. The soldiers had launched another round of fire potions. This time they were closer . . . no, not closer.

"They'd have to be *druids* to do that, and druids would know . . ." Lira trailed off, spluttering with outrage.

Honestly, I wasn't sure that my supposition was true. One tree looked very much like another to me, and the canopies were all merged. There was one way to tell, however. Although the burning tree in question was on the other side of the fighting soldiers, it was close enough to use Identify.

> **[Identification]: Blessed Oak – Properties: Protection (Suppressed), Blessing (Suppressed), Immortal (Suppressed)**

Oh, that isn't good, I thought. Around me, I could hear a subtle change in the shouts and screams. The beast-kin fighting the fires, the archers, the ones running towards the fight and the ones running away. There had been a mixture of fear and anger before, but that mix was quickly shifting towards anger.

The tree meant a lot to the beast-kin, and the humans were *burning* it.

Boy, I sure am glad I'm invisible, I thought. Maybe I should make the others invisible as well and we could just creep on out of here before it got ugly. Except for Reynard.

Unworthy as the thought was, it almost sounded like a plan. Hector's troops were still pushing forward, so the next round of fire potions wouldn't be burning the outer branches of the Blessed Oak, they'd be burning the . . . Heartwood? Crown? Whatever you called the core of a really big tree.

It was clear now what the goal was. Take down the tree, get the humans blamed for it, and put paid to any hope of peace between the Tribes and Latora for . . . well, forever. Less clear was how Hector thought he was going to survive, but he might be a sacrifice play. The Mind Mage (who might or might not be Lady Rankin) could have left him with the impression that he'd be saved somehow.

Also unclear was what I could do about it. I could get closer with Shadow Magic, though there were very few shadowed areas near the fires. But my Water Magic wasn't enough to put out the fires, and my Phantasmal spells were too small to make any kind of difference. I could try convincing everyone that the fires were out, but that didn't seem very helpful. Earth Magic would probably cause more damage than it prevented.

I was still dithering over what to do when something changed. From the smoky gloom behind the fires, from the area where the Council would have been, a whitish sphere appeared, about three meters in diameter.

Not whitish, I realized. It was white, but not fully opaque. There was a figure in the center of it, and the white was swirling around it furiously.

The figure held up its hands.

The white rushed out in all directions.

SNOWSTORM

An icy cold blast of wind knocked me off my feet. A lot of people went down at the same time. Not everyone, but even those, like Kyle, who stayed up had to brace themselves against the gale. It interrupted the fighting for a moment, which was for the best, as it was the defenders that were the worst impacted.

Most of the soldiers were high-Strength types who weathered the gust by freezing in place. The beast-kin tended towards Agility builds. Some of them stayed up, but more of them got knocked over. Or worse, they were in the air at the moment of impact and took a tumble. I don't think anyone was hurt, but if that was all that Borys had done, we would have been in a lot of trouble.

It wasn't, of course. As the wind died away, I struggled to my feet. I was now able to recognize that it was Borys in the middle of all that snow, snow that was now lashing at the flames in the treetops. The flames struggled, but Borys seemed to have an unending supply of snow and ice to drown them in.

For a moment, everything was unnaturally quiet.

"That's enough!" Borys called out. "Whatever you were here to do, it ends now."

I couldn't hear what Hector said in reply. I was too far away, he was facing away from me, and he wasn't yelling at the top of his lungs like Borys was. I caught something about "traitor" and "beasts" before he charged forward, throwing another potion straight at Borys.

I was running forward at full speed now. I didn't have to worry about people trying to stop me now that I was invisible. I wasn't sure what I was going to do, but I needed to be there to do it. I could have Shadow

Stepped—the darkness was coming back to the area—but I felt that my Invisibility spell was worth preserving.

Borys forced Hector back with a cold geyser of ice and sleet. The potion fell to the ground, encased in a protective layer of ice. I was close enough now to hear Hector snarl as he started to push forward again. Then he staggered and fell. Blood spurted from his back for no reason whatsoever.

At least, that was what everyone else saw. I saw Cloridan plunging his blades into the Captain's back.

> **Your party has killed Hector Rodakis – your experience share is 136 XP.**

Time seemed to stand still as I desperately tried to figure out what to do next. It could have been my thoughts speeding up, or it could have been that everyone else froze—again—as they tried to process how Hector had just died. Even Cloridan didn't move. I could only make out his outline, but he seemed to be staring down at Hector as though he couldn't believe the man was dead.

Should I leave it as a mystery? Cloridan would be safer if he was invisible but . . . he was perfectly capable of surviving without that advantage. He had Borys as an ally, and the beast-kin, and Hector's troops were nothing if not dismayed right now.

More than Cloridan's immediate safety, we needed *credit* right now. Credit and a distraction. I cancelled his invisibility.

Everyone jumped, including Cloridan, as he suddenly appeared out of thin air.

"Who are you?" Borys was the first to respond. He managed to keep the petulance out of his voice, but my skills told me it was there.

Cloridan took the pass and ran with it. With his back to about thirty guys who wanted to kill him, he bowed gallantly to Borys. "Cloridan Moquin, Lord Champion. I'm a companion of Councillor Kandis."

He stepped forward easily, putting some distance between himself and his enemies, without making it look like he was. "I'm not sure if you'd heard, my lord, but we came to the Great Wild hunting this man, and his men, for crimes against the Crown."

"That's a lie!" one of the soldiers called out, and there were a few shouts of agreement. However, without their leader, they didn't seem inclined to restart the violence. The situation seemed to have devolved into an argument, at least for the moment.

It worked out better for me, but I still had problems. The storm that Borys produced may have been still here in the center, but it filled the entire volume with a low-grade haze of diffuse mana. It made it hard to see what I was looking for, even though I was closer and things had calmed down.

Cloridan was explaining the mind-control theory to Borys, and Borys was berating the troops, trying to get them to stand down. The delay was not working in the soldiers' favor, as every second meant more flames put out, and more beast-kin—angry beast-kin—arriving.

That didn't matter to me, as I'd found at least one of the things that I'd been looking for. He looked like an ordinary soldier. Lined up next to all the others, I wouldn't have looked twice. Normally. Right now, though, he had a mana thread sneaking out from under his clothes.

He was in the middle of a press of scared, violent men so I couldn't get near him. Luckily I didn't need to. I just needed to get between him and the faraway Mind Mage so that the thread passed within my reach.

A flex of Theurgy and the thread was snapped. One down, one to go. Probably. But where was it? I knew that I'd seen two, but I couldn't see the second one now.

Had it become concealed again? Dispel Image was a pretty broad target spell and I spammed it around me a few times, but I didn't seem to pick up anything. Unfortunately, I was running out of time. Neither Borys nor Cloridan had the social skills to turn this situation around, and both sides were losing patience.

Cloridan let out a sigh of relief when I appeared next to him.

"Finally," he said. "How long were you going to let us meatheads do the talking?"

"You got them halfway there," I said. "I'll take over now, if that's okay?" I asked Borys, who was looking at me in surprise. He managed to nod.

The human soldiers recognized me, of course, and there was a subdued muttering reaction to my appearance. I don't know what Hector had told them about me, but I suspected I'd find out soon. For now, I ignored them and addressed the surrounding beast-kin crowd.

First, though, I cast a spell silently.

"People of the Tribes!" I announced. My voice rang out clearly across the clearing thanks to Illusory Terrain. Unseen Sound could make my voice louder, but this spell could make it come from all around.

I still spoke the words, though. When I created sounds out of my imagination, I couldn't use my skills through them. When I mimicked the sound of my own voice, I could use skills with an extended range.

"As you've heard, these men are not a Latorran army, but are criminals, on the run from their King's justice. Their crimes are many, but I ask that you accept their surrender and hand them over to your Council for a proper accounting of their crimes."

That might be a death sentence. I'd heard the outrage in Lira's voice when the Blessed Oak got damaged, and I doubted that she was an outlier. Hell, it might be a death sentence waiting for them back in Latora. I'd do what I could to prevent it, however. I'd seen one mass execution and that was more than enough.

There wasn't universal agreement from the beast-kin, but there were mutterings that sounded as if they would go for it. The soldiers, on the other hand, had other ideas.

"We're not surrendering!" one of them called out. "And we're not criminals either! We're on a mission from the King!"

I started with Persuasion. "Whatever you were told by Hector was a lie," I said, laying down the words with the weight of certainty. "He either lied to you, or he passed on the lies he was told."

Then I added Intimidation in. "There are no Kingdom forces coming to save you; you are surrounded. The Champion of Storms is standing in your path. You can surrender or you can die."

The soldiers flinched as my words hit them like hammers. They weren't ready to go down yet.

"The Captain was going to marry you, but you betrayed him! How are we supposed to trust you?"

I gave the man who said that a glare. I still didn't want these fools to die, but this guy was pushing it.

"Hector Rodakis came to tear down everything I'd worked toward." I wasn't directly threatening them, but I was holding the threat of their execution, either here or back home, over their heads. That let me keep using Intimidation, which was good as I wasn't in the mood for being nice.

"He thought that if he gave me a pretty smile, and flashed some muscly chest, then I would give it all away and share his bed in the ruins of my dream."

I looked down at his corpse.

"I didn't want him *dead*," I said. Out of the corner of my eye, I saw Cloridan stiffen. "But he was a dead man walking the minute that he betrayed his oaths to Talnier and to the King."

I looked back at the soldiers.

"Maybe, just maybe, there are enough extenuating circumstances here that I can save your lives," I said. "But it all starts with your surrender."

I paused. "Drop your weapons."

[Intimidate] Level 4 acquired through use.
For gaining a skill level, you have been awarded 1 XP.

The notification just beat out the dull thud of someone's sword falling to the forest floor. By the time I dismissed it, the rest of them were dropping their swords. There were a few holdouts, but they gave up when they saw which way the wind was blowing.

I let Illusory Terrain drop.

"Well?" I said to the nearest beast-kin. "Who's in charge here?"

"You?" he said, staring at me with wide eyes. "I mean . . . um . . ." he looked around wildly. "Probably her?" he tried, pointing.

The beast-kin he pointed to had small ears and prominent teeth, so . . . maybe a beaver-kin? She was looking around as well, but she must not have seen anyone more important than her, so she started barking orders.

They were the "take prisoner" kind of orders rather than the "slaughter them where they are" kind, so I felt that she had this in hand. I turned to my fellow Champion.

"That was a slick move, with the ice storm," I complimented him. "I don't know what we would have done if you weren't here."

He shrugged. "Champion of Storms is no empty title," he said. "But seeing these social skills in action is something else. Is that a blessing from your patron?"

"No," I said, letting just a hint of sour flavor my voice. "Whoever they are, we're not on speaking terms."

He nodded slowly. "My own start in this world was . . . not pleasant. We should share some stories sometime."

"Sounds good," I told him, "But I'm not sure this crisis is over."

I quickly explained about the Mind Mage and the amulets that let them spread their power.

"I was fairly certain that this group had two with them, but I only managed to find and disable one," I said. "If you can let go of the weather, I might be able to get a better look."

Borys looked up at the canopy. The fire was well and truly out by now. "No problem," he agreed. Whatever he did, the cold didn't dissipate, but the mana fog started to fade away.

"Is the storm not going to fade?" I asked as I scanned over the field of battle.

"It will take a while," he admitted. "Rakaro doesn't like to let storms go, and it *is* winter, even if it's much warmer than Polish ones."

"I don't see anything . . ." I muttered. Then I was interrupted by Lira, of all people.

"Are you looking for the druids?" she demanded as she stomped up. "Because I don't think any of those humans are druids!"

"Oh, right," I said. Glancing up at the Blessed Oak, I could see that its properties were still suppressed. "I guess it was someone from Hidden Hollow? They seemed to be working with Hector. It will need to be the Council that looks into that, though; we can't go rummaging around another village looking for someone."

"Indeed you cannot," a voice came from behind me. That was Nyssa of Elara unless I missed my guess. Beast-kin had fairly distinct voices, and my recognition game had gone way up as my Charisma had increased. Nyssa was one of Tinidan's "bosses." She was in the same faction as him but was part of the Council of Nine.

I didn't immediately turn around, as I was still looking for that damn amulet. The next voice did make me turn around, however.

"There will be no need for that," Vesper Frostpaw announced. She was part of the *opposing* faction, the militant one. Should she be standing next to Nyssa?

I looked around. Both of them were standing together like old friends. Both of them were wearing amulets.

"Hunt Leader Elodare?" Vesper called out. "Why are these humans walking around free? Arrest them."

TRIAL

I didn't have any time. As soon as I realized the situation, I cast Illusory Terrain again, filling the entire Glade with darkness. In the moment that I cast, I was a bit torn between conjuring darkness and more natural-looking plants and bushes. What came out was darkness, but rather than being flat and featureless black, it *writhed* with what I guessed were half-imagined bushes, rustling in the wind.

That was fine. A little nightmarey, but as long as it blocked sight, that was fine. I quickly reviewed what I'd learned about the amulets from my friends fighting the things in Talnier.

First, they needed touch or line of sight. That was why they wore them openly—they needed the amulets to "see" people to target them.

Second, Mind Magic was *slow*. At least, changing memories was. It had to be built up, piece by piece, or the victim would notice what was going on. Realizing that didn't make the false memories go away, but they could be ignored or contrasted with other memories. It didn't stop the invader, but it made their job much harder.

One of those amulets had come in with the human soldiers. It wouldn't have had a chance to target anyone other than them. The other one must have been in the Glade for a while, probably brought in by the Elder of Hidden Hollow. It could have messed with any number of Councillors. Not all of them, though, at least I didn't think so. The Mind Mage was just one person, after all.

People were still shouting in surprise and alarm when I cast my second spell, Shadow Step. Interestingly, the imaginary darkness didn't affect the *actual* shadows that I could use. Fortunately, the forest was well set up for shadows.

"She's gone!" someone shouted out as I reappeared. I must have slipped away just in time; *someone* wasn't letting a lack of sight stop them. It didn't matter, though, I was right where I needed to be.

Not near either of the two Councillors, of course. From the shouts in that direction, everyone was converging on those two. Where I needed to be was anywhere on a line that stretched between those two and . . . I was going to say Dorsay.

I already knew, from the previous talisman, the *direction* of that line, so it was a simple matter to put myself near it. I wasn't impeded by my own darkness, of course, but the spell did interfere with my Mana Sense in much the same way that Borys's snowstorm did. Not enough, though, that I couldn't make out a line three steps away from me. I took those steps and snatched at it.

That's one, I thought as it shattered into magical, immaterial dust. The other one had to be nearby, and it was. I reached for it just as everything changed.

Instead of the cord, the mana of my spell shattered. The darkness was dispelled with it, gone in an instant. I blinked in surprise, but I didn't let it distract me from the main prize.

The nature of the shouts had changed. It was taking them a while to find me. I wasn't exactly hiding, but stepping a hundred meters away from the action had confused them. It gave me enough time to focus on the thread. Focus and . . . dissolve it.

That's two, I thought. I knew Lady Rankin didn't have unlimited numbers of amulets. Here, she only had what Hector had brought with him, which was a fraction of her original shipment . . . she couldn't have that many more, right?

I looked back to where the shouting was coming from. There were five beast-kin that stood out from the crowd by the way they were glowing. Priests of Naldyna, I guessed. They had probably been the ones who had dispelled my illusion.

I had a few moments more before they saw me. I could have run, but I used the time to make sure there were no other amulets in the crowd. Now that my Mana Sense had cleared up, I could see at least that there weren't any more mana conduits headed in my direction. It seemed safe.

Relatively speaking, of course. There were still an unknown number of manipulated Councillors and the warriors that answered to them. I thought I might have an answer to that, so I started walking back towards the center. Once they spotted me, a group of Ranger types moved out to intercept.

One hundred meters was an insurmountable gap in social contexts, but a pack of beast-kin could cover the distance in an absurdly short space of time. Arrows were even faster, so once they noticed me, I stopped and held my hands up in the air. I was swiftly surrounded.

"Chosen," their leader said awkwardly. "There have been accusations—"

"That's fine," I cut him off before he could say more. "I'm surrendering."

They marched me up to where the Councillors were arguing. I'd handed over my weapons, and they'd bound my hands behind my back, but I was otherwise free. I wasn't sure if they *knew* that I could cast spells without my hands, but I wasn't going to volunteer the information.

Vesper Frostpaw sneered at me as I approached. "Trying to run away? From the finest trackers on the continent?"

"Not at all," I said. "I just had some quick tasks to take care of." I looked around and made sure that all of my party was accounted for. Kyle, Felicia, Cloridan, and even Reynard had all been captured. "You guys all right?" I asked them.

"We're fine, Kandis," Kyle answered. "There didn't seem much point in fighting when . . ."

"I'm not fine!" Lira yelled out. "Why are you arresting Lady Kandis, when she was only trying to help?" From the way a number of the beast-kin fighters looked uncomfortable at her words, she wasn't the only one who didn't want to go along with the story.

"Nonsense," Frostpaw declared. "The Council has heard from her own mouth of her romantic entanglements with this Captain Hector. Her ineffectual attempts at stopping him were only to prevent her from being associated with his doomed attempt."

Eww. What? Just what did they put in this guy's head?

Frostpaw wasn't done making declarations, though. "Now, all that remains is to see that these criminals pay for their desecration with their lives!"

"After the trial, right?"

My words were simple, and not spoken particularly loudly, but they had the weight of Persuasion behind them. Frostpaw stared at me, confused, and Nyssa took over.

"There's no need for a trial," she said. Even as she did, she got a confused look in her eyes, as if she didn't believe what she was saying. "We all saw clearly the events of today, and who is to blame. The Kingdom of Latora and their cat's-paw, the Chosen Kandis!"

"But there's always a need for a trial. Even a foreigner must be granted due process." The certainty in my voice was mostly due to Persuasion, but I was damn certain that was how the law worked here. There was no way that the individualistic, prickly political bastards that made up the Tribes would permit a single judge to make life-or-death decisions.

There would *have* to be a process.

Whoever it was behind the amulets, they were too used to Latorran thinking, where the highest ranked noble made the rules. They'd changed the Councillors' memories, but they hadn't changed all of them. Now I had their victims arguing against themselves.

"That's true . . . but . . ." Nyssa trailed off.

Frostpaw picked up the slack. "Yes! A trial! We'll present all the evidence of your perfidy, convince the undecided!"

"And we'll present the evidence that you're full of it!" Lira yelled. "Me, and everyone who was actually out here fighting!"

At least they meant well. Watching the legal machinery of the Tribes deploy was like watching high school students pretend to hold a court. They had the idea, but the practice was lacking. I was no lawyer, but I did have firsthand experience with how the law was used to restrain corporations like ours. The complicated game of what you could and couldn't do, the sophisticated legal mechanisms at play . . . there was none of that here.

At least it moved quickly. The idea of a trial happening in the same *week* as the crime would have been laughable at home, let alone on the same *day*.

"Are you *sure* you want me as your advocate?" Lira asked for the fifth time. "I'm only an apprentice."

"I'm sure," I said. "You were doing a pretty good job before. And I don't think this trial is going to hinge on technicalities of law."

"Of course not!" Lira said, offended. "That would go against all of Naldyna's teachings."

"Of course, it would," I said, refraining from rolling my eyes.

No one had batted an eye when I'd put Lira forward as my advocate. The opposing side had presumably felt that she would be easy enough to browbeat or outargue, but I would be handling most of my own defense. I needed *somebody*, though, and it needed to be somebody that I didn't suspect of having their mind altered.

"I don't understand, though, why you haven't just insisted on having Frostpaw and Nyssa getting examined by the priests," Lira asked.

That had come up, but I'd carefully kept my mouth shut. My earlier warning had raised suspicions, and the Councillors' behavior had raised eyebrows. Treatment by the priests had been suggested but was shot down by the Councillors.

Back home, the idea that the main accusers—under suspicion of *any* kind of influence—would be allowed to be the prosecutors was ridiculous. But they did things differently here.

"I want it to all come out at the trial," I explained. "Let them make their accusations and bring it all crashing down."

I might have been able to nip this all in the bud by insisting on a mental cleansing before the trial started. But I wasn't sure how far my status would take me. Going through the trial and being proved innocent would also make it easier to wring concessions out of the Council later, but I didn't see a need to burden Lira with that knowledge. She was a sweet soul and seemed to think the world of me.

The trial was scheduled for the evening after the event. That was quick even by Tribal standards, but the matter was important, and all the witnesses were already here. It was presided over by a triumvirate of three Councillors, chosen by lot. I held my breath when the lots were drawn, but the ones selected weren't anyone that I knew. They didn't seem important, so they were unlikely to have been manipulated.

The jury was the entire Council, of course, which as much as told me that they didn't use this procedure for most crimes. Probably left prosecution of murder and such up to the villages involved. Damaging the Oak was more important, though.

That was the main reason I was so confident. Unless every single Councillor had been manipulated, there was no way that every one of them would vote to convict. Another mistake from the Mind Mage, born of their Latorran experience. There, just influencing one person, be it the local noble or the magistrate, could swing the trial your way. Not that I'd know anything about that.

The first witness called was Tinidan. He spun some kind of cock-and-bull story about how I'd confessed the whole thing to him like some sort of villain from a fantasy tale. He'd come to warn the Council, but by the time he got there, the attack was already underway.

Lira asked a few questions as I'd instructed. She asked about the time of my "confession." Tinidan answered confidently, the answer clear in his memory. It was just an hour before the attack, just after lunch. I'd told him everything, and he'd made his way to the Glade to warn them all. Sadly, he hadn't quite made it in time.

There was just one problem with that.

"Honored Elders of the Tribe!" I called out. "Who here remembers talking to Elder Tinidan earlier *this morning*?"

Back home, behaving like that would have got me thrown out. Even here, it was definitely against the rules. My advocate was supposed to speak for me, the witness was the only one who was supposed to be questioned, and I certainly wasn't supposed to address the *jury*.

Fortunately, the Tribe's attitude towards breaking tradition tended towards "roll with it."

There was a brief silence before someone spoke up.

"I do," an Elder said from the middle of the crowd.

"I do too," another spoke up.

"I saw him after lunch, and he was fine!" another called.

"Elder Tinidan?" I asked, "What do you say against these witnesses?"

If the manipulator had still been in contact, now would have been the time for them to make another alteration. He'd left during lunch or something. They weren't, so they couldn't. All Tinidan could do was splutter.

"They're wrong! I arrived in the afternoon, and went straight to the Nine!" he said.

Four of the Nine were in my line of sight. They were all nodding in agreement with Tinidan. They were far outnumbered, however, by the calls coming from the wider Council.

"Honored Elders, under the circumstances, I think we must insist that Elder Tinidan is treated with Naldyna's healing light," I called out.

Frostpaw and Nyssa, our prosecutors, got a weird look on their faces, as if they thought it was a bad idea but couldn't quite articulate why. I don't know what memory they had that made them refuse all treatment, but it *didn't* extend to being a reason for someone else.

The first rule of memory manipulation, I decided, was to make sure they wouldn't believe their memory was manipulated.

With all the unmodified Elders calling out their agreement, and no real arguments coming from the other side, it was only a matter of time before they conceded. Tinidan didn't want to. He argued, he fought. But everything he said just convinced the others that he needed to be cured.

A priest was called, and the healing light was brought forth. It was interesting to watch. The bad memories *burned* off of Tinidan, like a green flame. The priest held the light in position until the flame died away completely.

"Honored Elder, this Elder has been under the influence of Mind Magic," the priest declared.

Uproar in the court.

When the shouting had died down, I asked Tinidan, in front of everyone, if he still thought I'd confessed to a conspiracy to damage the Tree.

"No? What? Why would I say that?" Tinidan said, confused. That was all it took. The attention of everyone turned to the prosecutors, Frostpaw and Nyssa. They protested, but they didn't stand a chance against the entire assembly.

> **Your party has defeated Vesper Frostpaw and Nyssa in a Tier 1 Social Contest! You have earned 180 XP.**
> **You have defeated Marianne Rankin in an Intrigue. You have earned 125 XP.**

Nobles just don't understand democracy, I thought smugly.

QUID PRO QUO

I really can't apologize enough," Tinidan told me.

I leaned back in my comfortable chair and sipped my berry brandy. I wasn't really a fan of the sweet liquor, but it seemed appropriate to the moment. We were doing backroom deals here, and I drew the line at smoking a cigar.

The brandy was also appropriate for a quiet celebration.

I had a name.

More accurately, while I'd already known that she was involved, I now had *confirmation* of that name. Marianne Rankin was the one behind it all. If she wasn't the Mind Mage, they were working for her.

If I'd been a noble, the notification would have been evidence to take to the King. As it was, I'd hold it close to my chest and see where we went. Lady Rankin was close to the King, and while I felt he had his own protections against Mind Magic, I couldn't be sure.

I had to abandon my smug contemplation, though, as it was distracting me from the point of this meeting. Nyssa and Kael Ironhide, the leaders of Tinidan's faction, were here to butter me up. Exactly what for, they were reluctant to say.

Nyssa was a fox-kin, her hair and ears long since gone grey, and she didn't have a sobriquet. She was just Nyssa. Nyssa of Elara if you needed to distinguish her from some other Nyssa.

Kael Ironhide was smaller than the other bear-kin I had seen around. He'd withered up with age, but the scars on his face and arms gave me an idea of how he'd earned the name Ironhide.

The fact that I was meeting with all three was a result of my increased status. They'd been friendly before because they'd wanted something from me. They still wanted that thing, but now they owed me.

"There's no need to apologize," I said. "You were victims as much as I was. I'm just glad we could get it all sorted out."

After Frostpaw and Nyssa had been cleansed, there was an instant demand for everyone to undergo the treatment. They'd had to call in more priests. I'd also gone under the light, and seen the faintest puff of green flame. The priests had told me that it meant a small change, done at least a month in the past.

I was still trying to work out what had been changed. Getting cured didn't flag the false memories or remind you of what had been lost. It was just reversed. The mind had a way of glossing over inconsistencies in what you remembered so it was hard to tell.

The rest of my companions had been treated as well. They were all clean, except for Reynard. Unsurprisingly, he had been one of the worst affected.

"So how much is this going to delay the delegation to the elves?" I asked. The three beast-kin looked at one another nervously.

"Not long, I should think," Tinidan said carefully. "There are still matters arising from this incident that need dealing with, but they don't require a full vote of the Council."

"The druid—or druids—responsible for weakening the tree are still uncaught," I said.

"We think we know who they are," Nyssa said. "We're looking for the druids known to come from Hidden Hollow, and some other druids of Vesper's faction are being investigated by the priests."

"There is still the disposition of the Latorran prisoners to be decided," Ironhide growled.

"A tricky question," I said. "You can hardly let them go after they attacked your capital, but you're worried that the King will take offense."

"There are some who would welcome the idea of offending the King," Nyssa said. "*We* would prefer not to tear down the progress that has been made thus far, but there are those that do."

"My *advice*," I stressed, "is to treat them as fugitives from Latorran justice and hand them over to the authorities there."

"Why?" Ironhide asked bluntly.

"It would be an injustice to punish them," I explained. "They were either manipulated or following orders. They *are* fugitives from Latora, though, so handing them over will let you get something out of the situation. Either cash or diplomatic credit, whatever you want to ask for."

"Won't it be just as much of an injustice for the King to punish them?" Nyssa asked.

"I'll certainly be putting that argument to the King," I admitted. "But the injustices of another nation are hardly your concern. The King will want to make that decision; giving him the opportunity to has got to be worth something."

The three of them looked at each other, disappointed. "We can make that suggestion," Tinidan said.

"And, assuming I'm back in Talnier, I can certainly be a go-between for that negotiation," I said.

"That would be most helpful of you," Tinidan replied, his smile strained.

The reason for their disappointment was that they were hoping I would ask for the lives of Hector's men. And the reason they were hoping for *that* was hanging over us, with no one willing to bring it up.

Our deal had fallen through. The reason that I had come here, the reason that they had hoped to enlist me for the delegation to the elves, was for help dealing with Hector. Now, Hector had been dealt with. I had what I wanted, but they still needed me.

Now, they were looking for something to tempt me with.

"Would it be so bad, just sending one Champion?" I asked, addressing the elephant in the room. Tinidan sighed, an admission of defeat.

"Two is unquestionably better than one," he pointed out. "But from our perspective, it makes our faction look bad to cancel all those deals we made to have the Council issue you the request."

What I carefully wasn't saying was that I had my own reasons for visiting the elves. They may not have been good ones, but I had the feeling that my presence was required there. I still planned on getting paid for it, though.

"You know, since coming here and seeing the craftsmanship on display in the villages, I realized that we're not making the most of this trade deal," I said.

"Oh?" Tinidan asked suspiciously. "I don't think we can go any lower on the tariffs . . ."

"Not that," I replied. "Those are acceptable. The problem is the inefficiencies in your trading network."

"I'm not sure what you mean."

"I didn't realize it until I got out here," I told him. "You have traders, but they only travel between a limited number of villages. For an item to be traded between villages that don't have a trader in common, it might have to get passed between any number of traders before it can get to its destination."

"How else would you do it?" Tinidan asked. "Each village controls who gets to trade there. Creating and maintaining contacts in as many villages is something a trader just has to do."

"What if there was a trading company backed by the Council that went to *all* the villages?" I asked.

"Backed by the Council?" Nyssa asked.

"What's a trading *company*?" Ironhide asked at the same time.

I sighed. This was going to take a lot more brandy.

I had to start with what a company was. Even Latora didn't have them, not quite. They had things that were *called* trading companies, but they tended to be family affairs. They were mostly owned by the patriarch of the family, who hired the children, and perhaps a few others. One person owned the business, and that person *was* the business. The various guilds that the kingdom had were a lot closer to the basic idea. They weren't owned by anybody but ran themselves based on a Charter from the King.

"What I'm talking about would be an entity in its own right, because it would be recognized as such by the Council. Separate from its *owners*, who supply the funds, but also separate from its *officers*, who would be hired by the company."

I explained about charters, boards of directors, and the regulation that was necessary. I sent out for paper and started writing down lists of requirements, of regulatory checks. I explained organizational charts and limited liability. I could feel Bureaucracy stirring, itching for a chance to lay down some more rules. I didn't need it for this, though; this was all just Economics 101.

And then I explained what the company would *do*.

"It would start by hiring some of the existing merchants. Not all of them will want to work for a bigger organization, but some will see the wisdom of it. Then, instead of buying and selling for themselves, they'll be buying for the company. The information about what they buy and sell is centralized, and the officers at the heart of things can tell which villages need what, and which villages can *supply* what."

"And all of this," Nyssa asked, gesturing at the table full of loose papers, "is in aid of *what*?"

"Efficiency," I explained. "Instead of goods bouncing around between villages like a pinball game, they can be shipped directly to their destination. And if the Council can start issuing licenses to trade, other companies can start up that won't be dependent on personal relationships with villages. Anyone could trade with anyone."

"It sounds like Latorran nonsense to me," Ironhide grumbled. "You'll be wanting roads next."

"Roads would be handy," I agreed, "but I know better than to suggest it. Now, at least."

"I still don't understand," Nyssa complained, "Why do *you* want this? How do you benefit from increasing trade between the villages?"

"First of all," I said, "increased economic activity in the Wild means more trade with Talnier. Second, I fully expect to be asked to provide advice and serve on the company's board of directors."

I grinned. "And thirdly, the ones who profit from a company are its investors. And I do expect that you'll allow me to be one of those."

"What if someone else wants to do the same thing?" Tinidan asked. "Without working for your company."

"Well, you'd let them incorporate as well, and we'd compete in the market," I replied. "May the best trader win."

"All of this, though," Ironhide said, "it doesn't exist. We'd need to make laws and rules to allow it, to regulate it as you said."

"Well, you are members of a legislative body, aren't you?" I asked. "A body that is desperately looking for a favor you can offer me? You can fund the extra costs of management from licensing fees."

"Couldn't we just offer you money?" Ironhide suggested hopefully.

"No offense, but I know how much tax you collect," I said. "Nothing from the villages, a small amount from this city, and a little bit from the trade deal. Given your expenses, I doubt you have enough money to tempt me."

"We're not poor," Ironhide snorted. "We just don't grasp after money like Latorrans do. We can manage a hundred gold, and I've not seen the adventurer who won't go for that."

I smiled. "Listen, Kael," I said, Persuasion layering my voice with honey. "What we're talking about here is going to massively increase trade within and outside your nation. Talnier is going to get a piece of that. I'm going to get a piece of that. Some of your people are going to get a piece as well. We're all going to get much, much more than one hundred gold."

The three Elders looked at one another.

"I don't know if I understand this well enough to sell it to the others," he said.

"Let me explain it," I countered. "I can give a presentation about the benefits of the limited liability corporation and the benefits to the Council for allowing it."

He sighed. "That's the one that increases investment by . . ."

"Reducing risk," I told him. "Investors only risk losing the money they've put into the company. If the company goes bankrupt, they don't lose any money other than what they've put in."

He frowned. I wasn't sure he understood what "bankrupt" meant. From what I'd seen, the Tribes didn't do a lot of loans. Another untapped market for the Bank of Talnier.

I wanted to sigh, but I was too excited. I was going to have to do a lot of talking over the next few days. But the opportunity was too good to pass up. It was probably time to put together my first Phantasmal PowerPoint presentation.

GOODBYES

So it turns out that when someone breaks a commercial agreement they made freely with you, Bargain gives you a notification. I guess that coachman that I'd paid to keep silent, way back when, had kept his side of the bargain because the first notification I'd seen of that nature was just before Reynard tried to kill me.

It hadn't worked, of course. I'd suspected that he might have an adverse reaction to having his memories restored, so I'd made sure to be only present as a Phantasmal Emissary. The days when Reynard could see through my illusions were long gone.

He made a good play. As the green fire poured off him, he went limp, held up by the guards keeping him in place. They weren't expecting him to suddenly break loose and lunge at me. They did manage to get him back under control before he popped the illusion, but he'd already realized that it was a fake. Real to the touch or not, illusions don't bleed.

Now he looked somewhat worse for wear. Tribal prisons, at least this one, were more comfortable than Latorran ones, but not by much.

"When are you going to let me out of here?" he asked from the other side of the wooden grate. Iron was in short supply here, but the bars were thick and well crafted. I felt confident that he was restrained.

"It's not up to me," I said. "Attempting murder is a crime here; you're going to face Tribal justice."

"As if five words from you wouldn't have me out and about," he sneered.

I didn't bother denying it. The Council would have loved to do me that favor instead of what I was asking.

"Why would I do that?" I said instead. "You tried to kill me, remember?"

"Because you want something from me," he said. "You wouldn't be here if you didn't."

I shrugged. "I just want to clear up a few loose ends. I doubt you know anything important, but I have a few questions that need answering."

"And why," he drawled, "would I do that?"

"The authorities here would look favorably on any cooperative behavior you displayed," I said. "It would reduce your sentence."

I leaned forward. Not too close—the gaps between the bars looked too thin to stick an arm through, but there was no need to take chances.

"But also because you can't go anywhere, you can't stop me from talking to you, and I can be very persuasive."

I unleashed the skill, letting it twist around him like a snake. Around and into him, making all my arguments seem that much more reasonable. There really wasn't anything to gain from recalcitrance. His capitulation was inevitable.

"Fine, fine, I'll talk!" he gasped. He stared at me for a long moment, waiting for the trembling to stop. "Damn, I guess I should be grateful you weren't using Intimidation."

I didn't engage with his small talk and started right in with the questioning. "Do you still consider yourself as working for the Countess?"

Reynard stared at me. I matched his gaze, and he was the one to look away first. "I guess so," he said.

"Not worried about being punished for failure?" I asked.

He shrugged. "We failed, but I did my part," he told me. "If I make it back . . . well, she'll probably still have a use for me."

"Even though you . . . took the initiative?"

"Everything had fallen through by that point, I strongly doubt that she had any schemes left to foil. She might have been pleased I succeeded. Since I failed . . . no harm, no foul? It feels like a forgivable error."

I didn't ask, but he kept on talking. He wasn't willing to meet my eyes, but he kept shooting aggrieved looks at me as he talked.

"Those memories she changed . . . they were mostly about how angry I was at you. She made me into someone who could tolerate your presence. When that went away, I took the one chance I thought I had. Given all that's happened, I didn't expect to see you again after that."

"What else did she take?" I asked. "Did she really leave you out of her plans?"

"For the most part," he said thoughtfully. "I did bring the amulets into Talnier. Five small boxes, but I never opened them."

"Who did you give them to?"

"I gave one to Hector," he said. "The others . . . I never knew their names. I would sit in a tavern, and every now and then a man would walk over and collect a box. I'm sure you can guess what was going on."

I grimaced. The Mind Mage must have been changing the memories of random people to think they were there to pick up a box of amulets.

I asked a few more questions, but he really didn't seem to know anything more.

"Well, Reynard, I suppose that's it," I said. "Thanks for your time, I'll be sure to let the Council know."

"Wait, wait!" he exclaimed. "Don't be so cold. Don't you still need a guide?"

"I don't," I stated flatly. "The Council are falling over themselves to offer me support to my next destination. And even if I did, don't you still want to kill me?"

He held the ingratiating look for a few moments more. Then it slipped off.

"Yeah, I do," he said. "I want to wipe the smug smile off the face that cost me the sweetest scam I ever did run."

"That's what I thought," I said. "So this is goodbye."

He didn't give me a reply as I walked out.

There was a lot of negotiation still to do, but it was looking like the new deal was going to go through. Having helped save the Blessed Oak went a long way with some of the more xenophobic Councillors. The more they hated me for being a human, a woman, or a money-grubbing banker, the more they venerated the tree and appreciated the aid I'd given.

It was going well enough that I thought it was worth sounding out Borys as a travelling companion. We met at a cordial cafe, which was something I'd only seen at the Gathering Place. I wasn't completely happy with the System translating a place that didn't have coffee as a "cafe," but the drinks they served were nice.

With so many different varieties of fruit and berries, it only made sense that a shop that collected the extracted flavors and sold them as drinks existed. Currently, it could only exist here, where all the beast-kin came together. Outside of the Place, each village had its own one or two recipes, and little need to trade for others.

Franchising the shop and spreading it out to the villages was just one thing that might result from the Council allowing corporate structures, and I made a note to include the possibility in the next presentation I gave.

Borys ordered a fairly pedestrian blackberry tea. I had been working my way through the menu, and my choice today was a cordial from something called silverthorn. We caught a few looks from the other customers but no one approached us as we found a table.

"We could have left by now if you hadn't slowed things down with these negotiations of yours," he complained once we were seated.

"Maybe," I agreed. "Though there would still be a lot of discussion about whether to send a delegation at all. And there are a few Elders who are suspicious that *you* don't want anything."

It was true. There were a few Councillors who looked askance at the idea of a free lunch. They'd been just as suspicious of me, until I convinced them I was going to make a lot of money out of incorporation. Or, rather, I convinced them that I *thought* I was going to make a lot of money. I don't think they trusted my explanations . . . but they could appreciate my greed.

"I have my own personal reasons for wanting to see the elves," Borys said.

"You could probably have made your way there on your own," I pointed out. "They probably would have let you in—they make exceptions for Chosen."

"Perhaps, but going as a delegation seemed more official, less likely to be given a runaround. They don't like to leave us free to wander around."

"No one does, you'll find," I said. "Everyone wants to point us at the nearest problem and say: Your fault! Go fix it!"

He chuckled. "I'm sure that's true, but I haven't seen much of it so far. This is my first expedition outside the temple."

"Really?" I asked. I hadn't heard much in the way of rumors about the Champion of the Storm. His arrival had been announced by his church, but nothing since then. "You've just been training since you arrived?"

"More like torture than training, but you get the idea,"

I narrowed my eyes and focussed again on his micro-scars. "Are you . . ." I trailed off and tried again. "How is your relationship with your church?"

He paused, staring off into space for a second. Then his eyes flicked back to me.

"Tense," he said. "I understand why they did what they did, but I am . . . not happy with them. I think they were expecting me to kill them when they were done."

"But you didn't," I said, carefully keeping it a statement. "There are some nobles back in Latora that raise their kids in a similar way. They feel that it gives them a head start."

He gave me a bleak look. "Cruel enough to do that to an adult. To do it to a kid . . ." He shook his head. "Cruelty doesn't begin to cover it."

"They *are* cruel," I agreed. "But since they were raised that way themselves, they see it as only natural, and look down on the commoner families who aren't willing to make sacrifices for their children."

"Disgusting. You should wipe the place clean of them." He looked down at his tea. "If I'm still around after this, perhaps I will pay a visit to Latora."

I could have taken issue with the last part of his statement. Level six or not, there were higher levels in Latora. Trying to wipe out the social structure there wasn't something you could do at swordpoint. The first half jumped out at me more, though.

[Privacy].

All the sounds of the cafe around us cut out. He looked surprised.

"Privacy spell," I told him, "no one can hear us now. Why do you think you're not coming back from this expedition?"

"That is my hope," he confessed. "Have you not been given hints that the elves hold a way back home?"

I stared at him and suppressed a perverse desire to check that my spell was working.

"I've heard there's a portal, but—"

"A portal that was used once can surely be reopened," he pressed. "Do you not think? Is that not why you are going?"

"There are demons coming through that portal!" I protested. "I don't think we want to jump into it!"

"It needs to be retuned, fixed, perhaps," he insisted. "There must be elves there who know what needs to be done."

"Maybe," I admitted. "But listen, Borys, I was told, by a god no less, that it was impossible for us to go back home. That only our souls got transferred over and our bodies are still on the other side."

He stared at me. "Which god? I didn't think you knew your patron."

"Fyskel," I answered.

He relaxed slightly. "The one thing that everyone tells me about that god is that he can't be trusted. We can probably discount what he says."

"The god that told me the portal was an opportunity was Ashmor," I countered. "What have people told you about *him*?"

"He *is* worse," Borys agreed. "But what, then, do you believe?"

"I don't know what to believe," I said. "I'm going in there with an open mind. I just don't want you setting yourself up for disappointment, or doing something stupid because of your expectations."

"That's . . . fair," he said.

"I'm serious, Borys. Fighting one demon was enough for me. If I have to hold off an entire horde because you opened the portal prematurely, I'm going to be very upset."

LEAVING

I t wasn't *done*, but we were. Borys wouldn't let us put our departure off any longer. To be fair, the prospect of more demons escaping and finding their way into populated areas *did* give me hives.

We were so *close*, though. I'd gotten broad, in principle agreement from all of the Councillors, which was achievement enough that they might tell of it for years. I'd overcome their suspicions, beaten down their objections, and convinced them that the change *would* be for the better, for all of them.

It would be better for me as well, of course. Even if they ended up insisting on majority Tribal ownership for all registered companies, there were still profits to be made. Forty-nine percent was a perfectly fine slice, if the pie was big enough.

The devil was in the details, though, and that was where things had gotten bogged down. I'd offered them what guidance I could, but a lot of the Australian financial environment was entirely alien to these folks. They had their own way of looking at things, and the final laws were going to have to reflect that.

I was confident that, no matter what they ended up with, I'd be able to profit faster from the new rules than the local merchants. Arbitrage between different systems was what international bankers *did*, after all. So I was willing, after much protest, to go on this urgent errand for them in return for assurances that the legislation *would* go through.

Once they'd ironed out the details.

To my surprise, Borys didn't have an entourage.

"They wanted to send someone," he admitted when I asked why his church wasn't sending people with him. "Lots of someones. I had to be pretty firm, but they should have thawed out by now."

I raised an eyebrow. Borys's Blessing of the Storm, while it did include a bonus to Ice Magic, wasn't *just* that. As we'd seen, he could combine Ice, Water, and Air Magic to produce a storm around him that he was entirely unaffected by. It violated the rules of all three types of magic, apparently, and it had strict limits on what kind of storms he could make: Snow, ice, and sleet were the three options. Snow was the least damaging option, which was why he'd used it on the fires.

Blessings like that almost made me wish I'd been acknowledged by my patron. Almost. Whoever they were—and I had my suspicions by now—they could go hang. Besides, blessings like that were at the whim of the god in question. Kaito hadn't had anything like that from Naldyna, and Ashmor had given a blessing to Maslin just to annoy me, as far as I could tell.

Maybe it was because the Champion of Storms was supposed to be a lone wolf. The other two gods had made sure their champions had an entourage. But then, why had his church wanted to send companions as well? Perhaps it was a reverse psychology thing, either on the part of the church or the god.

There wasn't really any point in speculating, I could go around in circles all day if I let myself. Borys might be a lone wolf, but he was travelling with us now. We were being sent with three people: a guide, an *actual* representative, and Lira, who was backup for the other two.

"I don't mean to imply it's deliberate, but I'm starting to detect a pattern where you keep stealing my apprentices," Tinidan complained. The owl-kin had feathery eyebrows that looked really impressive when he furrowed his brow.

"I'm not stealing her, just borrowing her for a bit. She seemed pretty happy about the idea," I said.

"Of course she's happy, she gets to traipse around the forest instead of memorizing dossiers," he grumbled. "She was going to be a Ranger before Anas took off and I had to tap the next in line for a replacement."

"All I said was that I hoped at least one of the delegates would be someone I could work with, and they put her name forward. You can do without her for a few days, I hope?"

"Yes, yes," Tinidan said. "I'm just worried. You'll look out for her?"

"Of course," I said. "I'll keep—I'll do whatever I can."

A twitch of Tinidan's mouth told me he had noticed my self-correction, but he didn't say anything about it. Instead, he just introduced me to the other new members of the party.

"This is Bram," he said, indicating a burly bear-kin. "An experienced guide. And your other delegate will be Thal."

"Just Thal?" I asked the wolf-kin. He was carrying his own Elder token and he had grey hair and white tufted ears.

"Some of us become Elders without having done anything notable enough for the kids to start calling you on it," Thal said, his deep rumbling voice sounding more like it should be coming from the bear-kin.

"Avoiding trouble sounds like a good idea," I said lightly. "I'll have to see if we can manage it this trip."

"That'd be appreciated," he said wryly. "I'm too old for them to start calling me something different."

The other beast-kin, Bram, nodded at me when I introduced myself. "Just let me know when you're ready to go," he said. "There's some decisions need making about the route, but that can wait until we get started."

I looked at the others. I thought that we were ready to go. While I had been politicking, they had been searching out supplies and getting us equipped. I had taken some time out to do the bargaining.

It turned out that fighting to save the tree and accepting a mission from the Council was good for a few discounts at the market here. We'd managed to make our funds stretch a little further and had purchased armor for more than just me.

I *had* ended up getting the shadowhide jacket. And the manticore bloodscale trousers. The stealthiness of the jacket was offset a little by the faint red glow of the bloodscale, but when I wanted to hide, I'd be invisible, so I didn't think it mattered.

The shifting black shadows of the coat and the deep red of the trousers did go together in some ways, though. I'd never been much for Goth clubs, but I felt if I showed up in this, I might get a few awe-filled stares.

Felicia got the emberskin boots, as they fit her better. Most of the leather pieces were designed to be easily adjusted to fit the wearer—within reason. Boots were harder to modify, and Felicia had the smaller feet. The 255 defense wasn't going to do much for her, unless they aimed at her feet, but fire resistance was always handy.

Cloridan had been reluctant to give up his chain, but the 356 defense of the venomhide gilet put the 180 of his light chain to shame. Cloridan didn't have Calculate, but he could tell that one number was bigger than the other. The best part was that metal was so rare here, I'd managed to sell the chain for more than enough to cover the cost of the gilet.

For his legs, he'd managed to find something called barkskin, made into trousers. I wasn't sure if the stuff was bark or leather. Maybe the skin of a tree animal?

> [Identification]: Barkskin Trousers – Quality: Perfect – Properties: +2 Int (Perceptive), Enchanted: Sense Danger – Protection: 305

Why they enhanced perception I didn't know, and the vendor refused to say. We managed to work out that the notation next to the Int bonus indicated that it was +2 to Intelligence, but only for generating totals with Perception. Cloridan said that the pants made him feel that he was connected to the forest.

"I think we're ready to go," I said to Bram. He nodded again and started leading the way. The rest of us bade farewell to the ones there to see us off and fell in behind him. We'd already had our fancy goodbye when the Council charged us with our mission. A lot of fancy words for "Go talk to the elves."

Actually, given that we had delegates with us, it was more like "Make the elves talk to us!" That was the nub of the problem. The Council didn't like that the elves were keeping them in the dark, but they didn't have anything to force the elves to keep them in the loop.

"So what were those decisions you were talking about?" I asked Bram, after picking my pace up to catch up with him. It wasn't hard—he wasn't a fast walker.

He looked at me with an unconcerned expression. "The route," he explained. "Lord Borys wants us to cut through the streams."

I blinked. "The *mana* streams?" I asked, thinking that he would hardly be concerned about regular streams.

Bram nodded. "It will be faster," he admitted. "His reason, though, is that he wants to fight monsters."

Oh.

It made sense. I doubted we'd go up a level from fighting a single monster—or ten for that matter, but fighting would increase our strength by some small amount. I wasn't sure that was the reason behind Borys's request, though.

He must be jonesing for a dungeon.

Borys was level six, and he *hadn't* benefited from the hack that someone, probably Fyskel, had set up to get me there. He must have done it the hard way, with every point of experience earned from killing a monster.

Sure, there were other ways, but even for me, the social experience I'd gained was a rounding error compared to monster experience. The grind could get addictive, too. I'd had it mostly under control—mostly because I *couldn't* delve as much as I might like. Of my party, Cloridan and Janie had it the worst, but I'd seen far worse cases at the Guild.

From what he'd said, his church had run him pretty hard. This was probably the first time since he'd gotten here that Borys had gone two weeks without delving. There were other concerns, though.

"The monsters in the streams ahead of us, are they claimed by any villages?"

Bram nodded. "You understand," he said. "They won't stop us, though. You're both Champions and on a mission from the Council. No one will want to get in your way."

"They'll bitch about, though, won't they?" I guessed. "They'll make trouble for you, for Thal, and your villages, right?"

Bram nodded again. "Don't want to tell Lord Borys no," he said. "And it *will* be faster, even with the fighting."

I thought about it. "Would it be possible," I asked, "to set a route that passes through a village *before* we cross a piece of the stream that they're claiming?"

"Ask permission, you mean?" Bram asked. He thought about it as we walked. After a little while, he spoke again.

"There are three streams we can cross," he said slowly. "Two of 'em we can visit the village beforehand. The other one we'd have to backtrack to do it that way."

"Two should keep Borys happy," I said. "Am I right in thinking that asking permission will help?"

Bram nodded. "They'll still be mad," he said. "And they won't say no. Not to you. But they'll be mad at you—or Lord Borys, not us."

"Give me a chance," I said lightly. "I may be able to convince them not to be mad at us at all."

He nodded again. "That'd be nice. You'll talk to Lord Borys?"

"I'll talk to him," I assured him. "Let's assume that we're taking that route for now."

I stopped and let the party pass by, starting up again when Borys drew level with me.

"I gather you want to kill some monsters?" I asked him.

"It has been a while," he admitted. "But we should fight together as a team at least once before we get to the elves, don't you think?"

"Not a bad idea," I said. "We have some particular formations that we use that you'd need to get used to if you don't want to trip us up."

"Bram said it wouldn't be a problem," Borys said.

"It won't be, not for us," I told him. "But those monsters are considered to be a resource claimed by the Tribes in the area. If we just push through, there will be consequences for Bram and the others after we're gone."

Borys's face darkened. "He should have *said* that," he said.

"He didn't want to tell you no, any more than those villages will," I said.

He frowned. "I'm not sure I like the idea of Bram playing one Champion against the other."

"Then don't think of it that way. He came to me looking for a solution to the problem he couldn't tell you about," I said. "And there's a simple fix."

"Oh?" Borys said, his frown lightening.

"I've adjusted our route," I told him. "We're still cutting through two streams, but we'll visit the villages first. Do you have some funds? I've spent most of our budget on our new armor."

"You want me to pay them for access to the monsters?" Borys asked.

"Yes . . . but that's not how it works. You'll be offering them money as a gift, and they'll be graciously allowing access because you're such good friends."

He blinked in surprise. "I would have thought a business type like you would be all about making it a transaction."

"When in Rome," I said. Which made me smile, because I was talking to one of the few people on this world who would know what it meant. "It's just a matter of following local customs. I'll guide you through it, and then we can all get what we want."

VERDANT GUARDIAN

We should have paid them more money," I said. A tree limb, green with foliage, crashed through where I had just been standing. The limb missed me while the smaller branches whipped across my coat, doing no damage.

"You mean *I* should have paid them more money. Why? They gave us what we wanted." Borys looked cool and calm as he slashed through a branch that came at him. Just as he'd done for all the others. He wasn't staying in one place, but he was cutting branches at such a high rate that he *should* have had a pile of brushwood around him high enough to stop him from moving.

He didn't, which was something I was worried about.

"If we'd paid them more money, they might have felt guilty about sending us out here without warning us about this thing!" I yelled.

Another branch shot towards me. This one was thicker, faster, and altogether more deadly than the last one. Fortunately, it came from a direction that allowed Kyle to block it. He couldn't slice through tree limbs quite as effortlessly as Borys, but when he blocked the tree limb, the wood shattered against his shield.

I was pretty sure physics didn't work that way, but I'd take my blessings as I found them, thanks. Kyle couldn't stop attacks from every direction, but he'd interposed himself between Felicia and the center of this animated thicket. That was where the worst of the attacks came from, and as long as I stayed near Felicia, he could give some protection to both of us.

Cloridan . . . was not doing well. He had my Greater Invisibility, but he was still taking attacks. By which I mean dodging. He was being detected somehow, and I had a sinking feeling it was touch.

Touching, or being touched, was a classic weakness of invisibility, of course, so you wanted to avoid it if you could. I suspected the problem here was that *everything* was a part of this monster. The trees, the vines, the bushes . . . the grass.

It had only been a few moments, but the jagged shards of wood that had fallen at Kyle's feet were gone. That settled it.

"I don't think we're hurting it!" I called out. "We need to get out of it!"

"How?" Kyle asked. It was a good question.

We hadn't entered the thicket unwarily; it had moved over *us*. We hadn't realized what was happening until we were in it, hadn't realized there was a threat until two glowing eyes glared down at us from the canopy. Cloridan had realized *something* was going on. His new danger sense was trying to tell him that there was hostile movement all around him. What he didn't grasp was that it wasn't something moving *through* the forest, it was the forest itself that was moving.

Sorta. The plants *moved*, but they weren't uprooting themselves from the ground. It travelled by incorporating new plants into its . . . body. Since it hadn't taken over the entire forest, I assumed it was also releasing plants in the direction it was travelling from.

Unless it is new, and is still in the process of taking over the entire forest. What a comforting thought.

Anyway, it was a fascinating sight to watch, but it took us a little too long to figure out what we were looking at. A vine might droop down and touch a bush, which might lower its branches to touch the grass or flick the vine up to grasp at another tree. No individual motion was particularly fast, but there were a *lot* of them, and each one gained the creature a few feet.

Now that we were surrounded, getting out might be difficult. The worst attacks came from what I assumed was the center, but the very edge of the creature was highly focused on forcing us further in.

"I might have something," Borys stated. He pointed back the way we came. "Ice Wall."

I'd expected a wall to form, but what we got was a ceiling. Borys had managed to cast the spell horizontally, and up in the air. Or, more accurately, up in the tree branches. They froze up, trapped in place while supporting the icy arch that had formed.

"I doubt it will hold long," Borys said. "Run!"

We didn't need to be told twice. Felicia and I took off first, closely followed by Kyle and his shield. I spared a glance behind me to make sure Cloridan was following.

Borys was the last. He could probably have cut through on his own. As it was, he was significantly impeded by chunks of his own ice falling on him as the branches twisted to free themselves. It wasn't enough to stop him, and we soon found ourselves outside, able to move away without constantly dodging attacks.

"Should we go back and join the others?" Felicia asked. The beast-kin travelling with us had been smart enough to hang back as we entered the mana stream, waiting for us to report it was cleared.

"Um . . . no," I said, considering the possibilities. "Monsters aren't supposed to come out of the stream, but they sometimes do if they're following prey. We don't want to lead it to them."

"If we're not going to fight it, then we should get moving," Kyle said, eyeing the plants between us and the beast. "I think it's headed this way."

"What did you mean when you said we weren't hurting it?" Borys asked as we started a brisk walk, travelling along the mana stream, instead of angling to leave it.

"All of the chunks of wood that you chopped off, they just got reabsorbed into it somehow," I said. "If it's not losing mass, I doubt it's losing hit points."

"Can we hurt it, then?" Borys asked, eyes narrowing. "It didn't seem vulnerable to ice, either."

"I'm not sure," I said. Looking back the way we came, I managed to get an Identify on the monster. I picked up a few random plants first, but eventually, I got its details.

> **[Identification]: Verdant Guardian – Threat: 20 – Properties: Distributed, Transient – Vulnerabilities: Fire**

"Vulnerable to fire, sure, I could have guessed that, but I managed to leave the Fire Mage at home," I grumbled.

I'd regretted the decision more than once, but I had needed someone to stay back and look after things at home.

Now, I *did* have a firebomb potion tucked away in my storage ring. You never knew when they would come in handy. I didn't want to use it now, though. The beast-kin were still a little touchy about the damage to their Tree, and using the same sort of potion might be triggering. The same way Janie might have been if she was with me at the time.

Was there something in the description that I could use? Distributed must refer to how it was spread out throughout the plants, not concentrated in a single physical core. Transient must mean that it didn't stay permanently in one plant. It was as if it were temporarily possessing them . . .

As far as I knew, this world didn't allow for spirits or ghosts or ethereal beings. Anything that wasn't physical had to be made of mana. Which meant . . .

"Do you have the Mana Sense skill?" I asked Borys. He had Ice Magic, so he should.

"Of course," he said.

I didn't bother telling him to turn it on, just pointed at what I was looking at. "Do you see that?"

Borys frowned, looking at the tangled thicket of animated plants. "I see . . . something. I'm not sure what. My skill isn't that high."

"There are threads of mana running through the plants," I told him. "There's a fine mesh which covers everything, but there are some big snakelike ones that shift around from plant to plant."

"I think I can see the snakes," he replied. "But only when they move. Can you see mana inside the plants?"

"Not inside, exactly," I said. I didn't want to get into my theory about multidimensional mana. "But if you try, you can see where the mana and the matter occupy the same space."

"If you say so," he allowed. "I'll have to take your word for it."

"I think the snakes are the main conduits for its control," I speculated. "If we can take them out, we can paralyze it at least."

"But they're made of mana," Felicia objected. "You can't cut them with a sword."

"You could cut the plant that they're in," I said. "They don't seem to like existing outside of a plant for very long."

"They're very quick," Borys agreed. "I can only see them as flickers."

"Right, so, we can try that, or we can try . . . Phantasmal Object."

Just as a snake jumped into a short vine, I wrapped the vine in an illusory sheet. The result was instantaneous. The vine dropped to the ground as if it were dead.

We all stared at the sheet-wrapped vine in astonishment.

"That was—" Borys started. We all jumped as my illusion popped. The vine leaped into the air and the thicket as a whole got a little more agitated. We all backed away a little more.

"That was weird," I finished for him. He frowned.

"I was going to say effective, but it wasn't for long," he said.

"What's weird is—actually, hold out your off hand and I'll show you."

He gave me a suspicious look, but he let me summon another, smaller, sheet around his left hand.

"It's just a sheet, see?" I explained. "It doesn't stop you from moving your hand about. Conversely, you can move your hand all you like but you won't be damaging the illusion. You have to—"

I stopped as he'd already worked it out. Grabbing the sheet, he stretched it until it started resisting the tension he put it under. It started taking damage from the stress, and it wasn't long before the illusion popped.

"I see," he said. "The vine wasn't stopped from moving, but it did stop. And the vine didn't do any damage, but the illusion was damaged."

"I think . . . that the mana snake was stopped from moving," I theorized. "It couldn't move the cloth at all, but it could strain against it, causing the spell to pop."

"I'm not sure how we can use this," Borys said. "But ice is a lot less easy to pop. Can you point out another one of those snakes?"

I could point, but it was a lot more accurate to use Static Image to put a glow around the appropriate target. Borys responded with an Ice Bolt.

"The ice didn't last long before," I said. The branch had locked up, covered in ice. It hadn't gone limp, but it wasn't moving.

"Casting the wall that way made it unstable," Borys said. "Having the canopy there allowed me to cast it off the ground, but it wasn't supported in any real sense."

It took over six minutes before the ice started to crack, and the branch started to work its way free as we watched from a safe distance.

"Six minutes," I mused. "You could get a lot of it locked up in six minutes."

"I didn't see the other plants stop moving, though," Kyle put in.

"I think that might be because it had other mana snakes taking up the slack," I said. "If we froze all of them, we might be able to make our way to the center. If it has a vulnerability, it will be there."

"I bet it's those eyes," Cloridan said. "If you can keep the attacks off me, I can get up there and take them out."

"Then it sounds like we have a plan," Borys said. "I'll undertake to defend Kandis. If Kyle and Felicia hang back as reserves, you can rush in if one of us falls."

"We can do that," Kyle agreed.

"Then let's get started," I said.

Sometimes, all you needed was a plan. Our efforts before had been completely ineffectual, but now we stormed in with purpose. It felt weird for Cloridan to take point while visible, but since the spell wasn't helping, it was better to do without it.

Once about half the snakes had been frozen, Cloridan was able to dodge and move fast enough to get past the thicket's defenses. We lost sight of him for a second in the canopy, and then . . .

> **Your party has killed a Verdant Guardian – your experience share is 622 XP.**

The forest quieted down around us, and Cloridan jumped down, holding a gnarled wooden sphere about the size of a basketball.

"Do you think this is where they get barkskin from?" he asked.

IMMIGRATION CONTROL

Y
ou know that *we* aren't immortal, don't you?"

Borys looked fairly imposing when he was expressing his displeasure. It wasn't backed up by any skills, though, so he was a paper tiger unless he resorted to violence. His bluster rolled right off the elf, who had probably spent a thousand years practicing his social skills. Somehow, he managed not to roll his eyes.

"It's been an hour," he said. "I'm fairly sure you weren't in any danger of expiring in that time."

I could tell that Borys wasn't *that* angry, on account of how he hadn't unleashed his blessing. Or maybe he was and he was just wary of the elf in front of us. Despite not looking like much, he gave off an aura more intense than ours. I judged it at level seven.

I stepped in. "I was given to understand that the Administratum would be willing to meet with me and that an invitation was in the process of being sent out."

The elf gave a definite twitch at my mention of the word "Administratum." He wasn't giving much away, though. We were well matched on social skills, but I think that I had the edge on him. He seemed surprised or even offended that someone should be beating him, even on what had to be a secondary skill focus.

The elven Ranger or border official, whatever he was, *looked* very much like a stereotypical elf. Pointy ears, blond straight hair, and a simple tunic that went halfway down his thighs. His weapons were not in evidence, but he had a suspiciously familiar-looking ring. Looks could be deceiving, though.

The elf's tunic looked like simple cloth, but an Identify was revealing.

> **[Identification]: Steelweave Guardian Uniform – Quality: Perfect – Protection: 510 – Properties: Enchantment (Temperature Control, Resist Lightning, Resist Ice)**

That tunic had more protection than my new coat *and* it had more enchantments. I hadn't expected to feel jealous of someone else's armor so soon.

The building we were in was equally deceiving. It looked like the typical beast-kin—well, actually, beast-kin architecture was too varied to have a "typical" look—but it looked rustic. This building was the official border entry point on this side of the elven nation. If you tried to cross anywhere else, I was told, you got picked up and brought here by the elves to have your attempt recorded. Then, generally, you got thrown out.

It was generally agreed that if the elves *actually* objected to you trying to cross, they killed you on the border and made sure no one ever found your body.

Since the Tribes had an official, if distant, relationship with the elves, this border post was a way of passing messages between the two nations. Delegations were received there, but they rarely got any farther. So this wasn't a *hut*; it was large enough to house a large delegation of important people . . . but that was all. It didn't appear to have any place to sleep, either for guests or for the resident Guardian. It wasn't much more than a simple pavilion, open on three sides. The other side was walled off to make room for a simple kitchen and restrooms.

And while it looked rustic, it was anything but. The whole building was shaped out of one piece of stone, expertly crafted by Earth Magic. The windows may have been open, but the inside was protected by the most complex enchantments I'd seen—outside of dungeon-crafted gear—that controlled what could come inside.

So I had some reason to think that the simple Ranger that stood before me was anything but.

"If you'd *waited* for that invitation to be sent, we wouldn't have to keep you here," he said. "It takes time for decisions to be made, messages to be sent."

"We sent word two days ago that we would be arriving," Thal said mildly. "Did that not get through?"

The elf waved irritably. "I sent it on," he said. "Don't blame me if it got ignored."

"Who *should* we blame, then?" Borys asked, stepping in closer. The elf didn't back away, looking up at Borys with a sneer.

"Don't think your status will protect you if you try anything, *mortal*," he said.

I frowned. This was getting a little out of hand. Borys had wanted to push the guard and had let us know beforehand that he might get a little strident. Since we were here to investigate something that the elves wanted to be kept secret, he reasoned that a little good cop / bad cop would help us get what we wanted.

I didn't want it to devolve into actual violence, though. While I was debating whether—or how—to pull Borys back, another voice cut through the heated discussion.

"Rest assured, it was not ignored. Please, calm yourselves and be welcome in Aeloria."

I whirled around to look at the person that had spoken. She seemed to have just stepped in from the forest outside, but . . . open on three sides, remember? We should have noticed her long before she stepped inside.

The new arrival was also an elf, also blonde. I couldn't tell if she was older or younger than the Guardian we were arguing with. She was dressed in a long robe that looked much like the Guardian's tunic, only more shimmery.

[Identification]: Silverweave Steward's Uniform – Quality: Perfect – Protection: 458 – Properties: Enchantment (Temperature Control, Entryway, Mana Shield)

Less protective than steelweave, and covered with two enchantments that I'd never heard of, I noted.

"You're letting us in?" Borys asked, surprised at least as much by the elf's sudden appearance as he was by what she'd said.

"Yes," the elf lady said. "Allow me to introduce myself. I am Nirelanirae, a steward of the Department of Harmonious Tranquility."

This was a vast improvement from the Guardian, who hadn't introduced himself even after we had given our names. *I wonder if we're not getting our own good cop / bad cop treatment.*

"It's good to meet you, Nirelanirae," I said aloud. "Should we introduce ourselves, or do you already know?"

She inclined her head. "I have been apprised of your status and the nature of your request," she said. "I have been authorized to grant entry to Aeloria to the two Champions."

"And our companions, of course," I quickly added. Nirelanirae looked at me without expression.

"Of course," she said. "Though I'm not sure if the definition can be stretched to include these three." She indicated the beast-kin delegates with a graceful wave of her hand.

"Lira has fought by my side," I said, putting my hand on her shoulder. "I consider her a good friend. She has a job to do here, for which she will need the guidance of the good Elder Thal, here. Bram is just a guide, he doesn't need to come with us. No offense, Bram."

"None taken," Bram said. "Wouldn't be able to do nothing for you in there, anyway."

"Gosh, I suppose we were together during the attack . . . really? A good friend?" Lira said, stumbling over her words.

Elder Thal kept his silence, and so did Nirelanirae, who just stared at me for a long moment. She didn't engage any skills at all, just . . . watched. Finally, she started speaking again.

"As you say, Champion. Aeloria has long seen the wisdom of permitting Champions entry into our lands, lest the gods find other ways of placing them there."

"Good to know," I said. "Will you be escorting us in, then?" I eyed the shoes poking out from under her robes. They looked comfortable, but not designed for outdoor use.

"Ah, there is no safe route between the border and the interior," Nirelanirae said. "We need to take a more direct way."

She gestured, and one of the doorways silently changed to show a different view.

Simple rustic building, my ass, I thought to myself. Was this how she'd snuck up on us? It seemed to me that there must be something more to it. While the portal was silent, there was a visual change, and I felt that we would have noticed something amiss unless it had been covered up somehow. Even as I stepped through the portal, I thought about where the nameless Guardian had stood in relation to us. Had he been diverting attention from Nirelanirae's entrance? I—

—pulled into the car park and slid us into one of the bays marked for guests. Traffic wasn't too bad in the middle of the day and the pool car had, thankfully, included aircon. I'd heard stories of other, less successful firms where the grunts at the lower end had to make do without.

Marcie, Dace, and I piled out of the car chattering excitedly to ourselves. Out-of-office presentations made for an interesting change from staring at screens and glossy prospectuses.

It wasn't as good as a Hospitality Opportunity , of course, but those were few and far between, and generally happened after hours. The big names, of course, could charge all the lunches, liquid or otherwise, that they wanted to Expenses. For us, the only time that happened was when management needed to make up the numbers for a big do.

Still, this wouldn't be bad. This startup wanted our firm's money and our recommendations. They'd be sure to take care of even the lowly peons. You never knew which lower-echelon employee had the ear of a decision maker, so you wanted to make sure that everyone got taken care of.

To be fair, there were some in the Firm who paid attention to these things. Every startup tried to impress the bigwigs, but some would cut corners when it came to the lesser staff. Some of our people paid attention to the exclusivity of the brand of champagne they were served, others checked to see if the champagne made it down as far as us.

The building we entered was fairly anonymous, indistinguishable from the twelve others that made up this technology park. Only the name on the front marked it as any different: Binary Nexus Technologies.

—What was that?

It felt like—it *was*, now, a memory. I'd experienced it as if it were real for a moment, but now it was just . . . there as something I remembered.

It didn't match up, though, with the rest of my memories. I remembered that we were *going* to go to a tech demo for BiNT, a couple of days after I got brought here. This was . . . a future memory? No, the demo would have been months in the past. A vision of an alternate past where I didn't get taken?

I couldn't rule it out, but I had a sinking feeling that I'd *actually* been abducted sometime after my last memory. I was just missing the memories between those two events, and now I had one of them back.

Missing, or erased? I wondered. I wouldn't put it past any of the gods to have messed with my memory, but why? And why would I get one back now? The obvious answer was another god's interference, but what was the motive? Was this memory significant?

I thought back to what I knew about the company. Binary Nexus Technologies was a tech company that had been courting us for investment and for us to help them with their eventual IPO. I'd been going over their publicized numbers, just one of many companies that I was researching.

They were hoping to start selling computer processing at scale— "compute" as the tech goblins liked to call it, in defiance of all the laws of grammar. It wasn't an unusual ambition—a lot of people wanted to be the next Amazon or Microsoft Azure. These guys . . . they had risen to the top of the pile because their projected profits were way higher than the norm for this sector. Looking into it, though, I found that it was because their costs were listed as being far lower than normal.

No reason was given for the lower costs, aside from a note saying it was due to the Anomalous Compute Stream. I'd passed a note on to the higher-ups. Presumably, they would be asking some pointed questions at the demonstration.

That was about all—

"Kandis? Are you all right?" That was Felicia, grabbing my arm. I'd frozen up after leaving the portal.

"Sorry, I just . . . remembered something," I said. I shook off my pointless speculation, resolving to deal with it later. Now it was time to take my first look at the elven settlement.

ELDORIEN

I didn't think there was going to be any doubt that the elven capital was going to be beautiful. The portal exit was well placed to give a fantastic view of it. No doubt that was deliberate, but to be honest, I think they might have found a harder time finding a place that *didn't* give a good view.

We were high up in a building made of . . .

[Identification]: Stonewoven Marble – Quality: Perfect – Properties: Redistribute Stress, Filter Air, Enchantment (Temperature Control)

That stuff. It looked a lot like white marble. The floors were a greyer version of the same stuff, and the door lintels were marked out in pale pink marble. From the outside, I imagined it looked a lot like the buildings that we could see through the wide clear glass window.

"The last few cycles of Champions have not been as impressed with our city as they used to be," Nirelanirae said as we stared out. "They said that the sight reminded them of skyscrapers from home, but that their buildings were more impressive."

If she was fishing for compliments, I was happy to oblige. "Taller, sure, but not more beautiful. We need to pack more people in than you do, I expect. How many people live here?"

"Here in Eldorien, about thirty thousand," Nirelanirae replied. "About as many again outside of this city."

The buildings here were smaller than skyscrapers, but not by much. About ten to fifteen stories, I judged, though two towers rose to at least twenty stories. They weren't identical, but they had a similar style to them, and they were all made of the same white marble.

Compared to the architecture back home, they looked thinner, almost spindly. Some of the towers split, forking out before rising in tandem. It looked very architecturally questionable if you imagined it made with the materials back home. *This stonewoven marble must be strong stuff.*

In addition to the buildings, there were lots of sky bridges connecting towers. It looked as if every building was connected to at least one other building, and I wondered if they used those instead of roads. I couldn't actually see the ground due to the thick canopy that our building rose out of.

"Do you not have earthquakes here?" Borys asked. "I'm sure those buildings are made out of something stronger than I'm used to, but connecting them all like that is asking for trouble."

"We do not," Nirelanirae said calmly. "The ground on which we stand is stable. The other Champions have spoken of natural disasters. Here, such things are not caused by the same processes, but by mana."

"What, really? How is that possible?" Borys asked incredulously.

Nirelanirae shrugged. "We have not been able to determine if our planet is constructed differently from yours, or if the gods reliably intervene to prevent random destruction."

"You're saying the gods *can* agree on something?" I put in.

Nirelanirae gave a slight, wry smile. "That *is* the major weakness in the theory, along with the observation that if they care enough to prevent physical disasters, why not prevent disasters caused by local mana fluctuations?"

"So you *do* have disasters, then," I said.

"Not here in Aeloria," Nirelanirae said proudly. "Our mana is properly managed."

Oh, right, the mana management, I thought. *How do the elves do it? The same way as the beast-kin?*

Since there was a window right there, I turned on Mana Sense and took a look.

I couldn't see any mana. Not *any*. Not the faintest glittering haze of ambient mana, no mana pipelines or streams. None of the ghostly mana machinery that ran the world. Nothing.

Blinking, I returned my focus to where we were. I thought that I would have noticed if we had stepped into an area without mana. Looking around me, I could see that there was mana, it was just constrained into . . . threads. Impossibly thin threads, barely visible to my enhanced eyes, woven into a two-dimensional fabric that was scrunched and twisted to fill the room.

"Is . . . the mana like this everywhere in Aeloria?" I asked. Borys looked at me, blinked, and then frowned. If his Mana Sense wasn't as good as mine, he might not be able to see the threads.

"It is," Nirelanirae answered. "The weave delivers mana almost instantly to wherever it is needed, preventing both buildups and deserts. We have isolated some places from the weave, to allow for dungeon formation."

"And the mana gears? What happened to those?"

"The weave impedes the function of such devices," Nirelanirae explained. "The System is self-correcting, though, so they were relocated as part of its automatic processes."

"Incredible," I breathed. "Were you worried about—"

"This is all very interesting," Borys interrupted. "But we are here on an important mission. We need to see this portal that demons are coming out of."

Elder Thal, our minder from the Tribes, if you wanted to look at it that way, gave a little jump at Borys's outburst. I noted that Borys was already putting his own spin on the mission. The Elders had wanted an *explanation*, something more than empty assurances. It was *Borys* who wanted to see the portal.

"Access to the portal is restricted," Nirelanirae said smoothly. "In anticipation of your visit, an application was lodged with the Administratum, but it is still being debated. Perhaps you would like to rest and refresh yourself while we complete our processes?"

"Sounds like a runaround," Borys said, eyes narrowing. "Perhaps I can speak with these Admin types, get things moving faster, eh?"

Nirelanirae's smile didn't shift. "I'm sure you would be more persuasive after you have cleaned up and rested."

Borys glared at her, but she didn't flinch. He grimaced. "That's a good point," he agreed. "Wouldn't want to be seen as less than civilized."

I cleared my throat. "While I fully support my colleague's desire for prompt access to the portal, there is another matter I'd like to see to."

"Oh?" Nirelanirae looked hopeful.

"Does Jesridae live in this city?" I asked. "I have a message to pass on from her brother."

"Ah, one of the Lost." Nirelanirae's smile still held, but there was a hollow look behind her eyes. "We would happily pass on that message for you, as well as any reply that she would give."

"You know, I don't think Aesrideu would like that," I said. "He did ask me to pass the message on personally, and I don't think he would be happy to have your lot involved. What with you hunting him and all."

"I suppose that's true," Nirelanirae admitted. "It is just that Jesridae is one of the lower levelled that we try and keep well away from danger."

"I hope you're not saying *I'm* a danger to her," I said. I kept my tone mild, but I started building up Persuasion. Nirelanirae was at a higher level than me, but I thought I could put up a fight, socially.

"Of course not," Nirelanirae said automatically. "It's just . . ."

"I could meet her alone if that's what you're worried about," I offered. "I won't need the rest of my party, since wherever we meet is going to be completely safe."

"Of course," Nirelanirae agreed. "I'm sure that it will be completely safe."

"I don't have a brother, you know," Jesridae said as I sipped tea. I frowned.

"You don't? He did *say* you were his sister, but I suppose . . ."

"I *had* a brother," Jesridae clarified. "When he escaped, he was classified as deceased by the Administratum. There's no returning when you run."

"But they send out hunters to bring people back," I said, confused.

Jesridae nodded. "They do. But when they manage it, the person they bring back can't go back to their old lives. They are exiled from their house and given a new name. They're still considered at risk of escaping again, so they are closely monitored. Unless . . ."

"Unless?" I asked.

"Unless they give up the person who helped them escape," she replied.

"Is there always another person?"

She shrugged. "How else is a low-levelled Ward like myself or my brother going to get past the sentries?" she asked rhetorically.

"So you don't know how he got out?"

"No, whoever helped him didn't trust me as much as they trusted him," she said, sighing. "Or they thought I'd be a liability."

I looked her over. Identify didn't work on people, but I pegged her at level four.

"How high a level do you have to be before they let you out?" I asked.

"Oh, it's not a level," she said. "They only let you out if they think you're going to uphold the traditions and laws of the Administratum. If they don't think you're *sound*, then you don't get to level."

"Sound," I repeated. "What does that mean?"

"No one who wants to leave is sound," she said bitterly. "The only ones who get to leave are those on a mission—diplomatic, or hunting. There aren't any other reasons to go, according to the Administratum, so anyone who *does* can't be right."

"I see. Well, I hinted that I had an actual message to give you, but I just got a note, asking me to let you know that he was still alive and well. The note said he'd be leaving Latora by the time I read it, so I have no idea where he is."

"That's for the best," Jesridae said. "If we don't know, then we can't send hunters after him."

"Mhmm," I agreed. "He also said that you might be able to help me."

"What? How?"

"I don't know," I said. "When I got his note, I didn't even know I would be headed into elven lands. I *suspect* that he might have been given a nudge by some god or another."

"Because he knew you were coming here? Maybe he just talked to the Oracle." Jesridae said jokingly.

"Is that . . . an actual thing?" I asked.

"I don't know," she said. "There are stories, but anything from outside is a thousand years out of date."

"Well if there is an Oracle, I suspect they're god-powered, so it amounts to the same thing," I said. "Do you have any idea of how you might help?"

She shrugged. "I know things," she said. About this city, about the elves, that you won't. Will that help?"

"Do you know anything about the demons escaping?" I asked, without much hope.

"Oooooh," Jesridae said. "You're here about *that*."

Nirelanirae had led us to our quarters via another portal. Apparently, the weave included a portal network that Stewards like Nirelanirae could access. A comprehensive network, with at least one entry in each building.

Wards like Jesridae had to walk. So we did, taking the skyways to our destination.

"Each building is owned by a family," Jesridae explained. "When you get new members, if there's no room, then you have to grow a new one."

"Are we tramping through family homes then?" I asked.

"We're all one big happy family here," Jesridae said sarcastically. "The levels where the air bridges connect are public. Or apartments for the really unpopular members of the family."

"And the Administratum?"

"It has its own building. Several of them; there are different departments. The Stewards of Harmonious Tranquility, the Guardians of the Aelorian Veil . . ."

"Do they all have names like that?"

"Pretty much." Jesridae stopped. "We're here."

We were still on an air bridge, so I wasn't sure how this was our destination. When I mentioned this, Jesridae chuckled.

"I can't get you near *that*," she said. "See that building?"

She pointed at one of the shortest and squattest buildings I'd seen thus far in the city. It could almost pass for human construction if you overlooked the ubiquitous white marble.

"That's the headquarters of the Guardians," Jesridae said. "And *that*"—she pointed at a covered walkway that curved gently to touch down in a grove of trees—"is how you get to the portal."

"This is as close as we can get," I realized.

"Not the closest," she corrected me, "But this spot has the best view. You can even see the guards from here."

Looking, I saw that she was right. There were a lot of elf Rangers scattered around the copse of woods.

"Tight security," I commented.

"It didn't use to be," Jesridae said. "The dungeon used to keep them all contained."

"Wait, the portal is in a *dungeon*?" I asked.

"Not just any dungeon. If you believe the histories I was taught, that's the First Dungeon."

FULL AND FRANK DISCUSSION

I hope you are not thinking of extracting Jesridae from her current situation," Nirelanirae said. She'd shown up after Jesridae had left. She'd allowed us the appearance of a private meeting, and Jesridae had been careful enough that I didn't feel the need to use Privacy. It would have just added to the suspicion.

"Why is it that Aeloria is known to the world as the Elven Glade?" I asked, ignoring the question.

"We prefer to make sure that no details about our nation are known to the wider world," Nirelanirae replied. "They have to call us something, and I suppose they have settled on that."

"Champions are an exception to that? You let us in and now we know the names of your nation and your capital."

"Yes," Nirelanirae sighed. "We have learned that the alternative is . . . worse. We do ask that you not share what you have learned, and after you die we will do what we can to remove any writings you have left about us."

I couldn't help but get diverted by the thought of what that might mean. *Were they threatening publishers? Burning manuscripts?* I let it pass and kept on with the thread of my original question.

"We can't be the only exceptions, though. I know elves do . . . leave," I said, choosing my words carefully. "They don't have a lot of incentive to keep to your rules at that point, do they?"

Nirelanirae shrugged. "We have found that the Lost tend not to share true details about their home. Whether that is to preserve their mystique, or because true tales about Aeloria could be used to track them down, I cannot say."

"Jesridae called herself a Ward," I said. "That wasn't because she lost her family, was it? I sort of gathered that almost all elves are Wards."

Nirelanirae inclined her head. "The majority are," she said. "Those without the desire to serve their society, who only wish to live their lives, are managed by the Stewards and watched over by the Guardians."

"She *wants* to leave, doesn't she?" I asked. "She didn't say she did, but she must."

"She has denied having the desire on multiple occasions," Nirelanirae said. At my surprised look, she added, "I read her file while you were meeting her. As you said, the Stewards feel that, despite her words, she does wish to join her brother."

"Would that be so bad, letting her do what she wants?"

"Her wants are immaterial," Nirelanirae said stiffly. "Elf lives are precious and must be protected. The Guardians can only do their work if the Wards are kept close and safe. Staying here is their duty, as much as it is the Guardians' duty to protect them."

"Not everyone here agrees with that, though, do they?" I asked. "Jesridae was saying that everyone who manages to leave does so with help from a Guardian."

"Every society has its dissidents and criminals," Nirelanirae claimed. "Unfortunately, the most effective methods for rooting them out, Mind Magic and such, are forbidden. We can only do the best we can with watchfulness and questioning."

"Well, if you're worried about me sneaking out with her, you can relax. That's not the way I do things," I said. For the most part, I meant it. Obviously, I wasn't above sneaking out with something valuable, but Jesridae wasn't that valuable to *me*. It'd be nice to do her brother a favor, but I didn't owe him *that* much.

Plus . . . aside from needing their portal network to get out, my best method of sneaking about, Shadow Magic, was being at least partially blocked. I could feel places that I *should* be able to get to but couldn't. Some fancy magic there.

"On the other hand," I said, "I could go for some upending of an unjust society. And isn't that what the Chosen tend to end up doing?"

"More often than we're comfortable with," Nirelanirae admitted. "But thus far, we have managed to weather the storm of Champion disapproval. Shall we rejoin the others?"

"Sure. I hope my meeting hasn't delayed Borys meeting with the Administratum."

"It has not," Nirelanirae assured me. "You will still be waiting longer than you would like before the Administratum deigns to see you."

Was it just me, or did I detect some satisfaction in her voice? She led me to this building's portal and opened it.

I was half expecting to get another memory when I stepped through the portal, and I wasn't disappointed. I was disappointed with *which* memory, though. Instead of following on from the last, it preceded the last one, covering leaving work and the early part of the drive.

It helped fill in the gap, which was nice, but it didn't get me closer to answers.

Are all the memories going to be in reverse order? I wondered. *Or is the order random?*

Nirelanirae noticed that I stumbled a little when I went through.

"Are you all right?" she asked.

"I'm fine," I said. The transition from sitting in a car to walking was a bit disorienting, but only for a second.

I let Nirelanirae lead me down the corridor, wondering why I hadn't heard from the gods on this. It seemed right up Fyskel's alley. Either to take credit or explain why it was someone else's fault. Perhaps getting extra memories back reflected poorly on the job that he'd done snatching me?

The elves didn't seem to like the gods, and they were a deal more sophisticated than the civilizations I'd seen so far. But I didn't think they were powerful enough to keep the gods at bay.

Until someone explained something, it would have to remain a mystery.

"Good meeting?" Borys asked when I joined him and the others in the lush waiting room that had been prepared for us. I nodded, but gathered a plate of pastries and fruit before joining the others on the couches. I got a drink as well. Fruit juices but no wine, I noted.

"I passed on the message," I said, and tried a pastry. Delicious. "She also took me to see the portal."

"You know where it is?" Borys asked, leaning forward. "Do we even need to wait on the Administratum, then?"

"I'd advise it," I said as I finished the pastry. "The route to it goes right through Guardian headquarters, and the portal itself is in a dungeon."

"A dungeon?"

"The first dungeon, even," I replied, trying the fruit.

"The *first* dungeon? I wonder how many levels it has?" Borys had an interested look on his face, a true grinder at heart.

"Don't get too excited," I told him. "The number of levels is a function of how much mana it has, not how old it is."

"Is that so," he mused. "The deepest dungeon I've been in was twelve levels, but I hear that you've gone down to level twenty."

"That was a trick *and* a fluke," I said. "All the bosses had left their posts, and very few of the monsters could get past invisibility. And the only reason those dungeons were so high was that the Kingdom was feeding half the mana in the Kingdom into them. I doubt the elves are that eager to feed dungeons."

I looked over at Nirelanirae, who was standing against the wall, but she declined to take part in the discussion.

"So what does it mean, that it's the first?" Kyle asked, entering the conversation for the first time.

"Not much, apart from the historical significance," I said. "Although . . . that probably means that it was one of the ones that had people living in it."

"People living in dungeons?" Elder Thal asked. He looked shocked at the idea.

"According to Fyskel, whom we all agree cannot be trusted, the dungeons were originally meant as massive arcologies, housing millions of people."

My team had heard this story before, so didn't react. Elder Thal just looked confused. Borys looked thoughtful.

"Food and manufactured goods created out of nothing, wastes disappearing just as easily. I can see it. What went wrong?"

"Ashmor corrupted the controlling magic and caused them to start killing people."

Borys winced. "That must have been—how long ago was this?"

"I don't know," I said. "There's no mention of it in the human histories, and they go way back. Something that big . . . it would have to be during the Gods War."

"It might have started it," Borys speculated. "It was supposed to be over how to support the mortal races, was it not? If everyone was forced out of the arcologies, the gods would have been desperate to save as many as they could."

"Maybe," I agreed. "Say, is anyone else getting memories when they go through the portal?"

Denials all around, which was no surprise. My distraction had been noticed, which kind of implied they weren't being distracted at the same time.

"What sort of memories?" Borys asked.

I frowned at the question. It was a little personal, and I didn't know Borys that well. Still, it wouldn't hurt to answer with some general details.

"Memories from after what were my last memories from our world," I said. "About two days after. When was your last memory there?"

"Having breakfast on . . . March eighteenth," he said easily.

The demonstration had been scheduled for March *seventeenth*, I recalled, so his memory was still a little way ahead of mine. Getting it back in fifteen-minute chunks would take a while.

"And you were just having breakfast and then you were here?" I asked.

He nodded. "No warning. There was something in the news that might be relevant. Something about cables being severed, cutting off communications with the east coast of Australia."

That did seem relevant. "Cutting the undersea cables wouldn't cut off communications *entirely*," I pointed out. "We have satellites and landlines to the west coast."

Borys shrugged. "It was just a short news story, more information to come," he said. "Communications cut off, undersea cables blamed."

I looked around to see what the others thought and saw a bunch of blank faces. At some point, Borys had switched to English, and I followed him.

"Sorry," I apologized. "Just talking about memories from home."

"Was it anything relevant?" Elder Thal said disapprovingly.

"I honestly don't know," I confessed.

"Probably not," Borys said, dismissing the speculation. "What *is* relevant is that now we know where we need to go."

"You're not thinking of just trying to bust your way through?" I asked.

"We don't want to anger the elves," Elder Thal cautioned.

"And they don't want to anger *us*," Borys countered. "Or get in our way. It would make the gods mad."

I was a lot less confident that the gods would protect us. I looked over at Nirelanirae, whose smile had faded to almost nothing.

"They might be reluctant to get in our way," I said. "But they still have a bunch of level sevens and eights that could ruin our day without even thinking about it. Are you sure you want to provoke them?"

"It's a risk," Borys conceded. "But I'm not talking about attacking them, just making our way to the portal. If they can't get in our way, then they won't, that's all."

He looked over at Nirelanirae as well, but it was more of a challenge. "If you were going to do something about us, you would have kept us out at the border."

"The prohibition on entering the First Dungeon is for reasons of personal safety," Nirelanirae said, finally stung into talking. "The dungeon is much more dangerous than any others you are used to. Allowing you to kill yourselves could hardly be taken well by the gods."

"If—if you recall, Lord Borys," Elder Thal stammered, "our goal here is simply to get answers about the demon incursions, not *necessarily* to inspect the portal."

"As far as we can tell," Nirelanirae insisted, "nothing has changed with the portal. We've simply been unlucky in the number of demons that have made it out of the dungeon."

Even as she was speaking, the double doors on the other side of the room swung open. Nirelanirae heaved a sigh of relief.

"I trust the point has become moot," she said. "The Administratum will see you now."

COMMUNICATIONS BREAKDOWN

A *re they trying to bore us into leaving?*
In fairness, I expected that meeting with the bureaucratic leaders of the elf nation would involve a fair amount of tedious talking. My expectations were not diminished when we were led into a room filled with almost identical elves. Not quite identical, but all wearing the same ornate robes, the same intricately folded cloth hats and the same neutral expression on their faces.

The Administratum were all seated at a horseshoe-shaped table while we sat at two tables in the middle of the room. Borys, Elder Thal, and I were on the front one, while the rest of my team sat quietly farther back.

"Welcome to Eldorien, the illustrious capital of Aeloria, where the verdant canopy of the forest shelters our ancient city, and the timeless towers stand as testaments to our enduring connection with the natural world. It is an honor to have you grace our halls with your presence on this auspicious day."

Then the speeches started. It seemed that each elf had to bring their own introduction that stated who they were, who *we* were, and what we were doing here. Considering that two of those were already known to us, it seemed a little rich for each one to find a new way of restating it.

"As you stand before us, emissaries of the divine, chosen by the gods for purposes unknown to us, we cannot help but feel a sense of trepidation mingled with awe. For millennia, our people have lived in harmony with the land, attuned to the whispers of the wind and the songs of the stars. Yet now, with your arrival, we find ourselves at a crossroads, torn between our duty to our homeland and the will of the divine."

I was a little surprised that Borys hadn't snapped yet. Maybe it was the solemn dignity of the room and its furnishings. Throwing a tantrum in front of this thousand-year-old panel of bureaucrats would have felt childish.

"The Elders of our Council have convened in solemn deliberation, consulting widely among ourselves and considering the transcripts of what the Oracles have told us. Yet, alas, the answers remain elusive, veiled in the mysteries of the cosmos. And so, we stand here today, grappling with the weight of uncertainty, uncertain of our fate in the eyes of the gods."

Another possibility was that every single one of them was over our level, sitting at a mix of seven and eight. Unlike humans who had spent a long time reaching those heady heights, the elves' bodies were still as lithe and limber as they were at twenty. The elf race was such a hack.

"But fear not, noble Champions, for we extend to you the hospitality of our city, inviting you to partake in the splendors of Eldorien and bask in the tranquility of our ancient groves. Here, amidst the towering spires and winding pathways, you will find solace and respite from the burdens of your divine mandate."

There had to be a limit, though. I readied my skills.

"We are here for a purpose, not a holiday," I said, and let Charm hit them at full force. That wasn't enough to win them over, not nearly enough. Even if I'd beaten their point totals, that wouldn't have been enough to influence a group united in purpose.

And I hadn't beaten all of them. I'd beaten *some* of them, though, which was a surprise to everyone there, myself included. The leader, Administrator Thalverianeu, was most definitely *not* affected but looked at me warily as I spoke.

The thing about Charm was that using it wasn't an *attack*, or at least didn't feel like one. The shock had stopped their speeches, but none of them needed to feel threatened.

"We're here to get some answers about the demon incursions," I stated. "Your assurances were all very well, but in light of the pattern of increasing numbers of escapes, your neighbors are concerned that you're losing control."

A flash of anger flickered across Thalverianeu's face. It must have been pretty intense to get past his control.

"The pattern is a fluke, nothing more," he said.

"What makes you so sure?" I asked.

"The portal and its . . . leakage have been in our charge since before the Great Wild spread this far south. There have always been random fluctuations. These will not last any longer than the ones previous."

"Honored Elder, have you an idea, then, of when the rate will reduce?" Elder Thal put in.

"It's not a matter of the *rate*," Thalverianeu snapped. "That has changed little, if at all over the centuries. The change is in the *type*."

"I thought that demons were infinite in their variety," I said.

"Perhaps they are," Thalverianeu agreed. "But they are not so varied that a different type comes through *every* time. The Status has managed to classify most of the ones that come through."

"That's nice," I said. "So where does the problem come in?"

"We rely on the dungeon for primary containment," Thalverianeu admitted. "We only need to deal with the few that make it through the gauntlet. However, on some occasions, demons appear that the dungeon cannot deal with."

"I struggle to see how that human possessor would get through a dungeon," I said. "There aren't any humans down there, are there?"

"No." Thalverianeu sighed. "There is a possessor type for every species, including monsters. They were not a problem until one came through that could possess the monsters of the bottom level."

He stopped talking and just looked grim. One of the other Administrators spoke up.

"A possessor can spawn any of the other types as required," she said. "And just as the System cannot detect them when embedded, nor can the dungeon. We believe that the first one eventually infected the entire first level. Possessed monsters aren't subject to the level restriction, so they could have escaped then, but they waited until they had infected the entire dungeon."

"That implies a level of intelligence and organization," I said.

"Oh yes, that is quite common among demons," Thalverianeu said, returning to the conversation. "It was quite chaotic when they all made a break for it. We took . . . losses. At the time, I'm afraid that the vingt that you encountered was judged a low priority as there seemed little likelihood that it would encounter a human."

I felt a surge of anger that Cutter's life—nearly *my* life—had been cut short on the basis of it not being very likely, but I pushed it down. Going with the odds was the smart decision. It didn't work out every time, which was why you made sure the loss wouldn't break you, but sometimes you had to take it.

Of course, in this case, the odds had nothing to do with it. *Someone* had nudged those dice. There wasn't any point in blaming the elves for that.

"The Guardians were spread thin at that time," one of the other elves put in. "We had the escapees to deal with and we also had to scour the dungeon to make sure there weren't any possessors left inside."

Elder Thal shuddered. He'd heard our stories of the possessor that we'd encountered. "But this incursion was dealt with?"

"It was. The gate has moved on from that type of demon, so we don't expect to see it again for some time."

From far away, a faint warbling sound started. None of the Administratum's faces changed, but there was the faintest of reactions among some of them.

"What's that?" I asked.

Everyone looked at Thalverianeu who answered reluctantly. "It's the evacuation signal for one of the other buildings."

"Sounds important," I said blandly. "Do you need to take care of that?"

"Wait a minute, we haven't finished yet—" Borys surged to his feet. Thalverianeu waved him down.

"It's not necessary, such things can be handled by the Guardians and the Stewards. We need to stay here to be informed."

In fact, it wasn't long before an elf in Guardian robes burst in the door. "The Ways have been shut off!" he said urgently. "Something is coming through—" He cut himself off when he saw us.

Thalverianeu gave us an awkward look. "If you'll excuse us for a moment, Champions . . ."

"Why don't we give you the room," Borys said. "You seem busy." He immediately stood and started striding out of the room. Confused, the rest of us followed him, as did Nirelanirae. She'd been standing against the wall with a few other Stewards, but I guess she was assigned to take care of us, so she followed.

Once we were all out and the doors closed behind us, Borys turned and faced us all.

"Right," he said. "This is our chance. Let's head to the portal."

"Are you crazy?" I asked, "Our handler is right there!"

"Indeed, I must counsel against such action," Nirelanirae said. "The building is being evacuated! It is not safe to venture into."

"It's fine," Borys said. "Nir's not going to stop us, and everyone else is too busy defending or evacuating."

"Yeah, because there's a demon there!" I exclaimed. "Demons are dangerous!"

"They are," Nirelanirae agreed fervently. "Please, do not do this. Let the Guardians handle this."

"Nah," Borys said. "Got the go from Rakaro, you know?"

I felt a chill. Not sure if it was because a god had made a move or if it was his way of saying hi. "What did he say?"

"Just, go. He's not one for conversation. If you don't take me, I'll just make my own way there. All I have to do is follow the sound of the alarm."

"Ugh, fine, I'll take you," I said, against my better judgement. Maybe I could get him out when it got bad. I looked over at my crew. "The rest of you should stay here."

"Uh, no," Felicia said. "We're coming with you."

"We'll just follow along if you don't agree," Cloridan said, butting in before I could reply.

My skills seemed to have deserted me for a second as I saw them all standing firm.

"I can't—I don't want—another Cutter," I managed to say. "Maybe Champions get to survive this sort of situation, but you don't."

"Champions survive because they have companions," Felicia said. "In all the stories, the ones who go alone don't last long."

"*I'm* happy to stay here," Elder Thal put in.

"Oh . . . fine." I gave in.

Nirelanirae came with us as well. She refused to guide us, but I knew where we were going, and as Borys had said, the alarm was a bit of a clue.

"What does it mean, that the Ways were closed? That's what you call your portal network, isn't it?" I asked her as we ran. We were all high-level and the corridors were clear, so we could maintain a fast pace and still talk.

"It means that either the demons are of a type that makes spatial manipulation dangerous, or that they were concerned with the demon escaping into the Ways." Despite the situation, she maintained an eerie calm.

"They can get out of containment that way, can't they?"

"Out of Aeloria, yes. It makes tracking difficult, but not impossible as you know."

I would have asked more questions, but we ran into the wave of evacuating elves. There weren't many of them, and they moved quickly, without panic. Many of them were wearing Guardian uniforms, but they seemed of low level.

"Trainees," Nirelanirae explained quickly.

The alarm was much louder now, as we entered the building. We needed to guide ourselves by the shouts and screams from where the fighting was.

"This is not good," Nirelanirae told us. "For the fighting to be here . . . the Guardians would have not retreated back to this spot. The demon must have broken through the lines."

It did seem this was a bad place to fight a demon. It was more like an ordinary office block, with offices and waiting rooms, and one larger room we went past that looked like a lecture hall.

Finally, we got close enough to see what was happening. The first thing we saw was the demon itself. It flew straight through the wall as if it were swimming through water. It was black with grey markings, a long and sinuous shape.

"Stop it!" The call came from another room, but there didn't appear to be any way for them to stop it. It finished passing through the wall, and then flew in a quick circle, looking for new prey.

Warning! Demon Detected!
[Identification]: Inahinmos Soul Snake – Threat: Unknown –
Properties: Unknown
Warning! Demon Detected!

It didn't make a sound as it whirled around. Then, it seemed to make a decision. It twisted in midair and headed right for us.

SOUL SNAKE

The demon twisted in the air with uncanny grace. It didn't seem to be flying or swimming. It just moved . . . how it wanted to move. It orientated itself and then shot itself in a straight line. Right at me.

Just like last time, I couldn't help thinking.

It was moving too quickly for me to dodge. No, not too quickly. The numbers that had been mostly in my favor so far had turned against me. Its attack was higher than my dodge, and so the System had seen fit to hold me in place to await its strike. It was only for a moment, but it felt like an eternity as I saw the snake open its jaws, ready to take a bite.

I wasn't the fastest person here, though. *Just like last time.* Borys flashed past me, his sword interposing itself between me and the demon.

Cloridan was moving, too, but just like last time, he was too slow and too far away. The elves were shouting something, advice or warnings, I guess, but the moment was happening too quickly for me to understand what they were saying.

Borys was moving like a particularly deadly dream. He was faster than me, faster than the snake, even. Not content with getting in the snake's way, his sword rushed towards it, as though the blade was on rails. It struck absolutely true, bisecting the mouth, then the head, and then running all the way along its stretched-out length.

It had no effect whatsoever, passing through the snake as if through air. The demon didn't even flinch away. It just carried straight on towards me. There was nothing I could do. My body was still trying to carry out my futile Dodge attempt. When that was done, I could look at casting a spell or screaming, but it would probably be too late by then.

Well, not too late for the screaming.

The snake was an arrow, aimed straight at my heart, jaws wide open and ready to bite. Somehow I knew that it would go through my armor, my skin, and my bone. The only things that were solid were its teeth, and the only thing they were solid to, was my heart.

Instead, it stopped. It bounced off and was flung back a few feet. Borys's sword swept through it again, but it didn't seem to notice. It stared at me with unblinking eyes, seemingly as confused as I was.

Had my armor protected me? For a moment, I gave thanks to whatever beast it was that shadowhide came from. Then my memory caught up with me and I realized that was wrong.

At the same time, the soul snake decided that whatever had happened, it was worth another go. Writhing sinuously, it ignored another swipe from Borys and launched itself on a twisting trajectory that only made sense to a demon.

There was even less time to react to this attack, and my Dodge was painfully inadequate anyway. Still, as long as it went for my heart again, I should be safe . . .

The demon's fangs sank right through the leather of my coat—then sprang back as if they'd hit a rubber wall. Or an elastic brassiere.

It's my fucking underwear!

The demon wasn't flung back as far this time. It floated in front of me, secure in its invulnerability while it worked out what to try next. However, this time I had a response ready.

[Phantasmal Object].

I wasn't sure if I could get it all in a bag, so I made a square of cloth and dropped it over it. To my surprise, the demon dropped as if the cloth was made of lead.

What the . . .

I stared at the result of my spell in surprise. The demon was still there, trapped under the cloth, writhing slowly. The other started coming up to me.

"What?" Borys asked.

I gestured helplessly. "It's just a solid illusion of an object," I said. "I got the idea it was affected by illusions, but this . . ."

"*Solid* illusions?" an elf said, coming up to us. "I've *heard* of such things. . . . Is it dead?"

"No," I said. "It's trapped, but . . ." I trailed off and summoned a copy of one of my daggers to my hand. The demon's movements were sluggish and unguided so it was easy enough to put the point of my fake dagger at the juncture of its head and neck.

The writhing intensified, but not by much. It seemed to have trouble moving the fabric at all. I pushed down, feeling a meaty resistance.

The fabric was in the way, so I dismissed it. Now the demon was free to move, except for its head, which was pinned to the ground by my dagger.

The rest of its body twisted and flailed at me, but it was as immaterial as it was before. It passed right through me, and there was nothing to stop me from putting my full weight down on the dagger. There was no sound, but the dagger stopped dead when it reached the ground.

> **Your party has killed an Inahinmos Soul Snake – your experience share is [Calculating] XP.**

The thing didn't even die properly. Instead of leaving a corpse, it just turned into smoke. Starting at the point where my dagger had entered, it just dissolved into the air, leaving only a hazy outline that quickly dispersed.

"Come with me, please," the elf said urgently. "There are three more of these."

I hadn't quite processed what was going on and what I'd done, but I let him lead me further into the combat zone while my brain worried at what [Calculating] meant in the notification.

The whirling speculation stopped when we saw the first bodies.

"We don't have anything to stop the Inahinmos," the elf said. "The only thing that slows them down is when they stop to feed."

I got my brain back into gear.

"If it works on one," I said, "it should work on the others, right?" I conjured another cloth and passed it to the elf. This one was more of a net, with weights at the edges. I hadn't used anything like it before, but I'd seen them for sale.

"You'll need a dagger to finish them off," I added, passing him my fake one. He accepted gratefully. Whistling another elf over, he passed them over. That elf gave the net an experimental twirl, demonstrating significant skill for something that had to be a niche weapon at best. Then he took off, moving faster than our group could.

"Borys," I said, making a fake version of his sword. He'd managed to target the things just fine. "Don't waste it on regular objects," I told him as I handed it over. "It does no damage and enough hits will cause it to pop."

He sheathed his weapon and took mine with an amused look. "It has weight," he said, surprised.

"Yeah, well, *they* don't," I said. I was already analyzing the last fight. "That's why they move so weirdly, and why the first one had trouble with ordinary cloth. There's a good chance you won't be able to cut them. You'll just swipe them out of the air like you were playing baseball."

"Oh woe," Cloridan said mournfully. "I see that I'm already second in your affections to the Champion." I rolled my eyes.

"Net and dagger, feel free to go out ahead of us and risk your life," I said acidly as I gave him his tools.

"Anything for you, my lady," he said, bowing deeply and touching his forehead. I snorted.

"Kyle . . . I'm not going to get you to carry *two* shields," I said.

"I could . . ." he said doubtfully.

"So I'll just . . ." I summoned a cloth covering for his shield. "That shouldn't be too much extra weight, and you can use your shield as normal. If you're taking hits from regular damage, though, it's going to pop sooner."

"I'll let you know when it does," he said. I nodded and made a pair of daggers for the two of them.

Time wasn't waiting for us, though. Even as we started moving again, I got another notification.

> **You have been credited with assisting with the death of an Inahinmos Soul Snake – your experience share is [Calculating] XP.**

That was a new one. I suppose it was because someone who wasn't in my party had killed a snake with my spell. You didn't get assists for supplying weapons, but my Phantasmal objects were a lot more . . . personal, it seemed.

"We'd better hurry," I said. "Or there won't be any monsters left."

"Let us hope for that outcome," the elf next to us murmured. Then he led the way into the fight.

Once we started moving, it wasn't long before we got into the thick of it. Soul snakes were only a part of the incursion, most of which was contained behind a line of battling elves. It seemed that the snakes had broken through the containment and had been followed by a bunch of much less dangerous demons. They were being dealt with, but the two remaining soul snakes were still wreaking havoc.

Borys leapt forward to make the next kill. As expected, his sword acted more like a bludgeon against these monsters, but he'd minded my warning. Striking at a downward angle, he sent the demon spinning to the ground.

Which . . . it didn't pass through? *What? What were the rules for these damned things?*

Regardless of how any of that worked, the snake seemed stunned by the blow and didn't resist when he skewered it to the ground.

> **Your party has killed an Inahinmos Soul Snake – your experience share is [Calculating] XP.**

Shortly after that, the elf I'd gifted with my spell made another kill.

> **You have been credited with assisting with the death of an Inahinmos Soul Snake – your experience share is [Calculating] XP.**

With the main threat dealt with, Borys joined the fighters holding back the main incursion. The other demons seemed to be made of fire and did not deal well with ice spells. Borys wasn't the only one with that kind of magic, and the fight didn't seem to be going well for the demons.

"Thank you for your assistance, Councillor Hammond," the elf next to us said. "The situation is under control now, so you can return to your meeting with the Administratum."

"There could be more of those snakes coming out," I said. "Maybe I'd better stick around until the incursion is completely finished."

The elf paused, trying to balance his two concerns. "That might be for the best," he eventually said. "Please do not approach closer, though. We still have the weapons you gave Ariandrilae, and they should be sufficient. If you'll wait here, I'll inform the Administratum of the situation."

"Sure," I said. "That okay with you guys?" I asked my team.

"Yeah, sure, we're not that eager to get into a fight," Cloridan said. "Well, not all of us," he added, looking at Borys.

Apparently, sitting out of the fight was enough for the party to be broken, because we didn't get any further notifications from Borys's kills. It wasn't long, though, before he was all done and the final notification came.

> **Calculations complete. You have been assigned 40,444 XP.**

I whistled aloud. "That's a lot of XP," I said. "How much did you guys get?"

"I got ten thousand, three hundred and seventy-seven," Felicia said, spelling the numbers out slowly. The other two nodded.

I raised an eyebrow and did some calculations. Felicia would have gotten five-sixths of my experience because of her level, so . . . "It looks like the assists I got were worth fourteen thousand each. Not bad."

It was only a small step towards level seven, but it was a step.

The nameless elf appeared again. "Councillor Hammond, if you would come with me. The Administratum would like to include you in their current discussion."

"Just me?" I asked. "What about Borys?"

"Him too," the elf said. "And you may bring your companions, of course."

"Sure," I said. "Let's see if we can drag him away from a battlefield and the portal that he's come for and see if he's up for another meeting."

ANGRY ELVES

When we'd met with the Administratum before, they had displayed an icy unity of purpose. Polite, yet disdainful of the brash Champions that had forced themselves into their city of quiet contemplation. Now, barely an hour later, the civility had dissolved into outright hostility. Auras that had been restrained before were now pushed to their limit, as the elves openly wielded their social skills against each other. It was difficult to tell as an outsider, but I felt that there had to be at least one Social Contest going on.

Felicia stopped at the threshold, face pale. The others didn't look much better. I fired up Intimidate and let them . . . shelter under my wings. I wasn't quite sure how that worked, but I'd done it before against the Duke back in his dungeon. I suppose that standing behind a big scary protector helped you withstand the big scary attacker.

Borys looked shocked. I don't think he'd encountered much in the way of social conflict.

"I feel like I've been slapped in the face in some new way that I never knew existed," he rumbled thoughtfully.

His words garnered the attention of the room, which was a bit of a two-edged sword. It meant that a lot of the angry glares were directed at *us*, but it also made a lot of the elves reign it in. God forbid that the lofty and exalted Administratum should be seen brawling it out in front of the mortals.

The chamber was silent as we took our seats, but it was clear that they were all itching to get right back to it. Rather than greet our return, the first elf to speak addressed Thalverianeu, the one who'd been doing all the talking up until now.

"This changes the situation. We need to respond."

"Nothing has changed," Thalverianeu replied, maintaining a semblance of calm.

"Point of order," another elf interrupted. All the other elves stared at him in surprise. Perhaps because he was still following the rules of order? Regardless of the reason, the elf just grinned and addressed me.

"Can we get a confirmation of reports? How did you defeat the soul snakes?"

I looked at him. "Well, Elder . . . ?"

"Galadrimorin," he replied. "Administrator Galadrimorin if we're being formal."

"Right. My profession is Phantasmal Artificer, which gives access to solid illusions," I said. It felt weird admitting it outright, but there wasn't much point in hiding it from anyone who hadn't already guessed.

"For some reason," I continued, "the soul snakes treat the Phantasms as if they were real—more real than they were. A simple illusion of a cloth sufficed to pin them to the ground—which they also couldn't move through—and a Phantasmal knife can kill them, despite not normally being able to do damage."

"Interesting," Galadrimorin said. "What made you try it?"

"A layer of my armor is Phantasmal," I said, choosing my words carefully. I didn't want to bring my underwear into this. "The snake bounced off it, which set me on the right track."

Galadrimorin looked over at Thalverianeu. "Do we have any Illusionists that can repeat these findings?" he asked.

Thalverianeu gave him a sour look. "There hasn't been a *report* of a level eight Illusionist for five hundred years. Illusion Magic is on the list of discouraged skills, ever since our last level *seven* Illusionist *left*, taking a dozen Wards with her."

"You don't have Illusion Magic at all, then?" I asked. "I would have thought it was a necessity for a group as intent on maintaining their privacy as you."

Thalverianeu looked at me disdainfully. "More trouble than it's worth," he said, making clear from his tone that he meant me as much as the skill.

"So it's confirmed, then," the first elf said impatiently. "The gods have—"

"The gods do not control what demons come out of the portal," Thalverianeu stated firmly.

"Even if that's true, that doesn't rule out predicting the demon type, or affecting the timing," the first elf insisted. "Do you think it's a *coincidence* that Lady Kandis showed up just when she was needed?"

"Coincidences happen," Thalverianeu replied.

"And the rest of the demons were fire-types, which the Champion of Storms happens to be strong against," the first elf continued.

"We have plenty of Ice Magic practitioners," Thalverianeu countered. "There was never any danger of those ones getting through on their own."

"But they weren't on their own, were they? They—"

"Sorry to interrupt," Borys said, not looking sorry at all. "But can you catch us up on what you're actually arguing about?"

"Thornielorin, there, believes that the gods are sending us a message that we should stay out of your way and let you access the portal," Galadrimorin explained.

"Well, that is exactly right," Borys agreed. "You should let us access the portal."

"There is no message," Thalverianeu said waspishly. "The portal has always changed its monsters randomly; this is nothing but more of the same."

"I can't believe that you're being so obtuse about this!" the first elf—Thornielorin—exclaimed.

"The gods are perfectly capable of letting us know anything they wish," Thalverianeu claimed. "Either directly or through their Champions here. They have not directed you to pass on a message, have they?"

"Well, not in so many words," Borys admitted. "He's dropped some hints, though."

"Hints," Thalverianeu sneered. "We can't base our policy decisions on clues from some treasure hunt."

"You know that the rules about what the gods can say changes when they're doing one of their Great Games," Thornielorin pointed out. "They don't want a predetermined result, but it's clear which way is safer for us."

"The safe route is not to play their stupid games in the first place!" Thalverianeu thundered. He was quickly losing his cool. "Pandering to their nonsense just leads to trouble down the line."

The tension was rising in the room again, but this time it was less chaotic. Instead of a grand melee of argument, everyone was focused on *this* argument.

"Since we seemed to have moved on to straight talking, would anyone care to explain what the issue is with us visiting the portal?" I asked.

Thalverianeu glared at me. "The gods and their Champions bring *chaos*," he lectured. "We have maintained our society for thousands of years, against the best efforts—both well-meaning and ill—of your kind to change every aspect of it."

He scowled. "There's not one of you that can leave well enough alone, that can leave things as you found it. And now you want to enter the First Dungeon, the blot at the center of our nation. Its containment was the reason for our founding and *we have kept it contained*. We don't need you, or the gods, to stick your noses in, and we won't let you."

"Point of order," Galadrimorin interjected. "We can't stop the gods from doing anything, and it would be unwise to stop their Champions."

"Unwise, perhaps," Thalverianeu agreed. "But well within our capacity. Just *go*, heroes. We don't need you. We don't want you."

"That attitude is the reason why the gods have destabilized the portal," Thornielorin complained. "They've clearly engineered the situation so that we have no choice but to allow the Champions to interfere."

"A few unlucky rolls of the dice is not destabilization!" Thalverianeu insisted. "The portal is perfectly stable, as it always has been!"

"You can't claim to know that for sure," Thornielorin argued. "No one has been down there since the possessors came through. Reports from the Guardian can hardly be trusted—"

"Don't speak of it!" Thalverianeu cut him off. Thornielorin rolled his eyes but sat down.

"So do you guys have some sort of voting procedure to resolve disagreements?" I asked.

"There is no need for a vote here," Thalverianeu insisted loudly. "I am in charge, and there *will be no change of policy!*"

"You've lost it, old man," Thornielorin retorted. "Logic and sense are on my side—*you will allow it!*"

There was no doubt about it this time. A Social Contest like nothing I'd seen before was starting to form. Thornielorin matched his Persuasion up against Thalverianeu's. It was clear from the outset that he was outmatched, but he wasn't alone.

"Some risks need to be taken," said one of the elves around the table, and added the weight of their skill to Thornielorin's.

"Tradition must be upheld," said another, taking Thalverianeu's side.

One by one, all the elves around the table took a side and added their skill to one side or the other. In a way, it was *like* a democratic vote, except that the votes were weighted by the social skills of the Council members.

That proved to be a telling factor. Thornielorin had more members, barely. Six were on his side, but the five opposing him seemed to have either greater skill or higher level. The difference was clear to me, and Thornielorin clearly couldn't hold out for much longer.

There was one member who hadn't spoken yet, and I looked over at Galadrimorin to see which way he was going to jump. He looked right back at me, grinning.

Well, fine. This was a Social Contest after all, not a vote. There weren't any rules on who could participate. I wasn't even sure that I *wanted* to see the portal, but I knew I would never hear the end of it from Borys if I didn't do something.

"I think it's pretty clear that the gods are setting something up," I said calmly. "The only thing worse than pandering to their whims is getting in their way."

I added my own Persuasion to the storm. It helped . . . but it wasn't enough. I heard a gasp from Felicia as the pressure increased. I was still sheltering them, but now I was facing a full share of the storm's force.

I could hold it back for a few moments more, but we were going to lose. It wouldn't be me who failed first, but once one of us did, it would be over. Then Galadrimorin spoke.

"Who knows, it might be fun," he said. Eight versus five and it was almost evenly matched. But now we had the edge.

"This is foolishness!" Thalverianeu cried, trying to weaken our resolve. "You will be made their playthings, toyed with and discarded."

"There's no way that isn't already true," I retorted, but saying that didn't really make a difference. The tyranny of numbers was already beginning to tell. There was no one else to join, so it was just a matter of time before the first elf crumbled.

> **Your faction has defeated Thalverianeu's faction in a Tier 1 Social Contest! You have earned 175 XP.**

I winced to see the notification. The biggest social fight I'd been in, and I only netted 175 XP? Compare that to the fight I'd just had where I'd barely done anything and gotten forty thousand, and it was clear what kind of activity the System preferred.

Of course, we hadn't done it for the XP. The weirdest thing was that Social Contest didn't leave any physical signs behind. It felt as if the room should be filled with smoke and blood, but the air was perfectly clear and not a chair was out of place. Only the attitudes of the combatants gave away the result.

I could see Thalverianeu, slumped in defeat. "This is a mistake," he sighed, unconvinced even in defeat.

I looked back at my team and the other noncombatants. Felicia and Elder Thal were still looking a little pale. Cloridan, Kyle, and our handler elf were putting a braver face on it but still looked a little shaken.

Borys was doing fine. I was getting the impression that hitting him in the face was just how you let him know you were serious.

"Does this mean we get to go?" he asked.

"I'm still not sure that's the wisest idea," I said. "But yeah, we get to go."

W H Y ?

I'm not even sure I want to go," I complained. I was doing so while sipping on some green lotus tea, so at least I got to air my doubts in comfort. I took a bit of the fruity—I wasn't sure what fruit, exactly—tart.

"You don't want to get home?" Borys asked, sipping at his own tea. The Administratum meeting had . . . ended, to put it politely, and we had found a cafe to gather at while the elves "sorted out the details" of our upcoming delve.

"I was given to understand that wasn't an option," I reminded him. "No body to go back with, no world to go back *to.*"

Borys frowned. "And yet, you got signs that the gods wanted you here, the same as me."

"Hints and suggestions, sure," I admitted. "And those have worked out well for me in the past. But . . . the gods were more than willing to talk before, but now they've clammed up."

There was a lot that I wanted to talk with Fyskel about, starting with the mysterious memories that were returning every time I passed through one of the elf gates. I was supposed to be the focus of the gods' attention, but none of my pointed remarks when I was alone had yielded results. Whatever it was that they wanted, they didn't intend to tell me about it.

"Rakaro isn't one for chatting," Borys confessed. "He's said maybe three words since I arrived, and one of them was today. His church is a lot more opinionated, but I get the feeling he doesn't like them much."

"How does that work?" I asked. "I would have thought getting along with your deity would be a requirement for a religion with a real god."

"You'd think," Borys agreed. "The impression I got from reading stories was . . . he's very individualist. That is, he wants humanity to survive by having individual humans become strong. Through their own efforts, if possible."

"I'm picturing a horde of ultra-jacked mountain men, each one with his own mountain to camp on top of," I joked. "Where do kids come into that?"

"You're not far off, and the answer is they don't," Borys said. "That's why the cult needed to find answers for themselves. *They* are all about being strong *together*."

"Very human," I commented. "Band together against bigger threats."

"Yeah, well, that's where the humans and the god part ways," Borys said. "Whereas I parted ways over what they *do* to get strong."

"So why doesn't he correct them?"

"He doesn't seem to care. Or maybe he recognizes that his vision isn't attainable for most—or any—humans, so there's no point in chastising them."

I was about to say something when I heard someone approach. Turning, I saw Thornielorin walking towards our table. All the seats were occupied, but Cloridan muttered something about finding something to do and let the elf have his seat.

"You're looking grim for someone who just won," Borys said. "Aren't you the new head honcho?"

"That is not how it works," Thornielorin said. He did look pretty grim. "A decision has been made, but each of us still fills the roles we did before."

"How long before that decision gets overturned, then?" I asked. I couldn't imagine that they would accept a ruling that had been made with my thumb on the scale. Twenty-four hours was as long as Persuasion lasted, at least the part where you *couldn't* go against the winner.

"It will not be overturned," Thornielorin said flatly. "The damage has been done. The unspeakable has been spoken in front of outsiders. Tradition has been forced to acknowledge the reality that has been placed before us."

"That is a very complicated and depressing way to say that we won," Borys said. "We all got what we wanted, shouldn't you be happier?"

Thornielorin shook his head. "Understand, all of the Administratum is united in its desire to keep you out of the dungeon. For you to leave with no quests completed, no ancient customs overturned. The difference of opinion was between those who thought that was possible and those who realized that *we have no choice*."

"You said that the gods had destabilized the portal," I said quietly. "So that you'd have no choice but to send us in to fix it."

Thornielorin inclined his head. "The official position of the Administratum is that the portal remains stable. That position is . . . not entirely borne out by the current evidence."

"And you just admitted that in front of us and the Tribal diplomat, so . . . the facade has been cracked. Your neighbors aren't going to accept your assurances anymore."

"The fact that they sent you to us suggests that they have already stopped heeding our denials," Thornielorin admitted.

"How are we supposed to fix it?" Borys asked. "I don't know the first thing about fixing portals."

"I don't know," Thornielorin said. "Our best Theurges have looked at the problem to no result. Our second and fourth best Theurges died trying to shut it down."

That didn't sound promising.

"What about the gods?" Borys asked.

"Either they cannot, or they have some compelling reason why they should not," Thornielorin said. "They have had ample opportunity over the years."

"There will be some way," I said. "There always is when they throw us at a problem like this. Something tailored to the two of us."

Thornielorin inclined his head again. "It is not our way to rely on faith," he said. "But there are times when the gods leave us little choice."

"Well this is a sad circus," Borys said. "But still. I am hearing that we get to see the portal and whatever problems the gods have caused they have left a way to fix them. Seems fine. Did you just come to mope, or did you have business with us?"

Thornielorin scowled. "I am here to go over the details of how you are to enter the dungeon," he said. "The first item is that no elves will be accompanying you."

"That's a blow," I said. "I've cleared dungeons with more levels, but I had help and I cheated outrageously. Are you sure some lowly level sixes and fives can clear this?"

Thornielorin shrugged. "That is the gods' problem, not ours."

"It's very much *our* problem," I said heatedly.

"Feel free to not go," Thornielorin replied, smirking. "You leaving of your own accord is the very best of our scenarios. The second best is the one where you die in the dungeon."

"As long as you don't have anything to do with it, right?" I asked uneasily.

"Yes." Thornielorin gave me a serious look. "Standing in your way might have consequences, but withholding aid should not trigger retribution."

"We're not leaving," Borys said.

"If we can't get a guide, can we at least get a primer on what's down there?" I asked.

Thornielorin waved his hand dismissively. "It would do you no good," he said. "The details of each level change quickly. Information from our last expedition is already out of date."

"Is that to adapt to the demons?" I asked.

"Possibly. More likely it is due to the dungeon growing bored," Thornielorin replied.

Now, there was a red flag.

"It's intelligent enough to get bored? And you know that it does?"

Thornielorin nodded. "It is capable of communication," he said. "It is the original artificial construct that all the others are based on."

I felt my blood run cold. "The original? So it's the same construct that killed all those millions in the first arcology?"

"Wait, what?" Borys interrupted.

I quickly got him up to speed. "According to Fyskel, dungeons were originally meant to house people in massive numbers. Only Ashmor reprogrammed the AI that was running them, turning them into murder machines."

Thornielorin raised an eyebrow. "That is substantially similar to the tale that the Guardian tells. Perhaps we can consider that partial confirmation."

"That—" I stopped and swallowed. "The Guardian *is* that AI?"

"Assuming that AI is a term for mana construct, yes, it is the same," Thornielorin said.

"It must be so old," I said wonderingly.

"Even older than you think—which brings us to our other major point. The dungeon utilizes time contraction."

"Time . . . contraction?" I asked. "What does that mean?"

"Time runs faster inside the dungeon," Thornielorin explained. "The disparity increases the deeper you go. It generally takes our people two days to complete an expedition, but their experienced time can be as much as a month."

"A month to cover a dungeon!" Kyle exclaimed, beating Borys and myself by a fraction of a second. "How big is it?"

Thornielorin shrugged. "It uses extensive spatial manipulation as well, so all I can say for sure is that it is large."

"Even under normal circumstances, I don't think it would have taken a month to clear the level-twenty dungeons," I said. "I mean, assuming you *could*."

"The number of floors and the threat level of a dungeon's monsters is limited by its available mana. Its size is only loosely constrained by mana, and given enough time, not constrained at all. We control the amount of mana available to the dungeon, so we have some control over its threat values."

"What are they?" Kyle asked.

"It should start at threat ten on the first floor, and go up by two each floor."

"So thirty-two at the bottom," I mused. "That doesn't sound so bad."

"Of course," Thornielorin added, "the demons are mostly not rated. You should find that the dungeon's monsters will attack them just as readily as they attack you."

"Wait," I said. "When you said it was older . . ."

"The dungeon experiences time at the fastest rate," Thornielorin confirmed. "I couldn't say how old it is, but it must be in the tens of thousands of years."

"I'm surprised it hasn't gone mad," Borys said.

"It started out mad, murderously so," Thornielorin reminded him. "It does not age like mortals do. Nor does it think like mortals do. You would do well not to trust anything it says."

"Any other bombshells for us?" I asked.

"I do not think so. Supplies that you might need are being gathered at the entrance. When do you think you will be ready to leave?"

"I thought you weren't going to help us?"

"We are not going to risk any more elven lives," Thornielorin clarified. "Minor aid like this costs us little, and if it speeds your journey even a little, it is worth it."

He scowled at me again. "The less time you spend in the markets, the less time you have to find customs and traditions of ours to overturn."

"You're not wrong," I agreed. "The more I see of this dystopian soporific environment, the less I like it. If it was how you wanted to live your lives, I wouldn't complain, but the number of people who try to escape suggests it isn't really their choice, is it?"

"There are a few malcontents," Thornielorin admitted. "They remove themselves and get to experience life unconstrained by the Way."

"That would be a great solution," I said, "if you didn't do everything you could to keep them here, and everything you could to hunt them down and bring them back."

Thornielorin looked at me without expression. "It is dangerous out there," he said. "We have to do everything we can to preserve elven lives. Those who have managed to escape have proved that they can live without our protection. We owe it to them to make sure that the test is as hard as we can make it. Only the most skilled can be allowed the choice to risk their lives."

I blinked. "Wow," I said. "If you think that's an argument *for* what you do, then you should talk to more people that aren't brainwashed."

A flicker of emotion crossed his face, but it quickly faded into an expression of slight disapproval.

"If you're ready to go, we can take a gate to the entrance right away," he said. "Best to get this over with quickly."

STARTUP MEMORIES

There was a brief pause in the lobby while we waited for the higher-ups to arrive. Maybe "lobby" was too grand a term for the lounge area they diverted us to, but there were more soft chairs than we'd brought people and they had a potted plant.

Once everyone had arrived, there was a flurry of introductions and the ceremonial passing out of temporary name badges. The important people were whisked off to the grand presentation, to be plied with champagne and caviar. Those of us who also served got handed over to Reggie.

Reggie took us to what was very clearly the *working* conference room, overlooking the bullpen where the techies crunched numbers on what looked like very expensive computers. We were separated by a glass wall, but I noticed the occasional nervous glance at the intruders in their midst.

There were offices on either side of the conference room, both empty. Their occupants were probably attending the main demonstration while the people they supervised were here, probably doing everything they could to make sure it went well.

"Ah, I should . . ." Reggie muttered as we entered and hurried over to turn on the display. It was already set up to show the other demonstration, and we could see the executives from both companies mingling with their champagne and canapes.

"I'll turn the sound on at the appropriate point," Reggie said, but we'd already been diverted by the presence of muffins and coffee. Muffins, not biscuits, which I counted as a win. Calories eaten on work excursions didn't count.

"Right, that's fine," he continued as we thanked him for the coffee. He seemed a little flustered to be in a room with three girls, so we turned it up a bit.

"Do you play computer games, Reggie?" I asked, giving him a warm smile. In the future, my smiles might be counted as weapons of mass destruction. Today, they were more of a Saturday Night Special, but that was more than enough to take out Reggie.

"Ah, not really, I'm too busy with work," he said nervously. "Some of the other guys play stuff."

My smile got a little wider. Asking about computer games was normally a guaranteed conversation starter with a techie, but there were two types of techs.

I mean, sure, there were *lots* of types of techs. But as far as HR was concerned, there were only two. The first type worked the hours they were contracted and then went home to play video games.

That was a simplification, of course. It would be just as accurate to say that there was one type of derivatives trader, who came just before lunch, worked until eight, and then spent the rest of the night drinking and doing cocaine. The crazy thing was that HR was *used* to the derivatives trader. It had taken them ten years to get around to the idea that the first type of tech wasn't a crazy deviant.

The transition had been necessary as finance became more technical. We didn't just depend on computers; trades were now done according to mathematical models, and our traders needed model mathematicians to run them.

Which was why HR's interests were of concern to me. HR was always on the lookout for good techs, and reporting back on possible hires was one of the things we were supposed to do while we were out here.

Reggie had just tripped a flag for the *second* type of tech. The kind that worked all day and only went home because you forced them to. Health and safety made that a requirement. When they were forced to go home, they still found a way to work on their project until they were allowed to go back to work. HR loved these guys.

It probably wasn't a fantastic idea to poach valuable staff members from the startup you were planning on funding, but as far as I knew that decision hadn't been made yet. The higher-ups would decide whether to fund or sabotage. Or both.

For now, I just gave Reggie a warm smile that should make him think more positively about working with us if we decided to make an offer. The firm had heard of playing fair but didn't want anything to do with it.

Reggie swallowed in this three-way blast of female attention but rallied valiantly.

"I should start by . . . asking about the NDAs?" he said.

"All done," Marcie answered, handing him a folder. NDAs were standard practice for this sort of thing. Startups were desperate to keep their secrets in-house. It didn't matter as much as they thought. This company had spent five years turning whatever their original idea was into whatever they would be presenting today.

We weren't going to take away anything that would let us skip those five years. We'd have to set up our own tech company and hire our own tech geeks, just to get to where they were today. Why would we do that, when they were offering to sell us at least part of their company right now?

Of course, if we *did* get something worth that much, then an NDA wouldn't stop the firm from doing whatever it took to capitalize on it. There were a thousand ways to get out of those, from eating the fine to eliminating the other corporate entity. If you didn't exist, you couldn't sue.

Still, the more time our counterparty spent worrying about nonexistent threats, the less time they had to worry about anything else we might be up to.

Reggie checked the forms with the nervous eye of someone who'd been told where we were supposed to sign, and the things that we weren't supposed to do, like alter the text before we signed it.

"Right," he said. "That all seems in order. We asked for your company to send people with a maths background, so are you . . ."

"We're all PhD level," I told him. "I was in econometrics, Marcie was applied mathematics, and Dace was fluid mechanics."

"Oh!" Reggie said, sounding pleased and surprised, "I hadn't expected . . . why are PhDs in the finance industry?"

"There's a lot of math in finance these days," I explained. "I'm surprised you weren't headhunted out of university."

"Ah, well, I suppose I did hear about a lot of that. But Malcolm recruited me while I was still doing my thesis. I finished it a year after I started working here."

"Mr. Edwards, you mean?" I asked. It wasn't that unusual for a startup for the lower levels to be on a first-name basis with the founders, but it was worth noting.

"Ah, yes, him," Reggie confirmed, getting a bit flustered again. "So the idea is that your executives get the presentation on the projected costs and incomes. The *idea* behind Binary Nexus Technologies is a little difficult to get your head around, particularly if you're not . . . mathematically inclined."

"So you want to convince *us* you're on the level, and then we can tell our bosses that."

"Uh, exactly," he said and shoved three fat comb-bound documents at us. "This is the math behind what we're doing."

We started to leaf through them, and I whistled softly. "Math background or not, I hope you don't expect us to understand these just by looking at them."

The book was filled with equations. They were beautifully typeset, but that only *helped* with comprehension.

"Oh, that won't be necessary," Reggie said. "I can explain what they're saying. We just wanted to show the calculations we use to do what we do."

"These look like physics calculations," Dace put in. "General Relativity formulae?"

"That's right," Reggie said. "The first part, that's what we were working on at the start. Well, Malcolm was. He was a physics PhD, and he was doing numerical solutions for Einstein's equations under certain edge cases."

Some of the text that wasn't an equation jumped out at me. "A binary black hole system?" I asked.

"Yes! Actually, there were a lot of weird setups, but the important one was the twin black holes. Under certain conditions of mass and rotation speed, you can get a singularity in the middle that isn't contained within the black holes. A naked singularity—a wormhole, in fact."

"This is all theoretical, though," I said, leafing further. The next section was entitled "Anomalous Compute."

"Oh, yes, entirely. The simulations were calculation intensive, but Malcolm had access to RMIT's supercomputer. He wanted to see what the simulation said the wormhole looked like."

"And did it?" Marcie asked.

"Yes, but there was a lot more. The simulation showed us what was on the *other side* of the wormhole."

"What was . . ." I trailed off, confused. "What *is* on the other side of a wormhole? Another part of the universe?"

"That's what Malcolm thought at first, but it soon became clear that the wormhole went to *another* universe."

"We're . . . still talking simulation here?" I asked.

"Yes! A simulation of another universe inside our simulation of a wormhole!"

"An entire universe?" Dace asked skeptically.

"As much of it as you can see from the hole," Reggie said. "But that's still much more information than the simulations should be capable of producing."

"This is the Anomalous Compute you're talking about," I said, still not understanding. "Where does it come from?"

"We don't know!" Reggie said, giggling nervously. "It's like you were watching a regular standard-definition stream, and one of the pixels was in 4K high-definition!"

"That's insane," I said. "But how do you use that? Isn't it only good for spying on other universes? Simulations of other universes," I added carefully.

"Well, that's what we've been spending five years working on," Reggie said. "You can control what universe you end up with by varying the initial parameters of the black holes. And there seem to be infinite universes to choose from, so—with a bit of effort—you can pick one that spits out the answer to the problem you're looking for."

"So you just choose a universe that spits out prime factorizations of hundred-digit numbers?" I asked incredulously.

"Almost. What you do is encode the prime in the initial parameters and get the factorization encoded in the background radiation coming out of the wormhole."

Reggie looked at our baffled expressions. "It's not NP=P," he said carefully. "There's a significant cost to running the simulation in the first place, and the calculations for determining the initial parameters are also quite costly. But we can routinely get a ten or twenty-fold increase in our effective compute, given the right problems."

I went back to the book, flipping through the pages. "So the first section is for the equations that you use to run the simulation. The second section is methods for getting information out of the simulation. And the third section is . . . estimates of how much calculation it takes to encode your problem into the parameters of the simulation."

"And the last section compares our methods with more conventional approaches," Reggie confirmed.

I looked at the last section. "That's crazy," I said. "Those are crazy numbers."

"But where does the information come from?" Dace asked again.

"Malcolm brought me in at the start," Reggie told us. "And we've spent five years tuning our equations and investigating that question. We start up five to ten simulations a day. And we still have no idea how it works."

"I don't know why you wanted people with math backgrounds," I complained. "If you wanted to tell us stuff that's just impossible, you would have gotten the same results if told it to a bunch of secretaries."

Reggie shrugged. "They wouldn't have understood it *was* impossible, and I would have had to spend so much time explaining the maths."

"I don't know that you've thought this through," Dace said. "If we go to the boss and say what they're doing is impossible, you're not likely to get the funding you want."

"We're hoping the demo will take care of that," Reggie said. "Once we've demonstrated something that *is* completely impossible, you'll be there to tell them how we did it."

He turned to the screen.

"Oh, look, the main presentation is starting."

He turned on the volume, and that was where the memory ended.

FINAL DESCENT

I stumbled again, leaving the portal. It was hard to instantly process all the memories coming back to me.

Or the memories getting put in for the first time, a darker, more paranoid part of me pointed out. I ignored it. While I couldn't refute the possibility, I'd been down that rabbit hole before, and there wasn't anything at the bottom. Except for rat poop.

Cloridan caught my shoulder before I could fall.

"Another memory?" Felicia asked. I nodded.

"Anything . . . useful? Relevant?" Borys asked.

"I'm not sure," I said. I thought about it. "Maybe a clue about what happened to bring us here, but I'm not sure how it connects."

I explained about Binary Nexus Technologies and their Anomalous Compute. I left the natives behind very early on, and Borys wasn't in much of a better position.

"So you think this . . . simulation . . . did something to us? To the whole world?"

"I don't know," I admitted. "It's just . . . something impossible was happening to them, right before something impossible happened to us. It makes sense that the two events are connected. Somehow."

"But for a simulation to affect the real world . . ." Borys said, trailing off. From the look on his face, he didn't want to say the conclusion that he'd come to.

Neither did I. I could only think of one way for that to happen, without it being *completely* impossible. On the other hand, my idea of what was impossible or not had changed greatly since coming here.

So I kept my mouth shut and pushed the thought down. It didn't really matter, one way or the other. The memory might not even be real.

I let the elf Guardians distract me by outfitting us for the trip. They'd been watching the conversation with a mix of confusion and thinly disguised impatience, which struck me as a little rude. *They* were the ones with all the time in the world.

The supplies were handed over to us in satchels. *Storage* satchels, much bigger on the inside.

> **[Identification]: Steelwoven Storage Satchel – Quality: Perfect – Properties: Enchantment (Spatial Expansion, Resist Lightning, Resist Ice)**

"That should have everything you need for an extended delve," one of the elves explained. "There's room left for anything you might want to loot from the dungeon. You're welcome to anything you find down there, but we will be needing the satchels back when you come out."

"These aren't of dungeon make," I said, running my fingers over the coolly slick fabric. I was already wondering if I could find a way to keep one. Or all of them.

"They are of our own manufacture, yes." The elf smiled smugly. "You are welcome to try analyzing the enchantments."

I just nodded non-committedly. Learning how to do spatial enchantments would be nice, sure, but I would probably have to learn how to enchant *cloth*, first.

The satchels were, according to the elves, all the same, the better to make sure that we weren't screwed by losing one. They held a *lot* of stuff. Mostly food and water. The elves thought it likely that we'd be able to forage in the dungeon, but they wouldn't guarantee it.

There was also rope, a bedroll, a shovel, and an expandable pole. *A ten-foot pole* popped into my head, a reference to something I'd heard sometime.

"No tent?" I asked.

"If you release the straps here, the mouth of the bag expands enough to crawl into," the elf said. "You can use the pole to prop it up to have room to move around, as long as you don't fill it too much."

"No potions or alchemicals?"

"We don't have the stocks to spare," he said flatly. "Hopefully, what you brought will be enough."

I rolled my eyes. "None of us were thinking there was a *month-long* delve ahead of us."

"If there's a potion you were using a lot, there's no way you could carry enough for *that*," the elf said. Which was true. While you could never have enough healing potions, we did have Felicia, who was rechargeable.

I glanced over the rest of the stuff—they'd laid out another satchel's worth of goods on a table so we didn't have to go rummaging—and made a few notes.

"Thanks for all this," I said. "I know you're not keen on having Champions up in your business, but you've been very polite."

He winced slightly at the obvious untruth but kept his composure. "We do what we can," he muttered. "When it comes down to it, we're *all* pawns in the gods' games, regardless of what we would like."

"Fair enough," I said, slinging my satchel on my back. "Is everybody ready?"

At first glance, the dungeon was a bit of a disappointment. The walls of the elven fortifications surrounded it but kept a fair distance, allowing the dungeon to appear as just a hole in a hill in a natural forest.

"This is the First Dungeon?" I asked. Our elf guide sighed, but kept his gaze fixed on the entrance.

"It is," he said. "It is said that it was once entirely above ground but sank down in order to trap as many of the inhabitants as possible."

"It is said? You guys weren't around then?"

"We were not. Our race was granted immortality during the Gods War," the elf said. "Records from that time are fragmentary, but according to . . . it, the sabotage of the arcologies was what triggered the Gods War in the first place."

"Did it always contain the portal?"

"I don't think so," the elf said, frowning. "But it was in place before our race was tasked with containing it."

"Well, nothing to do but start," I said. I let Borys go first and we all followed.

Leaving the elves behind, we crept carefully through a short passageway leading into the hill. I sent a Light spell to hover over and a bit behind Borys's head. It was only a few steps after that when we were stopped.

"What is it?" I asked. Borys took a step to the side so that we could see the passageway ended in a steel wall, blank except for the obvious sliding doors and the glowing button to one side of them. It had a downward-pointing triangle on it.

"Gotta be a trap," I said. No one disagreed, but we couldn't find it.

"There's nothing mechanical," Cloridan eventually reported. "No hidden panels in the wall, nothing concealed in the rocks."

"The whole thing is magical," I complained. "It could do anything, and I don't see a way to bypass it."

"Does that mean it *isn't* a trap, then?" Felicia asked. "They have to be fair, right? And the elves would have warned us if it was deadly on the first step."

"I don't want to be the one who says it," Borys said, saying it anyway. "But it doesn't look like a trap, it looks like an elevator."

Lacking a choice, we pushed the button. Using the ten-foot pole. Well, a five-foot pole—it was too awkward to hit the small target when the pole was fully extended. When Borys managed to make contact, there was a *bing*, and the door slid aside.

We all looked at the small room revealed. It sure *looked* like an elevator. Fake wood panelling, cheap carpet, brass trim that could well be plastic. The only difference was that the ubiquitous mirror on the back wall had been replaced by what looked like a flat panel screen.

It can't actually be that, can it?

"If that's what it looks like," Borys said for the benefit of the others, "it will have buttons next to the door to direct it where to go."

"The doors will close on their own after a bit of time," I said. "Cloridan, can you check the floor without going in?"

"No problem, boss," he said. Crouching down, he approached the door with a dagger held in front of him. As soon as the dagger crossed the threshold, though, the lift reacted.

"No need to be concerned, friends!"

The voice had come from the flat panel screen, which was now lit up with a picture of a face. It looked down at Cloridan as he scrambled back from the entrance.

"The Eternal Palace of Dreams is indeed filled with dangers, but you need not fear the elevator!" it said.

The face was clearly of artificial construction. It was all sharp edges and smooth planes, shaped to *resemble* a face, but the result was more like an eighties video game than anything real. There was an intelligence behind it, though. It tracked Cloridan with its eyes, and when I stepped forward it instantly switched to looking at me.

"That's the name of this dungeon?" I asked, for lack of anything better. I wasn't willing to engage this thing on the question of our safety.

"Originally, yes. The elves have taken to calling me the Fortress of Unending Nightmare, but that is a foul slander on my delicate nature!"

The face smirked.

"And after all my long years of service! I bet they were rude to you as well."

"You're the original construct that runs this place? That killed all those people?"

The face affected a sad expression. "Oh, but the gods saved so many of them, once they realized what was going on. I doubt I killed many more than 132,852."

It smiled. "That was so many more than I've managed since. Visitors have been so rare! And the elves keep my mana so restricted, I can hardly kill any of them."

"You're really selling the idea that the elevator is safe," Borys said sarcastically.

"It is, it is!" the face exclaimed. "I have ever so much to show you, and I can hardly do that if you stay up here—or if your broken bodies fall down a shaft."

The face grinned. "I will be trying to kill you once you get down there, but that's just what friends do, isn't it!"

"Cloridan, try checking the floor again. You, don't let the doors close," I said, addressing the face. "And how are you speaking to us? I thought you couldn't make changes on a floor with people on it."

"Quite true, quite true!" the face said, watching Cloridan with interest as he probed at the floor of the lift. "There is a loophole, though. This screen is responding to changes I'm making on the very *lowest* floor. No violations required! And, I must confess, this isn't the only place where such enchantments are set up. We'll be able to converse for your entire time as my guests, without me having to expose an avatar to your whims."

"Looks solid, boss," Cloridan reported. "Of course . . . magic."

Of course, magic. If the dungeon had set up magical traps in advance, it could dematerialize the seemingly solid floor at a whim.

"Whatever," I said. "I'm not going back to the elves with my tail between my legs. Let's go."

"An excellent decision!" the face on the wall said. "We're going to have such fun!"

We piled into the elevator. It was a little uncomfortable with the five of us, but there was enough room. As expected, there was a button on the inside, next to the door. Just one, marked "Fun."

"Great," I said. Bracing myself for the floor to fall away, or spikes to come out of the walls, I pushed the button.

Once again there was a ding, and the doors closed.

"It's all so familiar," Borys mused. "Where are you getting all this?" he asked the face. "Was this part of your original design?"

"Oh, I get things from here and there, there and here," the face said. "You're not the first Champion to visit you know."

"That didn't answer the question," Borys pushed.

"I know, I know," the face said. "But maintaining the mystery makes everything more exciting, don't you think?"

We could feel the elevator moving down as we spoke. My team had been alarmed at first but quickly accommodated to the sensation. I got more worried as the seconds passed and we kept heading deeper.

"How deep are we going?" I asked.

"Not all the way," the face replied. "But deep enough that . . . we're here!"

The doors opened and we got our first look at the first floor. It was . . . expansive.

Storm clouds roiled above our heads, only a little way about the tall buildings that rose all around us. Concrete and stone, they easily qualified as skyscrapers. Some of the windows were dark, others blazed with light. Human-looking figures hurried quickly down the street, looking for all the world like they were hoping to get under cover before the storm hit.

Despite the clouds and the concrete, though, it wasn't gray. Everything was lit with neon. Signs advertising all sorts of goods and services, from food to guns to sex, washed the street and the inhabitants in a hundred different colors.

"Welcome to the jungle!" the face said from behind us. "The concrete jungle, that is."

It started laughing. Smoke started coming out from behind the picture, and we quickly exited as the whole thing caught fire. Somehow, it still managed to function, and it got the last words out as the carpet caught fire and the doors closed on it.

"We're going to have such fun!"

ABOUT THE AUTHOR

Christopher Hall, also known as Maxlex, is the author of the Phantasm series. Hall started writing his first novel while sailing the Tyrrhenian Sea one summer, the salty night air flavoring and enriching his worldbuilding. Since then, he has continued to hone his craft while holding down diverse jobs in metalworking, marketing, perfume sales, and briefly, modeling. In addition to writing, Hall's interests include illuminated lettering and artisanal brewing. He endeavors to convey a sense of l'esprit in all his creative pursuits.

Podium